THE TURNING

I0648122

ARILIN THORFERRA

The Turning

Production copyright FurPlanet Productions © 2025

Cover artwork © Ken Sample 2025

Published by FurPlanet Productions
Dallas, Texas
www.FurPlanet.com

eBook ISBN 978-1-61450-671-3
Paperback ISBN 978-1-61450-670-6

First Edition Trade Paperback 2025

one
fifteen items or less

Despite being a week into spring, it's a stubbornly gray and chilly day in South San Francisco the morning Diana meets the goddess of love and war in a checkout line.

The sheep tosses two vegetable primavera frozen dinners in her cart, starts to wheel away, pauses, and adds two spinach lasagnas. The grocery store's selection of full vegetarian and low-meat dishes has been getting better the last few years, an unexpected silver lining to the way the neighborhood's segregation skyrocketed since she moved in eight years ago. They're not the highest-quality brands anymore, but they're within her budget.

She pulls her phone out of her purse and checks off "frozen meals," then looks between it and the cart. Laundry detergent, dish soap, breakfast cereal (she should have gone with something healthy but got Berry Honey Os, shut up), soy milk. Grapes. Dried dandelion trail mix. Bagged salad? Yes, there. Okay.

One of the wheels on her shopping cart fights her vigorously as she pushes it toward checkout. Grunting with effort, she holds it straight, making a beeline for the express lane. She should have a small enough basket. The stores in the richer, carnivore-heavy towns along the Peninsula mostly all have self-checkouts, but they haven't upgraded to those here yet. They're promised along with the remodeling, but she's skeptical.

It's not a long line, but it's moving slow, the stoat behind the cash register looking like he wants to be anywhere else but here making money. What's he doing here? Slumming? Or is his family too poor to move out? The mouse woman at the head of the line and the elderly squirrel woman behind her both look patient. The tiger guy directly behind the squirrel, the one Diana's right behind, doesn't. He stands out here, and he knows it. He looks rushed and maybe a touch nervous, like he's afraid he's in the bad part of town and might get jumped by, well, who, exactly? A tired middle-aged black sheep woman? That hasn't stopped him from pushing a half-full cart into the line, though. Figures.

A tall rabbit woman gets in line behind Diana, tall enough that the sheep does a double-take. She's taller than the tiger, so has to be, what, six foot three or four? She looks strong, too, but radiates a movie star out of makeup vibe—like she could make everyone in a room fall dead silent when she walked in if she wanted to, but it's a power she can turn on and off. She seems familiar. Maybe. From where?

The rabbit looks down at the black sheep's five-foot-six self and raises a brow. Diana smiles awkwardly. "Sorry, you're just...very tall."

"Yes," the woman says flatly, with a bare hint of a return smile.

The sheep clears her throat, nods, and looks away, drumming her fingers on her cart's handlebar. She's unexpectedly feeling a fraction more bisexual, and she's afraid she's going to put her hoof in her mouth if she keeps speaking.

The mouse gets checked out and the stoat starts lackadaisically sliding the squirrel's eight items through.

"I'm sorry," Diana says, turning back to the rabbit, "but..." She lowers her voice. "Don't I know you from somewhere?"

"I don't think so." The woman sounds amused now. There's a lovely lilt to her voice that makes Diana think of harp music.

"I don't mean that we've met, I mean..." She furrows her brow and sighs, waving a hand. "I don't know. Like I've seen you in a movie or on TV."

She shakes her head. "Not me."

"Hey!"

Both the rabbit and Diana look at the weasel who's gotten behind them in line.

"That's sixteen," he snaps, angrily pointing at Diana's cart. "You have *sixteen* items and this is a *fifteen items or less* line!"

Diana looks in her cart. Shit, he's right. "It's only one over."

"Rules are rules!"

The rabbit turns to him. "Don't you have anything better to do with your life?"

That draws him up short for a couple of seconds. He *is* short, not even Diana's height, so the bunny might be intimidating—although he seems to be staring right into her cleavage as he tries to put together a response. "You can't ignore the rules," he finally says, giving her his best glare. "What happens if everyone ignores the rules?"

"What happens if I snap you like a birch twig?"

Diana glances around, nervous. Yeah, people are staring. The tiger's looking back with an ugly smirk, a vixen one line over is glaring, the stoat has his hand on a phone behind the register like he's going to call over a manager.

"It's fine." She holds up a hand to the rabbit placatingly, and starts to pull her cart out of line.

"No." The taller woman puts her hand on Diana's cart. It's a casual motion, but she might as well have set a one-ton rock in the basket. Suddenly it's not going anywhere. "You only have one item over, and that tiger has at least two dozen items in his cart."

The tiger glowers at her. "I'm not the one making a scene."

"No, he is." She jerks a thumb at the weasel. "And about the sheep, not you."

"I didn't see his cart," the weasel protests.

"Come on," the rabbit snaps. "You have eyes."

The weasel doesn't say anything, just crosses his arms. The tiger snorts, shaking his head. Even the squirrel looks upset, but more in a shit-rolls-downhill way. The stoat still has two of her eight items to tally.

"Ma'am, you're going to have to get out of line," the stoat says.

Diana sighs heavily and starts trying to back up. The rabbit's hand remains on her cart. *Oh, come on, let it go, lady.* Standing on principle only causes trouble.

The rabbit locks eyes with the stoat. "Make them both leave," she says flatly, "or ring them both up."

"Or what?" The tiger turns to the sheep's self-appointed bunny savior, looking exasperated. "I don't know what it is with you herbivores. You know what? Rabbits are the worst, always acting like the rules don't—"

He disappears, along with his cart.

"I'm not a rabbit. I'm a hare. Hares are bigger."

"What the..." Diana looks around wildly. She can still kind of hear him, but distantly. *Squeakily.* The weasel who started it has disappeared, too.

The rabbit—hare—lets go of her cart. "Watch your step."

She looks down, then shrieks. Her left hoof dwarfs both the tiger and his cart. He's staring up, making incoherent mewling noises. Tiny mewling noises.

"Better yet, don't," the hare continues, looking down at the toy-sized, abruptly bluster-free cat.

"What? I can't step on him!"

"Of course you can. It's easy. Watch." The woman turns around and smashes her paw down on the weasel. "You could crush the cart, too, without hurting yourself. There's no stomp like a hoof stomp."

Diana watches, open-mouthed. She casually *shrank* someone and *stepped* on them just for being annoying? For being casually speciesist? For benefiting from species registries and all the discrimination built on top of them? Discrimination that created "Grasstowns" like this one? That created *decades* of shit that people like him—like the weasel, the stoat, the smirking vixen—never had to deal with and wouldn't see even if you smashed their faces against it, crushed them under a giant paw, ground them under a hoof—

She puts a hand to her muzzle. It's not that she's horrified at the thought of how easy smiting the tiger for his impudence would be, it's that she *isn't* horrified by it. At all. And *that* horrifies her.

And where the hell did "smiting him for his impudence" come from?

"You're up," the hare says, pointing.

Diana blinks herself out of her headspace, looking back and forth. The entire grocery store has come to a stop, everyone staring at her. Maybe they're staring at the hare. Maybe both.

"I. Uh." She rolls her cart forward, hesitates, and brings her hoof *right* over the tiger, holding it there like the threat of divine retribution.

"Please!" he yells at the top of his tiny little lungs. "I'm sorry!"

She feels her temper flare. "Tell me what you're sorry *for.*"

"I don't know! I don't know!"

She stomps her hoof down, *hard*, right next to him. He howls and faints dead away.

Snorting, she unloads her cart. "Are you going to give me trouble?" she says to the stoat, letting her tone fill with acid. She isn't the one who did any of this, she doesn't know *how* the hare did any of this, but right now she feels—powerful. She feels a thousand feet tall.

Good lord, Diana, what's gotten into you?

The stoat, eyes wide, shakes his head quickly, and starts ringing her up, for the first time as fast as he should be.

"I'd make a terrible goddess," Diana mutters under her breath, pulling out her credit card.

"No." The hare studies her. "I don't think you would."

Diana starts to flash a puzzled smile at her in return. *Don't engage, she's a super-powered psychopath, you idiot.* Clearing her throat, she takes her card and her bagged groceries from the clerk. "Are you...going to make him normal-size again?"

The hare shrugs. "Do you want me to?"

"Yes. Of course. I mean..." She looks down at him. "What I *want* is for him to not be the way he is."

The woman hands her single item—a bottle of single malt rye—to the clerk. "Ah, well. He'll remember that I shrank him and that you spared his life, and that might mean something. It probably won't, though. He'll convince himself it didn't happen, because nobody else will remember any of it." She pays, and strolls toward the exit.

Diana follows. "Including me?"

"Including you. Sorry."

"I..." She runs a hand through her thick hair. "But I want to remember."

They step out into the too-small parking lot and the oppressive heat, enveloped by the smell of asphalt and stagnant polluted puddles, the sounds of tires and brakes and car horns from the weary traffic crawling along the suburb's main thoroughfare. A battered grey sedan with a THIRD EYE SECURITY logo idles by the far entrance, the panther behind the wheel staring down at his phone with a bored expression.

"You're sure?"

"Yes," she says, unhesitatingly.

"All right, then." The hare smiles, and for a moment, the rest of the world vanishes, leaving only her. Only this tall, mysterious, murderous woman, the most beautiful being in the universe, favoring Diana with the delirious experience of being a veritable goddess in line at the grocery store.

Then it's over, and she's walking away.

But Diana *does* know her, she's sure of it, from somewhere. She can't think of the show or the movie or the song or anything else, but she can think of a name. "Moira," she murmurs.

The hare stops, goes perfectly still for a moment, then turns. "How did you know my name?" Her tone isn't threatening, isn't accusing. It's wondering.

"I don't know." Her mouth goes dry, but it's the truth. "I just... recognize you."

"Do you." The woman crosses her arms. "And you are?"

"Diana." She tries not to stammer. "Diana Lindsay."

"Nobody's recognized me for a very, *very* long time, Diana Lindsay."

"Are you..."

She waits expectantly, lifting a brow.

"A goddess?" Somehow Diana knows the answer is yes. She doesn't believe in gods, not like this, but it doesn't matter.

"This world doesn't have gods. Not any more."

That's not a no. "Maybe it should." It slips out sounding defiant. "It's not as if us mortals have done a great job on our own."

"No, you haven't." Moira's tone is matter-of-fact. "If you *did* have the power of a god, what would you do?"

"I don't—" Diana shakes her head. "Like I said, I'd make a terrible goddess."

"And I said you wouldn't. If I was one, wouldn't I know?"

"I'd think anyone who wants to be a god probably shouldn't be."

"I'd think it depends on why they want it."

"I don't know yet!" Diana winces at herself as soon as she says it. *Yet?*

Moira narrows her eyes, slowly looking Diana up and down, then uncrosses her arms and laughs. "That's an honest answer." She holds out her free hand.

The sheep reaches for it, then pauses, wondering if some kind of...offer has just been made. Ludicrous. But this entire afternoon has been ludicrous.

Biting her lip, she takes Moira's hand.

She's prepared for electricity, a lightning bolt, fire, ice, something, *anything*. Anything except what she gets: a tall, bewitching woman clasping her hand for a couple of seconds and letting go. That's it.

"Um." She looks at her hand. "Am I...?"

"Are you what?"

Diana lets out a soft chuckle. "Never mind."

"I hope keeping this memory gives you dreams, not nightmares." She lifts the bottle as if making a toast, and starts walking away. "Maybe it'll give you an answer to that question."

"And then what?"

The hare doesn't turn around, walking toward a crimson red Porsche Panamera. "And then you'll know."

"Just tell me who you are. *What* you are."

The hare drops into her car, gives the sheep that same slight smile as before, and roars out of the parking lot.

Diana stares after her, then pushes her cart toward her old Subaru. After she unloads it, she reaches for the door handle and stops. No. She has to see.

She heads back into the store.

Everything there's normal. Nobody's talking about the way two people impossibly shrank, the way a hare woman stepped on one and a sheep woman threatened to step on the other. The stoat checkout guy glances past her without obvious recognition. And wait. Isn't that the weasel Moira stepped on leaving the store, normal height, unharmed?

She couldn't have imagined it all. But—

Why *would* she want the power of a god, anyway?

Shaking her head at herself, she walks back out to her car. She's so lost in her thoughts she doesn't see the tiger until he literally grabs her, gripping both shoulders and spinning her around to face him.

"What the hell did you *do* to me?" he snarls.

She stares up, letting out an involuntary bleat, and pushes against him. "Nothing!" He remembers? But he wasn't—shit, that means—

"It wasn't you, it was the damned rabbit." He shoves her away, looking around wildly, and starts advancing on her, baring his teeth. "But you threatened to *step* on me!"

She backs up. "But I didn't," she protests. "Not that you deserved being spared."

Oh, why did she say that, she *knows* she shouldn't have said that. Now he's even angrier. She looks around desperately. A few bystanders watch: a couple of frightened mice, a sad-looking deer woman.

"Cunt!" he screams, swinging his fist at her face. She bleats again, raising her hands to block him. If she was really a goddess, this fucker would be staring up at her hoof again, he—

He vanishes.

Diana lowers her hands, eyes wide. She almost doesn't want to look down.

Almost.

She does, and there he is. He's fallen on his butt in one of the parking lot's noxious puddles, staring up at her open-mouthed.

The black sheep slowly leans over, watching him. The herbivores who were watching her have moved closer, their own eyes wide, and other people coming out of the store have stopped to watch, too.

"Help me!" the little tiger squeals. "Dammit, help me!"

She watches him, and she knows. She can *see*. He isn't sorry. He doesn't know what he should be sorry for, and even if he did, he wouldn't be. He's always behaved this way to herbivores, to women, to anyone he can. To anyone who can't fight back. And she's seen more than enough of this mortal.

"No. I gave you your chance." Straightening up, towering, she raises that almighty hoof and brings it down squarely on top of him.

Oh, shit. She just—oh dear God, how could she have—why did she think "this mortal," it's not as if—

—but she feels *something* in her, about her—

She looks around at the bystanders, at least a dozen people. They look shocked, but they're not screaming and pointing, not shooting live video, not calling the police.

The deer woman drops to her knees. Then the mice. Then, by ones and twos, the rest of them. Even the carnivores. Even the security guard.

Diana bolts back to her car as if demons were after her.

9

two
things that need
breaking

M oira gets down a double rocks glass, drops in two ice
cubes, and fills the glass up with the rye she bought yesterday, taking a seat on the couch.

It's a nice sofa, right? She tells herself that every time she sits
down on it, trying to convince herself this particular modern style
isn't ass. It's fine. It's just not her style.

The condo came furnished. She's been here three months.
Somehow, this is her first time living in the San Francisco area.
Maybe. Was she here during the Gold Rush? No. She was up north
of here for a while, but in one of her especially misanthropic
phases. She remembers nearly leveling a small mountain settlement. The bartender at the one saloon in town saved them by
giving her free drinks and good advice on where to go next.

She puts her paws up on the coffee table, takes a long drink, and
stares at the ceiling. The same question has cycled through her
mind for the past twenty-four hours and change: how did Diana
know her name?

Worse, how does she not *know* how Diana knew her name?
Sure, she's not omniscient, let alone omnipotent, but this is...

Well, if she knew what it was, it wouldn't be eating at her,
would it.

Okay. Hypothesize. Could Diana be a secret worshipper of the old gods? No. She was sincerely clueless about who Moira was. She recognized her, but she didn't *know* her.

So that recognition wasn't conscious. On some level, Diana believes that the world needs gods.

Great. Warm fuzzies for the forgotten goddess. But she knows damn well the sheep isn't the *only* person she's met in the last few thousand years who believes that. In her less antisocial decades, she drank with countless grizzled warriors and earnest monks lamenting how the world needed to return to the ways of the old gods. And not one of them ever squinted over their cups at her and called her by name.

"Then what *is* it about her?" she bellows. Her voice echoes around the living room, but doesn't come back with an answer.

Moira sits up, takes another long swig of whiskey, and rubs her face. She shouldn't have let Diana go. She should have brought her home and—and—what? If she genuinely didn't know why she recognized Moira, there was no answer to threaten or seduce out of her.

But, no, instead she let the woman remember Moira as the petulant, short-tempered goddess she is. She let her remember what it's like to have an enemy literally at her feet, and let her ponder what she'd do if she had the power of a god. Diana seemed to think Moira was about to *make* her a god, as if the hare could do that merely by taking her hand and wishing it.

She could have, once. But that wasn't just another time, it was another Moira. Even if she still could, like she said, the world doesn't have gods anymore. It doesn't want gods.

Maybe it should.

Abruptly, a wave of nausea washes over her. Moira hurriedly sets down the glass, and sprawls across the couch on her side, waiting for it to pass. What *is* this? It's been happening for weeks. She can't get sick; she knows she isn't pregnant. She'd been feeling better since finding a few local craft breweries—finally, good beer in this country—and feeling *great* since the run-in with Diana, better than she remembers feeling in years, even decades. Until she started thinking about it later. Maybe that's her mistake.

Why did she drive down to *that* grocery store, anyway? She could have walked to one of a half-dozen markets in the city, to a specialty liquor store or two. But no, she got up yesterday morning and thought *hey, time to visit South San Francisco.* Time to find somewhere a degree or two more hostile to herbivores, a degree or two more likely to piss her off.

Time to find somewhere she'd just *happen* to run into that sheep.

It's not that Moira doesn't believe in coincidences as a concept, but coincidences don't happen to her, don't happen to gods. What was it Briley used to say? A god's whim always means something.

Yeah, well. She's had nothing but whim to follow for the last few thousand years, nothing to do but kill time until the world ends. She wishes, not for the first time, that it'd hurry up and fucking end already.

Moira sits up gingerly. Enough. She's got to fill the hours with more than ale. She doesn't need money, but she needs work again. What's San Francisco known for? Mining's over, right? Bars, but she can't ruin liquor by making it a job. A great food scene, but— no. Too much, still. Lots of technology, but computers mostly piss her off, so she'd simply end up destroying a tech office. Although from what she's gathered, a lot of them could use a good stomping.

"There's no stomp like a hoof stomp," she murmurs, and shakes her head at herself, smirking. Diana might not have made a terrible goddess, but you absolutely do, Moira.

Okay, so then what? A few years ago, she could have paged through a phone book, but they don't have those anymore. That was a hell of a brief blip in history. They have temp agencies, though. She could check what one of those has. Hmm. Fashion agency? They'll tell her she's too tall and muscular to be a model, but if she wants to, she'll convince them otherwise.

If she wants to.

First step, though: get out of the condo and go somewhere besides a damn brewery.

She takes the elevator down to street level, walks out, and summons a jacket to pull around herself as she starts down the sidewalk. The old-to-mortals joke "the coldest winter I ever spent was a summer in San Francisco" is stupid—she's been in countless winters in the subtropics colder than it ever gets here—but she's sympathetic to the spirit.

Does San Francisco have a fashion district? It must. There's a clothing company or two headquartered here, she's pretty sure. No idea where, though. Maybe near the financial district, which seems to be where her paws are taking her. Or maybe that's divine whim again. Ha ha ugh.

In her experience so far, San Francisco thinks of itself as simultaneously more and less of a great world city than it is. Nothing mortals built here is awe-inspiring, but most of it's pretty. Dirty, too, but everyone pretends it's worse than the reality. Inequality, that's a real issue. But it's been one as long as she can remember—it's why she's stuck here, instead of having fucked off to wherever the other gods fucked off to. Still, the gap here startles her. There are probably more herbivores living on the street than there are in housing within the city limits. Ironically, San Francisco doesn't have that much blatant legal discrimination; this is all organically grown economic disparity.

She turns down Howard, walking right into the thick of the city's skyscrapers. What might other gods have thought of modern cities? Any one of these buildings would have been a true wonder of the world a few hundred years ago. Now they're high rise monuments to white-collar drudgery.

Pedestrians crowd the sidewalk here; it's a weekday, and the Financial District buzzes for twelve hours a day, five days a week. Five hours from now, past seven o'clock, it'll be quiet except around the hotels and the restaurants that cater to convention-goers, to business dinners instead of worker lunches.

So just where is she going? She stops at a corner and considers her own question. She hasn't gone job-hunting recently and she's gotten the impression much of it's moved "online" now, but she's been able to walk into an office and get a job for as long as there have been offices. Even in this computerized everything moment, offices are still staffed by mortals she can wrap around her finger with a few seconds of charm.

Okay. Looking up at buildings tells her nothing. She picks the tallest one at this intersection and walks into the lobby, studying the directory.

Financial companies, check. Tech companies, check. A construction company. A venture capital firm. Nothing that sounds like she'd want to work there, even for laughs. She turns and heads back toward the exit.

A woman in a wheelchair, a pika who couldn't be out of her twenties yet, rolls past her in the same direction. She's devastatingly cute in a kind of butch way: short sandy hair, denim shorts, faded t-shirt tight around both chest and biceps. Moira moves to hold the door for her, but the pika slaps the door open button as she rolls past, effectively holding the door for the hare. "Thanks," she says, walking behind her.

"You're welcome." The pika looks up at her, and tilts her head, slowing her roll and studying the hare more intently. "Do I know you?"

Again? Seriously? She shakes her head. "No."

"Okay." The pika nods and wheels ahead.

Moira makes it four more steps before a luxury coupe, a red and grey imported two-seater, screeches into a prime parking spot in front of the building—a space clearly marked with the blue and white disability sign. The car's hood slides into a no-parking zone before the driver slams on the brakes.

The pika slams on the brakes, too—from the way she jerks in the chair, as literally as wheelchairs get. She'd been heading for a curb cut that the front of the sports car now blocks. "What the hell, man!"

The driver, a tiger who looks like the asshole from yesterday but in a nicer suit, jumps out. He has to have heard the pika, but he doesn't even look at her.

"That's a handicapped space," Moira says, stepping in front of him close enough to force him to stop.

"Only gonna be here a half-hour. And I'm late." He steps around her.

"Asshole," the pika says, loudly enough that he gives her a dirty look. "You're parking illegally *and* parking like a dick, too."

He rolls his eyes. "Just go around." Clearly, to him the pika's the asshole for calling him on his shit.

"Move your car," Moira says flatly, "or I'm going to step on it."

He doesn't stop walking toward the building, but he turns to look at her incredulously. "What kind of crazy threat is that, bunnygirl?"

"That's a no, right?" She clasps her hands together and grins. "I've been wanting a good excuse to do this for years now."

He points at her. "Touch my car and I'll have your carrot-eating ass in jail." He turns around, heading into the building.

"Back up," she tells the pika.

"Oooookay." She does so.

Moira strides forward, rapidly growing as she moves. Her second step shakes the sidewalk. Her third adds new cracks to it. Her fourth takes her right into the street, cars in both directions braking to avoid hitting a paw as long as a delivery truck.

She pivots, bringing her other paw down right on top of the car. She lets it rest there a second, then begins shifting her weight.

The tiger runs out of the building, staring up at Moira, screaming. He's the only one running toward her. Everyone else is sensibly running away.

He stops in front of his car, pinwheeling his arms. She makes a show of it, letting each luxury tire blow out and each luxury window shatter as the luxury roof meets the luxury seats. It takes maybe five seconds for the whole luxury cabin to become one with the luxury floorboards.

"Holy fucking shit." The pika hasn't fled, either. She's staring up at Moira, dazzled rather than scared.

"No!" The cat screams. "No! What the hell—you can't—oh my God!"

"Goddess," the pika says.

Moira looks down at her sharply.

The tiger screams again. "A giant rabbit—giant rabbit crushed—"

"Not a rabbit," Moira mutters. A truck trying to inch past her taps its horn. She grits her teeth, but stops herself from giving it a reflexive kick. Instead, she picks up the flattened car, crumples it into a ball, and waves at the now-unblocked curb cut. "There you go," she says to the pika.

The woman keeps staring up at her, and barely whispers a name. *Her* name. "Moira."

Abruptly Moira returns to her normal size, standing by the wheelchair. She leans over, expression hard. "Why did you call me that?"

That gets the pika looking frightened, but for only a moment. "Myths. I love old myths and folk tales. And I know the ones about a beautiful hare, the goddess of love and war, sometimes as tall as the sky."

"And you think gods are real?"

"I didn't."

"I'm not the asshole!" the tiger wails.

"You are *totally* the asshole," the pika snaps before Moira can respond. "If I could make myself giant, I'd fucking eat you."

Moira smirks. "Honestly, I'd enjoy seeing that."

The tiger's ears flatten, and he pulls out his phone.

Moira waves a hand, and he freezes. Everything freezes, except for her and the pika. The pika looks around, eyes snapping open wide again.

"It's easier," Moira says simply. "I'm going to have to figure out a different memory to give everyone of all this, except him. Nobody will believe his car got crushed by a giant hare." She crosses her arms. "What's your name?"

"Hazel." She swallows. "You…you're really her, aren't you?"

Moira sighs, and nods curtly.

"*Please* let me remember this."

She knows that's a bad idea, but the girl seems so sincere, and at least she *has* an explanation for why she came up with Moira's name. Not a fully satisfying one, one that still ends with "I don't know, it's just you." But.

The same question she asked Diana pops unbidden into her head. *No, you sorry excuse for a war god, don't ask it.* Even though you want to know. *It's a fancy. It's toying with the poor woman's emotions.*

She looks up at the gray sky, and asks the damn question anyway. "What would you do if you had the power of a god, Hazel?"

The pika blinks several times, and focuses back on Moira. "Fix things that need fixing and break things that need breaking."

"That's a good answer." *It's the answer she'd have given a couple of millennia ago. Although seeing where it got her, maybe it's not that good an answer after all.* "All right."

"All right...?"

"You can keep the memory." She holds out a hand for Hazel. A moment later, the pika takes it, and breaks out into an adorably blissful grin.

As Moira starts to walk away, Hazel squeaks. "Will I see you again?"

"I don't know." Moira shrugs without looking back. "I'm in the area." She snaps her fingers, and the world picks up where it left off. Almost. Everyone but Hazel and the tiger resume their business as if nothing strange had happened over the last ten minutes. Or, rather, only one thing: a crushed ball of once-luxury car sits next to a handicapped parking space. Passersby stare, but nobody asks any questions. It's San Francisco.

The tiger still has his phone out, Moira guesses, from the way he launches into more cursing. She hears Hazel cursing back. Hopefully he's not going to cause trouble for the pika. There's still time to crush him like his car. On the flip side, Hazel seems like she can take care of herself, and Moira's caused enough trouble for the afternoon.

She's rounded the corner toward Market when she hears screeching traffic and horns blaring behind her. And a crash. Furrowing her brow, Moira turns back.

Hazel and her wheelchair sit dangerously in the middle of the street—but not dangerously for Hazel. The pika might have been five and a half feet tall if she stood, but now she has to be at least the size Moira was a few minutes ago, chair sized to match. She blocks traffic completely on one side of the street, but she's too preoccupied to pay attention. She's dropping her hand away from her muzzle, as if she's just stuffed something in her mouth. Or someone.

The pika makes a funny face, as if debating whether she *really* wants to do this, then tilts her head back and swallows.

Moira runs a hand through her hair. She should ask what the hell happened, but she can see what the hell happened. She can *feel* what the hell happened. What she doesn't know is *how* what the hell happened. There is, as of about two minutes ago, a new goddess in the world, and her first act of divinity was becoming giant and swallowing an idiot tiger whole.

Which, fine, Moira *did* enjoy seeing.

Hazel looks around her wheels now with obvious delight, although her ears dip when she sees the fender bender behind her. "Sorry," she calls. "I'll…uh…" She trails off, her expression shifting to wide-eyed confusion. The crowd that's left around her isn't running. They're dropping to their knees, looking up at her adoringly.

Moira strokes her chin. Hazel might get the hang of it on her own. She'll have to check if there's any news about this in tomorrow's papers. If the pika plays her cards right, figures out what to do, there won't be.

And if she doesn't, well. Maybe the world *could* use a new god who's up for fixing things. She's got an impressive head start on the breaking things part.

But—

Don't play dumb with yourself. It wasn't Hazel, it was you. It had to be you.

And it wasn't Diana…

Cursing under her breath, Moira tears her gaze away from the giant pika and hurries to the closest newsstand. She needs to check if there's any news about *yesterday* in *today's* papers.

three
weather report

F resh coffee at hand, Lily Parker opens the morning weather report.

The data it tracks isn't weather in the sense anyone outside her organization understands it. It has currents and patterns, ebbs and flows, but it's a far different mix than hot and cold air masses: it's the mix of order and chaos across the world. Law against lawlessness, calm against riots, hierarchy against anarchy. As with the natural climate, mortal actions influence it across the long term; unlike the climate, it's been slowly but steadily moving in the desired direction. More order, less chaos.

The silver vixen stops, goes back two frames, zooms in on a map of northern California, and frowns.

The mix is volatile, naturally, and she expects regressions. San Francisco remains too tumultuous for the company's tastes, although they're making some breakthroughs thanks to the tech billionaire class. This late in the project, though, there should be few truly unpredicted bursts of chaos.

And this outbreak isn't the kind she'd expect in San Francisco, not the quick flurry of an anti-authority street protest or the simmer of a temporarily successful collective. This burst is strong, with no antecedents they'd been tracking, and most alarmingly, it's *instant.* That's unusual.

That makes two in the same region, separated by a single day. She adjusts the date range to bring both of them into view. With a right-click on the southern one, she runs a quick news search for stories originating in that area since it happened. No headlines stand out. A right-click on the one within San Francisco, a day later, shows—hmm. One curious headline from a popular local blog about a traffic jam on Howard onlookers swear had been caused by...

A giant young pika woman. In a wheelchair.

Scowling, she sends the article to Torrance, the head of Celestial Venture Partners in Palo Alto, with a short note: *Have an explanation for this by 8:30 am your time.*

She presses a button on her desk intercom. "Ms. Storm."

"Yes, Ms. Parker?"

"I'm sending you two points of interest from the weather map. I want you to find anything about them online that the system's standard news search might not pick up. I particularly want anything that can verify the story about the pika woman."

"Got it. I'll get back with that shortly."

"Thank you." She pauses. "Do we know if Moira is in the San Francisco Bay Area?"

She hears the rat typing furiously for a few seconds. She's no longer wholly sure what research magic her assistant's capable of, but she's faster with answers than any search engine, and before that, any librarian. "Her last known residence was Rio de Janeiro, where she lived for twenty-eight years. But she left eight years ago. We have no later records of her."

"Hmm." She drums her fingers on the desk. "So she stayed entirely off our radar since. She was quiet in Rio, wasn't she, too? By her standards."

Ms. Storm sounds amused. "With that important qualification, yes, ma'am. Do you think she's connected with these?"

Parker smiles humorlessly. Quiet for Moira entails one or two incidents a generation when she rains down chaos because she's taken affront over something, rather than one or two a year. By that measure, she's been reasonably quiet going on a century. "I can't say yet. But these manifesting less than two weeks after the events at Test Site 3 sets my ears back. We only have half a year to finish."

"Yes, ma'am. I'll keep my eyes open for Moira as well."

When Storm disconnects, the vixen takes off her glasses and rubs her temples. She'd suspected for years that Moira had gone quiet in part because she'd grown ever less interested in mortal affairs, but also because she was as aware of the changing times as they were. In past times they'd discreetly contained her effects, keeping her out of the news of the day and keeping themselves from her attention. Moira had been doing more of the containing on her own for the past century or two, though, a decidedly mixed blessing. Mr. Nunwick simultaneously wanted the organization to keep close track of Moira's misadventures and to keep him from ever hearing of them. If she had to explain this level of chaos, now, it would be deemed a spectacular failure.

Her spectacular failure.

Yet if Moira *was* behind this nonsense, it was…different. Making a mortal giant so *they* could wreak havoc isn't her style; Parker doesn't need to flip back through case histories to know that. The damn woman wouldn't be so good at staying off their radar if she was that blatant.

She sighs, closing the weather map, and goes about the more mundane business of running a billion-dollar private equity firm.

It's over an hour before Ms. Storm calls her back. "Here's what I've found, Ms. Parker, and it's…somewhat unsettling. There are several cell phone photos of the pika woman on social media, and some commentary from witnesses who reported feeling compelled to drop to their knees around her."

Parker sits up. "Really."

"Yes. Fortunately, the stories haven't gotten much traction, and no major news source has issued any corroboration."

She knows that effect, and so does Ms. Storm: the compulsion a mortal gets around a god who's just performed a divine act. "You're sure they're referring to the pika woman, specifically."

"And to the sheep."

The vixen rubs her temples again. "The who?"

"The later incident you asked me to look into involves the pika; the previous one involves the sheep. A similar event in a super-market parking lot. She didn't become giant, but she apparently shrank someone and flattened him underhoof."

"And instead of running, bystanders fell to their knees."

"That's what several reports say. They're as unverifiable as the reports about the pika, I'm afraid, but…"

"But a sufficient amount of anecdotal data suggests real data, yes."

"I think so. None of the reports mention a rabbit or hare in either location."

As Storm speaks, mail comes in from the Palo Alto office, five minutes late.

I'm assigning an agent right now and we're getting security camera footage as I type this. Get back to you ASAP.

Security camera footage. Would Moira remember to erase that if she were involved? Not explicitly, but she was powerful enough that if she placed a geas of forgetting on the area it might well affect machinery. She supposes she'll give Mr. Torrance the benefit of the doubt for now, though. "All right. Ms. Storm, keep looking for any sign of Moira. She's never deified a mortal before that we know of, but she's the only one outside our organization that we know could. If she's changed her modus operandi after several thousand years, we need to know why. Fast."

"Yes, ma'am."

She drums her fingers on the desk again. Hopefully she can get a handle on this before Mr. Nunwick gets wind of it. More than anything else, Parker hates waiting for the next shoe to drop.

four
levitating plushies

Hazel's wheelchair appears on the sidewalk in front of her house with a window-rattling bang. From the jarring drop, it might have teleported in an inch or two over the sidewalk, not on it. She'll have to work on that.

An elderly dingo woman on the sidewalk a few doors down, holding a watering can, stares at Hazel open-mouthed.

Oh, she'll have to work on that, too. Dammit. She wiggles her fingers at the woman. "Forget everything." As soon as she says it, a voice in the back of her head screams, *you fool, she'll forget literally* everything *including her name!* Hazel starts to stammer out a retraction. Remember everything? No, that'd be worse. What about—

But no, as far as she can tell nothing happens at all. The dingo freezes for a full second, then drops the watering can and bolts inside her row house.

"I guess I should just keep taking the damn bus," Hazel mutters, rolling toward her door. Even with the nice street level entrance, one of the irritatingly few in the Castro without steps, it's a nuisance: a barred wrought iron screen door swings out while a heavy wooden door swings in. Her housemate likes the extra security of the second lockable door, though.

Hmm. She tries wiggling her fingers at the first door. "Open." Nothing.

Come *on,* she was a fucking *giantess* an hour ago. How did she do that? How did she change back? She pictured herself Moira's size, and later pictured herself back at normal size, right?

Picturing stuff. Maybe that's the key. She pictures the door swinging open.

It swings open.

Hazel bounces in her chair, clapping, and rolls ahead. She still opens the inner door by hand without even thinking about it.

Rhiannon's sitting on the living room sofa, laptop balanced across her crossed legs as usual. The room doesn't get much natural light, but the squirrel's got the knack of a gifted interior designer, accenting the white walls with pastel pink and blue decor. The couch is a neutral gray, but pillows, crocheted throws, and a half-dozen whimsical plushies—five of them Hazel's—stand out against it. She looks up, brushing long curly black hair away from her face. "I thought you'd be out longer."

"Yeah, so did I." Hazel starts to reach for the door to close it, but instead tries willing it shut. It slams closed. The pika winces.

The squirrel stares, setting down the laptop. "How'd you do that?"

"Magic. I guess. I'm still practicing."

Rhiannon narrows her eyes and walks over, smoothing down her skirt. She's tall, towering over Hazel (*for now,* ha), and she's chosen orange for today's theme: pale orange tank top, deeper orange miniskirt, amber-gold bangles around wrists and ankles. "Seriously." She studies the door and Hazel's wheelchair. "What did you do?"

Hazel scratches the back of one of her round ears. "This is going to take a while to explain, and even longer to convince you I'm not bullshitting you."

Rhiannon gives her a long, appraising look. "You're lucky I think you're so cute," she says with a sigh, dropping back into her seat and motioning for Hazel to go on.

"I *am* cute," Hazel says, locking the chair's brake. "It's a curse." She gets up, steadying herself for a second, and walks across the carpet to the couch and sits down on her end. "So. Do you know who Moira is?"

"Moira who?"

"Moira, the goddess of love and war."

"Oh, *that* Moira. Sure, we used to hang out at that dive bar over in Noe Valley."

Hazel picks up one of the plush toys, a cartoonish blue shark, and tosses it at the squirrel.

Rhiannon deflects it. "I don't remember much about mythology classes. What about her?"

"I met her."

The squirrel stares at her blankly, unmoving.

"I know how that sounds." Hazel raises her hands. "But I swear. I met her."

"You met a woman who told you she was Moira?"

"No, I had to pry it out of her at first."

Rhiannon covers her face and sighs melodramatically. "You mean *you* told *her* she was Moira, and she said yes."

"No. I mean, yes, kind of, but that's not—" She takes a deep breath. "Rhi, I have *powers* now. She did something to me." She points. "That's what I did with the door."

"Powers," Rhiannon repeats. "Like…superpowers."

The pika nods. "Yeah."

"Such as? Super speed? Strength? Or just the ability to magically close doors?" She holds up her hands. "Evildoers beware, it's the Incredible Door Closer!"

Hazel crosses her arms. She's got to come up with a better demonstration, but what? Nothing potentially dangerous, and nothing that's going to freak Rhiannon out. Much.

She bites her lip and concentrates. All the plush toys smoothly rise into the air and slowly begin circling Rhiannon's head.

The squirrel's eyes get wide, darting from toy to toy. She grabs one, searching it for hidden wires, then tosses it across the room. Hazel "catches" it and sends it back into position.

"How are you doing that?" The squirrel's voice is higher pitched, breathier than normal.

"I don't know. I just...picture what I want to happen and it does."

Rhiannon gives her a terrified look. "Anything?"

"I don't know," Hazel repeats, letting the plush toys drop back to the sofa. "Well, no. I'm pretty sure I'm not omnipotent."

The squirrel closes her eyes, holding her head in her hands and rocking back and forth. "This doesn't make any sense. What else are you going to tell me you've done?"

"Uh, I teleported back here from downtown." She clears her throat and adds in a mumble, "And I became a giantess."

Rhiannon snaps her eyes open. "What did you say?"

Hazel looks at the ceiling. She feels weirdly like her mom's caught her sneaking from a cookie jar. "There was a guy being a real asshole to Moira and me, and she got giant and stepped on his car, and I said to him if I could become giant I'd eat him. When Moira left, suddenly I felt like this, like I was *powerful*, like I was..." She takes a deep breath. "Like I was a goddess. And..." She trails off, not at all liking the way her roommate's staring again.

"You think you're a goddess."

"Well...maybe?"

"And you're telling me you became a giant. You know that's impossible." She narrows her eyes. "You didn't eat him, did you?"

Hazel crosses her arms. "Obviously not, if becoming a giant is impossible!"

"Hazel!"

The pika covers her face. "God, I'm hearing myself, and now I'm wondering if I'm going crazy. But it was... I could feel his hatred. *Hate.* Unredeemable hate. That's the only way to put it. Not of me, specifically, but of everyone he thought was beneath him. All the herbivores. Anyone lower class." She points at her chair. "Anyone with one of those."

"You're saying you saw into his soul. Because you're a goddess."

Hazel rubs the back of her ear, eyes widening. "Yeah," she mumbles. "Holy hell. I did."

She looks at the pika pleadingly. "You know how—how *insane* this all sounds."

"How do you explain what I just did? What you just saw?"

"I don't know, Hazel. I can't. But faking levitating plushies isn't exactly parting the sea."

"It wasn't faking." She sighs, shrugging. "I couldn't think of anything else to do that wouldn't freak you out even more, or damage something, or risk hurting you."

Rhiannon chews on her lip, then gets up. "All right. If this is real, we need to figure out what powers you have, how you *really* got them, and what you should do with them."

"We?"

"I don't have anything else to do until I get a job again, assuming I ever get one." She walks to Hazel's chair. "Can I ask a delicate question?"

Hazel pushes herself to her paws and walks to the chair, too. "If I'm a goddess—"

"—which you're not—"

"—do I still need this." It's not as if she hasn't already thought about it, but she's not sure whatever powers she has extend to curing the incurable. And she's been using it for over a decade. She sits down in it and looks up at the squirrel. "The truth is, I don't know. But there's something powerful about the image of a goddess using a wheelchair. Does that sound crazy?"

"No," Rhiannon says after a moment. "Honestly, if there *were* such a thing as gods, the world could do worse than to have one like you." She looks at the door. "Do what you did before, but without slamming anything."

Hazel looks at the door. Okay, think about gently opening it, reaching over and turning the knob, pulling it back...

The door opens, without slamming. She opens the iron door that way, too, and looks at Rhiannon triumphantly.

The squirrel slowly steps through the door onto the sidewalk, eyes wide. Hazel follows, rolling the chair along manually. She bets she can magically race along at freeway speeds, but she's not ready to try. Yet.

"Make yourself giant," Rhiannon says.

"What?"

"There's nobody on the street, and we don't get much traffic on it. You won't hurt anything. Make yourself giant."

"You don't think I can do it, do you?"

In response, Rhiannon waves her hands grandly toward the avenue.

Hazel grins, and rolls to the closest curb cut and out into the street. Okay. How did she do this before? She just did. She wanted to be big, and—

With a soft sonic boom, she's the hundred-foot tall pika woman again, enthroned in her appropriately sized chair—which sinks a few inches into the street as if it were sand. The blast of wind from air she displaces sends trash skittering down the sidewalks and blows Rhiannon's hair back like a banner for a second.

The squirrel stares up, mouth open, and steadies herself against a lamp post, looking weak-kneed.

Hazel leans over. "You okay?"

Rhiannon keeps staring up, breathing hard, gripping the post as if it's all that keeps her from collapsing. She manages a shaky nod.

A few people step out of buildings along the street to investigate the noise. They're all staring, too, naturally. A shrew woman Hazel's seen before a few times slowly gets to her knees.

"Still sure I'm not a goddess?" Hazel murmurs to Rhiannon.

The squirrel straightens up, but keeps a hand on the post. "You're a superhero."

"Oh, so divinity is nonsense, but physics-violating mutant powers are a-ok. Got it."

"It's a working theory." She takes a tentative step forward, then walks into the street in front of the wheelchair and puts her hands on her hips. "Although if you really ate somebody, you're a supervillain."

Hazel leans over more, holding her hand out for the squirrel, palm up. "I'm telling you, you don't understand how unredeemable he was."

"Still a supervillain." Rhiannon stares at the hand dubiously.

"C'mon, I'm not going to eat you."

That gets Rhiannon to look up at her, and the squirrel visibly blushes. Hazel grins lopsidedly. She didn't mean it as a double entendre.

"Not as reassuring as you might think," the squirrel eventually mutters, but she climbs onto the pika's hand.

"Okay, comics nerd." Hazel gently sets Rhiannon down on her thigh, which makes the squirrel tense up. "Should I set you somewhere else?"

"No. Uh, this is fine." She looks up at the pika, swallowing hard once, and slips into a more genuine smile. "So what do you plan to do with your newfound powers?"

"I guess if I'm a villain, I should roll over a bank or something."

She holds up her hands. "Please don't."

"I wasn't planning to." Hazel laughs. "Moira asked me what I'd do with the power of a god—"

"—superhero—"

"—and I said that I'd break things that need breaking and fix things that need fixing."

"Huh. That's clever, although we're going to have to figure out why this Moira gave you whatever power she did. Nothing this unbelievable comes without strings." She points out at the city. "Let's find things to fix."

"At this size?"

"Maybe a more manageable one."

Hazel carefully picks Rhiannon back up, sets her down on the sidewalk, and returns to her normal size. She pivots the chair to get out of the street, then blinks several times. Everyone outside who *isn't* Rhiannon is on their knees now.

As she rolls along the street, Rhiannon walking beside her, she looks up at the squirrel and grins teasingly. "Sure you don't want to fall to your knees and worship me?"

"See, asking that question even in jest clearly means you need someone who can smack you in the head when you need it."

Hazel laughs. "Deal."

five
checkpoint

When she gets up the next morning—fine, the next afternoon—and heads down to the newsstand to buy a paper, Moira doesn't find anything about Diana or Hazel. She didn't find anything yesterday, either. She's not sure what she's looking for, especially about the sheep, though. Maybe there's nothing to find. Maybe what she meant to happen is precisely what did happen: she let a mortal remember a chance meeting with a goddess.

But that's what she meant to happen with Hazel. It might not have happened immediately, but when she stood a block away looking up at the giantess she sensed what the mortals had—the new, wobbly, barely formed divinity of it all. That hadn't happened with Diana.

At least, not before she drove off.

Had she ever done this before? Three days ago, she'd have bitterly laughed off the idea, but now she wonders if she can make new gods by accident. Surely not. If this had happened before, she'd have eventually discovered it. Unless the new gods were as careful about hiding themselves from mortals as she'd gotten since the Industrial Revolution, there'd have been reports, legends. Hell, new religions. Yes, these were the first two mortals she could remember revealing herself to in centuries, but—

But, no, not revealing. These were the first two she could remember *recognizing* her. Ever. The world has gone *weird* all of a sudden, and she's the locus of that weirdness.

And she doesn't like it at all.

Maybe moving back to a big city was a mistake. She'd been happy enough leaving Rio to live in a trailer at the edge of the Mojave for a while, where she could go a season or two without seeing anyone chattier than a saguaro. (They had more to say than you'd think, but you had to know how to ask.) But she'd gotten restless, and set out hiking the Pacific Crest Trail until she hit the Cascades. By that point, she was itching to get back to civilization.

She flips back through the paper, scanning headlines, frowning at one. About a dozen states had passed "group area acts" in the last decade that divided up their cities and metros into carnivore-only, herbivore-only, and mixed residence zones; she'd known that, but she hadn't known the federal version had gotten as close to passing as it had. It'd still leave the divisions up to states and cities, but it *required* states to come up with group area plans for every "metropolitan statistical area" within their boundaries. California vowed to make all zones in the state mixed use if it passed, but some cities and counties were "reviewing legal options" for end runs around Sacramento. Fresno was about to pilot their version.

Fucking *Fresno*.

Tossing the paper onto the coffee table, she picks up the alt-weekly she'd also grabbed. Nothing about the new goddesses in here, either, but there's an events calendar. She hasn't gotten that strange nausea today. If anything, she feels more chipper than usual, like she wants to get out and socialize.

A music festival across the Bay, up in Vallejo, all day Saturday? That might be worth a trip. She hadn't kept up with music for years, not since she spent a decade as a folk singer. She got too close to actual fame for her tastes and backed off, but it'd been fun for a while.

Maybe she should drive around South San Francisco today, though, to see if anything looked out of place. New temples, suspiciously large hoofprints, that sort of thing. And where did Hazel live? Maybe somewhere in San Francisco proper, but without a sign, she can't narrow that down enough to be useful.

Sighing, she grabs her keys.

A meandering ride through the City down to South SF finds nothing out of the ordinary. The frustration with not being omniscient has been unusually high lately.

Well, there's one last check to make. She pulls into the supermarket parking lot, gets out, heads into the store. If anything drew her here apart from the opportunity to run into Diana, it's sure not obvious. Is that relieving or unnerving?

Slumming stoat boy isn't at any of the registers today, and a cursory check down the aisles doesn't show anyone else she remembers. There was that security guy outside, though, if he ever looked up from his phone.

She walks back out and looks for the Third Eye sedan. There it is, and it looks as if the same panther's behind the wheel.

Moira walks over, prepared to rap on the window, but he looks up from his phone when she's still a few steps away and rolls it down without prompting, flashing her a faintly suspicious look. "Can I help you?"

"Maybe. Did you catch anything strange out here in the parking lot two days ago? Tuesday, just after lunch?"

"Like what?"

"A black sheep woman doing anything…" She waves a hand, and repeats, "strange."

He swallows, ears flicking back an inch for a split-second. "Nope, sorry."

Okay, so that's a yes. She leans forward and gives him a big smile with a tiny push behind it. "I'm one of Diana's friends. I'm just trying to make sure she's all right."

He's immediately transfixed, staring at her so adoringly he's nearly forgetting to breathe. Oops, that might have been more than a tiny push. "She's…uh… I don't know, truthfully, my lady. She performed a miracle. A terrible miracle." He lowers his voice conspiratorially. "She's a *goddess*. We all knew."

"What did she do?"

"She *smited* someone!" His eyes are wide with fright and awe before he pauses. "Is that the right word?"

"I think it's 'smote.' Let me guess. A loudmouth tiger, a few inches shorter than I am?"

He nods. "Then he was a *lot* shorter than you were." He holds his thumb and forefinger a few inches apart, and finishes in a disquietingly reverent tone. "She brought her divine hoof down upon him."

"Dramatic. And then what happened?"

He shakes his head. "We all fell to our knees, and she ran to her car."

At least he's not referring to it as a fucking chariot. "All right." She pats him on the shoulder. "Thank you."

He slides his hand over hers, clasping it, and brings it to his muzzle for a gallant kiss. And another and another.

She clears her throat and pulls her hand away. She has *got* to work on her magic again, doesn't she? The only miracles she's performed for the last few centuries involved smashing things, so she didn't have to worry too much about finesse.

When she gets back home, she sprawls on her couch again. Okay, Moira, you've had a couple of thousand years of being the last god left in the world. No worshippers, no believers, drifting around on eternal vacation. Now, all the evidence suggests that you've accidentally deified two mortals in two days.

How do you *accidentally create divine beings?* And what do you do about it?

"Nothing" might be the easiest answer, but it might also be a valid one. They weren't going to stay hidden for long. Yes, they'd mess things up at first, but so what? With no other gods in the world, no mythic monsters or legendary heroes, nothing could kill them. They'd have time to learn. Once they got settled, she could…

Who knows. Watch from afar. Keep on keeping on.

Moira sleeps in longer than she should on Saturday, but gets out in the afternoon. Once she's through Treasure Island on the Bay Bridge, traffic thins. She moves into the fast lane and opens up the Porsche's throttle. She could easily make a Shortcut, turn off an exit and be right where she needs to be, but she's gotten to like driving again. This span is at least as pretty as the Golden Gate Bridge; it's just not as famous. Maybe they should paint it orange. She resists the temptation to snap her fingers and change its color.

If Moira's ever been to Vallejo, she doesn't remember it. It has more of a working-class vibe than where she lives in the City, but it's prettier than South San Francisco. Maybe it's the waterfront, the city nestled between San Francisco Bay to the south and the mouth of the Napa River to the west, running up into foothills along the east side.

The police presence is less attractive, though. As she approaches the riverfront park holding the festival, she passes cruiser after cruiser with lights flashing. Cops directing traffic, blocking off streets, corralling pedestrians, running speed traps. Lighted signs for festival parking warn about checkpoints. What fresh hell is this?

Fine, she won't make a scene yet. She follows the signs for parking, pulls in next to an SUV, and looks around.

Fences block off the neighboring park and the streets leading into downtown. Signs direct her to a gate with a short line in front of one of the blocked-off streets, with a police car parked there and a cop standing by the gate. There's *another* line a few yards past the gate, a much longer, slower one, leading toward a couple more police cruisers flashing their lights a block away. No, wait: there are two long lines, the slow one and a faster one alongside it.

When she gets in line behind a lanky, shaggy-haired coyote guy decked out in denim, he gives her a glance, then double-takes. Moira finds herself tensing up. *Fuck, please don't whisper my name to me.*

He doesn't. He clears his throat, looking self-conscious about staring, and says, "Hey." He's not recognizing her as a goddess, he's recognizing her as an attractive bunny who has about half a foot on him. He's cute, too, in a kind of cowboy way.

"Hello. So, is this normal?" She waves between the two lines.

"Last time I went was two years ago, and there wasn't anything like this. They're doing more ID checks to 'keep trouble down.'" He makes skeptical air quotes with his fingers.

"Ah." She studies the cop car for a moment; the logo on the door is weird. It has a typical yellow-and-blue shield design reading *Vallejo Police,* but in small print under the shield it says *Managed by NorthStar Enforcement.* Daranu's nutsack, the *police force* has been privatized. When did that happen?

It takes no time to get to the front of this first line, because the tiger's just scanning IDs and directing people into one of the other two lines. The coyote gets pointed toward the fast line; people at its head get waved through the fences. The cop points her toward the slow line.

"Why is one line so much slower?"

The tiger doesn't look at her. "One line's running IDs, the other isn't."

"But *you're* running IDs right here in this line. Why are all the herbivores in the slow line and the carnivores in the fast one?"

"I'm following directions, and everything will move faster if you do, too."

Another officer, a wolf, waves both the coyote and Moira along. "Hurry up."

The coyote looks flummoxed, maybe a little angry. "We're both going to the same place."

Moira gives him an appraising look. It's sweet to be offended on her behalf, but it's also naïve. Sure enough, the wolf gives him a sharp glare. "You're in the fast line, sir. Keep moving." He turns the glare on Moira. "And you, don't make this a scene. Move along, now."

"Fine." She slides her hands into her pockets and saunters past him into the fast line. The coyote tags along, looking nervous but impressed,

"I *said,*" the wolf growls, "don't make this a scene." He points at the slow line. The closest rabbits and rodents and deer watch now, with varying levels of interest and dismay. Some carnivores look back, but, well, their line's moving.

"I'm not." She shrugs, hands still in her pockets. "I believe *you* are, Officer."

"All right," he snarls. "That's enough." He grabs her arm, leading her toward the closest cruiser.

The coyote skews his ears, stepping out of line. "Hey!" The cops ignore him. Naturally.

The wolf gives Moira a shove. "Put your hands on the car and give me your ID."

"I can't give you my ID if my hands are on the car, now, can I."

He grits his teeth. "ID."

Shaking her head, she digs into her pocket and hands it over.

He studies it intently. "Moira…" He clears his throat. "Leannán?" He pronounces it as *lee-ann-in* rather than *lyann-uhn,* but she's heard worse. "I can't make out your birthdate."

"How old do I look?"

He narrows his eyes at her, and gets in the car, two-finger typing information into the onboard computer.

Moira realizes the coyote's still hovering around, looking anxious. She glances over at him. "Look, if you wait around here you're going to get in trouble, too."

"But I shouldn't. And *you* shouldn't. This is bullshit. I've never seen anything like this." He points at the two lines.

"The bullshit is getting worse lately. But there's a lot you might not have noticed because…" She scoffs. "You know."

He looks blank.

"She means because you're a carnivore," a stag in the herbivore line calls. A few people around him nod.

The coyote opens his mouth as if to protest, looks back and forth, and runs his hand through his hair. "I hear about the laws, but… I guess I don't…" His ears fold back.

"You don't have to think about them," a mouse says sourly, crossing his arms.

The wolf gets back out of the car, and gives Moira the hardest look he can muster, moving his hand to rest by his gun. If she wasn't who she was, it'd be downright intimidating. "You know anything about a disturbance in South San Francisco Tuesday, or in downtown San Francisco the day after?"

"You'll have to be more specific." How are they connecting her with any of that?

"It's a bulletin from Corporate." He sounds defensive.

"Did you like it better when you could at least pretend you were working for the people, or is it refreshing to have it all out in the open now?"

He bares his teeth, grip tightening on his gun for a moment. Then he slams her against the hood of the car.

"Hey! Don't you—" the coyote yells, but gets cut off when the tiger slams him down next to Moira. He looks thunderstruck.

"Okay, lady, let's do it your way," the wolf growls, forcing her arms behind her back and snapping cuffs around her wrists.

Moira grimaces, feeling pressure building inside her. It's not the odd, queer joy around Diana and Hazel. There's a joy to it, but no gentleness. She knows what's coming, but for the last few centuries she's quelled it. Tonight, though, she won't. Corporate hasn't seen what kind of disturbance she can *really* cause.

She takes a deep, ragged breath, and straightens up. The wolf lets out an annoyed, surprised bark and pushes her again, but this time she doesn't move. Not for him.

"Yes, let's do it my way." Moira straightens her arms, handcuff chain snapping like a brittle rubber band, whirls, and grabs him by the throat. "I accept your invitation to battle." She lifts him into the air.

He kicks, wrapping his hands around her fingers and struggling to pry them off. His ears go flat against his head.

The tiger draws his gun. "Let him go!" He fumbles to get a radio in his other hand. "I need backup at the Riverfront checkpoint. 10-33, repeat, 10-33!"

Moira drops the wolf. He staggers, drawing his gun, too. "Down!" he snarls. "Hands and knees!"

The hare moves in a blur, and now she's holding both guns, the two cops shrieking and holding their broken hands. She crumples the pistols and tosses them aside.

Both of the entrance lines have stopped now, staring. Some of the crowd backs away, breaking up, but others cheer, egging Moira on. More of the carnivores run. More of the herbivores clap.

The police car by the barricades at the front of the lines

switches on its sirens and pulls onto the street, heading toward them. Other sirens sound in the distance. "L-lady," the tiger stammers, "there's gonna be dozens of patrol cars here in a minute or two."

She grins, looking far more predatory than any of the carnivores around. That fierce, terrible joy surges in her. "Oh, I *hope* so." She claps once, hard, and electricity sparks along the fences, melting them away.

The crowd scatters in all directions—many heading into the now open-for-all festival areas, toward the stages and the street fair. Hundreds of others watch Moira and cheer, fists in the air.

The cop car coming up the street screeches to a halt. Two officers scramble out, guns drawn, and Moira *runs* toward them. They fire at her, squeezing off dozens of shots. The crowd screams.

She doesn't go down, though. She leaps into the air, somersaults, and slams her paws down on the cop car's roof hard enough to shatter its windows. They turn around barely in time for her to jump down and smack their heads together. She strides back toward the still-cuffed coyote.

He gapes at her, muzzle wide open. She can't tell if he's terrified, turned on, or both.

Moira effortlessly snaps off his handcuffs. "You really shouldn't have stayed."

"It, uh, seemed like the right thing to do." He rubs his wrists. "I didn't know you were...what are you?"

"A goddess." The sirens that had been in the distance aren't in the distance now, cop cars filling both the blocked-off street and the street she'd turned in on, coming across the grass. Officers on paw swarm through the crowd, too, shields out and riot control weapons drawn.

The wolf cop lumbers toward them, looking frenzied. "What the hell did you do!" He takes a swing at Moira and misses. She takes a return swing and doesn't, smashing him in the face. Her next punch audibly cracks his ribs. He topples over.

The tiger stares dumbly, and starts to back off. The coyote stays close to her, despite looking like he's on the verge of fainting. Meanwhile, the crowd's screams grow uglier and more frightened as the cops beat people out of the way, firing tear gas grenades, to move toward her.

Moira snarls. She'd have given them the dignity of a fair loss—more than they deserved—but not now that they've hurt innocents to get to her. She raises her hands over her head and claps them together again. The magic sweeps out of her, roaring across city blocks in a sonic boom.

All the cars, all the cops, abruptly shrink to toy size. Moira leans over, hands on her knees, catching her breath.

The coyote lets out a squeak, eyes as wide as golf balls. "Holy shit." The rest of the crowd is screaming and bleating, staring and pointing.

The miniature cars all still have their lights and sirens on as most screech to a stop. Some drive even faster, trying to weave between paws and hooves. The cops on foot, finding themselves ankle-high to the crowd they'd been bullying, lose their minds, half of them running haphazardly and half of them pleading their authority over the relative giants around them. For their part, the crowd's terrified, confused, uncertain, but you can watch the realization of the literal shift in power running through them in real time.

"Sure you want to stay with me?" Moira motions to the coyote and starts strolling down the street, hands back in her pockets.

"I-I…" He hurries after her. "I do, even though it seems lethally dangerous. I don't even know your name."

"Moira."

"I'm Stetson. Are you really—" He yips, hopping in the air over one of the cop cars, and points in front of her paws at another one. "Watch out."

"Good eye. Thanks." She kicks it out of the way.

"Oh my god oh my god oh my god," the coyote mutters, sticking with her but looking shellshocked now. "You are the most terrifying rabbit I've ever seen."

"I'm a hare. Hares are bigger."

"Right." Stetson laughs weakly.

They walk into the downtown area. Music's still going, people are starting to dance again. The flashing lights on the ground have been corralled in by a crowd, nearly all herbivores. Some of them lean down to pick up the cars, studying them in wonder. A wine-mom deer rolls a cruiser back and forth under one of her hooves, laughing incredulously. A cute red panda couple, guy and girl, have a car trapped between their muzzles, trying to fish the cops out with their tongues.

"Well, *this* hasn't happened in a while," she muses.

"It's happened before?" His voice is a hoarse squeak.

"People lose their inhibitions around me when I get wound up and do..." Moira waves a hand. "Goddess shit. Orgies, fights, a lot of flipped roles between predator and prey, dominant and submissive, all that. There's going to be dangerous magic in the air here until sunrise."

"Uh."

A few people—more than a few—have shed their clothes. And, yeah, there are actual fights breaking out. Some people are bigger or smaller than they started out as, too. She didn't mean to do that, but she's been on kind of a size kick for a while, and it's leaking through. Well, a night of role-reversal will likely do some good, and the ones who haven't fled—besides the police, who lost their chance—radiate embarrassed, ashamed interest.

"Is everyone changing size?" Stetson bursts out, sounding terrified again.

"Not everyone. I'm not. I mean, I *could*, but I'm not." She glances at him. "You are, though. You're smaller."

"What?" His voice rises an octave.

She moves to stand next to him. "You're barely chest-high to me now. Why'd you choose that height?"

"I... I didn't." His voice wavers.

"Mmm. Perhaps you find tall, terrifying women attractive, Stetson."

"I..." He trails off, glancing around the crowd. It's not exclusively big herbivores and small carnivores, but the balance definitely favors the herbivores. And many of them are dropping to their knees to stare reverently at Moira.

"What are you a goddess *of?*" he whispers.

"Tonight?" She grins, taking the coyote's smaller hand in hers. "You."

six
severe bullying

The mountain lion on Parker's screen looks disheveled, his shirt collar crooked and his tie—a clip-on, which seems perfectly in character—slipping. It matches the way his off-the-rack suit jacket hangs precariously on the back of his chair. He scans through the same reports she's looking at in another window. "From what we're seeing on social media so far, everyone affected appears to remember it as a dream. That's what Ms. Moira does, isn't it? Stays off the radar by—"

"Mr. Torrance." Her voice is tight, exasperated. "If this was 'off the radar,' we wouldn't be having this discussion. Festival-goers may remember this as a dream, but they're already noticing the similarities between those dreams. Ones that remember Moira specifically remember her casting magic. Far too many remember having magic themselves for a night, and using it to create a violently debauched bacchanalia. With twenty thousand attendees, thousands of whom woke up mere hours ago on the festival grounds after sunrise, how long do you think it's going to be before serious questions arise?" Her tone rises with her temper. "We don't even know at this point whether all those attendees survived, but we *do* know that ninety percent of the police force is unaccounted for. Do you know what happened to them?"

"I, uh, a few of the dreams seemed like they were about... bullying tiny policemen."

"Bullying," Parker echoes, and glances at highlighted posts in a social media feed. "Such as 'brb crushing cop cars under my hooves like fascist tinfoil' and 'maybe ACAB but they were so fucking delicious.'" She narrows her eyes at him.

"Severe bullying." He clears his throat. "Uh, we've contacted everyone we have in place at media outlets, and we're working on cover stories."

She drums her fingers on the desk. "Such as."

"Psychedelics in the food?"

"No. It would need to be an agent that everyone could plausibly be exposed to."

"So, uh, airborne." He scribbles that down.

Ms. Storm cuts in. Unlike Torrance, she's sharply dressed in a deep purple one-button blazer over a black blouse, the executive secretary who expects to own any boardroom she walks into. With few exceptions, she does. "There are no airborne psychedelics. Look at ones that can be absorbed through contact with skin and pads."

"Got it." He nods hurriedly, continuing to scribble.

"Now, tell me you've found *some* lead on Moira's whereabouts."

"We have not."

She narrows her eyes again.

"But, we *did* get a report from one of our security companies that she went back to the supermarket in South San Fran that you mentioned, and asked questions about the sheep woman."

"Go on."

He pulls up another window. "It's an odd report. An employee of Third Eye who *wasn't* assigned to that store said the guard who *was* assigned to it mentioned a rabbit woman asking about the goddess. When his coworker questioned what that meant, the guard started, quote, 'proselytizing about the sheep.'"

Parker takes off her glasses and rubs her temples, trying to quell a dull throb. "And what have you learned about the sheep and the pika yet?"

"Nothing."

She pulls up the day's weather report and zooms in on the SF Bay Area. There have been warm spots in South San Francisco and along Market Street in the last day, but nothing clearly unusual. Vallejo is another matter. If the chaos storm that had erupted there early yesterday evening had been physical, half of the town would have washed away. This isn't an effect mortals could create. It's not an effect she's seen from Moira in at least a century, long before instant global communication—and that last time, nowhere close to a metropolitan area.

So why *now*? Could Moira have become aware of them, tried to deliberately sabotage their plan? She couldn't rule it out, but subtlety wasn't the hare's style. Not that magicking tipsy citizens into literally eating law enforcement was "subtle," to be sure. But if Moira had decided to take on Celestial, she wouldn't come at them from the shadows.

"Ma'am?"

She snaps her attention back to the video call. "'Nothing' is not an acceptable answer, Mr. Torrance. There's no video from security cameras or traffic cameras available?"

"You didn't get the traffic camera footage?"

She closes her eyes, feeling the migraine throb. "No, Mr. Torrance, I did not."

"Oh. Uh, I'll send what we have to you now. We were able to catch it before any employees reviewed the footage, I think."

"You think." She opens the video and reviews it. Grainy, black and white, but exactly what she'd been promised: a giant young pika woman in a wheelchair, blocking traffic. No one had mentioned her decidedly predatory turn with the tiger before, though. Wonderful. "Surely, this is enough to identify who she is?"

"We're working on it."

She gives him a long, measured look. Who was it who hired Torrance again? He was one of Howell's chosen, wasn't he? "Mr. Torrance, I trust you watched that pika woman swallowing someone whole and alive."

"Uh, I did, ma'am."

"Do you have any idea what's that like?"

He blinks several times, looking even more nervous. "No, I don't."

"Ms. Storm, could you be so kind as to demonstrate for Mr. Torrance?"

"Of course, Ms. Parker."

Torrance holds up a hand, desperately. "Ma'am, please, I swear I'm—"

The rat leans forward, opening her mouth wide as if she were about to eat her video camera. The view fills with her tongue and teeth before going dark. On Torrance's feed, the mountain lion looks up in shock a moment before a shapely rat muzzle descends over him. He gets out a terrified yowl loud enough to cause microphone feedback as the jaws clamp shut and lift him up. The camera shakes, trying to focus on his empty, spinning chair as his jacket falls to the floor. Ms. Storm's feed brightens and refocuses on her as she leans back in her seat, the cat's legs kicking frantically between her lips. Tilting her head back, she snaps her jaws once, the legs disappearing, and swallows hard. A wriggling lump ripples down her throat.

Parker laces her hands together and lets out a slow breath. "And with that, my migraine fades away. All right, Ms. Storm. Psychedelics might be our best cover story for now. It's weak, but with luck we can use it to our advantage in a few months as we set the stage for Project Maelstrom."

Ms. Storm nods, shutting off Torrance's camera.

"Could you connect Max Howell in with the call?"

"Of course."

It takes thirty seconds for a new video feed to kick in, a dashing fox man who might have stepped out of the pages of a high-end clothing catalog. "Ms. Parker. What can I do for you?"

"I need you to take over an essential project from Mr. Torrance. He's no longer with the company."

The rat dabs her muzzle daintily with a silk handkerchief, brushing away the tiny clip-on tie stuck to her lower lip.

Howell's ears splay. "Of course." He grabs a pocket notebook and an expensive-looking pen.

"There are three subjects of intense interest to us in your area. One is a hare named Moira."

"*The* Moira?"

She nods. "And a pika girl and a ewe who we have reason to believe Moira has granted powers to. By the end of next week we need to know, at a minimum, where all three of them are and who the pika and the sheep are. With that information, we can discuss options going forward for dealing with them."

Max nods, scribbling in the notebook. "On it. It'll be my top priority for the next week."

"Thank you, Mr. Howell." She shuts off the feed.

seven
potluck

Moira sips coffee from a brightly colored mug, sitting in a shop a couple of blocks from her condo. While it's consciously hipster, it's the cluttered aunt's attic look: worn mismatched furniture, weird art, and punk flyers everywhere. Better than the minimalist style of spotless white tile, chrome and pale wood that's taken over lately.

It wasn't that she'd forgotten about her new goddesses as much as shoved them to the back of her mind. She still has no idea how the cops connected her to them, or even if they *had* connected her to them—but *someone* had the idea that a tall hare woman might be involved. While she'd filed that in the "get back to this quick" bucket, too, a disquieting voicemail on her phone yesterday had reminded her that the world's idea of *get back quick* wasn't hers. She pulls out her phone and looks at the transcript for the tenth time, instead of playing the voicemail back for a fourth time.

Hi, Moira. My name is Max Howell, with Celestial Venture Partners. Given your background, I'd love to talk to you about bringing you on board in some capacity. I know that may sound crazy, but we're aware of your recent work, and I truly think you could put your exceptional talent to better use. If we meet in person, I'm sure you'll understand what I mean. Please give me a call back at your earliest convenience.

If he hadn't opened with her name, she'd have dismissed it as a wrong number, and she still hadn't dismissed the possibility he'd meant to reach some *other* Moira with a background in whatever venture capitalists have a background in, finance or accounting or inheriting money from Daddy. But she hasn't stopped chewing on what the cop who slammed her against the car in Vallejo said: *it's a bulletin from Corporate.*

Meanwhile, whatever Diana and Hazel are doing remains tragically off the radar. Either they're too terrified to do anything but go about their normal mortal lives, or they've learned how to cover their tracks the way she does. That niggles at her. Why get that power and then lie low?

Well, why do you *lie low with it?* That's different.

Is it? They probably heard about Vallejo, too. Fine, voice in my head. So they're likely lying low.

But she didn't even know about what Diana did after she left the supermarket until she came back and heard it from the guard. A crowd saw it. A crowd saw Hazel become a damn giantess, too. Moira didn't try to cover their tracks for them, but there's been no news stories from them.

So maybe they *have* figured out how to cover whatever they're doing.

Putting her phone away, Moira turns back to the alt-weekly paper that came out today. She pages back to their coverage of the Vallejo festival story, headlined *Phantasmagoria* with a subhead of *How did everyone dream the same dream?*

She's seen articles in other papers about what happened two and a half weeks ago—what Vallejo's mayor dubbed a "psychedelic poison" that spread through the entire crowd, causing them to lose their minds and their inhibitions. Almost a thousand people cited for indecent exposure, lewd behavior, or disrupting the peace. No arrests, though, perhaps because Vallejo doesn't have much of a police force left. Officials made dire threats about the ongoing investigations, about how this might be attempted mass murder, about how they will *not* tolerate this anarchy, how they're forced to implement tighter controls on where people can go and when they can go there. So much of the official story is obvious bullshit (psychedelic poison? come the fuck on!), but everyone's going along with it as unquestioningly as they do with *her* tweaks, like making all the participants remember the night as a dream. So, terrific job there, hare: you may have given everyone who survived a night they won't forget, but now you've made their lives fractionally worse.

She skims over the article. It's short, and mostly a recap of earlier stories given a snarkier, more anti-authority spin. Nothing new jumps out at her until the end:

> *So just what did happen that night in Vallejo? The official line is that we'll never get a clear answer until and unless the missing partiers and police officers return. But this is merely the biggest and boldest "divine act" the Bay Area's rumor mill has ground over in the past two weeks, following incoherent but thrilling tales of miracles in the Castro and the suburbs of South SF. If the trend continues, the gods only know what we're in for next month.*

"Miracles in the Castro," she says aloud.

A maned wolf with exaggerated lashes, gloriously wild multi-color hair, and high heels to add another few inches to their already significant height looks over at her. "Hmm?"

Moira shakes her head. "Thinking out loud."

The wolf grins, leaning toward Moira and waving a hand with a flourish. "I live in the Castro, sweetie, and it's full of miracles. What kinds are you looking for?"

"These." She slides the paper over to them, pointing out the last paragraph.

The wolf makes a few *hmm* noises, then lights up. "Oh, they might be talking about her." They stride over to the closest wall and scan the flyers until they come to one and tap it.

Moira gets up with her mug and walks over. It's a grungy-gray photocopy of art that reminds her of a prayer candle, a fuzzily beatific image of a rodent woman in a wheelchair. The caption underneath reads ANGEL OF CASTRO. Her brows shoot up. "What's she been doing?"

"I couldn't tell you." The maned wolf shakes their head. "I'm not sure if she's even real. But I've heard people talking about seeing a beautiful mouse in a wheelchair before..." They wave a hand dramatically. "Small miracles happen. A new curb cut appears. A junker car gets mysteriously fixed. A business with a long tradition of fucking over their customers gets," they laugh and lower their voice conspiratorially, "mysteriously and *grandly* fucked over."

"Started happening about three weeks ago, I bet."

"That's what they say." The wolf looks at Moira speculatively, eyes sparkling. "You've seen her, haven't you?"

"I believe I have. She's a pika, not a mouse."

The wolf claps their hands together delightedly. "Lovely!"

Moira rubs her chin. Her new goddesses are off the radar of general news, but not indie news. Not of talk on the street. So the news about them isn't being suppressed *by* them; it's local authorities doing what local authorities do.

So the alt-weekly might be on to something, if by accident. There *are* three related stories here, all being hidden from, or by, mainstream reporters: what happened in Vallejo through disinformation, and what happened with Diana and Hazel through old-fashioned censorship.

"So," she says to the maned wolf. "I'm new in town and not up on the ins and outs with the place, but when I was in Vallejo the other day I saw the cop cars had 'Managed by', what was it, 'North Point' written on them. What's that about?"

The wolf rolls their eyes. "Oh, that was a scandal last year. Marin County contracted with a group called NorthStar to run the police department, oh, four years ago, I think it was. Half the other counties in the Bay Area, including good old supposedly progressive San Francisco, joined right in."

She sighs. "NorthStar. Right. Thanks." So all the corporatized cops *could* be coordinating with one another to keep a lid on it all.

And worse: "Corporate," meaning NorthStar, had circulated a bulletin about hares with her name or description, connecting her to Diana and Hazel's deification. Now a mysterious corporate finance jerk wants to chat about her "background" and "recent work."

Someone—not Diana, not Hazel, but someone *else*—knows who she is.

Downing what's left of her coffee in one gulp, Moira heads back out, fuming. *How can anyone know?* Sure, mortals study mythology, but as stories. Folktales. Or heresies, if they follow that kind of religion. Either way, nobody thinks, "Hey, that goddess of love and war from the history books might be kicking around the mortal world after all this time." Do they?

No, but is it possible somebody tracked her through her moves, passing the task down from generation to generation, stalkers who proved even better at remaining hidden than she has? Maybe, but she just has to keep mortals off her trail; they'd have to keep a *god* off theirs. That's tough.

Unless they're a god, too.

Is that even possible? Could another deity have stayed behind, kept tabs her on all this time? She knows she can't rule it out, but if it's true, why risk exposure now? Why step out into the sunlight? She bets the cop wasn't supposed to blab to her about the bulletin and its contents—he hadn't been the sharpest knife in the drawer. It'd be to their advantage if she wasn't sulk-stomping down the sidewalk dwelling on it all. Still, if this *was* what was happening, they'd gone millennia without her catching on.

But Moira had gone millennia without creating new gods.

She stops, closing her eyes and running a hand through her hair. NorthStar might know who Diana and Hazel are, too, and now Moira can't assume that nothing in the world can harm them except for her. Even if NorthStar doesn't have an actual god on staff, they might still have a demigod. As crazy as it is to think they might have chosen heroes, the kinds that could kill lesser gods in battle, is it *really* that crazy? Is *anything* really that crazy now?

She was an idiot to send her two new goddesses off in the world on their own. Nine hells, she didn't even get the chance to send

Diana off on her own—she left without understanding what she'd done.

Track down "The Angel of Castro" first, or the sheep? Given Hazel's nascent cult, she's probably going to be a snap to find, so Diana's the one to start with.

She drives back down to South San Francisco, this time making a Shortcut to turn right from her street onto the one by the supermarket. Is there a coffee shop somewhere around here? If there are DIY posters of Hazel, maybe there are DIY posters of Diana. Although Hazel has a decidedly more punk vibe than Diana does, so maybe not.

She doesn't find a coffee shop, so she starts turning down random residential streets when they call to her. The neighborhoods have a working-class air: houses old enough to feel lived in but not old enough to feel historic, sidewalks with stains and cracks, overhead power lines and nice lawns with too few trees. No pedestrians now that she's out of the business district.

She rounds another corner, and finds the missing walkers. A jogger here, a woman pushing a stroller there, people...carrying pots and trays of food?

Huh.

She parks behind an SUV with a family of mice—mom, dad, three kids—all unloading food from the back. As they start walking, she follows behind.

They round another corner, and run into a crowd. A *huge* crowd, spilling out into the road curb to curb, overtaking several lawns. It's centered around of one of those small, well-kept houses.

While the crowd isn't all obligate herbivores, there aren't many predators. She can't tell how many live in the neighborhood; some surely just breezed in from the Financial District, while others might not live anywhere with a roof.

As Moira wades into the flock, she realizes it's a street fair. People singing folk songs, scratching chalk drawings on the sidewalk, selling tie-dye t-shirts—no, *making* tie-dye t-shirts. Plastic utility tables have been unfolded across the house's lawn, people setting down their food dishes. Many of those, interestingly, *are* carnivores: a tigress, a wolf, a fox, a coyote, an otter. The food looks and smells mostly vegetarian, though. People line up as if it's a church potluck.

Murmurs ripple through the crowd, and she slows as she feels the weight of stares—not unfriendly ones, but *is that her?* ones. Uh-oh.

A young mouse bounds out of the house and down the steps toward her, eyes wide. "You *are* Lady Moira, aren't you?"

She looks down at him, lifting a brow. He's cute. Actually, strike that. Handsome. Kind of jacked. "Yes," she says, cautiously.

He turns around and yells with a town crier's voice. "Make way for the Divine Lady Moira!"

Grimacing, she follows as he parts the crowd. She'd wondered over the years if she missed all the worshipful pomp and circumstance she used to get in the mortal realm. She's relieved to find the answer is: fuck, no.

"Lady Diana has told us all about you," he gushes, leading her up toward the house's front door.

"Lady Diana doesn't know me."

Before they reach the door, it swings open under its own power. A roar rises from the crowd. Diana stands there, dressed in simple red sleeveless robes bright against her ebony wool, hands clasped in front of her. Simple, but resplendent. She shines. For a woman who'd been mortal three weeks ago, she's got the divine aspect down cold. Moira hears worshippers bursting into ecstatic tears behind her.

Diana's eyes widen when she sees the hare, but she doesn't lose a drop of composure, smiling and pulling Moira into a hug. The crowd's cheering intensifies. Then the sheep spins the hare around, entwining her fingers with Moira's and lifting their linked hands overhead as if they'd taken a gold medal.

She addresses the young mouse. "I'll be out soon, William. Lady Moira and I need to talk. Everyone should begin eating."

"Of course, your holiness," he squeaks.

Diana steps back into the house, pulling Moira along with her. She pushes the door closed, locks it, takes a deep breath, and slams Moira back against the wall with a furious expression. "What the ever-loving hell have you *done* to me?"

Moira winces. That slam actually hurts a little, and if she gets a bruise it's going to take time to heal, isn't it? Gods can hurt other gods. Awesome. "Ah. Yes." She looks around the house rather than meeting Diana's eyes. The inside is as well-kept as the outside, a nice combination living and dining room, comfortable furniture. A few worn mythology books with library tags lie across the dining table. "I think I made you a god."

"You *think?*" Diana lets her go, putting her hands to her head.

"It looks like you've taken right to it. You're dressed the part more than I am."

"They made me the robes!" Diana waves her hoofed fingers toward the front door. "It was only a few of them out there at first, but now it's *that*. Every day."

"What are you doing that's bringing them here?"

"I don't know!" Diana throws her hands up in the air. "I don't know anything! William asked me if he was my high priest!"

"Hmm. He did have that air. I think you've made him your chosen hero."

"My what? I don't…" Diana shakes her head. "You asked me what I'd do if I had the power of a god and I didn't have an answer, and you made me one anyway! You know the first thing I did with that power?" She stabs a finger toward Moira accusingly. "I killed somebody!"

"Did he deserve it?"

"I don't want it to be up to me to make that call, except that now it is, because I'm a fucking *goddess*." She bursts into tears. "Why *me?* Why did you do this to me?"

Moira puts her arm around Diana, guiding her to the sofa, and sits down with her. "I don't know why you."

Diana wipes her eyes with the back of a hand, looking horrified. "You don't… You did this to me on a *whim?*"

"Did you do that on a whim?" She points at the front lawn.

"At first? Yes! Worshippers just—just showed up. Hungry. I offered them food and drink, to be a good hostess, but I don't cook. You saw what was in my cart. If I had to do it all on my own, I'd be in the Parable of the Endless Hot Pockets."

Moira covers a grin. Diana continues, "So word got around that if people brought food, I could multiply it, a little potluck miracle. And now..." She waves at the front lawn again.

"Your whim is a *god's* whim. Coincidences and chance don't happen to us." She sighs. "I didn't even know what I'd done to you until the next day with Hazel. When I say I don't know why you, I'm telling you the truth, as bad as it sounds. But it's also the truth that there's got to be a reason."

"And you left me to fend for myself? I don't even know what I can do, but I know I'm *not* a good goddess." She buries her face in her hands. "How can I be, if I'm a killer? And I don't feel bad about it. I don't *like* not feeling bad about it. I feel bad about not feeling bad, about feeling so far above m... m... I can't even say it."

"Mortals."

"Yes!" She points at the front door again. "I'm above them, but I'm *responsible* for them. Why the hell do I feel this way?"

She shrugs. "Because you're a goddess."

Diana groans, and leans back in the sofa, crossing her arms. "So, tell me this. You really are the goddess of love from that mythology." She nods toward the books on the table.

"As hard as it is to believe."

Diana makes a point of looking up and down Moira's body. "It is not. And you're also the goddess of war, because you overthrew the war god, led a failed rebellion, and got exiled."

"Yes."

"So where are the other gods?"

Isn't *that* a great question. She takes a deep breath. "I don't know. I don't even know when they left. Every one hundred years on the winter solstice, I sent a raven off to the gods to ask if Daranu had gotten over himself. In so many words."

"The books say you were asking for forgiveness."

"I was asking for *understanding*. I wanted him to understand why I rebelled. I wanted him to talk to me again. To listen." She looks down at the floor. "The ravens always came back with the same message: no. No, he didn't understand. No, he didn't want to talk or to listen.

"Then, long ago by now, my raven came back with the message I'd sent with it. It couldn't find the other gods. And..." She shakes her head. "And that was that. I've been drifting ever since."

Diana looks maddeningly sympathetic. "Who's Hazel? Another god you created?"

"So it would seem." She looks at the sheep. "Diana, I'm sorry I left you alone through this. I thought you'd do well enough on your own. You're level-headed, now you're immortal, and I have enough faith in myself that I figured I'd picked you for a reason, even if I still don't know it. But I think there's another group that knows about us, about *all* of us, and I don't know what they want—or what they can do."

"Am I in danger?"

"It's possible."

"Even though I'm immortal."

Moira nods.

"What do we do about it?"

"Besides keeping our eyes open and staying in better touch, I don't know yet. But we have to find Hazel and bring her in on this, too."

Diana sighs, getting up and pacing around the living room. "So you've given me a gift of immeasurable power that I didn't ask for and don't want, it's put me in danger, and I'm terrible at using it anyway."

Moira shakes her head. "Not the last one. For all your worries about being a mean goddess, you're using your powers to not just feed multitudes, but to help them feed each other. To turn them into a community."

"That's small. Any of you could have done it in your sleep."

"But we *didn't*. It's a small thing none of us would have thought of. I was fighting for downtrodden mortals, for equality, but I was still focused on the gods. You have a perspective none of us did, that I still don't. That I can't. You were born and raised as a mortal."

Diana goes still, considering that silently for a long time. "Let's go find Hazel."

eight
beleaguered
roommate

"Hmm." Diana looks down the street Moira's driving along, part of the Castro's business district. The hare says she's just letting intuition guide her, like it took her toward Diana's house. Unlike Diana's street, there's no obvious sign she's going the right direction. "This is so…colorful." She's watching a particularly flamboyant pair of femboy foxes sashay down the street as she says that. One of them sees her looking and waves enthusiastically. She grins and waves back.

"You don't come up here often, do you?"

"Maybe twice in twenty years."

Moira lifts a brow. "I've lived here about three months, and I've visited a half-dozen times."

"I'm not much of a party person." Diana looks around. "Is it my imagination, or do most of the accessibility ramps and railings look new?"

"Hazel did say she wanted to fix things that needed fixing." Moira gestures toward a corner full of concrete rubble; imprints in the wreckage suggest colossal tire tracks. "And break things that needed breaking."

They round the corner, and Diana sucks in her breath. The angle reveals the newly exposed wall of the building next to the debris-filled lot—and its new two-story high painted mural of a beautiful pika woman in a gleaming, throne-like wheelchair. Light radiates from her as if she outshines the sun. Small figures sit or climb on her shoulders, in her lap, in her open hands; those figures are mostly herbivores. The cops and riot police and men in business suits down by her wheels and paws are mostly carnivores. It's clear from everyone's expression who the pika's protecting—and who she's smiting. "Goodness." She looks at Moira. "If that was a scene from real life, it would have made the news, wouldn't it?"

"One would think, hmm? It might be metaphorical. I haven't been trying to keep you two out of the papers, it doesn't seem you've tried to hide your tracks, and Hazel most certainly hasn't been hiding hers."

"Mmm. How do you keep yourself out of the papers?"

"Mortals mostly do it for me. They don't want to face anything too far outside their worldview. But it's not the mortals I'm concerned with now." Past another block, they reach a residential area; Moira takes a left, then parks the car. "Here we are. Maybe. What do you sense?"

"What do you mean?"

"Just that." She gets out of the car and looks around at the row houses. "If there's a god here, this close, we're going to sense them. So tell me if you feel anything."

Diana gets out, putting her hands on her hips and scanning the area. "All I feel is that I should have brought a jacket."

Moira crosses her arms. "Diana."

"All right, all right." The sheep crosses the street and starts down the sidewalk, looking up at each building.

Then she stops, looking intently at a house with an actual first floor rather than a garage and entrance staircase, and a front door level with the sidewalk. She looks back at Moira questioningly.

Moira nods. That's got to be it; there's a distinct presence there, strong divine energy. So Hazel is home. Or they're going to surprise someone (or something) most unexpected.

The row house has a wrought iron and screen door with the real, wooden front door behind it. Diana looks back at Moira again as she walks up, and reaches for the doorbell buzzer. Her hoofed finger hasn't touched the button before the door swings open.

A tall squirrel woman peers out through the screen, leaning on the door frame. She's built like a ballerina and dressed like a bohemian: midnight blue patterned maxi skirt, off-the-shoulder white blouse, denim jacket, turquoise jewelry everywhere—necklace, bracelets, anklets. Unbound wavy black hair falls down to her midriff.

"So," the squirrel says, looking past Diana to the hare. "You're Moira." Her gaze shifts back to Diana. "You are…?"

"I'm Diana."

"And you're involved in all this somehow. Great." The squirrel flicks her long tail, then unlatches the screen door, motioning them in. "She's been expecting you. Sort of. More hoping for you. Moira, I mean."

Diana clears her throat. "Are you, uh, Hazel's high priestess?"

"Oh, you are a *funny* sheep." She remains perfectly deadpan. Moira smirks. She thinks she likes this one.

The squirrel leads them through a small living room toward a dining table being used as a makeshift office. Two laptops and a big external display take up half its surface, surrounded by scattered books and a few prescription pill bottles. Hazel sits in front of one of the laptops. She doesn't look much different from when Moira last saw her: jeans, T-shirt, tough yet super cute. She looks over as the three enter, pushing herself up to a standing position, and grins. "You're here! Oh my god! Er, goddess. Whatever. Finally!" She looks at Diana inquiringly.

"Hazel? I'm Diana. I'm another, uh…" She motions at Moira.

"So you're super-powered, too." Rhiannon sighs, crossing her arms.

Moira lifts a brow.

Hazel gestures. "Moira, this is Rhiannon, my roommate—"

"My full title is 'beleaguered roommate.'"

"My beleaguered roommate. Rhi, this is Moira, goddess of love and war."

Rhiannon gives Moira a skeptical look, and turns to Diana. "And you claim to be goddess of…?"

Diana blinks. "I don't know." She looks at Moira.

"Stomping," Moira says. Diana makes a choking noise and narrows her eyes at the hare, who continues unfazed. "Honestly, I don't know if Hazel and Diana are goddesses of anything. This is new territory for me."

Rhiannon sighs melodramatically. "So I've gone from being in a house with one super-powered crazy woman to *three*. What even is my life now."

Hazel grins. "Exciting!"

Moira heads to a sofa and sits down, folding her hands in her lap. "Hazel, I shouldn't have left you and Diana alone to work through this. Especially you, since I saw what happened."

Hazel sits down by her laptop again, but faces Moira. "You did?"

"It's not as if you were a model of restraint. But that level of power flooding into a mortal has to be overwhelming." She sighs. "And I shouldn't have left you on your own. Even if you truly *are* fixing things that need fixing."

"And breaking things that need breaking," Hazel adds.

"You rolled over an ice cream truck," Rhiannon says flatly.

"It was an accident!"

"No one was hurt, were they?" Diana asks, eyes wide.

"It was gruesome." Rhiannon looks over at the sheep with exaggerated horror. "Ice cream sandwiches splattered over the pavement. Waffle bits and rainbow sprinkles everywhere."

Hazel groans. "Everyone was fine, okay?"

"Regardless," Moira says sharply enough to cut off any more conversation, "I'd believed the only thing on the planet that could hurt either of you was me. But now I'm not sure that's true. The corporation that runs half the police in the Bay Area wants to question me about 'disturbances' in South San Francisco and downtown —in other words, about you. I don't know what they know or how they know it, but they might know what I actually am—and what, and who, both of you are."

Diana looks shocked. "A corporation runs the police?"

Rhiannon nods. "NorthStar." She looks askance at Moira. "How do you know the cops want to talk to you?"

"A policeman tried to stop me in Vallejo. Well. All of them tried."

Hazel's eyes widen. "That *was* you up there!" She looks to Rhiannon. "Told you."

Rhiannon grunts, and sits down in front of her computer. "That confirms a bunch of my suspicions. The question is how Celestial knows about you supers."

"Supers?" Diana looks confused.

Hazel sighs. "She thinks we're superheroes."

"Or supervillains," Rhiannon interjects.

Moira holds up a hand. "What do you mean, 'Celestial'?"

Hazel answers. "I got email from somebody at 'Celestial Venture Partners' wanting me to interview for a job I can't be *remotely* qualified for. They said it was because of my background, but I'm a part-time webmaster at a non-profit. When I pointed that out, they said not *that* background, and I'd know what they meant if I met them in person."

Moira narrows her eyes. "Someone from that same group left a message on my phone with very similar phrasing." She looks at Diana. "You?"

"I haven't checked my phone in days."

Rhiannon rolls her eyes. "Look, I've been doing research on both CVP and NorthStar." Rhiannon pulls up a web page on the big monitor. "Celestial Venture Partners is a division of a financial services company called Celestial Capital. NorthStar, the police company, is controlled by a company called Celestial Private Equity, which is *also* a division of Celestial Capital. You know what else they own?" She doesn't wait for an answer. "In addition to Celestial Venture Partners and Celestial Private Equity, there's Celestial *Public* Equity, Celestial Consulting, and Celestial Logistics. If you trace out from all of those companies, through shell companies and offshore accounts and reverse mergers, they own news organizations, banks, web hosts, television networks, streaming services. And they're *big* into government services. Schools, police departments, prisons, road maintenance, even water treatment. Everything."

Moira looks at the page over Rhiannon's shoulder. "And who runs Celestial?"

"The CEO is Darren Nunwick, a lion who's excellent at staying out of the spotlight. They're a closely held private firm, they've been around about forty years, and their mission statement uses way too many words to say nothing." She taps on her keyboard, bringing up another website, and reads from it, dropping her voice to mimic the deep, blandly reassuring voice of financial service company television ads: "'From our founding, we have held to the conviction that there is a different way for an investment firm to create value. Our commitment to create lasting impact means that we work differently, tenacious in our desire to unearth the fundamentals that drive businesses and markets over the long term. And it means that we partner differently, aligning our interests with those of our investors for lasting impact.'"

"That is some bullshit." Moira sits down again. "A male lion, though, hmm?"

"Like Daranu," Hazel says, and squints. "'Darren Nunwick' even *sounds* like Daranu."

Moira nods, crossing her arms. "It does."

Diana lifts her brows. "You don't think…"

Rhiannon makes a time-out gesture with her hands. "Who's Daranu?"

"The creator god I led a failed rebellion against. He'd do whatever it took to enforce his idea of the natural order. Herbivores under carnivores. Women under men."

"I'm going to guess he wasn't big into LGBTQ rights, either."

Moira shakes her head. "No." She smiles faintly, then slouches in her chair. "I don't think the name similarity is a coincidence. But I don't know what it means. I'm not ready to believe Daranu secretly stayed behind all this time to become a corporate CEO."

Rhiannon shifts uncomfortably. "You're really committed to the idea of being a goddess, aren't you?"

"You've seen Hazel do miracles, and frankly, she doesn't know a fraction of what she's capable of. I'm going to guess there've been worshippers here. And you *know* this is all supernatural, impossible. You can rationalize superheroes, but not gods?"

"I don't know what the hell I can rationalize. All I know is that ever since you did whatever you did, I've had a supporting role in a crazy dark comedy and I can't figure out if my roommate's the plucky heroine or a cosmic horror. So thanks for that." She looks down at the floor. "You want to know why no gods? Because if there were gods, it'd mean they *let* the world get this way. There's so much beauty and so much ugliness. Maybe you can't have one without the other. But through all my short, mortal life, the balance has been tipping. There's always been corruption, but it's getting more open. Our leaders call laws against discrimination the *real* discrimination, the anti-fascists the *real* fascists. There are too many places I might get arrested—or worse—for just using a public restroom."

She takes a ragged breath, and looks up, glaring at the hare. "So no, I can't explain what Hazel can do now, or what I guess you and the sheep can do. But as insane as it is to believe you're superheroes? If I believe that you're a goddess, and you've been here a thousand years just watching? That you didn't help us? That you didn't *stop* us?" Her words drop to a broken whisper. "That's so much worse."

Moira goes still. The *temerity* of a mortal to lecture her about the condition of the world, after they made it for themselves. *They* turned their backs on her and all the gods. She ought to—

Diana and Hazel both move back, the sheep visibly cringing. Rhiannon clearly feels it, too. She trembles, ears lowering, but stands her ground.

After several long moments, Moira closes her eyes. She feels lightheaded again, that sense of nausea gods should be thoroughly immune to returning. Dammit, wasn't she past that? "I don't like this," she mutters.

Hazel speaks hesitantly, unusual caution in her voice. "Don't… don't like what?"

She opens her eyes. "Feeling for mortals again," she snaps.

"Feeling that Rhiannon is right. Except that it was longer than a thousand years, and I wasn't even watching."

She holds her stomach. The nausea is strong enough she wants to lie down, but she fights the impulse. "I don't know what to do. I haven't known for centuries. To my eyes, the world's been broken a long time. I thought the only way to fix it was to overturn Daranu's damned natural order, and I failed. I failed, the other gods abandoned me, and you all stopped believing in gods anyway. So, no. I haven't done anything but wait for the next Turning, and I don't know if it'll ever come." She swallows. "Maybe there's something I could have done, should have done earlier. And I'm sorry."

Rhiannon watches, silent, expressionless.

The hare straightens up, taking the squirrel's hand gently in hers. "I wish I could tell you I knew what to do now. I don't. The world has changed, though. Something's coming, and I don't know how to be ready for it. But I know I'll need help from two young gods. Or three."

"Three?" Diana and Hazel say at the same time. Moira doesn't say it out loud, but it echoes in her head simultaneously. *Three? Oh, for all the stars' sake, what are you saying, Moira? What are you doing?*

Rhiannon's eyes widen, and she pulls her hand away from the hare. "No. No no no."

"Answer me this." Moira's voice drops to an earnest whisper. "What would you do with the power of a god?"

"Give me power and you'll have a major supervillain on your hands, I swear! I'd... I'd..." She runs a hand through her hair, looking lost in thought.

The nausea is gone, just like that.

Moira holds out her hand again. Rhiannon stares at it as if it were a snake, gives Hazel a long look, then slowly puts her hand in the hare's.

nine
interview

When Moira steps into the restaurant, the disdain from the *maître d'* as he looks her over is palpable. "May I help you?" Please. He's judging her outfit at a restaurant full of Silicon Valley techbros? She knows how she looks: fabulous. Yes, she's in jeans, but they're jet black and unfaded. She's got nice sandals on her paws. She's in a blouse for the first time in damn it *has* been a while, hasn't it. And, oh yes, she's the fucking goddess of love. She could be wearing a bright orange trash bag and still command the attention of everyone in this room if she wanted to. "I'm meeting someone at the bar. Do you know if Max Howell is here?"

The stoat arches a brow, and his whiskers twitch. Shortly he offers a stiff smile. "I haven't seen Mr. Howell today." He motions toward the lounge area.

Moira shakes her head and heads into the bar. It's hipster, but in a markedly different way than the bars she's preferred lately. All soft light, soft wood, and hard currency. By her estimate, everyone here falls into three groups: young tech nerds with startups trying to convince investors to back them, middle-aged tech nerds who lucked into a big stock payoff and want to gamble on those startups, and spectators looking for flings with rich people. Everybody here wants to hook up with someone, none of them for sincere reasons. It gives her hives.

She leans on the bar and glances over the cocktail menu, lifting a brow. They look overpriced, even for this time and place.

Then she stiffens. There's something—

"Moira?"

She turns to see a fox walking toward her, and her eyes widen.

It's not that he's unusually attractive—he *is*, in a fashion model way, but she's used to that. It's not the perfect haircut, the thousand dollar tailored blazer, the whole "Ivy League bad boy" vibe; those all just make her want to deck him. No: it's that she can tell that he's not mortal.

"Max Howell, I presume." She straightens up, and takes his offered hand.

"Yes. Wow. You are one tall rabbit." He grins, and motions toward a secluded booth. "Let's take a more private seat."

He's tall, too, eye level to her. "I'm a hare."

"Ah, sorry. I admit I've never been clear on the difference. Hares are bigger?" He glides into the booth.

"Right." She takes the opposite side. After studying him a few moments more, she leans back. "So what are you, Mr. Howell?"

"Call me Max, please. And I'm a junior partner with Celestial's venture capital group."

"You know that's not what I'm asking."

He laughs. "Yes, I know."

The waitress, an attractive squirrel (although not as cute as Rhiannon, in Moira's estimation), comes by and prompts them for drink orders. "I'll have a Last Word," Max says, and looks at Moira expectantly.

"Do you have a double IPA?"

"We have a Lagunitas—"

"One of those."

The squirrel nods and heads off.

"So..." Max rests his hands on the table, lacing his fingers together. "Yes, we really are a VC group, but we're a division of Celestial Capital, which is...an unusual company."

"From what I know of them, they own half the world economy and half the governments."

"Mmm. I don't know about *own*, but it's reasonable to say we have influence over most of the world. But that's not what makes them unusual. The CEO, Darren Nunwick, is…like us. And there are others across the executive ranks."

A company run by gods. She tries not to let the shock show on her face, but she's not sure she's successful. "How many?"

"Only a handful of true ones," he motions with a hand between himself and the hare, "and dozens of higher-ups you might call elevated."

They stop talking for a moment as the waitress drops off the drinks. In her day, they wouldn't call them "elevated," they'd call them "legendary heroes" or "favored ones," but she understands what he means. Diana's elevated her high priest mouse, William, although Moira isn't sure the sheep understands she's done it.

"You're not one of the gods I knew from my pantheon."

He shakes his head. "None of us are."

"How?"

"How did new gods come about, or how did you not know?" He smiles knowingly.

She glares. "Both."

"Do you know why the old gods disappeared?" He swirls his drink around, as if it were wine instead of a cocktail.

"Do you?"

"They no longer matched the world. And we think they knew it. Maybe they stayed in your Otherworld and stopped coming to mortal realms, maybe they went somewhere else entirely, maybe they just faded away like the gods of the last cycle. But that doesn't mean there isn't a space in modern times for gods, Moira. It means the space looks different. Not stone and wooden temples and churches, but concrete and steel banks and skyscrapers. Not shaping the mortal world through smiting enemies and blessing supplicants, but through manipulating the levers the mortals themselves built."

That's a long-winded way of saying "no." She keeps her eyes on him, but stays silent, waiting for an answer to the other half of the question.

"As for how you didn't know…" He gives a slight shrug. "In part because we don't advertise ourselves, but in larger part because I think—hmm. I'm not sure how best to put this. The firm's been aware of you since long before I joined it, and there's been talk before of whether to bring you in."

"But they chose to keep me in the dark."

"Moira, *you* chose to keep you in the dark." He sighs, leaning toward her. "You've gone from the legendarily rebellious goddess of love herself to…what? An immortal drifter. For a thousand years, you've barely used your magic, as far as we can tell, except for petty feats. Making yourself barely wealthy enough to be comfortable, reinventing yourself every few decades, stomping poor saps flat when you fly off the handle. Frankly, we doubted you still had any ability to do meaningful divine work. So." He leans back again and crosses his arms, looking into her eyes. "What changed?"

She shakes her head. "I don't think anything has."

"Come now. After *millennia* of quiescence, you deified two women in two days, then turned an outdoor festival into a violent magic-powered orgy. We're having to do a lot of work to deal with the fallout from that, you know."

She shrugs. "Everyone who was there remembers it as a dream." Best not to correct him about the number of goddesses she's created.

"Everyone who survived, you mean. Eighty-nine out of one hundred three police officers are still missing. And that dream was *shared*. It's left more than a few wolves and tigers deeply confused about why they're now attracted to the idea of being led around on a leash by mice and sheep. Not to mention leaving more than a few mice and sheep bold enough to hold those leashes."

She can't help but grin at the idea of a cute mouse with a leashed tiger at their paws. Her grin earns her a slight frown from the fox. That makes her laugh, which makes his frown deepen.

"All right, Max." She takes a long draught of her beer. "Why does a group of divine financiers gung-ho about law and order see a cranky old goddess causing magical chaos and think, why, *there's* someone we want to be working with? If you hadn't brought me in before, why now?"

"That's a sharp question." He tilts his head. "Approaching you—and your new companions Ms. Harcourt and Ms. Lindsay—was my idea, and if I'm honest, it's not one my superiors are fully comfortable with. It's my understanding the man at the top doesn't like you."

"He doesn't know me."

"He knows your reputation. I do, too. And to me, you got that reputation by—" He stops and laughs. "As painfully corporate as 'thinking outside the box' sounds, it's true. I don't want to say that's a skill our C Suite lacks, but in the relatively short time I've been with them, I've found a…well, a certain *rigidity* in their outlook. That's admirable in a group that's, as you said, very gung-ho about law and order, but I don't think they have much idea what to do about you now. So I'm taking initiative. We obviously don't want to risk an open conflict—"

"Obviously." She keeps her tone perfectly flat.

He falters for a moment before picking up where he left off. "—but what are the alternatives? Keep doing what we've been doing?"

She sets down her beer and laces her fingers together, in conscious imitation of him giving his opening statement. "What *have* you been doing about me, Max?"

His ears tilt down. "It should be clear we've left you to your own devices," he says. "There are times, especially over the last century, when you became a touch…careless in your dealings with mortals, and we had to do a little cleanup work. That's all." He sighs, brings his ears forward again, and holds up his hands. "Look. *Something* in you is itching to make a difference again. Isn't working toward a real goal better than just letting out random bursts of magic? So far, all you've done is decimate a small-town police department and plunk a giant wheelchair in downtown San Francisco."

The charge of being careless isn't one she can argue with, but what does it mean to do cleanup work? And why? She doesn't buy for one second that it's for *her* benefit. "So what do you and Celestial Capital consider real goals?"

"The mortal world's adrift. Off course. I know you can feel it, just like we can." He spreads his hands. "We can take the helm. We can reshape the nature of the modern world, using all the state and corporate infrastructure built up over the last few centuries. We helped build it!" He gets more excited as he talks. "The energy, the divine magic of the modern world, is *money.* Capital. And Celestial's better at using it than any mortals, because we can see what mortals can't, take actions that mortals can't."

He leans forward. "Reshape the world with us, Moira. Use our magic. Rule the way modern gods do." If he's not being genuine, he's one of the best actors she's met in three hundred years and change.

She rubs the back of her ear. "Gods aren't rulers, Max," she says at length. "They're gods."

His brow furrows.

"Sure, we spent time down here in the mortal world meddling with this, nudging that, having petty fights, bestowing favors, hurling curses. But we're *archetypes.* Legends. Sometimes role models, other times cautionary tales. We're not kings or presidents or prime ministers. Or...or bankers."

Max opens his muzzle, closes it, and takes a long time to digest that. Then he crosses his arms. "With all respect, how did that work out for you? Your fellow gods are gone, and you've been abandoned down here for half of recorded history. People don't know me as a god, no, but I'm on the cover of business magazines. You're in musty history books. I fly private jets to private islands. You careen between odd jobs and dive bars around the world."

"What does Celestial think of Daranu's natural order? His insistence that the way things worked for our unevolved ancestors needs to be reflected in our society, both mortals and gods?"

He looks confused. "I don't understand the question."

"Of course you don't." She sighs. "I'll be blunt. We both know I have no idea how to be a divine financial analyst or whatever absurd job title you have in mind is. I don't think you're as interested in me joining you as you are in making sure I'm not fighting you. That's a good call on your part, but I'm not sure if it would be one on mine."

"If you leave this bar without saying yes, I won't be able to make this offer again."

"I'll take that risk." She starts to slide out of the booth.

"And the risk to your new friends? Diana and Hazel?"

She freezes, slowly sits back down, looks at him levelly. "Is that a threat, Max?"

"I'm just asking questions." He smiles, humorlessly. "But you don't want to stand in our way. You may think you know who you're dealing with, but I assure you that you don't."

Moira clenches her fist under the table. Her patience with patronizing carnivores is the lowest it's been in many a year, and she's finding that unexpectedly refreshing. "You're right. I don't. But do you know who *you're* dealing with?"

She reaches her other hand across the table, takes him by the wrist, and *yanks*. He yelps, now dangling by one arm held between her thumb and forefinger, less than two inches from ear tips to paws. She drops him in her pint glass.

Max shrieks, sinking into the beer in a trail of foam and bubbles before swimming to the surface and spluttering. He stares up at her, stricken, and tries to simply teleport himself out. She can feel the tug, but it's like someone trying to lift her hand with a feather. "What—" He wheezes. "I can't—"

"You can, if your will to get out is strong enough. If it's stronger than my will to keep you there." She lifts the pint to her mouth and tilts it back, letting the cascade of beer bounce him against her lower lip for several seconds. Then she holds the glass up in front of her eyes, studying the soaked fox. "You seem to be the one standing in *my* way, Max. In the way of me finishing this delicious pale ale."

This time the tug is harder, that of a young child pulling on her hand. She lets him try to exercise his divine will on her a few seconds longer, then takes another drink, slower, but deeper. His head slides between her lips twice before she sets the glass down. The remaining beer's only hip-high to him now.

"This isn't funny!" he gasps.

She crosses her arms, resting her elbows on the table and smirking down at him. "It's hilarious."

"You're a herbivore! I'm—I'm—"

She licks her lips exaggeratedly.

Max's ears flatten. "I'm a god! Gods can't kill other gods!"

She lifts the glass up again. "I killed the god of war, Max, and I assure you it was a lot harder than this. And not nearly as refreshing." She opens her muzzle wide and tilts the glass all the way back.

Max wails, managing to brace himself with his hands on her bottom teeth, the wail rising as the beer drains past him. She shakes the glass until he loses his grip and tumbles into her mouth, then swallows.

She sets the glass down, wipes her lips, and looks at his half-finished cocktail. Shrugging, she finishes it, too, then puts down enough money for both drinks and a generous tip before walking out of the lounge.

ten
low profile

"You...you *ate* him?" William bursts out. The mouse had stayed silent through most of Moira's retelling of her meeting with Max, but that revelation seems to be a bridge too far.

"You've got to know some of the old myths by now." She arches a brow. "They're all about giants striding across the world, and every third or fourth one ends with someone going down an angry god's throat."

"Y-yes, but those are mortals. And *bad* mortals. Ones you've judged."

Moira shrugs. "I judged Max."

"He was a bad god?"

"He couldn't even get out of my pint glass, so I'd say he was pretty shit, yes."

Rhiannon gives her a look.

"He made a threat to me—the goddess of war—against all of you. I even gave him a chance to retract it, and he doubled down. No apologies."

Hazel snickers. "Killing a god just returns them to being mortal, anyway."

William's eyes get wider again. "It does?"

"See, Hazel knows her folk tales. Yes, but it's more as if...hmm. A mortal incarnation of the god replaces the divine one. There's a mortal Max now, but he wouldn't have a memory of having been a god. He might have a far different life than the pre-deification Max did." She shrugs. "Anyway, we're getting off track. Max said he was trying to recruit us without telling anyone, so this may buy us a little time."

"Did he?" Diana arches a brow. "You said he claimed the people over him didn't like the idea of bringing us in, but even if he was telling the truth about that, it doesn't mean he didn't tell them he was going to try."

"He said he was 'taking initiative.' Isn't that business-speak for going rogue?"

"Maybe. It *does* have a kind of 'easier to ask forgiveness than ask permission' tone to it." Rhiannon looks to Moira. "But what does that buy us time to do?"

"Research more about them."

"And train," Diana adds. "We need to know how to use our powers."

Moira runs a hand through her hair. Nobody trained her on how to be a goddess. She just...was. "I don't know if I know how to do that."

Hazel lights up. "No, that's a great idea! I'm already doing all this, and you said that's just a fraction of what I'm capable of, so *damn*, let's go!"

"Yes." Rhiannon crosses her arms. "Only you can teach Hazel how not to destroy the world if she gets overexcited."

Hazel pouts.

"Okay." Moira sighs. "I'll think of an exercise, and we'll go out tomorrow."

Diana stands up and walks to the front door. "We'll call it a date. Meanwhile, I have loaves out there to multiply."

"They're hoagies from Dan's Deli, m'lady," William corrects.

"Not as poetic, but more filling." The sheep heads out, the mouse close behind.

The next day, Moira drives them up to the Financial District. A fully deserted space would be safer for mortals, but William claimed there'd be a park here that should be all but empty on a

Saturday, and he wanted to shop at a nearby farmers' market while they trained.

When she arrives, though, she instantly finds a hole in the theory. The FiDi doesn't look crowded, but the Ferry Building Marketplace is a madhouse. "Is it really worth fighting through this?"

"Yes, m'lady." William nods firmly. "There's no other place in the Bay Area where you can get produce like this. The fruit from Harvest Dance is divine."

"So to speak." She drops him off and heads to the park a couple of blocks northwest, pulling into a handicapped parking space and hanging Hazel's rarely-used hangtag on the mirror. She hmms, rubbing her chin.

"What?" Hazel says. She's riding shotgun.

"Let's make this your first test. Get your wheelchair out of the trunk and roll it over to you."

The pika gives her a skeptical look. "Do what now? How? Teleport it to me? Open the trunk from in here and levitate it out?"

Moira shrugs. "Doesn't matter. You pass the test if you do it without hurting my brand new, expensive sports car." She leans over the pika and fixes her gaze on her. "Do *not* hurt my brand new, expensive sports car." She magics up whatever money she needs at any given moment and has no real attachment to the car, but she doesn't have to let Hazel in on that.

Hazel's ears fold back and she smiles nervously. "Ah, heh. Okay." She looks behind her. Diana and Rhiannon look back from the back seat, both also nervous.

"I've done this before with the door. Shouldn't be too difficult. Right?" The pika scrunches up her eyes, then pauses, looking at Moira. "I don't know how trunk locks work."

"Do you know what your wheelchair looks like?"

"Of course."

She points at the sidewalk. "What would it look like if it were right there?"

"It'd…well. It'd…"

"Don't tell me, show me."

Hazel looks at her doubtfully and looks back at the sidewalk. She scrunches her eyes again.

"Just relax and see it."

"That's easy for you to say." Hazel closes her eyes, takes a deep breath, and opens her eyes again, staring hard at the sidewalk.

And, with a soft clatter, her wheelchair is sitting there. The car rocks gently. Hazel squeals and claps her hands.

Rhiannon stares. "Huh."

They all get out of the car. Hazel drops into her chair, and Moira leads them into the park on a slow stroll. "That trick is what I call visualizing. It's not the only way to use your power, but it's the most straightforward way." The path they're on leads up a gentle hill. Rhiannon puts a hand on one arm of Hazel's wheelchair, pushing it along.

"So what *are* the limits to our powers? I've changed size, changed the size of others, and pulled off that never-ending potluck trick. But I can't just go..." Diana lifts her arms, palms up, and says in a commanding voice, "And now, *world peace!*" She drops her arms. "Can I?"

Moira shakes her head. "You can put 'visualize world peace' on a bumper sticker, but you can't actually do it."

Hazel hmms. "While I can change size because it's so easy to visualize a skyscraper at my knee height."

"Right."

Diana's eyes widen. "You haven't been that big, have you?"

"Not yet." Hazel grins. "But what are the limits on that? What if I visualize myself big enough to eat the planet like an apple?"

"Don't," Moira says. She's watching Rhiannon, who's looking more sullen than usual. Given her annoyance at all things divine, that's significant.

Hazel looks excited. "Because I couldn't, or because I could?"

Moira eyes her. "Because you can't visualize how hard I will kick your ass if you try."

The pika clears her throat and nods.

"I'm not getting it," Rhiannon says abruptly. "I haven't used power once since I've supposedly become a goddess."

Hazel looks back at her. "You just pushed my wheelchair with one hand about two hundred feet up an incline. You'd have been panting halfway up a week ago."

"That's not the same thing."

"If you couldn't do it before," Diana says, "then—"

Rhiannon starts talking over her. So does Hazel.

Moira stomps her foot once. She doesn't change size, doesn't make a big show out of it. She merely puts a dash of *power* in the stomp. Not even a three on the earthquake scale, but the sidewalk at the base of the rise cracks. The air fills with the sounds of car alarms, loose branches falling, frightened birds taking flight, and a few hundred people whipping out their phones and texting one another QUAKE? messages.

Diana and Rhiannon both stumble. Hazel's chair wobbles and starts to roll until the pika recovers, "grabbing" it with a wave of her hand that jerks it to a halt.

She looks at Rhiannon, folding her hands behind her back. "Diana and Hazel are right. You haven't used your power *much*, but it's there."

Rhiannon grunts, and slowly turns around, looking down the hill. Her tail twitches behind her like a storm warning. "Right then I visualized being big enough to pound this hill into a sand trap, but I'm still the same size."

"One, good, because we're supposed to be keeping a low profile right now. Two, no, you didn't."

The squirrel glares. "I did!"

Moira shakes her head. "No."

"Dammit! I'm seeing myself—the hill—"

"If you're seeing yourself, you're visualizing what someone else would see." Diana spreads her hands. "How does it all look like to *you* when you're that big?"

Rhiannon holds her hands out in front of her, fingers curled. "It looks like this!" she shrieks. "It looks like—"

The sonic boom of displaced air almost distracts Moira from the now monster-sized Rhiannon losing her balance in shock. The hare grabs the sheep by the hand and the pika by the chair, bolting backward. It helps, but the sheer force of several thousand tons of angry, startled boho squirrel hitting the ground sends all three tumbling down the hillside: Diana bleating, Moira cursing, and Hazel wailing as she fights to keep her wheelchair upright while it does a credible F1 imitation.

Rhiannon pushes herself up, clumps of grass, several trees, and one park bench falling away from her hips, shoulders, and chest. "Like...this." Despite its new force, her voice trembles.

Moira gets to her paws, muttering under her breath. "I just said 'low profile.'"

But the squirrel's staggering to her full height, too, shaking off her hands, taking an unsteady step, then a steadier one, watching the effects her paw has on the ground as it sinks in. "Oh my god oh my god," she mutters. She takes another step. Then she starts walking away, toward the crowd, toward the city.

"Where's she going?" Diana runs a hand through her hair.

Hazel's recovered from her wild ride, but she's still breathing hard, staring after her roommate with a haggard expression. "I don't think she's handling this well."

"I picked up on that." Moira scowls, striding after the squirrel, breaking into a run. Getting giant herself is tempting, but *two* monster movie size women will be damn hard on the city if Rhiannon steps out of the park.

Rhiannon steps out of the park.

"Oh, come *on*." At least the squirrel didn't step on any traffic, but she's already caused one accident—make that two—just by being there. Three. The park's surrounded by skyscrapers on three sides, too, most of which stand even taller than the mega-squirrel. Silver lining: she's hidden from most of the rest of the city. Unless she trips again.

Diana hurries toward the hare. "Can't we visualize her small?"

"I tried it." Hazel's rolling along, too. "It didn't work for me. Lady Moira?"

The hare sighs, watching the squirrel come to a dead stop and try to decide what to do next. She hasn't yet noticed that she's picked up a crowd of worshipful admirers trailing behind. "Well, the first thing you did was eat somebody, and the first thing Diana did was step on someone, so this is relatively innocuous so far." She motions for them to follow the squirrel.

Diana hurries ahead of the hare as they cross a wider avenue. She doesn't wait for traffic, instead holding her hands out to either side. Cars screech to a halt, drivers gaping in awe rather than honking. A few get out of their cars and drop to their knees.

"Man, she is *good* at whatever the hell she's doing," Hazel says, rolling next to Moira along the path Diana's temporarily cleared.

The hare nods. "It really is like she was meant for it."

More people get out of their cars. Hazel glances from side to side, then over at the hare. "Why can we just melt into the crowd sometimes and other times get this?"

"Usually we're not calling attention to our divine aspects."

"So it's when we do magic?"

"Accent on 'we,' not 'magic.' Diana's given William power, even if she hasn't noticed yet, but no one's going to fall to their knees for him."

Rhiannon's making her way down a fortunately low-traffic side street. "Divinity is complicated," Hazel mutters. "Maybe she just wanted to take a walk as a giantess? I won't lie—I'd probably kick over a skyscraper or two if I could."

Moira glances down at her. "I've seen you stand. And walk."

Hazel rests her hands in her lap, letting the wheelchair roll itself, now that she can. "For short distances, unless it's a bad day. Although I don't have those often now." She shrugs. "But I was telling Rhiannon, it feels important to remind everyone you can still be powerful this way."

"Fair."

Rhiannon's stopped in front of a relatively short office building, ten stories or so high. Her fists clench. The crowd that's been trailing her looks more agitated, too, as if tuned to her anger.

Hazel squints, and lets out a groan. "Uh oh."

Diana looks at her worriedly.

"That's the HQ of the software company she worked at. When she filed a harassment complaint a year ago, they made it so miserable for her that she quit, and she thinks they're making it difficult for her to get another job."

"She doesn't need to work now," Moira murmurs. "But I understand her feelings."

The goddesses navigate through the crowd, this time letting Hazel lead. The pika doesn't have the same *let me through, my lovely worshippers* panache as the sheep, but the mortals still back away respectfully. Moira's impressed.

Rhiannon hasn't moved much, past breathing hard and swishing her zeppelin-sized tail back and forth. She tenses up, relaxes, tenses again, then crouches slowly, eyes on the approaching gods. Mostly on Moira. "I kept myself from smashing it just because I could."

"And do you feel better?"

"No." Her softly booming voice is matter-of-fact. "I still want to. But if I'm going to help keep you in line, I need to be able to keep myself in line."

Diana looks up at her, brows lifting. "With all respect, I don't think Lady Moira intended to appoint you group conscience."

"Yeah, but I see the value of testing. And this is a difficult one." Hazel glances up at Rhiannon. "I remember how furious you were after you'd gone to HR about your coworker, and the lady went on about how maybe the real problem was you not keeping your 'trans ideology' to yourself."

Rhiannon frowns, looking down at Hazel, back at the building, back at Hazel. "Yes, I do, too," she says curtly. She straightens, looks up at the sky a moment, takes a deep, slow breath, and starts walking away.

After three steps, she whirls around and slams her paw into the side of the building. "Fuck you, Joanne from HR," she snarls.

The crowd of quasi-worshippers collectively decides a safe distance is about two blocks. In short order, only Moira, Diana, and Hazel remain, watching the facade of the building crumble and slide down in an urban avalanche.

Rhiannon brushes her long hair away from her face and takes a deep breath, then returns to her normal size, staring at the damage she's done.

"Feel better?" Moira repeats, crossing her arms.

The squirrel gives her a curt nod. "Yes."

They head back through the park. All of the crowd's watching them now—but mostly watching Rhiannon. Some drop to their knees, many loudly whispering about the goddess, singular.

"So," Hazel says, giving Rhiannon a too-wide grin. "Low profile."

"Shut up."

eleven
peaches and cream

Diana looks up from her computer worriedly. "This one mentions my place."

All four goddesses, old and new, are at Diana's suburban house-cum-temple. In what she's realizing is Moira's frustratingly typical way, the immortal hare won't come out and say they should all stick together for safety, so she put her hoof down over it. And together means here. She's seen how small Rhiannon and Hazel's home is, and it's palatial compared to Moira's loft. (Even though the loft must have far and away the highest rent of the three. Moira hasn't explained how she does that with no visible income yet; is she visualizing money?)

"Yeah, I'm reading it, too." Rhiannon looks over from where she's sitting on the couch near Hazel, both of them with laptops. "That's not good."

"No." Diana quickly scans the article, the third one about the "apparition" of a giant squirrel woman seen around a collapsed, fortunately unoccupied office building. No one has clear pictures of Rhiannon, only the damage. But this is the first story tying it into the string of "odd occurrences over the last month," including the psychedelic mess in Vallejo; the "Angel of the Castro" and her murals, along with new ramps and other affordances mysteriously popping up around the neighborhood, and the disappearance of a few notoriously awful landlords and businessmen (and occasionally their places of business, too); and, quote, "a neighborhood in South San Francisco becoming the epicenter of a personality cult around a reclusive woman who claims to be a goddess."

Moira gets up, pacing slowly. "Celestial's minions are losing control of the narrative."

"That's good, isn't it?" Hazel says.

"Yes and no. They'll feel compelled to move against us more directly, and I don't think anyone but Max was keen on trying to bring us inside the tent." She wiggles her nose, looking at the kitchen. "Is your mouse William making coffee?"

"Yes." Diana sighs. "And he's not 'my mouse.'"

"Call him your high priest, your page, your chosen hero, or your magic butler, but I assure you that he's given you his absolute devotion, and in return you've given him a touch of your power."

That can't be right, but that names precisely what she's been feeling about William for days, isn't it? He unfailingly knows what to do and when to do it around the temple. Er, house. Even if it's as simple as making coffee. Hmm.

"I think they already are, with what this article says." Rhiannon gestures at her computer. "The mayor's bringing in *more* security consultants to, quote, 'coordinate a response to the grave and immediate danger of local anarchists and cultists.' The consultants are from a company called Third Eye."

"They were outside the grocery store I met Diana at. Wild guess: they're owned by Celestial."

"They are, and they came up in my research the other day when I was looking into Presage. That's a data analysis and surveillance company that works with intelligence and counterterrorism agencies, majority owned by Celestial Private Equity. And, they have a big contract with Third Eye."

William enters from the kitchen, clearing his throat softly. He's balancing four bowls with the skill of a waiter. "This is a sort of, ah, mid-afternoon snack, your graces, to complement the coffee." He sets them down around the table. "At least *this* is going right. The magic for the potluck outside is a mess."

Diana heads over. "A mess?"

He shakes his head. "Some of the food's turning into other things entirely when it multiplies. It was fine when a pot of baked beans became jelly beans, but a lentil loaf became a loaf of packing peanuts. And a cherry pie tried to bite someone."

"I'll...take a look." Diana shakes her head, and looks at the bowls. "Peaches and cream?"

The mouse nods. "This farm's always got the best fruit I've ever had, and I wanted to share it with all of you in its best form. And they wanted to share it with us! They gave me these peaches for free."

Diana raises a brow. "Because you're such a good customer?"

"I suppose so, m'lady."

Hazel stands up and walks over, Rhiannon by her side. "Hmm. I'm not a big fan of peaches, but I'll give it a try, sure."

"I'll get the coffee." The mouse disappears back into the kitchen.

Moira keeps pacing. "So what does that mean they're going to do? If they're so committed to staying in the shadows, not acting like gods..." She waves a hand in exasperation.

"A PR war, at least at first." Diana takes a seat, frowning. "We'll all be portrayed as 'anarchists and cultists,' according to that article." The peaches and cream look good and smell even better. She slips a spoonful of peach into her mouth, and—

—and she's a lamb, barely knee-high to her mother, standing in one of the last surviving orchards from the time the Santa Clara Valley was known for agriculture instead of computers. She didn't know back then what an "heirloom peach" was, but she knew it was the most incredible thing she'd ever taken a bite of. Even the best peach she'd tried as an adult hadn't measured up, and she'd written it off as a memory colored by being so young and naïve. Maybe it was. But this peach brings that memory back so intensely it's oversaturated: the taste, the scent, the texture, the warm sun on her wool. This peach is that good. This peach might be *better* than that good.

William has come out from the kitchen, setting down cups of

coffee. She puts a hand on his wrist. "William, what did you *do* to these peaches?"

His ears color and he shakes his head. "Like I said, it's the quality of the fruit, my lady."

"I don't know PR." Moira grunts. "What does that even *mean*? Getting people to think that feeding the poor or helping your neighbors is bad?"

Hazel adds, "Or standing up against corruption." She gets a spoonful of peaches, too, and sticks it in her mouth. Her eyes widen. "Holy shit, I think I might have just come."

Diana manages not to choke on a sip of coffee. William goes bright red.

"For god's sake, Hazel." Rhiannon sighs. "And, anyway, it's not as if it's going to be difficult for Celestial to spin a giantess stomping on buildings as bad." She picks up her bowl of peaches and takes a spoonful absently, then double-takes at them. "Whoa. Okay, these really are incredible."

William beams, although he's still blushing.

Moira stops pacing and looks over to the dining table, clearly irritated. "There may very well be other gods we know nothing about preparing for battle with us, and you're all rhapsodizing about dessert."

The mouse looks down, abashed. Diana pats his shoulder and loudly whispers, "Don't worry, she gets like this. It might be a war god thing." She hopes it isn't a love god thing.

"Lady Moira, we're talking about..." Hazel waves her spoon in a circle. "Everything. But the only god we have any experience with is you. A month ago, I was an agnostic, Rhiannon was an atheist, and Diana was a..." She looks over at the sheep inquiringly.

"Divorcee who hasn't been to a church since her marriage."

"I may still be an atheist," Rhiannon mutters.

"So," Hazel continues, "our insight on divinity is pretty limited. I've read folktales about your pantheon—I was sort of an Aronn fangirl—but it's just not the world anymore. There haven't been gods striding among the mortals openly doing miracles since..." She trails off.

"Yesterday," Moira says dryly. "And what do you mean you were a 'fangirl' of the god of death?"

Hazel leans forward, eager. "Was he cool?"

"No. He was a melancholy, morose drip." She heads to the table and picks up her bowl of peaches and cream, looking at it skeptically.

Rhiannon leans back in her chair, crossing her arms and looking pensive, huge tail twitching behind her. "What does being against Celestial *mean*? Are we trying to overthrow the new gods, and just get it right this time?"

"No. I don't…" Moira sighs heavily, and stirs her bowl of fruit.

The squirrel looks straight at her, keeping her voice matter-of-fact. "When we first met, you ranted about how you've started to feel for mortals again, how you didn't know what's coming but you needed us to be ready for whatever it was, and how much you hated Daranu's 'natural order' shtick. Everything we're learning about Celestial suggests *their* shtick is modernizing and refining that."

Moira stabs her spoon into the peaches and takes a bite, looking petulant about it.

Then her eyes widen in shock and she nearly drops the bowl.

Hazel smirks. "We told you they were good."

Moira swallows slowly and sets the bowl down, visibly shaking.

Diana frowns. "Moira, what's wrong?"

"Where…" She stares at the bowl, expression so dismayed it edges into alarm, then looks at William. "Where did you get these peaches?"

"T-the farmers' market we were—"

She leans toward him, eyes locking onto his with the intensity of an anguished lover. "What's the name of the farm?"

"Harvest Dance. Th-they're up in Sonoma County." He holds up a finger and dashes into the kitchen, looking terrified, and comes back holding up a receipt. "See? Here's the phone number and address."

The hare grabs the receipt and studies it, and looks away with a distant expression.

"Moira," Diana repeats more firmly, standing up. "What's wrong?"

"It's..." She takes a deep breath, closes her eyes, lets the breath out shakily. "I haven't had fruit that tasted like that since...since I was exiled. Not since my last visit to the Otherworld."

Hazel looks down at her bowl. "Are you saying that when William said the fruit from this place was divine, he was accidentally being literal?"

"No. Maybe. I don't know."

Diana looks to William. "The guy there gave these peaches to you, right? To you specifically."

"H-he said the owner wanted us to have them."

"Us," Moira repeats. "Not 'you,' but 'us'?"

He furrows his brow.

The hare rubs her forehead, then heads to the door. "I'm going to the farm."

All the other goddesses get up. "William," Diana calls, "take care of things while we're away."

Moira stops, hand on the doorknob, looking back with a cross expression. "This isn't a group road trip."

"It should be," Rhiannon says. "You might need our help."

Diana bites her lip to keep from saying anything. That might be the worst possible line to use with a war goddess. But Moira shakes her head, stepping through the door, and doesn't stop them from following. The ever-present crowd of worshippers parts for them, giving them cheers and blowing kisses, as they get into Moira's Porsche. This time, Diana gets into the passenger seat.

The hare starts the car and pulls away from the curb. The moment she's on a main street, she stomps on the accelerator hard enough to slam all three of them back in their seats. In short order she blows past a half-dozen stoplights, all of which stay green—or in two cases, turn back to green—for her, and one cop car, which has all four tires blow out just as it flips its siren on.

Diana starts to glance toward the speedometer, but decides it's better if she doesn't know. "Goddesses can't die in car accidents," she whispers to herself. "Goddesses can't die in car accidents."

Moira pulls onto the freeway and accelerates again, cutting across four lanes of traffic from the entrance ramp to the carpool lane. A coyote in a pickup truck honks angrily, which she ignores until he manages to pull in front of her, flips her off, and slams on his brakes.

She doesn't slow down. Instead, she makes a grabbing motion, and the truck disappears. She holds that hand out to Diana. "Do something with this."

Diana takes the truck, now toy-sized, and gapes. The tiny coyote gapes back. Shaking her head, the sheep lifts her hand up to her muzzle and blows on it. The truck, and the coyote, appear unharmed on the side of the road in the emergency lane.

"See, she's being a good example," Rhiannon says to Hazel.

"Fine, Little Miss Building Kicker."

Moira takes the next exit ramp. They've only been on the freeway for a few minutes, but this ramp *isn't* on the south side of San Francisco Bay; they're already in Sonoma Valley. Diana looks around, confused.

"It's a Shortcut," the hare explains, as if that explains anything.

"There wasn't anyone in that building when I brought it down," Rhiannon says.

"But were you *sure* of that at the time?" Hazel persists.

"Well, no, but…" The squirrel trails off, and makes an uncomfortable chitter noise.

Diana turns around. "You just realized you're not bothered by the possibility there might have been, and that seriously bothers you, doesn't it?"

Rhiannon swallows, looking at her, nodding a fraction.

"I've been there. I still am. It's…a lot."

She turns around, looking out the window. They exited onto a state road, and just turned onto a county one; the scents of exhaust and concrete have faded into the scents of grass and wildflowers. Along the left side of the road, rows of grape vines cling to weathered trellises. An orchard, maybe almonds, runs along the right side.

Moira comes to an actual stop at the next stop sign. "This is probably going to be a mortal farm with someone who doesn't have any idea what they have."

Diana tilts her head. "So you're coming out here on a divine whim."

The hare grunts.

It takes another five minutes to reach a dirt road marked by a sun-faded HARVEST DANCE ORCHARD & FARMS sign. At the road's end sits a small barn, equally faded, with a house sitting farther back, and a pickup truck that's been sitting by the barn long enough to be invaded by weeds. Moira parks beside it.

"Are they even open?" Rhiannon murmurs as they all get out of the car.

"I don't know." Moira walks toward the barn, circling around to one of the smaller sides and finding the entrance.

Inside, baskets made from small half-barrels line wooden tables, each one burgeoning with fruit and vegetables—mostly plums, apricots, and, yes, peaches, as well as tomatoes, squashes, and chile peppers.

A portly grey fox looks up from a cash register on the far side of the room, lifting his paw in a wave. "Good morning! What can I help you with?"

Moira looks at him without saying anything. He doesn't seem fazed, walking over and continuing to talk. "We're usually not open on Sundays, but the owner said she had a feeling..." He trails off, studying Moira. "You okay, ma'am?"

She runs a hand through her hair. "Who's the owner?"

"I am." A mouse woman steps through a doorway behind the register, wiping both hands on a dirty green rag. She's on the older side of middle-aged, but her outfit's classic farm girl: plaid blouse tied under her generous chest, denim shorts, straw hat over tangled hair. Call it classic farm hot mom. The most striking thing, though, is her fur color, golden as a sheaf of wheat.

Moira's eyes go wide. The mouse looks at her, and swallows hard, taking a deep breath and letting it out in a slow sigh. "Hello, Moira."

Diana's eyes widen, too. She can sense a *presence* from the mouse, like she did with Hazel, and Rhiannon, and Moira. And the mouse's presence is more like Moira's than the others.

"You left!" Moira bursts out, clenching her fists. The words sound as if they're being ripped out of her, leaving big, bloody wounds. "You *left!* You *all* left!"

The mouse looks down at the barn's dirt floor. "*They* all left, Moira."

Moira turns away, fists still clenched, and storms out of the barn.

Rhiannon's tail twitches. "Could someone fill me in on what the hell is happening?" she murmurs, just above a whisper.

Diana shakes her head, equally lost.

The mouse looks after Moira sadly, then turns to the fox. "Take a break, Jerry."

The fox, looking utterly baffled, nods and heads into the back room.

Turning back to the group, the mouse puts her hands on her hips. "So three new goddesses. Once I saw y'all in the city papers, I knew it was either waiting for you to find me, or finding you first. So who are y'all?"

They look at one another. The sheep's the first to speak. "I'm Diana."

"Hazel."

"Rhiannon."

"Well." She waves around the room, gives them a wan smile. "Welcome to the farm. I'm Briley."

Hazel sits up straight in her wheelchair, eyes widening. "Goddess of the harvest?"

The mouse tips her hat.

twelve
great friends

"Oh my god, this is incredible." Rhiannon's just taken a sip of hot apple cider Briley poured for her, Hazel, and Diana, served in mismatched ceramic mugs. It's not as strongly spiced as the cider she remembers from when she was a kid, but it's bursting with sweet, subtly tart apple flavors, as complex as any wine. They sit around a wooden table in the kitchen of the house behind the barn. The appliances look state of the art for maybe 1945; she's seen gas stoves before, but never one like that.

"I'm pretty good with fruit," Briley says. "But wait 'til you try one of Jerry's pies." She fills a mug for herself and takes a seat with them. "So, to get to your question. The short answer is, I just never left. The long answer…mmm."

She takes a sip of her cider, then sets down the mug, lacing her hands together under her chin. "I always spent most of my time down here in mortal lands. On the farms, in the fields, in wild orchards. It just got more comfortable than being around other gods in the Otherworld. It wasn't about the worshippers, although don't get me wrong, those were nice. But the mortals I felt closest to were ones who lived directly off the harvests. And those were the ones the gods always seemed less concerned with."

"The herbivores."

The mouse nods. "Not to put too fine a point on it."

"Except for Moira." Diana sounds arch, a little indignant.

Briley smiles a small, curiously sad smile. "Except for Moira." She looks down, silent a few seconds, then picks up her mug again. "After her failed crusade, the rest of the gods just closed in on themselves. Like they became absent landlords, letting mortals go their own way. So folks down here stopped calling on them as much, folks up there saw that as a reason to pull back even more…" She takes a sip of the cider and shakes her head. "True for me, too. I mean, people stopped worshipping me, calling on me. But I loved everything here too much to leave, even when it didn't love me back. They came down here less and less, I went up there less and less. And then one day, after I don't know how many years, I tried to go back and I couldn't."

Hazel looks wide-eyed. "Did you forget the way, or was it… gone?"

"I don't think it was me. But six of one, half a dozen of the other, I suppose. I was on my own, and I guess I was okay with that."

Rhiannon hmms. "But Moira was here, too, and it doesn't sound like she knew you were here. Couldn't there be other gods neither of you know about?"

Briley tilts her head, considering, then shrugs. "I can't say for sure there's not, since I guess I just showed we can be around for a long, long time without running into one another. But the truth is, I can't think of anyone else who would, anyone who'd have the attitude toward y'all that I did. They felt pretty betrayed by y'all. Well, mortal y'all, not…" She waves a hand.

"The *gods* felt betrayed by *mortals*." Diana doesn't keep the skepticism out of her tone.

No, that makes a weird sense to Rhiannon. "Because we—uh, they—didn't believe. New religions rose that didn't ask as much of worshippers, and science came along and said maybe there weren't any gods at all."

Briley raises her mug toward the squirrel, nodding. "Me, I was never real keen on counting worshippers. Far as I'm concerned, any time somebody bites into a juicy pear and blisses out, that's giving me thanks. And agriculture just might be the original science." She grunts. "Granted, I'm not so keen on what y'all have been doing lately. Tomatoes as tough as rubber balls and with about as much taste. And do *not* get me started on supermarket apples, or I'll be stomping like Moira does."

Hazel laughs. "You know, the mythology books talk about the gods fading, or dying, or leaving for another land, depending on the folk tale. But they don't talk about you staying behind."

"Y'all know that not everything gets into the books." Briley shrugs.

Diana crosses her arms. "The books also say you and Moira were great friends," she says softly. "You knew she was here. Why didn't you reach out before today?"

The mouse looks distant. "We didn't part on the best of terms. I did try and get word to her once or twice after her exile, though. Never got a peep back."

And that was it? For millennia, that was it? "That was before you were the only two left." Rhiannon gives Briley a sharp look. "As far as she knew, she was the *only* god left, and you just—you just let her become a bitter drunk."

She hears the house's front door open and slam shut. Uh oh.

Briley doesn't meet Rhiannon's eyes. "I reckoned she didn't want my company. And y'all are proof she coulda just made new immortal friends when she wanted."

Moira pushes through the swinging door entrance to the kitchen. "I'm not a bitter drunk, I'm an angry drunk," the hare snaps at Rhiannon. Then she turns on Briley. "And you're damn right I wouldn't have wanted your company."

Briley sinks lower in her seat, but grits her teeth. "Oh, here we go."

"She said she did try to get in touch with you," Rhiannon pipes up.

"Not very damn hard." Moira looms over the mouse. "Before my exile, you wouldn't have left me alone even if I asked."

Briley pushes back from the table and stands up, somehow a head taller than Moira now. "Before your exile, you *wouldn't* have asked." Her voice still holds her country lilt, but there's a touch of sharp blade underneath. "If you're accusing me of something, come on out with it."

Moira's eyes narrow. "I'm not accusing you of anything." She takes a step forward, making Briley take a step back, and now she's a head taller than the harvest mouse. "It's just funny how in the last month I've learned there are new gods trying to run the world behind the scenes." She takes another step, and she's even taller. Briley backs up faster, looking alarmed. "And now I find out there's another old god still here, too."

Briley's expression returns to anger. She straightens up and shoves Moira back a step with both hands—easily, since she's a head or two taller than the hare. Or would be if she could stand up fully: now the ceiling's too low for her. "All I do is run a damn farm stand, bunny!" She waves a hand angrily at the other three goddesses. "You're the one who goes 'round deifying mortals when she gets bored!"

Hazel rolls back from the table. Diana and Rhiannon both follow. "Uh," the squirrel says, "I think you two should maybe take this down a notch."

"Or go outside," Hazel adds. Rhiannon gives her a warning glare.

Moira grits her teeth, balling her hands into fists. "Excellent idea."

Briley narrows her eyes. "Don't you dare."

Moira smashes up through the ceiling and roof, leading with her fists, now at least twice the height of the harvest mouse. Make it three times.

"Dammit, Moira!" Briley charges out of the house—through the side door, but she's so big, moving so fast, she knocks out some of the wall in the process.

"Maybe we should go outside, through another exit," Diana says hurriedly.

Moira's upper half isn't visible from their vantage point, but they can hear her. "What do you think you're going to do, farm—" She disappears, yanked straight up out of sight.

Shit. Yes, outside—now. Rhiannon visualizes the gravel parking lot, with Hazel and Diana by her side, and snaps her fingers. With an audible *poof!* all three of them are there. Perhaps she's getting the hang of this after all.

"Thanks," Hazel says, then looks up. "Whoa."

Briley stands at least fifty feet tall, towering over both barn and the house, and has the merely fifteen feet or so tall Moira in one hand. "Stop. Wrecking. My house!" she thunders.

"Mice look surprisingly intimidating when they're giant," Diana murmurs.

Rhiannon jerks a thumb at Hazel. "Yeah, I got that with the terrifying giant pika."

Hazel grins. "You say the sweetest things."

The grey fox—Jerry, she guesses—who'd been running the farm stand has run outside, scurrying toward them, staring up. "Oh, my goddess."

Despite her relatively diminutive size, the hare gives Briley a venomous glare. All at once she's twice the mouse's size and falling. Briley goes down under her with a literally earth-shaking crash, most of the farmhouse flattened under the harvest goddess's shapely rump. "Tell me what you know about Celestial," Moira growls, trying to pin Briley under a knee.

Briley groans, wincing, then reaches up and grabs Moira's shoulder, the mouse now suddenly half again as large. They roll over, away from the farm stand, and the mouse slams the hare against the ground. "I don't even know what that *means*, you straw-brained bunny! You ever seen me messing with mortal affairs?"

"Should we do something?" Diana runs a hand through her hair, looking worried.

Hazel raises her hands and a bucket of popcorn appears in them. She holds it out to the sheep.

"That's not funny."

"Not as funny as 'get between two legendary goddesses having a wrestling match,' sure." She shakes the bucket.

Diana sighs and takes a handful of popcorn.

Moira lifts Briley up off her with apparent ease, even though the hare doesn't grow this time. Briley looks nonplussed. "So you're just staying out of it all," Moira snarls, "and playing farmer." She sits up—a hundred-foot-tall hare holding a hundred-fifty-foot-tall mouse over her head—then hurls Briley away. The mouse skids through the fields, one of her paws coming dangerously close to taking out the farm stand.

The fox flinches, holding his hands to his head.

"You knew your boss was, uh…" Rhiannon waves a hand toward the two giantesses.

He nods after a second. "I did, ma'am. I've been with Lady Briley…well, I'm older than I look."

"Ah." She raises her brows. What did Moira call that? A chosen hero?

"And you—you three…"

"We are," Diana says.

Jerry's eyes get wide. "Briley's not one for worship, but, uh…?"

Rhiannon shakes her head. "Absolutely not me."

Diana smiles, but doesn't say anything.

Hazel nods. "Definitely. Kneel."

Rhiannon punches her shoulder lightly. "Don't screw with the mortals, Hazel."

"He's not technically a mortal. And that's literally our job." She holds the popcorn out to the fox. "The goddess says take some fucking popcorn."

He clears his throat and does so, munching on it nervously. Rhiannon rolls her eyes and punches Hazel's shoulder harder.

Briley sits up, wheezing, brushing soil off her. Then she gets up —way up, about two hundred feet tall—and charges after Moira The hare has enough time to get to her paws, but not enough to avoid being tackled. Both giants tumble, this time past the farm stand, over the comparatively tiny fence, out across the road. Briley struggles to hold Moira down. "Yes, I'm staying out of it, and if you had more common sense than a turnip, you would be, too!"

"That's what you've always been best at, isn't it?" Moira's still smaller, but she gets one paw under Briley and kicks. The mouse goes flying up with a yelp, landing in the field across the road with a crash that brings down trees and topples the Harvest Dance sign. Moira staggers to her paws, then stomps toward Briley, growing with each step. "I know better than to count on you, but you could have at least let me know I wasn't alone!"

Briley sits up, wheezing, and looks up at Moira, raising her hands in front of her face as if to ward off an impending kick. Instead, Moira stops, trembling, then hauls the mouse up by her shoulders, screaming in an anguished voice that has to carry for miles. *"Why didn't you let me know?"*

"Because I was ashamed, you idiot!" Briley bellows back. Then she closes her eyes, sagging. "I was ashamed."

Moira lets her go and sinks to a sitting position, looking defeated. Briley drops beside her, more of a slump than a sit, staring at the ground. "I *begged* you not to make that damn fool stand. I begged you."

"You said nobody else would stand with us." Moira still sounds accusatory, but the anger's draining out of her voice.

"And I was right." Briley's still looking down, voice getting thicker. "But so were you. I knew it. I should have been there by your side. I was just *afraid*, Moira. I've never been strong like you."

Now Moira sounds weary, sad. "I told you I—we—wouldn't die."

"And you couldn't know that. We *could* die, and I just didn't have your faith. You'd have died for what was right, even if it tore the universe apart. Me, I just couldn't—I wasn't willing to lose..." She sits up, waving both hands around to encompass the fields, the orchards. Then her voice cracks. "Instead of choosing you, I chose my damn fruit."

As Briley starts sobbing, Moira pulls the mouse into her lap, wraps her arms around her. "I shouldn't have made you choose."

Fumblingly, Briley clasps one of Moira's larger hands, and their fingers entwine. "I stayed behind to find you and I just couldn't—couldn't *face* you, and so I just—I just—"

Moira tilts Briley's head up gently, pressing her lips to the mouse's. Briley lets out another choking sob and throws her arms around the hare tightly.

Jerry's eyes get wider. "They...oh my."

Rhiannon wipes at one eye, and leans toward Hazel, speaking in a whisper. "So, uh, the mythology books said Moira and Briley were 'great friends?'" She makes air quotes with her fingers.

"Like she said, not everything gets into the books," Hazel murmurs.

thirteen
home front

"You were always so good at..." Moira waves her hand around, taking in the living room. "...this."

Briley sets the coffee pot and four mugs down on the table, and sits on the sofa by Moira as she fills each of them. "Decorating?"

"Visualizing?" Diana suggests. "I mean, you just willed this all back into existence the way it was."

Briley shrugs, sipping her coffee. "Lived here forty-odd years, so it was all pretty easy to picture. Most of it. Probably got a few bits and bobs wrong."

"Which I bet you won't fix." Moira picks up her mug, too. "I've never understood your fascination with *not* using your powers."

Briley pokes the hare's thigh. "I use my powers all the time. I'm just subtle. Speaking of subtlety, that brings up a question I've had for the last few weeks, you know, seeing stories in the papers about pika angels, giant squirrels, never-ending potlucks and violent magical orgies."

"Hmm?"

She sets down her mug. "What in ninety-nine fucks do y'all think you're doing?"

"Well, I'm—we—" Moira scowls. "We're preparing."

"Uh-huh. It just seems to me that if you think you're being called to lead another rebellion, now against new gods who are so good at keeping to the shadows you didn't know about 'em until a few weeks ago and I didn't know about 'em until an hour ago, you might wanna be staying a wee bit more, what's the modern phrase, off the radar."

"We need to have *some* idea how to be 'gods.'" Rhiannon makes air quotes with her fingers before picking up her mug and taking a sip. "Man, even this is the best coffee I think I've ever had. How do you keep doing this?"

Briley shrugs. "Coffee's a fruit. And I'm not sure you can learn how to be a god. You just are. You figure out what to do over time."

"We don't have that time." Rhiannon sighs. "Anyway, we've been learning about Celestial. It feels like since I've become whatever I am, I can almost... I hate to use 'divine' as a verb here, but I can divine my way through computer security."

Hazel lights up. "You're a literal hacker goddess!"

Rhiannon winces.

"I've been trying to figure out how Celestial fits into your mythology," Hazel continues. "And I have a theory. In some of the tales, after the old gods leave the mortal realm, monsters rise without anyone to fight them. What if Celestial *are* the monsters?"

"That could fit," Rhiannon muses. "Everything I'm finding out suggests they're keeping what Moira hated about Daranu's 'natural order' vision and throwing out virtually everything else. I think they're trying to build a version of the 'one world government' that conspiracy nuts always imagine, but doing it through corporate control."

"Max used the word 'reshaping,'" Moira says. "And I've seen what he means. I've barely been paying attention to mortal affairs, and even I'm starting to see the effects of all the laws you've been passing."

Rhiannon nods, looking sour. "With worse ones about to go into effect—written by Celestial lobbyists, enforced by police departments they run."

"But they're trying to run the world secretly." Hazel spreads her arms. "That's what we can take advantage of. They can't come after us without exposing themselves."

"They don't have to physically come after y'all, they just have to get people to be more scared of you than of them. That's what I'm trying to get at. Between you rolling over traffic, *you* kicking over a building, and *you* getting half of Vallejo riled up into a magical cop-eatin' sexfest, they ain't gonna have to work real hard at it."

"I know. But I can't help but wonder if I'm gearing up for a battle I didn't consciously know was coming."

"What if you had won?" Rhiannon says. "Your first one, I mean. Your rebellion. Say you got Daranu to agree to your terms. What *were* your terms? All I've heard is 'upend the natural order,' and I don't honestly know what that means."

"To let mortals find their own way. It's what I told Max: gods aren't rulers."

Briley snorts. "What Daranu used to say, until he figured out that letting mortals make their own big decisions means they might not decide things the way he would."

"Exactly. He stopped meeting his own ideals." Moira shakes her head. "And when the rest of the gods left, I figured that then, at least, mortals would move back toward equity, lose old prejudices. But they didn't. I despaired that Daranu had been right—that even if wolves no longer eat sheep, the sheep *do* have to be naturally subordinate to them, that it's woven into the fabric of the universe for this cycle and it can't truly change until the cycle turns."

Briley gives Moira's knee a pat. "If you ask me, that's why when Moira lets her magic loose, things go upside-down. Not only does everybody go feral, they go feral backwards, and you get the sheep eating the wolves."

Moira gives her a wry smile. "Or hoof-stomping tigers."

Diana clears her throat, looking up at the ceiling.

Hazel giggles, and drums her claws on her knees. "But maybe sheep eating wolves isn't bad, at least metaphorically. Maybe the cycle doesn't have to turn, the world just has to swing hard in the other direction before it comes back to a balance."

Rhiannon folds her arms. "That's going to be a pretty hard sell to the wolves."

"They benefit from the way things have always been," Hazel

retorts. "As far as the people on the top now are concerned, *any* change will be worse. Besides, you're the one who's been doing all the digging, so you know better than any of us how much Celestial's been reshaping the world and who they're shaping it for. That asshole jackal down the block from our house who rants about his taxes going to 'vermin' might buy into the idea his 'right place' is over you and me, but as far as people—or gods—at Nunwick's level are concerned, he's just as much vermin as I am."

Briley sets her mug down with a sharp *bang*, making everyone but Moira jump and look at her. "So y'all are circling around *why* you wanna take a fight to Celestial, but you're still not getting to the *how*. What I'm trying to get across here is that I don't see how little chaos explosions are a strategy."

Moira rolls her eyes. "Do I need to write 'I won't magically charm mice into terrorizing cats' on the chalkboard a hundred times?"

"Wouldn't dream of asking you to make a promise you can't keep, darling." She gives Moira a kiss on the cheek.

Rhiannon's tail twitches, and she bites her lip. "Are you going to stand with us, Lady Briley?"

"No," Moira cuts in sharply before the mouse responds. Briley looks startled.

No. No no no. She just found her again, and she's so happy *and* so angry *and* has far too much to work out. Far too many centuries lost. She takes both of Briley's hands in hers and looks into her long-lost lover's eyes. "I won't make you choose like that again. I shouldn't have then. I can't now."

Briley smiles softly, leaning forward and giving Moira a light but long kiss. "I'll support you any way I can. Even if it's just being your home front."

"I couldn't ask anything more." Moira draws her into a hug. She's so angry she's missed this so much.

Diana smiles, finishing her coffee. "Should we leave you two here to catch up?"

She shouldn't say yes, but she can't say anything else. But she doesn't have to. Hazel gives her an uncharacteristically bashful smile. "I think I'm seeing the love goddess more than the war goddess right now."

Moira clears her throat. "You know how you can get back to Diana's place on your own from here."

Hazel waves her hand, nodding. "Sure. Lots of options. Teleporting. Flying. Driving my chair down the freeway at a hundred feet high."

Rhiannon gives her a look.

The pika holds up her hands. "Kidding, kidding. I'd only be twenty feet high tops for that."

Moira looks at Briley. "You can help babysit, right?"

"Hey—" Hazel starts to say, but Diana grins and claps her hands. All three of the young goddesses disappear.

fourteen
the side of chaos

When Diana wakes up Tuesday morning, the air feels wrong.

It's been a month since her—what should she call it? *Deification* sounds clunky, but *ascension* is far too ostentatious. A month since she became a goddess, and she's still not sure whether she absolutely needs sleep, or for that matter, needs food, or to breathe, or anything else mortal. She *likes* sleeping and eating (and breathing), though.

When she teleported everyone back from Briley's farm two days ago, it was a cloudy day. Yesterday those clouds looked positively threatening, promising violent storms that haven't yet come. When she pulls back the curtains of her bedroom, looking out, the sky remains unchanged—but a fight's happening, right now, on the front lawn between a group of herbivores and a group of carnivores. William is wading into the middle of it, trying to break it up.

She hurriedly pulls on clothes the physical, mortal way (she suspects she could trivially learn to do that with magic, but that seems extraordinarily vain) and races out. She can smell coffee brewing. Rhiannon's looking out the front window. "Morning," she says, without turning.

"Not a good one, apparently."

"No."

Diana opens the front door, but the fight's already over. William looks winded, slightly scuffed, as he walks up to her. "My lady." He nods respectfully, turns, and sighs. "It's worse than yesterday."

She purses her lips, nodding. Every day this week, the worshippers have become more fractious. A few days ago the goddesses had "practiced" outside with Moira, learning more visualization and magic control, but that might have been a mistake. She can't tell if the crowd's angry they haven't done it again, angry they did it the first time, or both.

No matter the case, the happy chaos of a street fair has given way to the angry chaos of a street fight. More carnivores have been showing up; tempers have been flaring, tensions rising. And the wibble-wobbles with the magic, as Hazel put it, have been getting worse, too. The originals stay good, but magical duplicates go bad in progressively stranger ways when left unattended, becoming piles of leaves, or broken glass, or bees. Every so often they'll leap back off plates as if refusing to let certain people eat them.

"I think I'll walk around and see what's happening this morning. With luck I can be a calming presence, not an inflaming one."

"Yes, my lady." William heads in as she heads out.

As she walks through the crowd, most of them kneel or bow or nod their head, but the *something wrong* gets stronger as she looks around. A person? A group? Other magic from…somewhere?

Thunder cracks overhead, and she looks up, startled. But the sky hasn't changed. No rain, no lightning. No one else reacted, either. Was it silent? In her head?

No. It's real. The clouds are wrong.

Diana frowns at herself. What does that even mean? No funnel clouds, no unnatural colors. And yet—

The wind picks up. A bowl of fruit salad topples over, seemingly of its own accord, and the grapes and apple slices scurry away as if alive.

A woman striding down the sidewalk a block away catches Diana's attention: a silver vixen, midnight blue jacket and matching wrap skirt, wearing mirror-shade sunglasses. Long hair, black as a desert night sky, is pulled back in a tight ponytail.

As she gets closer, Diana stares. The vixen stands tall, well over six feet, as tall as Moira. But that's not all she has in common with Moira. Divine power radiates off her.

"Ms. Lindsay," she says as she approaches, voice raised over the wind.

"Who are you?"

"Lily Parker, Celestial Private Equity." She gestures at the house. "Let's chat inside."

Someone from Celestial, here? Now? With Moira gone? Oh, god. (Can she still think that?) "Let's stay outside."

"I know you can sense what's coming in the air. And I know you haven't been prepared for it."

She wishes she could snap back with a denial, but she knows she can't. "What is it?"

The vixen takes off her glasses and puts them in a jacket pocket, locking ice grey eyes onto the sheep. "Consequences, Ms. Lindsay."

"I'll give you five minutes. We may be new at this, but you don't want to face all three of us."

"Mmm." Parker walks behind Diana, quickly catching up to her.

Diana opens the door and Parker steps through, heeled sandals making each step of her digitigrade paws rap sharply against the floor. Hazel's in the room now, too, sipping coffee.

"Who, uh…?" Rhiannon looks wary.

"Lily Parker," Diana says tightly. "From Celestial."

Rhiannon narrows her eyes, huge tail twitching. Hazel, though, snorts, sets down her mug, and holds out her hand. The vixen blurs and appears in the pika's palm at a few inches high—

Hazel starts. No, there's a rubber toy version of the vixen in her hand. "What the…?"

The toy vixen expands like a balloon and bursts open, tiny spiders pouring out. The pika shrieks, flinging her hand—and arachnids—around frantically. William, Rhiannon, and Diana all jump, but the spiders vanish before they hit anything else.

"Now that we've had our fun, Ms. Harcourt, we need to talk. I'm not here to pick a fight with you, but a fight might well be imminent." She motions to the dining room table. "May we sit?" She looks to Diana inquiringly.

"Fine," the sheep sighs.

Parker nods, taking a seat. She motions to William. "Coffee, black."

The mouse nods, looking nervous, scurrying toward the kitchen.

"I'm sure she meant to add 'please,'" Rhiannon calls, and looks at Parker. "So are you treating him like that because he's mortal, or because he's a prey animal?"

The vixen sighs. "Because he's clearly staff and because we don't have that much time, Ms. Doran."

Diana takes a seat across from the vixen, looking at her intently. "No, we don't. I gave you five minutes. That won't be enough time for you to enjoy your coffee. So who are you, Ms. Parker? I assume you're not here to make job offers again. And if you're going to give us a lecture about the natural order, I'll ask William to find you a styrofoam cup."

"I'm the CEO of the Private Equity Group. What is it you think you know about Celestial Capital?"

"You're the most powerful institution on the planet," Rhiannon says flatly. "You control or outright own thousands of market-leading companies. With government contracts, your divisions run prisons. Welfare programs. Police departments. Actual military units."

"And you're apparently run by gods," Hazel adds. "New gods who want to double down on the shitty 'species is destiny' mindset of the old gods who kicked Moira out of their pantheon."

William comes back with Parker's coffee as well as a pot, refreshing the coffee in the other goddess's cups. "Thank you, William," Diana says, making a point to meet his eyes and smile.

Parker takes a sip of coffee. "Species is not destiny, Ms. Harcourt, it's *affinity*. A primordial predilection older than language, older than walking on two legs. Your very soul knows, deeply and inescapably, that in a distant time, being this close to a vixen would mean being snapped up." She smiles, widely and coldly, showing off sharp, brilliant white teeth.

Hazel looks nonplussed a moment. "Good thing this isn't a job offer, then. 'Work for me because I want to eat you' isn't a winning pitch."

"Only employees who come in at the lowest stack ranking at their annual review risk being eaten."

Hazel and Rhiannon both raise their brows. Diana thinks Parker's making a deadpan joke, but she can't honestly tell.

"So," Parker continues. "What happened to the world when the age of myth ended? Mortals drove themselves into the darkness. They burned civilizations to the ground in the name of imaginary gods and self-serving ideals. Genocides, sweeping atrocities. The Forty-Year War, which cost over a million lives across two generations. And more often than not, history's metaphorical monsters were herbivores unconsciously following Moira's lead in trying to upend the existing order. You—we, for I was mortal once as well—were spiraling toward doom, at an ever-faster pace."

Diana looks at the clock pointedly.

"After that war, we formed a small, secret group called the Order of Caeles. We'd found those wars and atrocities had become more numerous and more violent *after* the gods left. Worse, monsters of other kinds had grown in number and power. Plagues. Famine. Storms. And, yes, literal monsters. Not all the folk tales and legends of fantastic creatures are real, but more of them are than you think. We learned how to fight the growing chaos with order, and how to fight it behind the scenes. Ultimately, the only way to win was to fill the void left by the absence of old gods with new ones. To match our new, more secular time, we chose to be new, more secular kinds of gods."

"How?" Hazel crosses her arms. She looks like she's still trying to figure out how she can shrink Parker and stomp her flat. "And we're supposed to believe you did it all out of the goodness of your now-immortal hearts?"

A crash sounds from outside. Diana looks toward the door

worriedly, but before she says anything, William raises a hand. "I'll go check, my lady." He heads out.

"The 'how' isn't a story we have time for now, and call it enlightened self-interest, if you must." Parker sets her cup down, and looks around at them intently. "Chaos and order are tangible forces, and they can be tracked. Mapped. Influenced. Directed. Even the smallest mortal action creates a flow, one direction or another. Collective action, on the level of societies and nations, has massive effects. And *that* is what Celestial does. We influence and direct. Our goal is preventing the turning of the mythological cycle, forestalling the end of the world. Now that you are what you are, that needs to be yours as well."

Rhiannon narrows her eyes. "You're saving the world by secretly ensuring all the mortals fit into what you call their 'right place?' Please. You're just about making yourselves obscenely rich."

"Don't be naïve. I'm a literal goddess, as are you. I could snap my fingers and have trappings of luxury beyond mortal ken. You could, too, with actual training." She puts a slight emphasis on *actual*. "And you could have avoided creating the chaos nexus this house has become."

"Chaos nexus," Rhiannon repeats skeptically.

"It's fluctuated over the last several weeks, but since all three of you—four, when Moira is present—have been congregating here, using your powers, the forecast has grown...concerning. This morning, it became dire. We have moved from a tornado watch to a tornado warning."

Hazel runs a hand through her hair, then looks at Diana. "This is more than five minutes, isn't it?"

"I don't think you appreciate—"

Clattering comes from outside, followed by screams. The door opens, and William staggers inside. He looks *wrong*, but she can't tell why.

All of them stand up. Parker closes her eyes, muttering under her breath. "The weak link is *the assistant*. Of course." She opens her eyes and points at William. "Focus on him as he is. As he should be. Quickly!"

Diana looks at her in alarm. What does that even mean?

The mouse shudders as if in the grip of chills, and drops to his knees, gasping.

"I said we didn't have much time," the vixen snaps. "Whatever noble cause Moira has convinced you she's championing, being on the side of chaos creates monsters."

"Monsters like us?" Hazel snorts.

William takes a deep, ragged breath, and lifts his head. His eyes have gone solid red.

"No, Ms. Harcourt," Parker replies softly, eyes on the mouse. "Not monsters like you."

Rhiannon hurries over to him. "William, whatever's—"

He backhands her, throwing her across the room.

Roaring, the sound of an angry feral bear rather than a mouse, he begins to grow. From five feet tall to six. Seven. Eight. Muscles bulge. Claws sharpen. Teeth lengthen. With another, deeper roar, he smashes through the living room wall, charging into the crowd outside, setting off more panic. When he stomps on a wolf with a thick, wet crunch, he's already twenty feet high.

Rhiannon staggers to her feet, dazed, glaring unsteadily at the vixen. "What have you done?"

"I did not cause this, Ms. Doran. I came here to help you stop it."

"William!" Diana yells desperately.

The mouse—now forty feet tall and still growing—either can't hear her over the panic or doesn't care. He grabs a bobcat who had the misfortune to stumble near him. Her terrified yowl rises in pitch over the second it takes for him to shove her in his mouth and swallow her alive.

Visualize. Visualize William being himself. Small, demure, overly polite, infatuated—

The giant mouse thunders directly over her, crushing a packed car as it tries to pull away.

Diana covers her mouth, feeling a piercingly mortal desire to flee, to take shelter. Then she closes her eyes, steeling herself. "William!" This time she *commands*.

His eyes snap to her.

"Stop!" She walks ahead slowly, acutely aware of hundreds of eyes on her, murmurs in the crowd. Their goddess is here, back in control.

But is she? She should be able to will the mouse back to normal, to envision it and have it *be*. And she can't. The more she tries to focus, the more agitated he looks, the deeper the growl in the back of his huge throat becomes.

Diana looks desperately at Rhiannon and Hazel, through her demolished wall. They're arguing with the vixen. Hazel's looking smug, pointing at the sheep. "We know how to stop monsters *because* we've been monsters."

"But I don't!" Diana calls.

The two give her a shared dismayed look, and quickly move forward, Hazel dropping back into her chair. The pika points at Parker accusingly. "Stay the hell out of this."

Parker folds her arms.

"No!" William roars, crouching over Diana, baring jagged, uneven fangs. He swipes at a cluster of terrified carnivores.

The sheep turns back and holds her ground. "William," she repeats, holding out her hands, palm up. "This isn't you."

He snarls, stepping back and grabbing an attractive young coyote who'd been gawking a yard too close, holding the flailing woman up over his head.

"Put her down!" Diana grows to match William's size. Followers near her hooves scramble back, and she looks down, letting out a dismayed bleat.

Worshippers around her draw back, screaming. "Lady, *protect us!*" a gazelle wails, tone both beseeching and accusing.

The monster mouse shakes the hand he's closed around the hapless canine. "She isn't 'us,'" William snarls. "She's a *predator*." He hurls her at the ground, hard. She barely has enough time for a final shriek.

The crowd yells—some in fear, others in approval.

"Fucking hell." Rhiannon's outside now, staring up at the monster mouse. "It's like he's possessed."

"Possessed by her," Hazel mutters, jerking a thumb toward

Parker. "Maybe it goes back to normal if we take her out."

Diana looks back, too. The thought had occurred to her—but surely Hazel can feel how strong Parker is. Moira could take her out, probably, but—

Parker sighs heavily, walking forward. "He does not."

"I told you to stay fucking put!" Hazel growls.

"Come on." Rhiannon's voice is as sharp as the pika's. "Don't pretend it's a coincidence this happens right when you show up."

"Don't reverse cause and effect," Parker snaps. "I came here because you've been loose cannons for a month even *with* Moira's ostensible guidance, and because you have created a ticking bomb which I expected to explode this morning. *Which it has.*"

Diana takes a deep breath. "Rhiannon, get Moira. Hazel, watch Parker while I try to subdue William." She doesn't wait for a response, charging after the mouse.

As she grapples with him, trying desperately to keep both his claws and her hooves away from the crowd, she yells, "Get back!" Why aren't they running? Instead they're wailing—or cheering. Some clearly root for the monster mouse.

And they're starting to fight with one another. A few look distinctly bigger than normal.

Is the vixen somehow affecting them, too? Possessing them? But Moira hadn't *possessed* people at that festival. It was simply that—

—that chaos creates monsters—

Dammit. No. Don't let Parker get in your head.

William aims a kick at Rhiannon, then a stomp. He's missing her, but he's distracting her enough to keep her from teleporting. "Go! Go!" Diana shouts, trying to hold the mouse back.

And, abruptly, she's flying through the air.

Diana blinks dumbly in surprise before she lands with an earth-shaking crash, letting out a bleat that shatters windows. She's sliding through…crap. The house across the street.

She sits up, shaking her head woozily, watching Rhiannon grow rapidly, heading toward William. She raises her hands, but instead of fighting, heavy iron cuffs appear around the monster mouse's wrists and ankles, chains running into the ground. He topples with an angry, surprised roar.

Rhiannon hurries across the street.

Diana looks around the ruins of the house, rubbing her head. "Mrs. Henderson is going to kill me."

"You're immortal," Rhiannon says. "You okay?"

"Betrayer!" William howls, staggering to all fours. He's straining against the cuffs, but he can't get up.

"Yeah," Diana says. She staggers to her hooves, walking across the street again. "William. You have to stop. We don't hate predators."

"Overthrow the natural order!" He gasps raggedly. "I've heard you. I've heard *all* of you. We should be—we should be on *top*. They should fear *us!*"

Rhiannon scowls, pointing back down at Diana's house, at the vixen. "I don't know what that woman's put in your head, but you need to—"

William strains against his chains with a scream. "Rip the predator goddess to pieces!"

Hazel eyes Parker. "Feeding him lines to convince us? Seriously?"

That gets the vixen to shift her expression from pained annoyance to genuine anger. She abruptly slams her hands down on the arms of Hazel's wheelchair, nose to nose with the pika. "Moira and you three have turned this house into a chaos nexus, filled that mouse's head with the virtue of overturning the natural order, and exposed him daily to magic the world hasn't seen in a thousand years. We're *all* in more danger than you understand, and it is past time one of you show actual control."

Hazel's ears fold back during Parker's tirade. Then her eyes narrow. She puts her hands on top of the vixen's, lifts them, and *flings*. Parker rockets away, smashing into one of the intact walls hard enough to make it less intact. "How's that for control, jerkface."

William, despite the chains, manages to stand fully upright.

"Dammit," Diana breathes, dashing toward him. He's not

growing in height, but he's growing in muscle, moving toward the grotesque. As he strains, the chains begin ripping out of the ground.

She leaps for one of the chains, Rhiannon going for the other. Visualize being rock solid, the way Moira held her cart at the grocery store at that first meeting. Be an anchor.

The mouse swings her—and the squirrel—around like toys.

Diana wails. She can see other giants now, definitely. Ten, fifteen, twenty feet high. Mostly prey animals, chasing the predators who haven't fled. They're not *letting* the predators flee.

"Hazel!" she shrieks.

Hazel's already wheeling forward. "Visualize the monsters small," she mutters aloud. She focuses on the closest "monsters," a pair of mice converging on a panicked wolf woman. Both, *small,* right *now.* All at once, they're ankle-high.

The wolf, still panting in terror, stomps both of them repeatedly.

Hazel winces. "Not small. Not small, idiot. Normal-sized."

"You can't do it one monster at a time!" Rhiannon yells. "Let's all —focus on everyone—"

Hazel mutters a profanity under her breath, but lifts her hands slowly over her head. This time, no one gets flung. Instead, everyone starts floating up into the air. Up—and apart. Surprised combatants flail futilely at one another. Victims drift away from their tormentors. "Yes!"

William twists sharply, letting out an unearthly howl, and his chains snap as *things* erupt out of him, shooting in all directions. Pseudopods? Tentacles? Whatever they are, Diana and Rhiannon get grabbed in the length of a breath, wrapped up by sticky strands.

"Oh, shit—" Hazel doesn't finish punctuating the sentence before a viscous rope barrels into her, yanking her out of the chair back toward the no-longer-a-mouse. Frantically, she tries the same *fling* that worked on Parker. The tendril that's grabbed her oscillates wildly, but it hangs on to her. She gets pulled tight against the monster's body, grey but now furless, pulsing against her.

"Hazel!" Diana yells, but she's got enough of her own to deal with. She's been trying to shrink William or bind him or just knock him on his ass all this time, but the magic's making whatever's taken him over *stronger*. The twisting, sticky mass wraps around her wrists, her ankles, her chest, starting to envelop her. She can't break free, not with strength, not with magic. The monster is pulling her *into* it. From the screams of the other two, they're being pulled in, too. It's winning. Its howl is a howl of anticipation.

Can whatever William's become kill a god? Kill *three* gods?

The creature's roar turns pained. Diana finds herself sliding to the ground in a squelch of sticky ichor. She wipes her eyes clear to see what's happened.

Lily Parker stands *over* Diana's house, the silver vixen now as tall as the thing that had been William. She's looking down, sweeping her hands around. The mortals Hazel had levitated float down to the ground, drawn apart from one other. Her voice thunders out: "There will be *order*." Fences of hazy, crackling violet light shimmer into existence, separating the crowd from one another—and from the immortals. "Not. Chaos."

Parker kicks off her immense sandals and moves her hands in front of her, bringing them together, and a sword materializes between them, a cutlass that runs forty feet from hilt to tip.

Monster-William's roar becomes furious, and its eyes—more than two of them now—burn with hatred. It charges toward her, pseudopods exploding out of its mass.

Despite the blade's immense size, Parker swings her sword at a near blur, parrying the creature's liquid thrusts, chopping off its limbs as fast as they reform. The air fills with the sounds of sizzling, dripping ichor and falling chunks of flesh.

Diana drags herself to her hooves, standing by the other dripping goddesses, breathing hard.

"Sword-fighting." Hazel stares. "A goddess, in a business suit, sword-fighting."

Rhiannon grunts. "When we used magic, it just made it—him—stronger."

Monster-William charges again, and the vixen pivots, lopping off an arm. She's rewarded with another furious roar, but another arm bursts forth at a different place on the creature's body.

Parker's next dodge isn't as successful, the monster looping a tentacle around her sword hand. She grits her teeth, producing a dagger in her other hand and sawing the tentacle off.

Diana doesn't want to trust Parker, but the vixen might have saved their lives. At least their godhoods. "How can we help?" she calls, voice hoarse.

"Diana!" Hazel hisses.

"Use the *right* magic." Parker's voice strains. "You'll only be able to hold it for a moment, but that's all I'll need."

The sheep puts her hands to her head. Visualize—what? The monster back as William? The creature shimmers, fuzzing in and out, hints of murine features appearing and disappearing, but it's a signal that won't stay locked in.

"No." Parker steps back hurriedly. "Don't be concrete." The vixen takes another quick swing, chopping off one tentacle in a set surrounding her. One of the others successfully catches her ankle, pulls, and she topples onto her back with a pained yelp. Keeping her sword pointed up at the creature, she yells more urgently at Diana. "Focus on the end state!"

The end state? What the hell does *that* mean? Isn't that William back to being William? No fighting? Everyone back to normal? How can she focus on that without *seeing* it?

She closes her eyes, raising her hands over her head. Not the how, not the look, but the feeling. Peace. Serenity.

Yes, fine, all right. *Order.*

The sounds stop. She opens her eyes and drops her hands.

The creature still writhes, but seems less angry, three clawed arms and four tentacles slowly lowering.

She did it. She doesn't know what she did, but she did it. The other two goddesses stare up with the same happy-confused looks. Maybe *they* did it, all of them.

Parker scrambles to her paws, takes a deep breath, and plunges her sword into the monster at chest level, burying it to the hilt. The curved blade rips out its back, spraying ichor and blood.

Diana screams. Rhiannon puts her hands to her muzzle.

As Parker tilts the sword down, the creature slides off and begins to shrink, regaining murine features as it does so. The mortals trapped in Parker's fence-cages begin to normalize, too. A ragged cheer goes up. She raises her sword high, watching as the monster's bloody, ruined corpse returns to being a mere mouse. To being William. The sword shimmers the same purple as the cages, then it—and the cages—both vanish. The cheering rises in volume.

Diana runs to William, splashing through the blood, kneeling and lifting him up, cradling him. "William! Oh, Will..." She looks up at Parker, stricken. "Please."

The giantess kneels, too. "Not everything can be undone, Ms. Lindsay." Her voice is soft. "I am—"

"Don't say it," Rhiannon snarls, wiping back a tear. "Just don't."

Parker goes still, and nods once, looking into the distance before speaking again. "I hope that when—not if—we meet again, you appreciate the value in working with us rather than against us."

Hazel sets her jaw, glaring up. "Don't count on that."

"As you wish." She twists around, putting on her shoes, and stands. The mortals who haven't fled are on their knees for her now, predator and prey alike.

After a moment, she looks straight down. "Ms. Harcourt."

Hazel looks up to see the vixen raising a foot high over her wheelchair. The half-second she takes to think of what to do is a quarter-second too long. The sandal smashes down.

The scream gets caught in Hazel's throat. She's in the space between the sandal's heel and sole, mere inches to spare on either side. The stomp, hard enough to shatter the pavement, still reverberates through the ground.

"Actual control. Remember it." Parker vanishes in a burst of violet light.

fifteen
what changed things

"Your smile's as lovely as ever." Briley looks down at Moira's face, brushing her hand under the hare's chin.

Moira tilts her head up, still resting it against the mouse's bare bosom. Her smile—which truly *is* lovely—widens, and she laughs. "You're probably the only being left in the world who's seen it."

"Oh, I'm sure lots of mortals over the centuries have seen you smile real big. It's just the *last* thing they see."

They're resting on a hillside, not far from Briley's farmhouse but well away from the road. Moira's not sure whether Briley talked her into this or she talked Briley into it, but here they are, gods who've made love in the middle of a vineyard, bathed in the golden light of early evening. It's secluded, but hardly private. Anyone who managed to get close enough to see them, though, would be more than close enough to *feel* them, the full force of the goddess of love with her long-lost partner. That would put other things on their minds.

Briley sits up, too, and rubs along Moira's spine, down to her puff tail and back up to her shoulders. "I'd be more at ease if y'all had even a scrap of plan for what comes next."

"So would I." Moira sighs. "I told them that a goddess's whims mean something. What you used to say. But I'm not sure if I believe myself. Maybe I was just lonely for the company of a god again."

"Of course you were. So was I." Briley tilts her head. "But that doesn't mean you were lying. The world's been *off* for a couple centuries now. You've felt it, haven't you?"

Moira leans against Briley, stretching her legs out and crossing them at the ankles. "I have, but I drank enough to ignore it."

"Mmm. Things've moved faster since they got electricity running everywhere than in all the time beforehand. It's got to have made you suspicious."

"Why? We all knew they didn't need us to take care of them, even if we wouldn't admit it. That meant they didn't need us to screw up spectacularly, either."

"Think they could pull off the industrial revolution, all on their own?"

"I do."

"Corporate capitalism?"

Moira shrugs. "I don't see why not."

"Cryptocurrency?" Briley spreads her hands with a *come on* expression.

"All right, that one's a stretch." The hare runs her fingers through Briley's shorter hair. "But I've been thinking. Just a few months ago, I got the urge to move again and found a beautiful little apartment in the city. It turned out to be a few miles from where Hazel and Rhiannon live, and only a few miles more up the road from Diana. Why?"

"'Cause a beautiful little apartment in the city's better than an ugly little one?"

She nips the mouse's ear. "Why here, why *now?* I haven't even liked cities much the past century. When I got the urge out of the blue, it came at just the right time in just the right place to meet these three. And when I met them, I went 'poof, you're goddesses.'" She waves a hand dramatically, mimicking a stage magician. "I've never done that before."

"We get called. By worshippers, by dreamers, by the land itself. It's part of the deal. It's the *whole* deal. Just because you hadn't been called in a couple thousand years doesn't mean you got let off the hook."

"You can't retire from being a goddess, can you." Moira stretches and stands, holding out a hand to Briley. The mouse takes it, and they start walking back to the farm. "But if the land's calling me, I can't help think it got the wrong number."

Briley snorts. "Until a month ago, it was just you and me."

"No, it wasn't. There's Celestial. If they're not old gods—and now that I know you're here, I'm not as quick to rule that out as I was a few days ago—then who the hell called *them?*"

"You didn't have any kids you forgot about since the rest of the gods vamoosed, did you?"

"Please. I wouldn't forget giving birth." Moira thwacks Briley on the rump. "Besides, you're the fertility goddess."

"I'm the *harvest* goddess, jerk." She thwacks back. "Pretty sure Celestial ain't led by a divine rutabaga."

By the time they walk into the farmhouse, they're clothed again. The smell of baking olallieberry peach pie fills the air, a new recipe Jerry said he'd been working on. The fox is there, as he often is; he lives in a guesthouse on the farm, but seems to spend more time in Briley's house than his own. (Except, Briley noted with a grin, when his boyfriend visits from "out east.")

Before they sit down, Jerry hurries out of the kitchen, looking upset. "Rhiannon called a few minutes ago. I was about to, ah," his ears color, "go get you both."

"Glad we didn't make you blush even more." Briley grins faintly, but tilts her head. "What's wrong?"

"It was hard to follow, ma'am. She was talking about monsters and chaos and attacks, and she was crying, and—"

Moira's already on her paws. "I'm on my way."

"It's back at Diana's temple, isn't it?" Briley's brow furrows.

"Yes, if a two-bedroom house in the suburbs is a temple." Moira senses it too, now that she concentrates. "I shouldn't have left them alone."

"They're goddesses, not your grandkids," Briley says, moving to give Moira a hug.

The hare returns it tightly, giving the mouse a deep kiss, if a quicker one than she'd like. They both say "I love you" at the same time.

Then Moira hurries out to the car. She takes a different Shortcut than the one she'd made to get here, turning from the road to Briley's farm right onto Diana's street. It's reckless, but she has a mounting sense of dread, and it's not as if she's been a model of restraint lately anyway.

She hears sirens and sees emergency lights approaching before she turns the corner and slams on the brakes, parking by the curb and charging toward Diana's house.

Bodies lie in the street, sprawled amidst shattered asphalt and damaged—or fully crushed—cars. The house across the street is all but razed to the ground. Diana's home looks like a bomb went off in the living room. Dozens of dazed bystanders mill about, many clearly injured.

Diana sits on the curb, cradling a bloody body in her arms. William the mouse, the sheep's chosen hero, the lovely boy who made the peaches and cream. Rhiannon hurries toward Moira. No idea where Hazel is yet.

The sirens and lights flash from a fire truck, two ambulances, and three—four—five?—police cars rolling down two different streets. Terrific. In twenty seconds every nook and cranny will swarm with cops. If she follows her instinct to teleport them into a garbage pit or something, it'll freak out the other emergency workers.

"Moira!" Rhiannon yells. "Moira, everything—it—"

"Where's Hazel? We have to go."

Rhiannon blinks rapidly. "I, uh." She points in one direction, then another. Hazel's rolling toward the police like she plans on being a one-pika blockade. As fun as that'd be to watch, it's the last thing any of them need now.

Moira claps her hands over her head, and abruptly they're all in her living room.

Rhiannon chirps in surprise. Hazel's still rolling; Moira waves a hand to stop her before she crashes into the sofa. Diana looks startled, her arms still in the position they'd been in cradling the mouse's body. "William—" She runs at Moira, screaming, slamming her fists against the hare's shoulders. "No! You can't leave him! I can't—I can't—" She dissolves into sobs, still pounding at Moira.

"We could have taken them all on!" Hazel protests.

"Moira's right," Rhiannon says hoarsely. "More fighting is the last thing we need."

Moira wraps her arms around the sheep, trying not to wince. Pounding from hoofed fingers hurts. "Tell me what happened."

"Celestial happened, that's what," Hazel spits. "They waited until you were gone and sent someone after us."

Moira's eyes widen. "They killed William? All those people? Just—"

"No." Rhiannon shakes her head. "William killed them, Moira. He—he turned into a monster."

"After Parker showed up!" Hazel yells. "Come on!"

Moira holds up a hand, then guides Diana over to the sofa, sitting down with her. The squirrel and pika follow. "Rhiannon, your version."

"A vixen. Lily Parker. She said she was with…some Celestial division. She—"

"Private Equity," Diana mumbles.

"She showed up and started talking about how there wasn't much time, then gave us a kind of…sales pitch." Rhiannon crosses her arms. "In her telling, after the gods left, mortals went off the rails. Bigger and bigger wars, more and more chaos."

"Which she's *really* hung up on," Hazel adds.

"She says Celestial's holding back all that chaos by trying to strengthen Daranu's natural order, just in a new way."

"And if we keep screwing with their plan, actual monsters will get loose." Hazel rolls her eyes, throwing her hands over her head. "Like the ones tonight that just *happened* to burst onto the scene when she was here to save the day from our 'chaos nexus.'"

Moira lifts her brows. "Our what?"

Diana closes her eyes. "My house was full of magic, chaotic

magic, because of us three. Four, with you, Lady Moira. Hazel thinks it was all Parker's doing. She might be right. But...what happened here is a lot like what happened around you in Vallejo."

Hazel sounds frustrated. "When Moira's magic broke out into chaos, it wasn't just violence, it was orgies. People enjoyed themselves."

"The ones who weren't eaten," Diana mutters.

"Fine. What I'm getting at is that this was *all* ugly and nasty." She looks to Moira. "And you weren't even here! We don't have that kind of magic between us, and there's nothing special about Diana's house."

"No. There is." Moira runs a hand through her hair, bending down an ear. "Briley was right. It's a temple. Worshippers, pilgrims, a resident goddess performing miracles." She swallows. "A high priest."

"Okay, so it's a temple. So what?" Hazel looks impatient. "Temples don't turn on their worshippers by themselves. But gods *do* attack the temples of other gods, don't they?"

Rhiannon nods slowly. "But if Parker wanted to get rid of us, she could have let the monster take us. Let's face it, we weren't winning."

"She didn't want to get rid of us, she wanted to *use* us. Put on a show for the crowd. Demonstrate that our chaos caused the mess, and only her 'order' could stop it." Hazel slumps down in her chair, visibly fuming.

"And I guess she got it."

Diana looks over at her dolefully. "She could have been taking advantage of what we'd accidentally created."

Moira shifts uneasily on the couch. Diana had just put her own doubts into ice clear words. What Rhiannon had said this vixen, Parker, had said, wasn't as stupid as she dearly wanted it to be. "Magic can change mortals into monsters." She sighs. "And a mortal already touched by magic...but I don't know. Hazel's right to be suspicious of the timing. There aren't any old myths—"

Diana leaps to her hooves, voice abruptly rising to a shout. "We aren't living in the old myths!" She points at herself. "I'm not in the old myths." To Hazel. "You aren't in the old myths." To Rhiannon. "You aren't in the old myths. Lily Parker? She isn't either." She turns to Moira. "And the myths don't tell us what happened to you when you stayed behind. They sure as hell never said Briley stayed behind. All they say is that monsters rise, and they were right about that. Parker was right about that."

Hazel holds her ground. "Was she, though? The 'monsters' Parker was talking about were metaphorical, and the secret order that supposedly became Celestial sure wasn't doing a bang-up job of stopping them, given that the worst genocides in recorded history happened within the last eighty years or so."

"She mentioned literal monsters."

"The only example of one we have is tonight. What changed things? Us, or her?"

There's an obvious answer, and Moira hates it. She stares off into the distance, not at anything, most especially not at any of the others in the room. "I did." She finds her voice unexpectedly hoarse, and closes her eyes. "I made you gods."

Rhiannon's the first to break the long stretch of silence after that. "That's necessary, but not sufficient."

Moira opens her eyes again, looking at Rhiannon. Hazel and Diana both look at her too, confused.

"You gave us power because, even if you didn't know it at the time, you sensed the mortal world was falling out of balance. And it *does* need chaos. Things need fixing." She looks to Hazel. "And breaking."

Hazel smiles back, slightly.

"And this is all new—even for an old god like you. We don't know what Celestial's done to the world. We don't know what we're doing to it merely by existing, let alone by going out and getting all magical or giant or whatever. It's a wonder things aren't much more screwed up than they are."

Moira grunts. "It is, isn't it? That's depressing."

"I mean that if we're all here to change the world, we're going to have to expect the world to resist. Maybe what happened today was a weird explosion of chaos magic, but it might have happened less because of us than because of Celestial trying to straight-jacket the world into nothing but order."

Hazel nods, perking up. "We've done enough to be a real threat to them."

Diana rocks back and forth on the sofa. "And enough to be a real threat to the world."

Everyone falls silent again.

The sheep holds her face in her hands. "My house is ruined. I've got to be wanted by the police. What was left of my flock fell on their knees to Parker."

"She tricked them into—"

"She *saved* them, Hazel. You may not like it, but she saved them. She saved us, too."

Hazel visibly stews, but doesn't contradict her.

"I wish, I dearly wish, I could be as confident as you are that she's lying, that it was all an elaborate, evil show. But I'm not." She looks to Moira.

Moira looks back, then down at the floor. What can she say? She didn't even know she'd made Diana into a fucking goddess at first. She's just about the opposite of a font of divine wisdom. She's not confident of a damn thing right now.

"Right." Diana takes a deep breath and stands up. "I need to go somewhere for a while and just...sort things out."

"What do you mean—" Rhiannon starts.

Moira looks up as the sheep simply vanishes.

"What the hell?" the squirrel finishes. She looks at Moira, mouth open. "Where'd she go?"

She shakes her head mutely.

"What do we do now?"

"I don't know."

"I can try to find out more about Parker," Rhiannon offers. "Maybe we can figure out if anything she's said is true."

"Fine." Moira closes her eyes.

"Hey." Hazel leans forward. "We're not giving up."

"On what?" Moira shakes her head. She feels so tired. She needs to sleep. She needs a drink. "Just go home."

"And you'll get in touch with us." Hazel doesn't make it a question.

Moira looks at her, refusing to nod. "Go. Home."

Rhiannon trembles, then grits her teeth. She snaps her fingers, and both she and Hazel disappear.

Moira puts her head in her hands.

sixteen
off the board

T he floor-to-ceiling window to the right of Parker's desk, in the campus on Nunwick's city-sized estate, overlooks a small valley with a massive construction project going on at its floor. It's the culmination of a century's worth of work, or several hundred years' worth, or two millennia's worth, depending on when one cares to count from. The construction is ahead of schedule—if one omits the inconvenient fact that the first of two scheduled live tests, two months ago, failed catastrophically, and the next test is less than a month away from today. Three months after that, the magnificent, ridiculous machine being assembled on that valley floor must not only be complete but safe and fully operational. Ideally, capable of operating *without* replicating the Test Site Three fiasco on a literally worldwide scale.

"She's crawled back into an ale barrel, then."

Parker turns away from the window, toward Tierney Ironheart, Celestial's COO, the first high priestess of the Order of Caeles. "We don't know that. We still don't know what made her crawl out in the first place two months ago, but as I've said before, it's hard to believe the proximity to our last test is mere coincidence."

"So you think she'll reappear before the next test."

"I do."

"What about the other goddesses she's created?"

137

Parker shakes her head. "They've stopped performing miracles, or even being seen in public. Ms. Harcourt and Ms. Doran have remained in San Francisco but kept to themselves. Ms. Lindsay abandoned her home and her cult and has effectively disappeared."

"Yet you still think they might be threats."

"They're untrained and naïve, but they're still goddesses. As cagey as you and Mr. Nunwick have been about Project Maelstrom's specifics, I'm aware it centers Agent One. That means it centers chaos, and chaos is the bailiwick of Moira and her compatriots. They may have gone to ground for now, but I wouldn't underestimate their capability to grievously interfere."

Ironheart stands and walks to the window. "In turn, don't underestimate what Mr. Nunwick's work has led to." She points at the construction cranes visible on the valley floor. "We've long ago proven that divine magic can be channeled—but that also means it can be diverted."

Parker flicks her ears in thinly veiled irritation. The elder goddess often aspired toward mysteriously grandiose speech, but frequently fell short, instead hitting elliptically pompous. "Which means what?"

"Meaning that while we're proceeding with Maelstrom as planned, we're investigating new options." The lioness grins, eyes sparkling. "Taking them all permanently off the board, including Moira, might well be a possibility."

Parker lifts her brows at that.

"So. Mr. Nunwick and I are working full-time on Test Site Four's final preparation, building on your foundations, while your attention shifts to Maelstrom."

The vixen nods. This isn't a change; they'd implemented their most ambitious, arguably extreme, societal rearrangements in that metro area, ratcheting it up for years. Parker had run much of that pilot project, although she'd argued against the plan for the rollout. It made too many assumptions about how governments would react to unprecedented disasters, left too much up to chance. Arguments between Parker and Nunwick became arguments with Parker on one side and Nunwick and Ironheart on the other, though, and this one had been no different. "We've taken advantage of the situation by encouraging selectively edited stories about the actual events at Ms. Lindsay's former home rather than suppressing them."

"And connecting it to the previous stories about the goddesses?"

"We don't have to make those connections. Mortals excel at manufacturing conspiracy theories. So far, the few mainstream news stories on the subject aim to debunk the idea of magical monsters and demonic spirits, but that simply encourages suspicions, the idea that 'they' don't want the truth to come out."

Ironheart purses her lips, as if she's unsure how to process that. Parker doesn't know how long ago the lioness was deified, but she occasionally seems to have trouble understanding mortal thinking at all. Nunwick seems to do better, despite having made himself a god—somehow—long, long before. "Have you touched base with Agent One yet?"

"No." She can't keep the curtness from her tone.

Ironheart cocks her head, and half-smiles. "I'm aware you two have…different styles, but—"

"It's not a matter of style or aesthetics, it's a matter of her conflicting with our organization's entire ethos." Parker crosses her arms. "And no, I won't relitigate past arguments, but I trust you're not suggesting I oversee her."

"Not deal with her day-to-day, no." Ironheart turns away, obviously considering her words. "But both Mr. Nunwick and I have faith you're capable of subtly defining boundaries for her."

The expression in the lioness's eyes, equal parts faith and threat, forestall any further objection. Parker nods. "I'll do what I can."

"That's all we ever ask." Ironheart walks to the office door. "Keep me apprised of any new information about Moira."

"I will."

After the lioness leaves, Parker sighs, pulling up the information file on Test Site Four.

seventeen
still here

Moira downs the rest of her beer in one gulp, slamming the pint glass on the counter in front of her. "Let's try the imperial rye stout."

This microbrewery hews so closely to the common design tropes that it transcends stereotype and reaches archetype: a converted garage in a light industrial park on the edge of a gentrifying working-class suburb. It's irritatingly crowded, but the beer has been good enough to make up for it. The group of too-loud foxes playing corn hole are getting on her nerves, though.

The cat behind the bar walks over. He's in an unbuttoned plaid flannel shirt, because of course he is. "Wasn't that your fourth? You haven't been here even two hours." He takes her glass.

"Do I look drunk yet?"

"No," he admits, filling up one of the snifters they use for higher ABV brews. "I guess I'm stereotyping you based on other rabbit women."

She takes the glass. "There's your mistake. I'm not a rabbit, I'm a hare. Hares are bigger."

"Got it." He grunts thoughtfully as he heads over to a couple sitting down at the other end of the bar. "You know, you really look familiar."

"I have that kind of face."

He flicks his ears and nods, tending to the newcomers.

Moira stifles a sigh. Sure, she's been getting that since the literal beginning of time, but it's definitely been on an upswing the last month and a half or so. Most of the news stories around what happened at Diana's place raise questions about murder-suicide cults, with reports of giants and monsters written off as drug-induced hallucinations. Diana, the suspected cult leader, remains "on the run"; a few questions were raised, too, about possible connections between her and the mysterious Angel of Castro, perhaps because said angel hasn't been seen since.

But there's a *lot* of chatter across the fringier corners of social media about magic and monsters—and about how chaos leads to the latter, how it can only be defeated by order. Celestial's strategy of suppressing whatever shit Moira stirs up in action, she suspects.

So why give them any more ammunition? The new business gods may not be making the world better, but her adventure in popping off and making new gods demonstrably made things worse. Maybe Hazel, Diana, and Rhiannon can do better without her. She's been happier leaving them to their own devices.

"The thing about being a goddess is our whims mean something, right?" she mutters, and raises her glass. "Here's to divine bullshit."

"Lady Moira?"

She'd seen the canine walking toward the bar, but hadn't been paying close attention. A lanky coyote, short but cute, with shaggy hair and wary brown eyes. Oh, *right*, from her stunt in Vallejo. Stetson, right?

"It is you! I'd started to wonder if the news coverage was right and I *had* dreamed everything, even though I was sore for a week." The coyote looks self-conscious, then dismayed, and starts to drop to his knees.

She catches him by his shoulder. "No. Please. No. Just sit." She guides him to the stool next to her.

"Uh. Sorry." He rubs his shoulder, looks around, leans toward her, and lowers his voice. "That 'cult' in South San Francisco that people say might have involved magic—"

"It's not what the stories say."

He looks into her eyes. "The cult part's wrong, but the magic part isn't. What about the part about demon summoning?"

"I'd call it less 'demon summoning' than 'monster creation.'" She looks away. "I gave other people magic, and maybe I shouldn't have. Not that I did it on purpose. You're lucky I didn't accidentally turn you into a god." She pauses and squints at him. "I didn't, right?"

Stetson's ears skew. "Not that I've noticed."

"Just checking. You feel completely mortal to me, but I've been losing my touch. I finally got out in the world, stayed visible for a couple of months, and what happened?" She waves a hand. "A monster attack and a new set of ID laws."

The bartender cat comes over and sets a bowl of snack mix down by the coyote. "What'll it be?"

He scans the menu board quickly. "The barleywine."

The cat nods. "Good choice." He heads off.

"They were coming anyway." Stetson shrugs. "Fresno's had worse since the start of the year."

"Oh, let's not pretend it isn't my fault." She looks into her beer. "I'm the one literally hopping on police cars, and you all pay the price. As much of an asshole as Daranu could be, he'd at least have punished the right people."

The coyote fidgets.

"So." She straightens up, sighing. "What brings you to this garage brewery?"

"I live here in Concord. I don't own a car, and with the new ID checks, taking public transit or taxis between cities is enough of a hassle that I don't bother unless I have to. Fortunately, I really like this garage brewery."

The bartender drops off the coyote's beer. She sips her own, and smiles down at him wanly. "So, despite not having a car, I hope you've had a better past two months than I have, Stetson."

"It's been run-of-the-mill, other than the dreams." He gives her a lopsided grin. "Which are still...whew."

She takes another swig of her beer. "I'd say I'm sorry, but I'm not."

"I'm not, either."

Moira smiles, feeling almost...what's the word? Relaxed. Then the corn hole foxes all scream at whatever constitutes a good play when you're throwing beanbags into holes, she guesses. She twitches. "If they can't keep it down a little..." She makes a *hmmph* noise and shakes her head.

The coyote's ears twitch as he looks toward them, then back at her. "I don't know what you're thinking, my lady, but I'm guessing it would probably be both weirdly hot and a bit of an overreaction."

"That's my style, isn't it? Overreaction on the micro level, stagnation on the macro."

"I didn't mean that. You've done...a lot."

"Mmm."

"And, us mortals sometimes fantasize about doing horrible things to people who bother us, too." He chuckles and sips his beer.

"But you usually don't."

"Not me personally, but I don't know if that's wisdom as much as just the way I am."

"That's the same thing. Most mortals have *some* measure of humility that I'm not sure gods do. Empathy. If you don't, you're a...what's the word? Sociopath." She waves a hand. "I'd have guessed gods who'd been mortals the week before would still have that humility. Silly me."

"Well." He rubs the back of one of his ears. "All I've seen is what happens when you gave mortals a blast of unexpected power for a night, and I can't say that I saw a lot of humility on display."

"I guess not." She chuckles bitterly, and downs the rest of her beer. "You know what I am, Stetson?"

"An immortal, nearly omnipotent, drop-dead gorgeous hare. And if the mythology books I bought after we met are right, the goddess of love and war."

"I'm an anachronism." She waves the bartender over. "I'd like one of what he has." She jerks a thumb at the coyote.

"You've had a *lot* of beer in a short time, especially for a herbivore. You'd better take a break *mewp!*" The cat abruptly finds himself in the midst of the snack mix, not much bigger than one of the pretzels.

"Fine." Moira reaches into the bowl and pulls out a few bits of snacks. The cat wails, scrambling back through the peanuts and rye chips to barely stay away from her fingers. She tosses what she's caught into her mouth and crunches noisily, then holds out the bowl to Stetson. "Do you want any?"

The coyote stares into the bowl. "I…uh…no, thanks."

"Did you notice that he never brought *me* snacks like this, but brought you some before you even ordered? I noticed." She sets the bowl down, ignoring the cat's frantic apologies. "Anyway. An anachronism. I mean, I've tried to keep up. I'm not going around saying 'forsooth' and cursing electric lights as demonic. I like modernity. I have a nice car."

She picks up another handful of snacks, this time brushing the cat's legs. He shrieks. Stetson cringes. Moira studiously acts oblivious. "But it seemed as if… I don't know. As if everything had lined up to force me out of the background, as if I'd started taking action almost without knowing it because it was *time*."

Stetson glances around nervously. Nobody else in the brewery seems to have picked up on the cat's disappearance, although a couple at the other end of the bar are clearly looking for another beer themselves, wondering where the cat's gone. Another bartender, a maned wolf woman, is coming on shift. "Time for, uh, what?"

"My guess is as good as yours." She shakes her head. "I'd have thought the next cycle would have started by now. New world, new gods. That's what Daranu was afraid my revolution would bring about, you know. I guess I finally *have* made some new gods, but same old world. And my new gods? The first thing one did was stomp somebody under a hoof. The first thing another did was eat someone. Did I say, 'Hey, don't do that?' Of course not. I said, 'Ah, well, the victims were jerks.' I said, 'Kind of feels good, doesn't it?' What a grand example I've set for them."

"Well." Stetson's eyes flick to the cat, who's hugging a pretzel stick and sobbing hysterically.

"And then, and *then*, I learned that the world already *has* new gods." She waves her hand around. "And they might well be behind half the terrible stuff you all are doing to yourselves. They're at least pushing it all, taking advantage of it. Daranu's natural order, re-invented for a modern age. So that had to be what I was supposed to do, right? To fight them. I wasn't just making new gods on a whim, I had a purpose. A literal divine purpose."

"But?" he prompts after a moment.

"But what if I'm wrong? What if a god's whims *don't* always mean something? Maybe this is the new world after the gods that the myths promised, Stetson. Maybe everything *did* turn." She sighs. "And even if I'm supposed to be fighting, I don't think I know how anymore."

"I can't imagine the goddess of war is capable of forgetting how to fight." He rubs his ear. "You certainly haven't forgotten how to be the goddess of love."

She snorts, then fishes around in the snack bowl, hauling up both the cat and his safety pretzel. "So is this enough of a break, do you think? If I keep sitting here without a drink, I might just finish off the whole bowl."

"Oh god *goddess goddess* yes whatever you want please—"

Abruptly he appears back behind the counter, full-sized. Moira pops the pretzel into her mouth.

The cat stares at her, then scrambles to fill up a glass of barley-wine, beer sloshing over the rim due to his violent shaking.

Stetson glances around, ears skewed, and leans in toward the hare. "Why is nobody staring at the disappearing and reappearing cat?" he murmurs.

"You'd be surprised what people miss when you don't call attention to it." She picks up her beer and takes a big drink, then furrows her brow, setting the glass back down slowly. "What I just did with him was sociopathic, wasn't it? And to me, it's just being a god. I'm being a bad example without even thinking about it. Gods are sociopaths, aren't they, Stetson?"

"Oh, boy." He takes a big sip of his beer. "I don't...um. Lady Moira, I don't think you see things the way mortals do. I don't know if 'sociopath' can even apply. I appreciate the attention you give me, but I know that we're so far beneath you, individuals surely don't matter that much."

No. But yes. But—

She runs a hand through her hair, frustrated that being immortal doesn't help to put this into words. "In a way, no, they don't. If I leveled this bar, even this city, the world would just…go on. In the grand scheme of things, no one person matters *that* much, and most people come and go like sand on a beach.

"But in another way," she shifts in her seat to look directly at him, "mortals matter more than anything. You're the reason *we* exist. You're why we're here. We aren't here for ourselves. We're here for you." She scoffs, looking down. "At least, when we *were* here."

Stetson nods slowly again. "Why…" He trails off, takes a long sip of his beer, then looks back up at her. "Why did the other gods leave?"

"They didn't tell me. What I'd guessed matches what a…a close friend who was in touch with them longer than I was said, too. That they retreated because they thought mortals didn't want them. That you'd all decided you didn't need us anymore. But the truth is that I don't know." She starts to reach for her beer, but her own words crash onto her with an anvil weight. "It's been a thousand years," she whispers, "and I still don't know."

She doesn't realize a tear's escaped until she sees Stetson's reaction, his ears flattening, his look of dismay. He scoots his stool closer and puts an arm around her waist.

Moira stiffens. This isn't becoming of the goddess of love, let alone the goddess of war. She…

She puts her arms around the smaller coyote, sniffling.

The rest of the bar has gone quiet, except for other people starting to sniffle. Stetson glances around. "But *you* didn't leave," he murmurs. "You're still here for us."

"I'm still here because Daranu never forgave me for rebelling, and I was too proud to apologize to him."

"You didn't apologize because you were right."

She snorts. "That's ironic for a carnivore to say."

"It's true, though, isn't it?" He takes one of her hands in both of his. "Lady Moira, I don't know anything about divine whim. Until that night in Vallejo with you, I didn't *believe* in gods, and frankly, the world made far more sense that way. But you're here. You're still here, and I think it's because it's where you need to be."

She looks down into his eyes. They reflect the earnestness in his words. "It's been a long time since a mortal had genuine faith in me."

"Does that give a god any extra kind of power?"

"No more than it does a mortal." Tilting his muzzle up gently with two fingers, she gives him a light kiss. "But maybe that's enough."

He kisses back, tail wagging, then looks around and half-grins. "You're broadcasting emotions, aren't you?"

Moira looks around, too. Most of the bar is sobbing openly, even though half of them look confused as to why. "They'll recover. But it'll help if I head out." She chugs the rest of her beer, stands, fishes out five twenty-dollar bills from her pocket, and puts them under the empty glass. The bartender cat looks caught between terror and gratitude.

"Will I see you again?"

As soon as he asks, she knows she wants him with her, even though she's not sure why. Not to deify (she can tell that impulse isn't there), not as a lover (although he's the best squeaky toy she's found in decades), but...okay. Whim. Fuck it. She holds out a hand. "Come with me."

He downs the rest of his beer and takes her hand. "Where are we going?"

"To visit the new gods I created."

The coyote's eyes widen. "How safe is this going to be?"

"Eh. That depends on how angry they still are with me."

Stetson's ears fold down, but he follows her out to her car.

eighteen
staying grounded

I n the crisp mountain air, Diana's breath curls out as vapor, mingling with the steam rising from her coffee mug. She leans on the railing of her cabin's deck, looking across the sparkling mirror of a quiet lake toward distant snow-capped peaks, and wonders why she ever wanted to live in a bustling city.

But the city hadn't been her dream, had it? It had been her husband's—to be close to his office, to move into a newly refurbished loft townhome a few blocks off Market Street, to live the San Francisco startup dream. During the divorce, she hadn't fought him on keeping the house. But she hadn't expected to keep next to nothing. The divorce settlement had granted her barely enough money for a down payment on the tiny old house she'd found in South SF. She'd grown to like the place, but not love it, and having it become a de facto temple had made her kind of hate it.

And now even that's slipping away. The bank is repossessing the house, and she's not fighting. She can't. She's technically a fugitive. When she checked it on it stealthily last week, she saw they'd sent in their own repair team. It's nice that it won't be a neighborhood blight, but she suspects she's now history's first goddess with a bad credit rating.

She takes another sip from the mug, turns, and heads back

inside. Strictly by the numbers, the A-frame cabin has less space than her old house did, but it feels more open, more comfortable. It has that back porch deck, with the stunning postcard view. She relocated some undamaged furniture and her few irreplaceable possessions up here already. In barely a month, it's come to be more of a true home than she's had in years.

Setting down her mug, she heads to the front door and opens it.

The older sheep woman standing outside stops with her hand raised to knock, then shakes her head. "I've told you how disconcerting it is when you do that, Di." She's shorter than Diana, a few pounds stockier, but shares the same deep brown eyes. Her wool might have been the same black as Diana's once, too, but now shines silver around the edges.

"I thought you might need help carrying things in."

In response, her mother lifts a single paper bag, holding it by its woven handles. "Come on. I'm not that decrepit yet."

Chuckling, Diana holds the door open.

She beelines for the dining room, setting down the bag and unpacking breakfast onto the two-person table. "Already set the plates, I see. You have more of that coffee?"

"Of course." Diana heads to the kitchen, getting down another mug.

"Brewing it the old-fashioned mortal way?"

"Yes." She fills the new mug and tops off her own. "No reason not to."

"It's good to stay grounded."

Her mother finishes dishing out slices of red pepper frittata, hash browns, and fruit cups, plated as nicely as they'd be at the local café. "Especially when your head's sometimes literally in the clouds." She pours two glasses of fresh grass juice.

Diana takes a seat. "I haven't done that in a while, unless you count climbing the mountain. I'd rather not draw that much attention. You're the one who has to live here."

"Mmm hmm." Her mom sits down, too, and raises her coffee mug, holding it out expectantly.

Diana laughs, shaking her head, and clinks mugs.

"So." Her mother cuts into her frittata. "When are you going back? And don't make a joke about how eager I am to get rid of you. You know I'm not."

"I know, mom." Diana sighs. "But I don't know if I *am* going back."

"You said I'm the one who has to live here, which suggests you don't plan to."

"That's not…" She waves around. "This is the only house I have now. When or if I go somewhere else, I don't know where that's going to be. But I need to figure out the *why* first."

"You are what you are now, that's why. You might still deign to use an old electric coffee maker, but you remodeled this place—and moved all your furniture in—with your bibbidi-bobbidi-boo. I'm pretty sure half the town has figured something odd's going on up here, too, not that they'll ever let on."

"Because they'd be too terrified to?" Diana says it lightly, but can't keep an edge of bitterness from her tone.

"Because they're good neighbors, and part of being a good neighbor is knowing when not to say anything. Anyway, I doubt anyone's thinking 'oh, that quiet sheep woman who fixed up that old house by the lake's probably secretly either a serial killer or a goddess.'"

"Surprise, she's both," Diana mutters, stabbing at her cantaloupe.

"Di, you are *not* a serial killer." Her mother's voice takes on that brook-no-disagreement parental cadence. "I told you, I've read the articles you've linked, and I saw all the good you did. Stop blaming yourself for how that ended."

"I'm not blaming myself."

"Who are you blaming? Apparently not your irresponsible bunny friend, and not that mysterious vixen ninja, either."

"What? She wasn't a ninja."

"You said she had a ninja sword."

"I said she had a sword, not a *ninja* sword, mom. It was more like a cutlass."

"All right. You're not blaming your irresponsible bunny friend or that mysterious vixen pirate, either."

Diana rolls her eyes, but chuckles. As she returns to the food, she looks more contemplative. "Moira isn't irresponsible, she's just..." She trails off.

Her mother raises her brows, then continues when it's clear Diana can't finish the sentence. "You know this is all so fantastic it's hard for me to believe, even after seeing what you can do. But I've seen enough to take your word for the rest, and you've had words about that bunny. If you'd gone out kicking over skyscrapers, she'd have given you a brush to sweep the concrete dust off your hooves."

"She thought we'd all find our way naturally. Nobody had to teach her how to be a goddess."

"She grew up in the age of mythology, or sprung up fully formed, or whatever gods do. But you didn't any more than I did. I didn't even remember the names of these old gods you've been talking about." She waves her fork around. "I'm at least an occasional churchgoer, and we don't talk about magic, only parables from a thousand years ago."

Diana nods. "A few of the church ladies I remember would be dragging me off to get exorcised."

Her mother makes a rude bleat. "Some of them would have done that after you got divorced. This congregation's solidly liberal, thank the stars." She takes another sip of juice. "Also, don't think I haven't noticed you sidestep when I ask if your apparent godhood means the church is a fraud."

"The truth is, I don't know. Moira sidestepped whenever any of us mentioned it. A lot of 'not necessarily' and 'it depends on how you understand things.'" She shrugs and musters a wan grin. "You're getting more religious in your retirement, aren't you? I've heard that happens."

"I don't know if I'd say that, but one does think more about mortality the longer the clock runs." Her mother furrows her brow, as if contemplating what it means that her daughter is presumably immortal now.

Immortal. She can't wrap her head around that. Will she still look the same in ten years? Thirty? A hundred? Will she have to keep moving from town to town so as not to attract suspicion? How does Moira do it? How have the gods at the top of Celestial been doing it?

Diana drums her finger-hoofs on the table, then shakes her head. "I guess… I guess I still don't know my next move. I'm at a crossroads with no map. I helped people, but I also put them at risk." She holds up a hand. "And it's not about blame, it's about effect. I have power I still don't understand, and I still don't know what to use it for."

"Are you worried you haven't been good at taking up that rabbit's old causes, or worried that they're lost causes?"

"She's a hare. And I don't know. Both."

Her mother finishes her frittata. "I fought so many fights when I was your age, even younger. To get into college. To get my first job. My first promotion. At every turn, there was a gate I had to break down because I was a woman, or because I was a sheep. But…" She waves at the panorama outside the cabin's sliding glass doors. "My mother, your grandmother, wouldn't have even been able to buy a house in this town, you know that?"

"I do, mom."

"It wasn't just that they were still redlining against herbivores, even after they made it illegal. Women couldn't get credit except through their husbands. No loans, no bank cards. We've come so far in the last century. And your Moira should know that."

"I'm sure she does. But she has a much longer view of where we're regressing, too. And the last few decades…" She shakes her head. "It's been a lot of 'one step forward, two steps back.' Laws popping up about what we can say, where we can go. And more and more, I don't know, conditioning."

"What's that supposed to mean?"

"Look at pop culture." She finishes her coffee. "Find me a single new show with a rebellious mouse or squirrel bucking the system."

"There's one that just started a couple of months ago," her

mother protests. "The one about the young lawyer doe who takes up cases against big corporations."

Diana stands up and goes to get the coffee pot, refilling her mug and topping off her mother's. "And tell me who the villain is in the pilot episode."

Her mother crosses her arms. "It's an old family company owned by tigers. Yes, there's a nefarious rabbit accountant who gets involved and pushes them to cut corners, but…" She sighs. "Don't read so much into everything, Di."

"I said that exact thing to Hazel, when we were having this same conversation and she was playing the role I am now." She sip-laps gently at the coffee. "So I know how it sounds. But once you start seeing how many shows and movies critique the status quo with 'it's only a few bad people,' or 'it just takes one strong and true man to set things right,' it gets hard to unsee."

Her mother listens, pursing her lips in the way she does when she's contemplating the uncomfortable, then changes the subject.

They talk for another half-hour. As she walks her mother to the cabin's front door, the older sheep turns. "You've still never said when you were going back."

"Mom." Diana can't keep the exasperation from her voice. "I told you, I still don't know when or where or even if. Don't push."

"And like I said, you are what are you now."

Diana fidgets.

"I know you didn't ask for it. As much as I hate to say it, though, that doesn't mean Moira was wrong. It doesn't mean you weren't meant for it." She takes Diana's hand and squeezes it lightly. "It's all right that you don't know what you're meant to do. But we both know it's not sitting around a remote mountain town having takeout brunches with your mother."

Once she's alone, Diana goes back out on the deck, staring over the lake, and remains still for a long time.

Her mother's right about one thing. (Many things.) Diana's found quiet here, a place that feels like home, a measure of peace. But what she'll never find here is answers.

She won't find them with Moira, either.

Diana heads back inside and locks up, then pulls up a New York City address on her phone, switching to the street view. There's undoubtedly a key to doing this without being so literal, so concrete, in her visualizing, but this should work. She hopes.

She twirls around the virtual camera, fixes the image in her mind, and steps forward.

All at once the cool, clear air becomes warm and thick, reeking of exhaust, hose water and garbage. She chokes, rubbing her eyes—

Someone slams into her, and she lets out a startled bleat.

"Oh! Excuse me!" The wolf woman looks apologetic. "Didn't see you there."

"I wasn't there a moment ago," Diana explains. But the woman's gone, striding down the block, quickly lost among other pedestrians. No one pays any attention to the sheep who's just teleported in, or to one another. Welcome back to city life.

Giving her hair a quick run-through with her fingers, Diana looks up at the skyscraper ahead of her, its base taking up half the block. She has a fleeting image of standing taller than the building, just to check if the air is cleaner when she gets higher up, although she knows it won't be.

As she heads for the revolving door entrance, an elegant mouse woman steps out, giving Diana a skeptical glance as she hurries past. What—oh. She's still wearing sweatpants and a faded t-shirt, isn't she? With a finger snap, her outfit changes to a tan wrap skirt, matching blazer, and white blouse.

Once she's inside, she checks the directory, then heads to the elevator bank. It takes her a moment to figure out that the call panel makes you enter your floor on a keypad, then directs you to the proper car. The trip to the twenty-third floor is short, though.

The elevator brings her to an austere lobby, the minimalist bespoke look of new money rather than the clubby ostentatiousness of old. There's no signage, just a softly backlit constellation behind the young lynx receptionist. She doesn't acknowledge Diana until the sheep stops in front of the circular desk. "Good afternoon."

"Hello. My name's Diana Lindsay." She takes a deep breath. "I'm here to see Lily Parker."

"Do you have an appointment?"

"No. But she'll see me."

The lynx frowns, studying Diana keenly a few seconds, then picks up the phone.

nineteen
welcome back

Hazel stretches in her seat on the sofa. "Finding any more information on Black Oak?"

Rhiannon shakes her head. "The more I look for it, the less information there is. References I could find to it a week ago aren't there anymore. And that's not the craziest part."

Hazel tilts her head.

"It's disappeared from *printed material* published decades ago."

"That's..." The pika frowns. "Only a trick other gods could pull off, isn't it?"

"That's my guess." She looks at Hazel. "We're going to have to go back there and do more serious digging."

"When?"

"Maybe tomorrow. We should—"

A hesitant knock sounds at the front door.

Hazel and Rhiannon look at one another. In theory, no mortal should be able to simply walk up unannounced unless they had specific business. In practice, that kind of magic "visualization" is a feat both of them still have to work on; people slip through the cracks.

Shrugging fractionally, Rhiannon gets up and opens the door a fraction.

Moira stands there, wearing her familiar jeans and T-shirt. A short, lanky coyote stands behind her, ears laid back.

The squirrel opens her mouth, but no sound comes out.

"Who is it?" Hazel calls.

The hare meets Rhiannon's increasingly angry glare. "Hi," she says softly.

After a moment, Rhiannon opens the door fully, remaining silent.

Moira walks into the living room, Stetson trailing behind her. Hazel gives her a shocked stare, even more piercing than Rhiannon's, as she sits down. The coyote takes a seat pressed up to the hare.

Hazel squints at the coyote. "You are?"

The coyote's ears still haven't lifted. "I'm Stetson. Nice to meet you. Please don't kill me."

She gives him a look that clearly communicates *no promises,* and turns to Moira. "Just visiting, or planning to stick around this time?"

"Stick around, if you'll have me."

"Now you're finally concerned about rejoining the fight you started and put us in the middle of? Now?" Rhiannon stomps her foot, and the entire room flashes with lightning for a split-second.

Stetson yelps, tail bottling out.

"I didn't—" Moira starts, voice as hot as the squirrel's. She catches herself, clenches her fists, and looks down at the floor. "Rhiannon, I don't even *know* what kind of fight I've started, and when the first actual battle happened, I wasn't even there. You could have all been killed."

"We'd have just become mortal again."

"There'd be a new mortal Rhiannon, a new mortal Hazel, but they wouldn't truly be *you.*" She looks up. "I'd have still lost you, and I'd have lost you because I put you in that situation."

"Well, we're in it whether we like it or not."

Moira nods slightly. "I know."

Hazel grunts. "Look, I've gotten over being drunk with power—mostly—and I'm doing my best to do good. But it's a whole fucking lot of responsibility, and I don't have much to go on for guidance other than old mythology books…and you." She leans forward. "Maybe you don't understand this fight. Hell, we certainly don't. But it's not just that you made it our fight, it's that you literally *made us for this fight.* All that 'divine whim' stuff, even if at the time your whim was just that a hundred-foot tall pika woman in a wheelchair demolishing traffic would be spectacular." She glances at Stetson. "Which it totally was."

He nods hurriedly. "It sounds surprisingly terrifying, ma'am."

"It's just…" Moira spreads her hands. "Suppose my whims *do* mean something. Don't Darren Nunwick's, too? And this Lily Parker's? Maybe it was *her* divine whim to show up that day, specifically."

Rhiannon sighs heavily, and looks over at Hazel. "So apparently goddesses get their midlife crisis at around, what is it, four thousand years? Five?"

"I'm not having a midlife crisis!"

"You did get a sports car," Hazel points out, then gestures at Stetson. "And a boy toy."

Stetson's ears turn bright red.

Moira puts an arm around him, and looks between Rhiannon and Hazel. "If there's anything I should have known not to do, it was to make you feel abandoned. I truly am sorry. I can't promise to be everything you want, but I promise to be here for you now. And for whatever comes next."

Rhiannon rubs her ear. It *is* kind of exactly what she wants to hear, but it sounds sincere enough, in a slightly begrudging way. She glances at Hazel, who gives her a slight nod, and back at Moira. "That's all we can ask."

"No, it isn't," Hazel says. She points at Stetson. "What's his story?"

"Uh." He clears his throat. "Lady Moira and I met in Vallejo when she did…all that, then—"

"No. I mean, why are you here?"

Stetson's ears skew, and he looks up toward Moira.

"Divine whim," Moira says.

Hazel rolls her eyes. "Oh, fuckballs."

After a few seconds of silence, Rhiannon asks, "Have you heard from Diana?"

Moira shakes her head. "No."

"Neither has Briley. Hmm."

The hare lifts a brow fractionally. "You've been speaking with Briley?"

"Occasionally. You aren't?"

Stetson clears his throat. "Who's Briley?"

"Goddess of the harvest," Hazel says. "Mouse. Moira's old lover. Total MILF."

Rhiannon glares. "Hazel!"

"What? Am I wrong?" She flutters her eyelashes, then shifts her gaze to Moira. "All right. So instead of waiting for you to tell us what to do, let's figure out what to do together."

The hare smiles, tiredly but genuinely.

"And do it fast," she adds, "because I think something big is happening."

Stetson speaks hesitantly. "What, ah, like what?"

"As frustrating as it is, we don't know." Rhiannon shrugs. "But Celestial seems like they're seriously ramping up their power consolidation. Maybe it's a direct response to us, maybe we're just a pretext, maybe it's just coincidence, albeit in Lady Murderbunny's 'divine whim' way."

Stetson looks blank.

"As in maybe the new gods were moving things into their end game, and I unconsciously picked up on that and set a response in motion by deifying new goddesses of my own." Moira frowns. "And what do you mean, 'Lady Murderbunny?'"

Stetson flicks his ears. "They're creating new gods, and you're creating new gods? How easy is it to create a god, anyway?"

"There were only three of us who could deify mortals—Daranu, me, and Aronn. As far as I know, Aronn and I both only did once before I met Diana."

Hazel hmms. "And Daranu?"

"He made some demigods, but no more full gods."

"By 'made some demigods' you mean he banged a few mortals, right?"

"Right."

Stetson furrows his brow. "Um. So, then...where did Celestial come from? It has to be another god who stayed behind, apart from you and Briley, doesn't it?"

Hazel waves her hands in the air. "Welcome to our unsolvable existential question, boy toy."

"What about the demigods?"

"They can't make gods," Hazel says.

"I mean, did any stay behind?"

Everyone looks at Moira.

"I don't think so. Nobody ever got in touch with me, I can say that for sure." She leans back in her chair and stares up at the ceiling. "I still don't believe that Daranu secretly stayed behind and created Celestial as a second try. The modus operandi is just too different. And it doesn't fit with what Briley said, either, about the other gods becoming resentful at not getting enough attention from mortals."

"So what does that leave?" Rhiannon says.

"I don't know."

"And what do they want?" Hazel chimes in. "I don't believe Parker's crap about them doing this all to save the world."

Moira sits up straight again and sighs. "It's hard to guess that, either. Saving the world makes more sense than Max's 'this is how new gods rule' marketing line. Gods aren't meant to rule mortals, they're meant to shape them, directly and indirectly."

Stetson whispers, "Who are Max and Parker?"

"Gods with Celestial," Moira whispers back. "Parker is powerful, Max wasn't."

"Wasn't?"

"I ate him."

"Of course." Stetson clears his throat and folds his hands in his lap.

"Yeah, well." Hazel crosses her arms. "We can't fact-check most of what Parker said that night, but if that 'Order of Caeles' that became Celestial was supposed to be stopping atrocities, they've done a pretty bad job."

Rhiannon nods. "I give her a little more benefit of the doubt than Hazel does, but in that 'villains are the heroes of their own stories' way. She might believe what she's saying, but that doesn't mean she's not a villain."

"And I think she knows she's one of the villains." Hazel shrugs. "Anyway, we haven't found much about the Order of Caeles, other than oblique references to it from monks a few hundred years ago as a heretical secret society."

"Heretical?" Stetson tilts his head. "Like, the way a new religion looks at an old religion as a heresy?"

The pika waggles her hand in an *eh* motion. "There's one—but only one—reference to it being an old cult of Daranu. There are more references to it being a mystic sacrificial cult, though, devoted to the idea that its practitioners can ascend to godhood."

Moira lifts a brow. "Well, that's suggestive."

Stetson chews on his lip. "When you say 'sacrificial,' you mean..."

"They didn't give details, but whatever awful thing you're imagining? Probably that." Rhiannon holds up a finger. "And that brings us to the mystery of Black Oak."

The hare lifts both brows now.

"We've been lying low, but we weren't just sitting on our divine butts for the last month." She stands up, and the living room fades to near-black, dim light coming from...somewhere. A map appears behind her, like a huge projected slideshow.

Stetson yips, ears folding back. "What the hell?"

"Rhi is the goddess of PowerPoint," Hazel says.

"Please." She turns, pointing at the map. "Right here, about halfway between two big-by-Midwest-standards cities, sits a town called Black Oak. About five thousand people. It's been there a century and a half, famous in mining times—"

"Wait wait wait." Stetson makes a time-out sign. "I went to college in one of those cities, and I've been on that highway you're pointing at dozens of times. There's no town there."

"You stole the punchline." She finger-guns at him.

"Huh?" The coyote lowers his hands. "No, really. There's just a ghost town or two. They're not uncommon out there." He rubs the back of his head. "I remember… I remember stopping at a hamburger joint somewhere around there, with burgers topped with crazy things like peanut butter and jelly."

"Shorty's Burger Shack?" Rhiannon asks. "In an old service station, with picnic tables out front and in what used to be the garage?"

"Yes, that's it! It was in…uh…" He furrows his brow, starting to look worried. "I can't remember."

"No, you can't. Suddenly nobody can. And all the references to it have disappeared from archives, both online and off. *Except* in a couple of documents I found on the internal, secure networks of what company? Go on, guess."

Moira grunts. "Celestial."

"Yep. And, I think your coyote here just confirmed the ghost town Hazel and I found a couple of days ago is—was—Black Oak." A photo of a decaying old service station, clearly abandoned for decades, appears over the map. It's barely possible to make out "Shorty's Burger Shack" on the rusted sign out front.

Stetson gapes. "But…"

Moira crosses her arms. "So what, Black Oak is Bumpkin Môrdinas?"

"Isn't Môrdinas fictional?"

"No." Moira shakes her head. "It was my favorite mortal city for centuries. I wasn't the only god who thought that way, either. I still miss sitting on the cliff outside Bara's Café with an absinthe coffee and a kouign amann."

Hazel's eyes cross. "Did you just mix up like three cultures at once?"

"It was extremely cosmopolitan. At least, before it disappeared and mortals started treating it like a children's story."

"What happened to it?" Rhiannon waves a hand, dismissing her divine slideshow, and looks toward Moira excitedly. "I don't know if they're connected, but it might be a clue."

"I don't know."

"What?" Hazel, Rhiannon, and even Stetson all say it simultaneously.

"I don't know. It happened after my rebellion." She grunts. "As I said, other gods liked the city, too, and that made it less comfortable for me. Soon the only welcoming places left were my temple and one of the demigods' palaces, until he and I had a falling out. I stopped going back, and later got word there wasn't anything to go back to."

"One of Daranu's sons kept talking to you after the rebellion?" Hazel lifts a brow. "Why?"

"Because he developed a massive crush on me when I was towering over him in my silver dress once."

Stetson looks her up and down. "I've never imagined you in a dress."

"I'm not sure that I *can* imagine her in a dress." Rhiannon plucks at her skirt in illustration.

"I can." Hazel grins. "I've seen a couple of classic paintings."

Moira looks back to the squirrel. "Have you two been to where Black Oak is? Or was?"

"Briefly. That's how I got the picture of the former Shorty's."

"We visualized the section of highway it was supposed to be on," Hazel adds. "We were off by about ten miles, but not bad, I guess."

The hare nods, frowning in a prettily brooding way for a few seconds, then says. "I think I need to see it."

"We were planning to go back."

"Good." Moira stands and claps her hands over her head. The world goes black.

Rhiannon squeaks. She knows she's teleporting, but it's still disorienting. She feels her ears pop. When the world comes back, she mutters, "We were planning to go back tomorrow morning, not right now."

The air hits her first, even warmer and stickier than her first visit. The overcast sky blends into the gray landscape and what's left of the deserted buildings. The closest structure is the gas station from her photo; it doesn't look like it's been used in fifty years. None of the other buildings do, either.

"So, this is Shorty's," she says, then turns to find herself facing a sleek, long tan paw bigger than she is. "Whoa." She joins the others in gawking up at Moira.

The hare not only towers over the landscape, she's in a silver dress. *That* silver dress. It falls to the midpoint of her calves, and shimmers with each of the giantess's movements, fluttering like a sail in the breeze. As much of her as it covers, it reveals even more: the fabric isn't sheer, but it clings. Where it touches her fur it's translucent.

"So." Moira puts her hands on her hips, molding the fabric to her form even more closely, looking over the town from her higher vantage point. "A town that's been abandoned for decades, yet this burger stand was open for business just a few years ago."

"Ah. No, just a few..." Rhiannon has trouble focusing on anything but Moira's body. "Uh, a few months ago. Just a week before you deified Diana and Hazel."

Moira looks down, frowning. "Really. That's...hmm."

"You do, uh, look spectacular in a dress," Hazel stammers. She drops into her wheelchair, still staring up.

The hare crouches, leaning over to place one palm flat on the ground by the group, and the other on the gas station roof. "I know."

Stetson makes a strangled warble, squirming and readjusting his jeans as if they've become very uncomfortable. Moira flashes the coyote a teasing smile, and sits back on her heels. "The question is, are there any clues here to how this happened? Or why?" She shakes her head. "A place that became a decaying ghost town impossibly fast, and a cover-up that involves literally making mortals forget it all existed. Whatever the secret is, they *really* don't want it to get out."

"Welcome back!" Rhiannon says, spreading her arms wide.

twenty
the silver rose

"**M**s. Lindsay?"

Diana turns, startled. A tall, brunette rat woman, with both the body and style of a fashion model, stands on the opposite side of the reception desk. "Follow me," she says, holding open a door Diana hadn't spotted as she'd looked around the lobby.

She leads the sheep down a wood-paneled hall, past a dozen or so unmarked doors, to a separate, smaller reception area. Walking past the desk—the rat's desk, Diana guesses—she heads to a halfway open office door, pushing it fully open, and motions Diana inside.

As she steps in, Parker comes toward her from around a mid-century modern executive desk. Diana had forgotten how tall the vixen was. Assuming that was her natural height, of course. She's not any taller than Moira, but she somehow has a more imposing air—no mean trick, considering. Perhaps it's the clothes. As far as she's seen, "formal" for Moira means black jeans and a blouse rather than faded blue jeans and a T-shirt. Both times she's seen Parker—at her house, and now—the vixen's worn a tailored business suit that likely runs in the thousands. Today's is an electric blue blazer with a matching skirt and a cream-colored blouse. She looks depressingly stunning.

The office is huge and well-appointed, neither of which surprise

Diana. The window forming the entirety of one wall doesn't surprise her, either. The panorama out that window, though: that floors her. Instead of looking out over the city, it looks out over an ocean, as if from a high cliff. The sky is brighter than New York's, a saturated deep blue, sunlight filtered through cotton-white clouds.

"I usually look out over another city we have an office, or at least interests, in, but there are times I want at least the view to escape urban life." Parker turns to the rat. "Ms. Storm, hold my calls for the afternoon."

"Of course, Ms. Parker." Her secretary nods and steps out of the room, closing the door behind her.

"I have to admit, this is a surprise." Parker waves toward a sofa rather than a desk. Like the rest of the furniture, the couch sports a restrained, subtly retro look, the future as envisioned fifty years ago: curved, minimalist oak frame, black leather cushions.

Diana sits down. "It's one to me, too. But I wanted to talk."

Parker heads to a small bar and pours two glasses of water, setting them both down on the coffee table in front of the couch, then sits by the sheep. "And what would you like to talk about?"

She glances around, back out the floor-to-ceiling window overlooking a brilliant azure sea untold miles away. It shouldn't be any harder for her to do that than it was for her to walk to Manhattan through a photograph. Maybe it isn't. But she'd never have considered it. All that's in her head right now is just how far out of her depth she is. She'd had an answer to Parker's obvious question a mere hour ago, but it's a struggle to recall it now. "That night, back at my house." She keeps looking out the window rather than at the vixen. "How much of what you said was true?"

Parker folds her hands in her lap. "Whatever answer I give you, I'll have only my word as proof, which rather puts us at an impasse."

"Did you really want to offer us jobs? Here?"

"The late Mr. Howell took that initiative of his own accord. I'd asked him to keep tabs on you, Ms. Harcourt, and Moira. We've been watching her off and on for centuries, but she'd never before done what she did with you two. Later, three. We did *not* intend for him to make contact, particularly with Moira."

Diana glances at the two water glasses. Parker hasn't taken either one; she realizes the vixen's leaving the choice up to her. She takes one, but doesn't sip yet. "If it had been up to you, how would you have handled it all?"

Parker leans back, crossing her long legs at the knees. "Bluntly, Mr. Howell had his priorities as backward as his eventual place on the food chain. You, Ms. Harcourt, and Ms. Doran remain connected to the world in a way that Moira hasn't been for at least a millennium. You're not set in your ways, and you all have *some* experience with modern corporate structure. And at least at first, it appeared that Moira was taking a hands-off approach to you." She sighs. "But I made a mistake by not making a pitch to you myself, before…events overtook us."

"I don't have any experience with corporations like this." Diana waves her free hand around. "And especially like that." She gestures toward the magical window.

Parker inclines her head in acknowledgement.

"Why—" Diana frowns. "Why does a secret society of new gods *stay* secret? Why didn't the Order reveal itself? You were part of it, weren't you? Why move from tiny arcane cult to enigmatic global megacorporation?"

"The world still needs gods, Ms. Lindsay, but it doesn't want them. It wants business leaders. Industry titans." The vixen leans forward to pick up the remaining water glass and sips from it. "I think you've come here with questions your mentor either won't or can't answer. What being a goddess even means in the world now. Not just how to use your powers, but *when* to use them. *Why* to use them."

"So you're making a job pitch after all."

"I'm making a point."

"Holding back secret knowledge isn't Moira's style." Diana tilts her head. "But so far it's very much been yours."

Parker falls silent, looking distant for several seconds, then sets her water down, pushes her glasses back up her muzzle, and stands up. "Then let me reveal some to you, Ms. Lindsay." She walks to the glass wall, reaching a hand out to it, and—opens a door.

Diana stands up slowly, staring. *Is* it a door? It's still a pane of glass, but it's the size and shape of one. It swings open like one. And it lets in a blast of warm air with a distinct briny tang to it. So outside is, as far as she can tell, exactly what it appears: the ocean. "What...?"

The vixen indicates the doorway with a hand. "After you."

"Just...walk through?"

"Just walk through."

The part of her that had been against the idea of reaching out to Parker at all—that judgmental yet often sensible part—roars back, louder than ever, warning about how this could be a trap. Yet she's *here*, in Celestial's building, in the vixen's office. If this is a trap, it's already sprung.

She stops at the door and risks a look down. She doesn't normally get vertigo, but she sees exactly what she's afraid she will: the sheer side of the building dropping over twenty stories to...to what? The sidewalk? The sea? All she can make out below is fog.

Diana smiles crookedly, trying to hide her nerves. "This feels like a trust exercise."

Parker doesn't return the smile. "It is."

All right. She can trust that she's still a goddess. She can surely visualize herself flying rather than hitting the ground. No: hitting the ground unharmed, landing in a dramatic pose, cracking the sidewalk under her hooves. Nice image.

Steeling herself, she steps out, starts to fall—

—and immediately stumbles. She's dropped only a couple of feet, landing hard on a weathered wooden floor. Dock? Deck? Deck.

Parker lands next to her, with the grace not merely of a vixen, but a vixen who knew what to expect. "And here we are." She has to raise her voice to carry over the wind.

"It's..." It's a sailing ship. A *big* sailing ship, a grand wooden one straight out of adventure movies. They're standing on the ship's rear deck—aft deck? poop deck?—right at the stern railing. A towering mast, one of three she can see, lies dead ahead, past another railing; an old naval flag she dimly recognizes from history books, or maybe those movies, hangs off a spar a few feet above a huge square canvas sail. A lower deck stretches out between that mast and the next.

"A frigate. The *Silver Rose*. She'll be sunk less than a year from now, but this summer she's still one of the most feared pirate ships in the tropics."

"A pirate ship. We're on an actual pirate ship."

"We are. And no, none of the pirates can see us." Parker walks toward a ladder leading onto the lower deck, motioning Diana to follow. "Here, we're ghosts from the future."

The sheep walks a step behind the vixen, following the railing on the ship's right side. Er, starboard side. Now she can make out another, smaller ship, not so far in the distance, flying a different flag. "If any of us can change the past—"

"The past is fixed. The most powerful of us can hold it still for a length, but neither you nor I nor any other god can change it. At most, we can revisit it." They reach the bottom of the ladder and walk out onto the quarterdeck. "This past is a memory I know well."

Before Diana can ask what the hell that means, she comes to an abrupt halt, staring up at the ship's captain: a tall, silver vixen, the wind whipping both her burgundy overcoat and her long, unbound hair. She faces the smaller ship, taking its measure, preparing to pounce. "Hard to port!" she yells, raising a gloved hand high as she points. Her voice is unmistakable, as is the cutlass at her side. "Full sail!"

"Yes, Captain Lily!" several crew members shout back, scrambling into position.

All the ship's sails unfurl, and it starts a sharp turn starboard and picks up speed. Diana turns wide eyes on the vixen. The modern, goddess vixen. "When you were mortal, you were a fucking *pirate queen?*" she blurts.

"No, Ms. Lindsay." Parker is, for the first time Diana's seen, grinning openly as she watches her earlier self stride across the deck, directly past them, barking quick orders at crew members. "I was *the* fucking pirate queen."

They're not as far away from the other ship as Diana had thought. As they set an intercept course, the crew hurriedly lowers the naval flag and replaces it with a new one, solid black except for the outline of a rose.

Parker looks up at the flag, smiling with clear fondness. "The ship we're overtaking will recognize the flag. *My* flag. At this point in our career, we rarely had to do battle."

"What, other ships were so scared of your reputation they just surrendered?" But even as the sheep asks, she sees the other ship's raising a white flag.

The vixen leans on the railing, watching as the ships draw alongside each other. Several pirates throw grappling hooks, pulling them together, while others—including Captain Lily—draw swords, daggers, or pistols. "It's easier for all concerned. No one has to die."

"No one *has* to be a pirate."

"No. I could have taken the path my parents had set before me, to marry a minor nobleman not much younger than my father and certainly no kinder. And these men here could have been sailors in one royal navy or another, or merchant mariners. In some ways, easier lives. But lives of hard labor for minimal pay—all but indentured servants. On the *Rose,* they followed me by choice, splitting the plunder equally. While I would have been rich in the life I was born into, I would have lived entirely at the sufferance of others."

"That's—oof." Diana hangs on as the two ships smack into one another hard, and the pirates swarm over the railings. "You know that you're saying you chose a chaotic life where everyone could live equally rather than—"

"Rather than a life of prescribed order." Parker's gaze grows distant again. "Yes. But this is only part of the story." She motions Diana to follow her as she begins walking.

A billow of fog envelops them both. As it dissipates, the surface under Diana's hooves changes from wood to cobblestone. It's night, but the air is warm, heavy. The road they walk along has shops, all shuttered, to one side, and a high iron fence to the other, an imposing three-story stone building set far behind it. Gas lamps cast a deep, flickering orange light.

"It took half the royal navy to catch me, but catch me they did. Tonight—the night before my scheduled execution—a mysterious Lord Nunwick visited my cell, and talked of gods and monsters, much like you and I have talked. And, much like your Moira, he transformed me and left me to choose my path."

"He just…left you here, in prison? He didn't worry you'd choose the monster side, all things considered?"

Parker laughs, the sound echoing oddly and fading. Diana turns in one direction, then the other, blinking. She's alone.

The fortress shatters.

It's not an explosion. There's no dynamite, no blast. Instead, there's an enormous silver fox woman crouched in—and over—half the building, clothes ragged, hair and eyes wild. Walls and furniture and little people, soldiers and other prisoners, rain off her toward the ground. The new giantess glances around frantically, taking in her incredible new situation, and slowly straightens up, still breathing hard.

Then she grins.

Diana's been around Moira—and, for that matter, Hazel—long enough to see terrifying giant grins before. The vixen's rivals any of them. She shows more and more teeth, until she raises one arm and snaps her fingers. Her clothes shimmer into the seafaring uniform she'd had on deck, the tops of her gleaming black calf-high boots higher than the roof level of the rest of the garrison.

Taking two steps ahead, she smashes a boot down on the building, bringing her other around through the rest in a swinging kick. The entire fort erupts in panic, soldiers running, prisoners scattering, rifles firing. The pirate goddess smashes another building under her boot, and puts her hands on her hips, smirking at the ineffectual response.

Her next step comes down in the midst of the soldiers. The remaining resistance crumbles, and the troops run full tilt for the gate. The sheep backs away as men break through, scrambling past her. Should she intervene? No. She couldn't even if she wanted to. This all happened long ago.

The giantess laughs, waving a hand, and the gate slams shut with enough force to cut the unfortunate lead soldier in two. "No permission to leave, boys!" she thunders. "Turn and fight!"

Most of them don't listen, pounding on the gate fruitlessly as she strides toward them, walking directly over the sheep. Her smirk turns into a feral snarl. "If you won't die like soldiers, you'll die like bugs."

She starts stomping. Diana covers her eyes. The sounds are horrifying enough.

When the noises stop, she risks a look, then gapes. There's no mistaking it: the giantess is looking *directly* at Diana. She crouches, reaching for the sheep.

Diana starts scrambling backward. "No no no you can't see me I'm a goddess—"

The vixen's hand closes around her and the world goes dark. She bleats, scrabbling in instinctual panic, until she rolls onto her back and blinks in bright, artificial light.

She *is* in the vixen's hand, still, but she's back in Parker's office. The businesswoman looks down at her through her glasses, expression distinctly amused. "I'm in no position to blame any of you three for toying with the monster side, Ms. Lindsay. We all have demons to exorcise. The question is whether we stay monsters."

Diana's still panting, feeling considerably more self-conscious and less powerful than she has in months. "I don't..." She swallows, sitting up in the vixen's hand, and translocates to be standing in front of Parker's desk at her normal size again, collecting herself. "It's difficult to see how you get from *that* to goddess of the status quo."

"I didn't, at first. Being a pirate meant freedom. Being a goddess meant being unstoppable. And I freed others, in my own way. The town went from royal port to pirate haven overnight and stayed that way for thirty years, with sailors telling folk tales about me for another thirty more."

She sighs, folding her hands on her desk. "But I also empowered scores of criminals, slavers, tin pot dictators, and rebel leaders who often proved worse than the tyrants they rebelled against. I'd say that I'd begun to fear that Mr. Nunwick, who'd always left the door open at the Celestial Trading Company for me, was right, but that wouldn't be honest. I'd known he was all along."

Diana nods slowly. "But...isn't the real value in balance?"

"Chaos is a wildfire, Ms. Lindsay. You preserve balance by fighting against it." She spreads her hands. "We have many divine beings working for us, from powerful ones such as the late Mr. Howell and my secretary, Ms. Storm, to elevated mortals closer to your unfortunate mouse assistant. But this time last year, we knew of only five true gods, gods such as you and me, in the entire world. Now we know of three more—all acting as agents of chaos along with Moira. The balance you value is already irrevocably shattered."

Diana crosses her arms. "So this is all a long way of saying more or less what Hazel accused you of saying that night. That if we don't join with Celestial, you think we'll bring about the end times."

She leans forward, looking more intently into Diana's eyes. "I think, Ms. Lindsay, you've already started to."

twenty-one
four questions

"Another one." Hazel points. "That truck hit a telephone pole and was just…left there."

Rhiannon looks back the way they came. "So that makes, what, four abandoned car accidents, including a head-on collision that probably killed both drivers."

"Or they were already dead." Stetson shivers, glancing from side to side. "Everything here is dead. Even all the plants are dead."

They stand in what should be the middle of downtown Black Oak, but there's no downtown left to stand in the middle of. Like Shorty's, everything's aged decades past what it should be. Stetson's right about the plants, grass to trees to windowsill flower beds.

Moira nods. The hare's shifted back to jeans and T-shirt, but remained giant. "But no bodies. No skeletons."

"Someone came in and took them," Hazel suggests. "A cleanup crew."

"Maybe." Rhiannon sighs. "They've done a hell of a good job, if that's the case, though." She sweeps her arm around. "There's just nothing here, other than abandoned, prematurely decayed buildings. We might be looking in the wrong place."

"Maybe not." Hazel rubs her chin. "You don't want anyone here to know there's anything nefarious happening, so whatever you're doing will be as hidden as possible. You stick your secret evil laboratory inside a normal office building, or a strip mall, or even a house. Maybe *under* a house. Make it secluded enough to hide comings and goings, but still have easy access to the main highway. If it's a house, it's going to have something...off about it."

Moira puts a hand on her hip, and looks around the town from her vantage point, this time toward the highway, such as it is. She strides toward the east side of town, where bigger, more secluded houses sit on full-acre lots. "Secluded" is a stretch, given the town's pancake-flat, wide open layout, but it's as close as anything nearby gets.

How can she tell if a house that's been magically aged fifty-odd years is new? She guesses there should be a clue in the design, the look, that stands out. But she's not the goddess of architecture. These honestly all look about the same to her.

Hmm. Nearly all the houses are—well, were—two-story wooden squares with angled roofs, right out of some insipid children's book about glorious pre-electric prairie life. One, though, and *just* one, is a single story, what she thinks they call "ranch style." It's on a corner lot that's got to be closer to three acres, letting the house sit back well from the road. And it's in better shape than the rest.

Two driveways, too, and one comes up toward the back through trees. The back driveway ends at what could be an RV pad, but there's no rusting Winnebago back there. She waves at the group. "Come give this one a look." She shifts back down to standard size, returning to her jeans and T-shirt style. This doesn't look like the right kind of place to keep being a Renaissance painting.

There's fencing along the property line, but it looks pretty normal—it might have literally been white picket fencing at one point. Definitely not electrified with ominous KEEP OUT signs. Maybe it's just, well, a big house with an RV pad. She follows the crumbling street to that back driveway, walking up it.

Hazel's the first one to reach her, wheelchair kicking up clouds of dust as it squeals to a halt. The pika follows Moira's gaze to the back of the house. The overhanging roof hides what she's looking at from above, and the house's design hides it from the street, but—

"Is that a *loading dock?*"

"That," Rhiannon confirms as she sprints over, "is a loading dock."

It takes Stetson a half-minute to catch up. He's the only one who looks winded.

Hazel grins. "You should have asked me for a ride."

The coyote stares, still breathing hard. "I can't imagine any... way for you to do that which wouldn't...leave me blushing profusely."

Her grin widens. "I can't, either."

Moira walks down the slope of the loading dock, frowning as she looks up at the rolling door. "I can't say that I'm up on current home design, but this isn't normal, is it?"

"No." Rhiannon walks along the side pathway that stays at ground level, heading to a door by the garage, then hesitates, pointing up at the corners of the dock at small, dusty black domes. "Security cameras. And they look brand new."

"Are they running?"

The squirrel closes her eyes a moment, focusing. "Maybe. There's an operating electrical field around here."

Stetson eyes them. "If they're running, we're already within their field of vision."

"Great." Rhiannon touches a keypad by the door. "This is a serious lock, too." She concentrates again. "But it *doesn't* have power. It's stuck in the locked position."

"We're not going to stop here." Hazel crosses her arms.

"No, but I don't know... Oh, what the hell. Time to play super squirrel." Rhiannon spreads her arms and slams her hands into the door, digging her claws into the metal, then pulls. She rips the door off its hinges.

Stetson stares, tail twitching.

Hazel bounces in her seat. "I need to get you to be a badass more often."

Moira grins, walking on in. Hazel rolls right after her. Rhiannon follows, with the nervous coyote bringing up the rear.

The room inside dispels any remaining illusion this might have been a normal house. The floor and walls remain unfinished concrete. The vast space is entirely empty but for a small forklift parked against one wall and a few dollies and hand trucks in a corner. The equipment looks used, but none of it's decaying; whatever affected the rest of the town didn't do its work here. Elevator doors—massive ones, sized for freight—take up part of the back wall, next to a door that looks like an office building's fire exit.

"Hazel, I think you got it spot on." Moira looks around, then down at the floor. "We're on top of the secret evil laboratory."

Rhiannon looks at the elevator. "I can't sense any power up here. I could get the control system running, but that might wake up other systems we'd rather leave off." She glances over at Moira. "Any other divine magic ideas?"

The hare shrugs. "Visualize it running on magic, not electricity. Force the doors open and levitate down the elevator shaft. Transform to mist and flow through the ventilation."

Stetson clears his throat, holding the fire exit door open and pointing. "Take the stairs, and teleport Lady Hazel down?"

"Or that." Rhiannon walks to him. "Huh. Well, I guess we just need a light."

The pika wheels over. "Eh. I don't need the teleport. I'm good at magicking things into being chair-friendly."

"Got it." Rhiannon concentrates, and a glowing baseball-sized sphere appears in the stairwell, casting a blue-white glow over the concrete walls and steps.

"A will-o-wisp." Hazel grins. "Ominous!"

"It's ball lightning, goof."

Hazel laughs, and rolls her wheelchair right onto the stairs past Rhiannon. The squirrel stifles a gasp, but the chair stays balanced and level, front wheels in the air and back wheels against the stairs as if they formed an even, smooth slope. The ball lightning drifts serenely ahead of her.

Rhiannon watches her go. Moira walks past and Stetson stops beside her, tilting his head questioningly.

"I sometimes forget I have an amazing roommate," she murmurs, and pads downstairs.

He tilts his head the other way, nods once, and follows.

The stairs lead down about three stories, air turning cold and musty as they approach the bottom landing. Hazel waits by the exit door for the rest. Moira doesn't. She opens the door and shoos the light through, following right behind.

Once they're all in, the will-o-wisp drifts toward the exposed metal beams of the high ceiling, brightening as it climbs.

They stand in a single, large room. High-walled cubicles line one wall in a single row, and other doors lead…wherever they lead. Machinery housing fills at least a third of the space: metal cylinders, cubes, frames. All sealed, all bolted to the floor. Long, low control consoles run just short of wall to wall in the back. Behind them, a huge, strangely medieval mechanical clock overlooks the scene, a half-dozen concentric dials ending at a sun and moon phase display in its center.

Painted on the concrete floor between the machinery and the consoles stretches a wide, white circle, another smaller circle inside it. In the center of the smaller circle sits a chair. It's a nice chair, or at least, it used to be before fire left it pockmarked and charred. There's more machinery on the ceiling over the circle, ending in what looks for all the world like a giant ray gun pointed at the chair.

"So," Hazel finally says. "What the hell are we looking at?"

"I don't know. Some of these look like generator or transformer housings." Rhiannon gestures around at the machinery.

"So we're standing in a secret underground power plant that's lost power? I love the irony, but what's it for?"

The squirrel points up at pipes along the ceiling. "Half of those are electrical conduits. But I don't know what the other ones are. Hydraulic lines, maybe."

Moira kneels to study the paint lines, tracing a finger around barely visible symbols between the inner and outer perimeters. "I know what this is. A ritual circle."

"Ritual?" Stetson pads over nearby and looks down warily. "Like summoning demons?"

Hazel grunts. "The giant retro sci-fi gun kinda makes me think ritual sacrifice."

"Mad science *and* dark magic?"

"What you get when your arcane secret society reincorporates as a venture capital fund." Moira stands, spinning the executive chair around. It squeaks in protest. "The question is, what were they trying to do."

"And who exactly 'they' are," Hazel says.

Rhiannon stares at the ray gun. "And if they succeeded."

Stetson looks at the ceiling. "And what it has to do with what happened to the town up there."

"Fine. The four questions." Moira waves at the control panels. "Can you do your computer god magic and get any information from these relics?"

Rhiannon walks to one, frowning as she walks along its length. "This looks like a mission control center from an old space race documentary or something. It's electronic, but...you'll have to give me a few minutes."

Hazel looks toward the staircase door. "Did you hear that?" She keeps her voice softer than usual.

Rhiannon shakes her head.

The next sounds, though—footsteps—everyone hears. Moira narrows her eyes, first pointing at the consoles and motioning for them to duck, then pointing at the will o wisp. Rhiannon nods, crouching and waiting for Moira and Stetson to do the same, while Hazel rolls to position herself behind one of the big machines. After she's there, the squirrel waves a hand and the light evaporates. The chances are they can more than handle whoever it is, but they might be able to learn something before the fight starts.

Flashlight beams shine through the doorway. Unexpectedly, an engine somewhere above rumbles to life, echoing through the pipes.

Emergency lights switch on, square, amber-orange bulbs set in the room's corners. Dim, but still bright enough to illuminate the room—and the police filing in. Four of them. No, five. Six. Seven. Eight. All carnivores, all men, mostly canines, mostly big. The first one in the room, a massive wolf, motions at the others, pointing silently around the room. They fan out.

Wait, *are* they police? They have the uniforms, but the logo looks like Third Eye Security. And while none of them have a divine aura, someone with them has been touched with power.

Well, time to improvise. Moira stands up. "Hello."

Instantly, they stop and pivot, pistols out and trained on her. "Hands in the air!"

She rolls her eyes, raising her hands half-heartedly.

Another hulking wolf behind the first scowls. "You and your friends are trespassing, ma'am. And this place has been abandoned for god knows how long. It's dangerous." A fox next to him, slim but just a few inches shorter than the two wolves, is the only one out of uniform; he's in a black suit. He's giving Moira a wary glance. Does he recognize her? He's definitely the one with the hint of magic. Not much, but enough to be unpredictable.

The other five officers resume their search, shouting at Stetson and Rhiannon within a handful of seconds. They stand up, too, looking toward Moira for cues. Hazel rolls into view under her own power and puts her hands in the air, smirking.

"Which god?"

The fox stares at Moira suspiciously.

She lowers her hands. "Which god knows how long this place has been abandoned? I know Nunwick and Parker by name, but there are a few others, aren't there?"

The two lead wolves look at one another, puzzled, then at the fox.

"All right," the fox growls, "I know who you are now." The wolves look even more confused, but he ignores them. "And I warn you, I'm no pushover. Don't make this hard on you all."

Moira smiles. "If you truly *understood* who I was, you'd know not to invite me to take anything you say as a challenge."

He looks nonplussed for a moment, then narrows his eyes and snaps his fingers. Abruptly, Moira's entire group is together, around her—and all barely ankle-high to him.

The fox lets out a breath, looking smug. He holds out his hands and a plastic "serving saver" type box appears in it, with a few holes punched in its top. "We'll put you all in here for safe keeping." He turns to the other wolf. "Get upstairs. The moment you get a signal back, let Agent One know we have the rabbit." He reaches for Moira.

Moira grabs one of his fingers with both her hands and pulls hard. His eyes widen, and he crashes to the floor face-first. All at once, she's back to normal size, moving at a blur. The two wolves barely have time to point their guns at her before she grabs the pistols by their barrels, yanks them out of their paws, and gets the wolves in a headlock, one under each arm. Then she stomps a paw down on the fox's back, making him squeal in pain.

By this point, the other security guys have their guns out. They fire, creating a brief fusillade of petunias. They quickly stop and stare at their pistols.

"That was you, wasn't it?" Hazel says, returning to her normal size.

Rhiannon returns to hers, too, and grins. "Never gets old." She snaps her fingers at Stetson and he re-sizes, too. The coyote's panting, looking deeply unsettled.

The officers who aren't among the three held by Moira start to charge toward them, until Hazel holds out her hands and shouts, "Alakazam!" The serving saver appears between *her* hands, the guards sprawled inside it.

Moira glances at her. "'Alakazam'? Seriously?"

"Hey, I'm improvising." Hazel looks down at her basket of gunmen and shakes it, making them all yelp.

"So." Moira looks down at the struggling wolves and fox. "You're *exceedingly* bad at making things hard for us, so just tell me who you are. Run-of-the-mill cops wouldn't have been able to remember this place even existed, let alone do magic."

"We're not talking," the fox wheezes.

"The pika might start eating the goons she's got."

One of the wolves Moira has in a headlock snorts. "Come on."

Hazel keeps her eyes locked on that wolf as she picks up a tiger, shoves him in her mouth, and swallows.

The wolf's ears flatten and his tail tucks between his legs.

"Like I was saying, the pika might keep eating the goons she's got."

"Look," the other wolf stammers, "w-we just got a call to come here and check out this site, okay? We don't know what this site is, we don't even know the name of this town, we didn't even know there was ever a town here. None of us except for Guerrero." He nods frantically down at the fox, who groans.

"Guerrero, with the magic, hmm?" Moira looks at the fox. "You work with someone who gave you power. Who?"

"I work with Third Eye Security." He lets out a pained cough and closes his eyes. "That's as much as you're getting from me, and the rest don't know anything."

"With, not for. So who's your employer?"

"He's with Presage," one of the wolves gasps.

"See, you know something after all, don't you." Moira clucks her tongue. "I'm getting tired of holding you two like this, so I'm giving you to Hazel." She's abruptly holding tiny wolves, one in each hand, and walks over to drop them in Hazel's serving saver. The pika looks down and exaggeratedly licks her lips.

Guerrero rolls onto his back with another pained wheeze, and sits up as Moira walks back to him. "Go ahead, do your worst." He manages a sneer.

"Oh, my. You really don't want that." She shoves her hands in her pockets, looking down at him. "Look. I'm going to try the carrot rather than the stick. Make a bunny and carrot joke and I will kick your muzzle clean off your head."

He looks up at her warily.

"Now. You know who we are, but either your bosses at Presage didn't know how to prepare you to deal with us, or they don't care if you die horribly." She leans over. "I'd take a few moments to think about that."

He looks away, silent. At length, he mutters, "If I encountered anyone in your group, my directions were to not engage and to report the encounter directly to Agent One."

The tiny officers squeak angrily at this revelation. Hazel nods down to them. "He's kind of a jerk, huh?"

"They'd already seen us," Guerrero snaps. "What was I supposed to do?"

"What you could do *now* is tell us what you know about this machinery."

He looks around and gestures angrily, ears flat. "I don't know what the hell any of this is. And the only times anyone mentioned this place, they just called it Test Site Three. They tell us as little as possible."

"So if you get caught, you can't give much away," Stetson says. The coyote hasn't quite joined the group, but he's watching from a few steps back.

"Yeah." Guerrero looks down. "Not how they pitched it, but, yeah."

Moira purses her lips. Test site. Great. "Testing what?"

"Dunno."

She looks back at the huge wall clock. She recognizes it now. Sort of. It's an astrarium, a mechanical astronomical clock. Something seems off about it, though. "Who's Agent One?"

"A 'special assignment contractor.' I don't know what that means, I've never met them, don't know their real name, nothing. I hadn't worked with them at all before a few months ago, and we've just sent a few emails back and forth. All I know is that people who know them talk like they're the devil."

"Okay," she says. "One last question. If we take all of you guys outside Black Oak, do you forget the place exists?"

The fox's ears lift. "I won't. But they will." He swallows. "Does this…uh…mean you're leaving the rest of us alive? I heard you never did that."

She eyes him, then lifts her arms and claps her hands together. Abruptly they're all standing outside Shorty's. "Hazel, give the man back his fake cops."

The pika sighs melodramatically, rolls over, and holds out the container. Guerrero takes it like it might be a venomous snake.

"All right." Moira runs a hand through her hair. "I guess we regroup." Rhiannon nods, and she, Hazel, and Stetson move to Moira's side. "And Guerrero, look around this town and contemplate just what your employers might be testing."

He looks away again, brooding.

Moira snaps her fingers, and the goddesses and Stetson all disappear in a burst of light.

twenty-two
scouting out the enemy

The way Parker's offices in downtown Manhattan leaned into postmodern hipster minimalism had been impressive, but Diana has to admit that the way the mothership, Celestial Capital, goes all in on old money excess might be even more so: it's not an office building, it's a country club, somewhere north of Boston.

The marble-floored, high-columned lobby Parker's leading her through offers more than enough space for an elegant cocktail party; given the couple of dozen elegant business types—mostly, but not all, carnivores—lounging with complimentary sparkling wine and hors d'oeuvres, it might well be an all-day one. They cross it to reach the top of a wide double staircase. It curves down on either side of an extravagantly grand restaurant space: chandeliers, polished parquet floors, and white-cloth table settings. Floor-to-ceiling windows form the far wall, revealing a commanding view of rolling hills with a golf course threaded throughout the greenery.

"And Celestial *owns* this club? The golf course, everything?"

"Mr. Nunwick owns the land, but leases this part of his estate back to Celestial."

"Estate? Are you saying he lives here?" Her hoof clacks a touch too sharply on the parquet, leaving a tiny mark behind. Can she discreetly magic it away? Before she makes the attempt, a maid hurries over, kneeling to rub at it with a cleaning cloth. Diana stares a beat too long before hurrying after Parker.

"He does." They walk through the dining room into a separate bar area right out of a period mobster movie: all mahogany, brass, and leather, a bar running at least twenty feet along one wall with a mirror spanning the entire length. "His mansion's five miles to the northeast."

"You can travel *five miles* from here and still be on the estate?"

"It's over twenty thousand acres." Velvet ropes cordon off the empty back of the bar, a stoic-looking black jackal standing at attention. He nods to Parker and unhooks the rope to let her and Diana pass.

"Now," Parker murmurs. "Be polite, but direct. 'Be yourself' is a cliché, but Mr. Nunwick will see what I see in you." She smiles, and it's radiant enough that the sheep's heart skips a beat. She smiles back and nods, taking a deep breath. They step behind the rope together.

A few more steps take them to a deep, lushly cushioned booth. Two people, lion and lioness, sit with drinks—a Manhattan for him and a Brandy Alexander for her, both served (naturally) in old-fashioned coupe glasses. Their dress is as formal as the room and equally as old money, just on the right side of timeless versus out-of-fashion. It's not merely their style that radiates power, though. They watch Diana and Parker as the two approach.

"Ms. Lindsay, this is Darren Nunwick, our CEO, and Tierney Ironheart, our COO." Parker indicates each in turn. "Mr. Nunwick, Ms. Ironheart, Diana Lindsay."

"It's nice to meet you both," Diana says, trying to keep the hesitancy from her voice. Ironheart inclines her head, offering a barely perceptible smile; Nunwick gives the most perfunctory of nods, motioning at the space by the lioness. Diana smooths down her dress and takes a seat. Parker sits next to Nunwick.

Just like Parker and Moira, both lions stand unusually tall. Should she start presenting herself at six foot something? Is this a divine fashion choice nobody clued her in on? Nunwick might be an inch or two shorter than Parker or Moira, actually, but it's not until she's sitting that she appreciates how *wide* he is, how broad his shoulders and chest are, how massive his forearms are. Ironheart doesn't have her boss's weightlifter physique, but she still has well-delineated muscles under that tailored outfit, and a disquietingly predatory focus to her gaze. She perfectly matches her ludicrously dramatic name. If Parker had introduced her as Nunwick's body-guard rather than another executive, Diana wouldn't have questioned it.

A mouse waitress appears seconds after she's seated. "What can I get you, ma'am?" The mouse is faultlessly professional, but far back in her eyes there's a mix of awe and terror, as if she can sense she's not merely in the presence of some of the highest-power executives on the planet, but of true immortals.

Yes, she's a goddess, too, and based on what she saw of Moira she can hold a prodigious amount of liquor. But she'd never developed much taste for booze. "A gin fizz, please." She's never had one of those before, or even heard of it before today; Parker had suggested it as a low-proof drink she might like.

The mouse nods and turns to Parker. "And your customary daiquiri, ma'am?"

"Excellent."

The mouse nods again and steps away.

Nunwick takes a sip of his drink, sets the glass down, and faces her. Dark eyes study her intently long enough to let the silence grow uncomfortable. "So. Ms. Lindsay." His voice is exactly as deep as she'd expected, but crisper. He rests both his hands in front of him, massive fingers laced together. "Why are you here?"

One of Parker's tips about meeting Nunwick was that when he asked a direct question, she should answer just as directly. Not doing so might "end poorly," a phrase the vixen had refused to elaborate on. Answering with *because you asked to see me* would be technically correct, but she knows that's not what he means. *I'm still trying to figure that out* would be honest, but unwise. "To learn, Mr. Nunwick. What we've discovered on our own about your organization only goes so far, and while Ms. Parker's telling might be biased, it...raises questions."

"Of course her telling—our telling, as I doubt we'll contradict one another—is biased. Your divine benefactor Lady Moira's telling is just as much so, you realize."

"I'm sure it is. But her telling didn't include you."

"No." He grunts. "So you're scouting out the enemy, then." It's difficult to read his expression, but his voice remains conversational, light. Maybe that's wishful thinking, though.

"Perhaps I'm learning if you truly are the enemy."

The lioness tightens her grip on her glass, claw tips showing. Diana does her best to ignore it.

Nunwick, though, looks amused. Marginally. "Oh, I am." He picks up his drink again. "Certainly as far as Moira believes."

She tilts her head. "You make it sound as if you know her."

"Of course I know her. The goddess of love who claimed the mantle of war to try—and fail—to launch a grand assault on the king of the gods himself, all in the name of freeing the oppressed." He swirls his cocktail, gazing into the glass. "Only the tenderest of hearts could conceive of such a brutal folly."

Of all the descriptions Diana might come up with for Moira, *tender-hearted* wouldn't have been at the top of her list. She tries to keep the surprise off her face, but Nunwick glances up from the glass with a small, knowing smile. "That doesn't match the Moira you know, does it? But I speak as a historian with the gift of immortality. I know the old gods better than anyone left in this world besides Moira herself."

All right, that implies one answer she'd wanted: he doesn't appear to know about Briley. And it sounds less as if he knows Moira than he knows *of* Moira. "It doesn't," she admits. "She's not who she used to be. But you know that, don't you? You know those history books, certainly better than I do. It's your tale that's the mystery, Mr. Nunwick. A secret order that led to new gods—who choose to remain secret."

The mouse waitress returns, setting down Parker's daiquiri and Diana's gin fizz, which looks for all the world like an orange cream soda in a tall, narrow highball glass. She takes a sip and her eyes light up, and she nods, very slightly, to Parker in appreciation. The vixen gives her a matching slight smile in return.

"Legions of true believers would only make our work more difficult. And perhaps you're right, that Moira isn't who she used to be. Yet, that old self-righteousness of hers has returned, hasn't it? For the first time in millennia, gods openly walk the world. And now we stand on the brink of a new war between them, all because of her."

"Ms. Parker said much the same, and in even more apocalyptic terms." She takes a longer sip before setting the glass down and looking back to Nunwick. "But I confess I don't see how fighting for equality leads to the end times."

"A goddess should know that better than anyone else that equality is a fantasy."

"The existence of divine beings doesn't prove that."

"The behavior of mortals proves it!" He sounds indignant, exasperated. Then he lets out a short sigh, tone shifting toward patient professor. "It doesn't matter how oppressive a kingdom or a nation may have been to those on the bottom of its hierarchy, nor how noble the plans of the revolutionaries are. Revolutions lead to new kings, new dictators, who grow *more* oppressive, keeping the language of egalitarianism while ensuring only 'party leaders' have anything resembling true freedom. In the worst case, it descends into feral pandemonium—a foreshadowing of what happens at the end of this cycle if we let it turn."

She remembers Hazel and Moira both talking about cycles in mythology. When the gods left, this current cycle should have ended, turned, should have become…what? She should have asked one of them, or maybe Briley. Now she might never have the chance. Stifling a pang at that, she looks down, speaking more softly. "My mother grew up believing the world was becoming, if not more equal, at least more fair. But through all her life, we've just watched it become ever more sorted into rich and poor, strong and weak. Now we've reached a point where just talking about basic *equity* makes half the world think you're a crazy radical. And in the last few years, it's become much worse. More authoritarian.

Even dystopian. And whenever we trace these pushes back to the source..."

He smiles humorlessly. "It's me."

"Not personally. But it's often tied to a Celestial-owned company." She looks all around the club, hands spread. "This kind of wealth is unimaginable to billions of people. Even sitting here, it's barely imaginable to me. A year ago, if someone had asked me about all this sorting, this hierarchy, I'd have just said that's simply the way the world was. I'm honestly ashamed it took becoming a goddess for me to ask if it's the way the world *has* to be."

Unexpectedly, Ironheart speaks, her voice a quiet lilt. "Centuries ago, when I was mortal, my family were merchants, the beginnings of a middle class—neither noblemen nor serfs. After they were swept up in a great revolution, after all the glorious breaking of chains, what happened? The serfs still worked the fields. The merchants who hadn't been driven out or butchered with the nobles had lost everything. And the *new* glorious leaders just built new palaces. All in the name of the people." She looks down at Diana coolly. "When you say revolution, Miss Lindsay, what I hear is petty class resentment inflamed into self-mythologizing violence."

Nunwick nods approvingly to his COO. "We don't claim the world is perfect as it is—but hierarchy is closer to perfection than anarchy. The time of the nation-state is coming to an end, and the corporate state must rise to take its place. It's a different order, but the world *needs* order."

Diana leans back, furrowing her brow. "Maybe," she says slowly.

"But?" Parker prompts, looking resigned.

She clears her throat. "It's not that I don't appreciate the appeal of a world where everyone slots into their 'right place' and is perfectly happy there. It's that I can't help but think that vision is more appealing to those whose assumed place is at the top of the hierarchy."

Ironheart looks down again. "Do you think that makes the vision wrong, or are you uncomfortable with knowing you're now at that top along with us?"

Diana fidgets. Her honest answers are *I'm not sure* and *yes,* respectively.

"The closer you are to the top of that pyramid, the more responsibility you have to those below." Nunwick grunts. "Now, as much as I may be enjoying this philosophical conversation, you and I have a more pressing concern. While I appreciate that you're not feigning eagerness to join our organization, you don't seem committed to either reviving Moira's rebellion or stopping it."

She doubts he's been enjoying the conversation, but she's likely been combative enough. "I don't want war, Mr. Nunwick. I don't think..." She trails off.

He smiles grimly. "You want to say you don't think Moira does, either, but you prefer not to lie."

"No one *wants* war. She didn't want it the first time."

The lion frowns, then harrumphs, gazing off to the side. "She chose that fight. She rejected love. Never forget that, Diana."

She fidgets again.

"You've read those myths, haven't you? How the battles caused the seas to boil, the air to burn, threatened to crack the heavens open?"

"I have."

"Those battles were her standing alone against the other gods. This time, she has a sisterhood of goddesses who owe their divinity to her on her side. And this time, any battles won't take place in the land of the gods. They'll happen right here, in mortal lands." He leans toward her. "Prophecy is *not* destiny. We—the Order, Celestial—have kept this cycle from turning, kept the end times from arriving. But my ultimate goal has always been to *break* the cycle, to forge a new path. My gathering of power is a means to an end."

Diana looks between the other three at the table, and shifts in her seat uncomfortably. "You think it's starting to turn because of Moira rediscovering her cause. And...because of deifying us."

"It's not a matter of 'think.' You've seen what's starting to happen. You've personally suffered from it. We're now in a race with Moira and her goddesses to break the cycle before it can turn. And I'm well aware this risks bringing us out into the open, disrupting nations, causing turmoil for hundreds of millions. When the alternative is a war of the gods, though, I make no apology for taking that risk."

Visions of what her worshippers became, what William became, snap into her mind, along with the other bursts of chaos Moira caused. That Rhiannon and Hazel and, yes, she caused. But visions of the new checkpoints in cities across the country aren't far behind. Reports of new ID laws, of food lines, of laws—written by Celestial's lobbyists, enforced by companies that Celestial controls —that amount to apartheid.

She shakes her head, feeling an uncomfortable pit in her stomach. "There has to be a way that isn't authoritarian dystopia on one hand or cosmic war on the other."

"If there is," Parker says, "you may well be the only being in the world who can help us find it."

Diana straightens up, startled. Parker looks dead serious, though. Nunwick does, too, sharp eyes locked onto the sheep.

"There's nothing I can promise," she says hesitantly. "Especially on anyone else's behalf."

Nunwick smiles.

twenty-three
zero tolerance

When the doorbell rings, Guerrero looks up suspiciously from the dishes he's washing. It's nine o'clock at night, and nobody pays him social calls, anyway. Could one of those goddesses have figured out where he lives and decided to come after him?

He crosses his small apartment's living room as quietly as possible and looks through the peephole. A short woman stands there, waiting patiently. He can't tell exactly what she is. Weasel? Badger? She looks kinda cute, at least. Okay, fine. The fox cracks the door open.

"Good evening!" she greets him cheerfully. Fully revealed, she's more than kind of cute; she's downright hot. Black and grey fur, wild bone-white hair, and dressed to kill in a tight red one-piece with a neckline plunging to just above her navel. She holds a small box of chocolates in one hand. "Mr. Guerrero, yes?"

"Yeah?"

"We haven't met in person before, but we've talked in email occasionally. I'm Agent One." She beams a bright, sunny smile full of predatory teeth.

His ears fold back. This can't be good. "Oh. Uh. You're—uh. H-hello, ma'am. What, uh, what brings you out here this late?"

"Your report on Black Oak. I have feedback of the sort that

requires a personal touch. Let's go on inside." She motions with her free hand. Her claws aren't any less intimidating than her smile. Honey badger, he realizes. She's a honey badger.

He steps out of the way, and she glides in, beelining for his couch. He can't help but watch her tail. God, why did she have to be attractive?

She sets the chocolates down on his coffee table and waves him over. "Sit down."

He closes the door and manages a weak nod as he pads over to sit down on the couch, as far away from her as possible.

"So." She folds her hands in her lap. "Management didn't take my advice to promptly level the Black Oak facility to keep it away from prying eyes, which I'll take up with them shortly. It would have saved everyone so much bother, hmm?"

He nods uncertainly.

"What I have to take up with *you* is your choice to engage with Moira's group, against my advice to you. Management, sadly, gets to ignore my advice. You, Mr. Guerrero..." She fixes him with her gaze, steel-grey eyes locking onto his and holding him in place like a vise. "You do not."

"We w-weren't sure who they were, ma'am. Civilians have found their way there since the test. By the time we knew who we were dealing with, I had to—I had to use my best judgment."

"I understand. I believe you. That's the whole problem, you see." She lifts her brows. "Your best judgment is, clearly, just terrible."

His ears fold back.

"Civilians might have seen a curious ghost town they'd forget as soon as they drove away," she continues. "But the moment that group successfully located the actual facility entrance, they all but announced who they were. And you engaged with them after they managed to get inside."

"We—I don't know what else we could have done."

"You could have done the easiest thing in the world, Mr. Guerrero: literally nothing." She waves her hands in exasperation. "You could have left. Ideally, you could have left before you got all your coworkers shrunk and eaten for your failure." She waves a finger at him in a *tsk-tsk* motion. "I'm sorry, but I have zero tolerance for idiot minions."

"What? No." He swallows. "The crazy pika lady only ate one of them, and there wasn't anything—"

"Oh, no, no. I ate the others. Although I still have three left, I think." She picks up the box of chocolates and opens it, peering inside. "No, two." She smiles brightly and holds the box out to him.

He stares. Yes, just two: two chocolate figures of security officers, both frozen with terrified, pleading-for-their-lives expressions.

The ratel picks one up between two fingers, and lowers her voice to a conspiratorial whisper. "They *are* still alive. They can't move, but they can hear, and see. And feel." She pops that officer into her mouth, leaving her jaws open.

Guerrero must be imagining the terrified expression on the confection becoming even more terrified as the chocolate begins to melt on her tongue. He must be. "P-please. I won't—give me another chance! I won't fail you again, I swear!"

She tilts her head back and crunches up the chocolate cop, swallowing, then licks her lips. "I think you've forgotten what I just told you, dear." She gives him a pitying smile, and touches a finger to his nose. "Zero. Tolerance."

He tries to plead more, but he can't open his mouth. His lips have fused shut. "Mmmph! Mmmph!"

"Now, now. We wouldn't want your screaming to disturb the neighbors. That wouldn't be, well, neighborly." She leans forward and grabs one of his arms, dragging him back toward her on the couch, forcing his head down against her lap. "And I'm going to make you scream, Mr. Guerrero." She gazes down at him, expression almost affectionate. "A lot."

"Mmmmmph!"

Agent One sinks the long claws of both hands deep into his sides, and hauls him up toward that beautiful, psychopathic grin, jaws opening wide.

She's true to her word. He screams a lot.

twenty-four
bona fide
blast zone

A single taste, and Rhiannon's eyes widen. She stares at her bowl of gazpacho in awe. "I got to go to a Michelin-starred restaurant for lunch once, paid for by the company I worked at then. I started with gazpacho there. This makes theirs taste like they dumped it out of a can."

Briley laughs. "That's sweet, dear, but don't go overboard. I just have good ingredients, is all. Other restaurants can get tomatoes as good as these."

Moira looks across the supper table at her. "Only if they get them from you." She waves her spoon at the mouse. "And don't pull that aw-shuck-my-husks act on us. You've been cooking since—since there's been cooking. And baking! Your cardamom mango cake is, and I say this as the goddess of love, absolutely orgasmic."

Briley blushes.

Stetson clears his throat, ears slightly red, and pays studious attention to his bowl. "It is truly amazing soup, Lady Briley."

"Thank you." The mouse looks from Stetson to Moira, and stage-whispers, "He's so damn cute!"

Stetson's ears twitch, and he shifts in his seat, smiling awkwardly.

The main course is a salad of four different greens, with roast carrots, roast chicken, and a crumbly cheese all served on the side ("so you can decide how omnivorous you're feeling," Briley says). True to the harvest goddess's style, it's simple, yet somehow built on the best possible version of everything.

Near the end of supper, Hazel looks to Rhiannon. "You've been quiet, Rhi."

"I'm usually quiet."

"That's debatable. But let's say quieter than usual."

Rhiannon shrugs. "Sorry. I guess my mind's drifting to that philosophical tail-chasing you tease me about."

Hazel grins. "It's one of your more endearing qualities."

"So what's your mind been drifting to?" Briley says. "Questions about your mysterious missing town?"

Rhiannon waves a hand in the air self-consciously. "Like, I don't know, is there really such a thing as love at first sight?"

"Oh, going right for the easy ones, aren'tcha." The mouse laughs.

"I dwell on questions that don't have answers, I guess. That one's just—"

"Yes," Moira says.

Rhiannon stops and furrows her brow at Moira.

"Yes," Moira repeats, tone gentle. "But not the way most people mean it." The hare tilts her head to the side and smiles. It's a small smile, but it's sympathetic, compassionate. "It's easy to fall in *lust* at first sight. But love at first sight is a seed. It doesn't grow and bloom in the snap of a finger. It takes time and attention."

Rhiannon bites her lip, expression shifting as she fully digests that she just asked a question about love to one of the few beings in creation who wouldn't treat it as rhetorical. She swallows, then words tumble out of her in a rush. "How do you find the right person? Does everyone only have *one* right person? Is it possible you *never* find them?"

Hazel gives her roommate a confused, skeptical look, but Moira just sighs, still smiling. "There are lots of right people for anyone, for everyone. But 'right' means so many things. People are..." She spreads her hands. "They are what they are. Proud, shy, frightened, foolhardy. But when you meet someone who might be right for you, whatever that means in your heart, you'll feel it. You'll feel the seed."

Looking away, Rhiannon twists a hand in her hair, then nods. She looks back, realizing most of the table's looking at her, and clears her throat. "Like I said, philosophical tail-chasing." She shrugs. "I had a period in high school when I was secretly reading romance books, and I guess they stuck with me."

Briley smiles. "When Moira and I met, we knew we were the seeds for each other's flowers." She laughs. "Which probably sounds both stereotypical harvest goddess and kinda saucy."

Moira chuckles. "Kind of."

The mouse finishes her salad. "Not to change the subject, but I don't suppose any of you took a photo of that star clock."

"No." Rhiannon looks relieved at the subject change. "Did you think of something?"

"Maybe. I don't know." The mouse leans back, folding her arms. "Moira said something about it seemed odd, and that keeps tickling the back of my mind."

"The context is what's odd," Hazel suggests. "A giant mechanical clock with multiple nested dials, on the wall of a secret laboratory, under a house in a rural town."

"No, there was more to it than that." Moira purses her lips, back to her harder-edged air. "I don't suppose either of you have a photographic memory." She glances between Hazel and Rhiannon.

"She does," Hazel says, jerking a thumb at the squirrel.

"I don't," Rhiannon protests. "It's not fully eidetic."

"Let's see what we can do with partially eidetic, then. It's time for a magic mirror." Moira motions Rhiannon forward, and takes her hand when she's close enough. "Picture what you saw as we walked down that staircase last week and entered the weird laboratory."

"Fine." Rhiannon sighs, closing her eyes. "We walk in that door, and the will-o-wisp goes to the roof and lights up all the machinery—"

"Open your eyes and make the view look that way."

Rhiannon opens her eyes. "The what?" She sees what she's

facing—a floor-to-ceiling glittering black square—and literally jumps. "I can't just...uh." She swallows, facing the square, and her huge tail twitches. "We need a will-o-wisp." She points and a bright spot of light appears, floating in the blackness. "And, uh. It goes to the roof, and lights up the machinery." The light floats up in the blackness, and gradually the room starts to appear.

Moira turns to Stetson and Hazel. "Does it look right to you two?"

"Spookily," Stetson says. "What's actually happening here? Are we seeing Lady Rhiannon's projected memory?"

The mouse waggles a hand. "That's probably the best way to put it. We could walk in there, if we wanted to, look around like time travelers. But we couldn't change anything."

"Because it would break time?"

Briley grins at the coyote. "Turns out time's damn hard to break. Despite all those stories y'all tell about paradoxes and flapping butterfly wings, nobody gets to change what's already happened. The only way the past ever gets rewritten is when a god dies, and only just as much as it needs." She gestures at Moira. "For instance, when she did in Segomo, the god of war, he became a mortal wolf who'd already been around a few decades. Born before his immortal original was done in."

"That's mind-bending."

"Gods." Hazel shrugs.

Rhiannon bites her lip. "Okay. Read-only time travel. Let's see if we can get a good look at the clock." The view pans to center the clock, the will-o-wisp moving to hover over it.

"Hmm." Briley stands, looking at it. "What'd you think was odd about it? Looks pretty normal."

Hazel snorts. "That's normal?"

"For a star clock, sure." The mouse points at the outer ring. "Twenty-four segments along here for the hour. Matches this hand here." She moves to the next ring. "This is a calendar. Twelve segments, twelve months, on this hand." The next ring is also twelve segments, offset. "The moon and the sun's position in the zodiac. The sun and moon phase in the center, around a minute dial." She hmms. "Don't see minute dials too often on these, though."

"Okay, maybe that's all normal for a medieval clockmaker, but this is a mad science lab."

"True enough," Briley admits, stepping back and rubbing her chin. "Don't see how it connects in with all that modern equipment."

Rhiannon purses her lips. "Nothing in that room looks modern."

"We're using different scales for 'modern,' dear." Briley shrugs after a few more seconds. "But nothing about this one stands out beyond that minute dial, and that ain't *that* unusual."

"No. Wait." Moira moves closer and points at a bronze triangle at the twenty mark on the outer ring, another on the zodiac ring, and a third on the minute dial. "Those arrows. What are they?"

"Markers," Hazel says, studying them. "Together they're marking out a specific date and time. Three-oh-four p.m. on...no idea."

"The zodiac signs. Twelve equal parts, thirty degrees each." Moira gestures. "We're in this house now, this is two houses back, maybe...six days past its start point. So roughly eleven or twelve weeks ago."

Rhiannon's eyes widen. "Right before all the evidence of Black Oak's existence started disappearing."

"Along with the town." Briley grunts. "You don't pick a wackadoodle time like four minutes past three in the afternoon without a good reason. Somebody knew something was going to happen right then, and they had to take advantage of it."

"So it's a giant astronomical alarm clock." Hazel crosses her arms. "Letting them know exactly the right time to do whatever the hell they did."

Rhiannon nods. "But why that instead of just, you know, a clock clock?"

"It might be a switch," Stetson says hesitantly. "Like a sprinkler switch."

Briley and Hazel look confused. Moira arches a brow. "Fire sprinklers?"

Rhiannon lights up. "No. Lawn sprinklers. I've seen light timers like this, too. They're simple analog switches tied to a clock dial. You set one slider to the time the sprinklers, or the lights, are supposed to come on, and another to the time they shut off."

"Huh." Moira studies it for a couple of seconds. "But there's only one time this can set, isn't there?"

Stetson nods. "They might have only needed it to come on, and just run until it was finished."

Briley makes a *huh* noise. "Did the clock keep running afterward? Was it still going when y'all were there?"

They all look at one another.

The mouse shrugs. "Maybe it's not important, but I'm wondering if the markers ever moved."

"That's worth checking." Moira claps her hands, and the view changes to: nothing. Instead of the underground bunker, it's a flat, featureless plain under the prairie sky.

Stetson blinks. "What are we looking at?"

"I don't know. The view should have changed to the same location it'd been at, but at the present moment." She holds her hands out, palms to the ceiling, and raises them. The window's view changes, as if from a drone flying straight up.

With the expanded view, what they're looking at seems like a dry lake bed—at first. The higher the view gets, the more it suggests a crater, with a big jagged crack running roughly along the center.

Briley leans forward and grunts. "I'd ask if you were sure you've got your magic camera in the right place, but I'm gonna guess somebody got their knickers all in a knot when they realized their magic history eraser button didn't work on immortals."

"Well, we knew we were on to something when security showed up." Rhiannon sighs, and waves a hand. A second, small floating window appears in front of her, this one more like a computer screen. She reads for a few seconds. "There are reports of an anomalous earthquake in that area last week—the day after we visited. I guess that's the story for anyone who felt the demolition, although I can't figure out what the hell they used."

206

"A paw." Moira crosses her arms. "Somebody stomped it."

"What?" Hazel gapes. "Even setting aside how gigantic somebody'd have to be to pull that off, nothing there looks like a paw print."

"She didn't say a step, she said a *stomp*." Briley leans closer, squinting at the crater rim. "You get big enough and smack your paw down, you don't get a nice, pretty outline of your pads. You get yourself a bona fide blast zone. All that air under your paw has to go somewhere, and it does it real fast and real hard." She traces a claw tip along part of the crater surface. "And I think that *is* a faint outline of the side of the paw. Can't say what kinda paw, though."

Rhiannon half-smiles. "Should we be disturbed that you're talking about this as if you have firsthand knowledge?"

Briley laughs. "Not that I can't get showy if I put my mind to it, but that kind of thing's not my style. I got to see a few 'crater lakes' at creation, though, and they're not all from volcanoes or space rocks."

Stetson rubs his face, muttering under his breath. Moira gives him a quizzical look, and the coyote clears his throat, looking away. "Sorry, it's hard not to picture one of you four at a thousand feet tall now."

Moira shakes her head. "We'd have to be closer to a mile to do that."

The coyote makes a soft strangled noise.

"Oh, he's even cuter when he's flustered, isn't he." Briley grins. "Anyway, seems like somebody sure wanted to keep you from doing another search around there."

"Yes." Moira drops back into her seat and grunts. "But we have a date, a time, and a location to look up. That's at least something."

Rhiannon snaps her fingers. "Of course. Maybe we don't need *that* clock." She steps away from the group, summoning a few more virtual computer windows.

Briley sits up straight. "Môrdinas."

Moira looks blank. "What about it?"

"That's where I saw an astrarium with a minute dial set up just like that one. It was new when I saw it, too."

"Did it have the sprinkler switch bits?" Hazel asks.

"I can't say." Briley shakes her head apologetically. "And I don't remember enough of the place to do that time-walking trick."

"And I only really knew the parts around the coastline," Moira says. "Which didn't include any astronomical clocks. Where'd you see one?"

"A temple, maybe?" Briley thinks. "I don't know. It was after all the other gods had left. I only went back a couple times." She looks down, clearing her throat. "Kind of afraid I might run into you."

Moira winces, but pats Briley's knee.

The mouse puts her hand on the hare's. "Um. Môrdinas had a passel of tiny temples to demigods nobody cared about. Daughter of the music god, son of the ocean god, that sort of thing."

Hazel drums her fingers. "So Môrdinas was full of proto-hipsters. A demigod of clocks or planets or stars, something else astronomical?"

Moira rubs her chin. "That all mostly fell under Daranu's aspect, as the god of the sun. But it could have been one of his children."

"Maybe. What's worrying me is the thought that I first caught sight of that clock not too long before Môrdinas disappeared."

"Hmm." Moira furrows her brow, leaning back.

"If they're connected," Hazel says, "maybe this underground facility was a temple to the same demigod?"

"It wasn't a temple." Moira shakes her head. "I'd have felt it. *You'd* have felt it, even if you didn't know what you were feeling. But if Briley's remembering right, it definitely might mean something."

Rhiannon looks over from her nest of floating windows. "I think your figuring out what that clock was has helped me figure out something else, something I got in my raid on Celestial's networks where I found out about Black Oak in the first place. The same data store had a small list of times and codes, and one of those times matches the mystery markers on that star clock. So the codes might be geocodes. Location markers."

"You might have a list of other locations they're doing the same thing." Moira sits up. "Past, or future?"

"Both, I think. There's two on the list *after* what we're guessing is Black Oak. I'd been trying to figure out if there was anything special about that location, but couldn't come up with anything. No concentration of natural resources, no seismic activity before that mega-stomp, no history of supernatural events, no ley lines. Ley lines are bullshit, aren't they?"

"They're bullshit," both Moira and Briley say together.

"I figured, but still mildly disappointing. But there *is* something interesting about the time and location together: that's when the moon rose on March 20th—the vernal equinox."

Briley frowns. "That can't be a coincidence."

"No. But, we know what one location code is, we know how to read the time codes already, and that should be enough to start cracking the other ones." She concentrates, and more windows start flying around her head.

Hazel straightens up in her chair. "Rhi, you said the Order of Caeles was some kind of cult that worshipped Daranu, and its followers want to ascend to godhood."

"Mmm-hmm," Rhiannon says, distracted.

Moira gets it, though, staring at Hazel. "You're saying it's not that Nunwick *is* Daranu, but that he intends to *become* Daranu."

Hazel nods. "I think so."

"Dammit," Rhiannon abruptly says.

Everyone looks over at her.

"This won't be as easy as I hoped. If I can figure out a second location, I'll have the pattern, but I think this is... I don't know. Some ancient mariner shit on how to mark locations." She rubs her face. "This might be a while."

"That's fine," Moira says.

"No, it isn't. Like I said, I know how to read the time codes already, and..." Rhiannon spreads her hands.

"And?" Stetson prompts.

"Whatever happens next happens just before midnight on the summer solstice. That's a week from now."

twenty-five
a sliver of trust

"We're not open for walk-ins right now, ma'am. Could you come back in maybe a half-hour?"

Parker pauses with her hand on the salon's door handle, turning toward the rabbit. The doe is standing outside the building and well back from it, in a group of three others. They all flash Parker nervous looks. She tries the door anyway. Locked.

"I'm not here for an appointment. I'm here to speak to one of your customers, who should be finishing up," she glances at her watch, "any moment."

The rabbit swallows, eyes darting to the salon's windows and back to Parker's face. "We only have one customer right now and we, uh, we close the shop for her."

"We *really* want to give that woman space," a coyote who looks like he stepped off a fashion magazine's cover says, shivering melodramatically. The receptionist shoots him a panicked glare.

Parker sighs. "I commend your caution, but assume I won't hold you liable for my own actions and unlock the door."

"I really don't think…" The receptionist trails off, looking into Parker's eyes. The vixen doesn't use any magic. She doesn't have to. The look is enough. With a soft whimper, the bunny opens the door. "I didn't know you were like her," she mutters.

"I assure you, I am not." Parker heads inside without waiting for a response.

The salon is empty, except for two people. Agent One sits in a chair, holding a hand mirror in front of her face, moving it from side to side critically. A cougar stylist stands behind her, stock still. He gives Parker an alarmed look.

The honey badger keeps moving the mirror. "What do you think?"

"Your next victims will no doubt be enchanted by how well-groomed their destroyer is."

Agent One looks up at her at that and pouts, then stands, handing the mirror back to the cougar and beaming at him. "Thank you, dear. See you in six weeks." She gives him a kiss on the cheek, making him flinch visibly, and heads toward the front door.

Parker leans toward the stylist and says *sotto voce*, "Did she tip you?"

"She doesn't pay. But she didn't hurt me this time," the cougar whispers back, voice strained.

Parker pulls a hundred-dollar bill out of her purse, thrusting it at him and stalking after the honey badger.

"So as I doubt this is a social call, Ms. Parker, what tremendous office emergency requires you to seek out your least favorite operative?" Agent One says as she catches up.

"You were supposed to meet with me this morning." Parker glances at the rest of the staff, who shoot the two women fearful glances as they scurry back inside.

"Oh." The ratel shrugs, grinning. "I must have missed that on the calendar."

"I'm glad it's nothing so petty as you avoiding my meetings because you don't like being chastised."

"Let me guess." Agent One clasps her hands together. "You don't approve of the way I sealed off Test Site Three."

"I can think of few less discreet approaches to 'sealing off' an area than becoming several kilometers high and stomping it hard enough to register a six on the magnitude scale."

"I wasn't asked to be discreet, I was asked to be effective." She waves a hand dismissively. "That place is—was—absolute middle of nowhere, and I did it at night under a new moon. I'd have been all but invisible to higher-flying planes, and there was almost no traffic on the road."

"'Almost' is not 'none.'"

"No. It was two cars, a minivan, and one bus." Agent One tilts her muzzle up toward Parker, leaning in. "I don't have any tires stuck in my teeth, do I? I try to floss, but you know how it is."

Parker grimaces.

"Oh, take the mast out of your ass, Captain." Agent One grins widely, and rests a fiercely clawed hand on Parker's shoulder. "I sometimes think you forget you're not my boss, no matter how much you expect me to act like you are."

"I'm quite aware you don't technically report to me, *Agent One.*" Parker's growl makes the pseudonym sound like an epithet. "But I've been told to keep my attention on Project Maelstrom, and whether we like it or not, that means keeping my attention on you."

"Keep your 'attention' on it." Agent One laughs. "If this is your way of asking *me* for more information about it, I'm afraid I've been given even fewer specifics than you have yet. All I know is what I've known for years. We're going to fuck shit up, and Celestial's shell companies and puppet governments will use it as an excuse to turn the authoritarian knob to 110%." She rolls her eyes. "Assuming the next test proves that insane theory will actually work."

"Based on past tests, it's not insane."

"Mmm-hmm. I wasn't sent to clean up after Black Oak because of how brilliantly successful it was, was I?"

Parker has no response for that, so changes the subject. "What instructions have you been given about the new goddesses?"

"If you don't know, maybe I'm not supposed to tell you."

Parker narrows her eyes.

Agent One raises her hands in mock surrender. "All I'm doing is playing spy, since they're clearly gathering information on us. And I've been asked to report back if they show off divine power more publicly again."

"I trust you're *not* to stop them if they do that."

"I wasn't asked to, but I wasn't asked not to, either." She laughs. "And you'd be first in line to remind me I'm not someone you call in on a stealth mission if you're *not* expecting trouble. Besides, aren't you the one who should be telling me what I should prepare for? They sound disappointingly amateur. An uncontrolled orgy or two and a mouse-monster? Please."

"Moira is the goddess of war. She could kill you more easily than I could, and I assure you I could kill you easily."

"Wouldn't that be fun to test." The ratel looks Parker up and down. From her grin, it's difficult to tell if she's judging the vixen as an opponent or picturing her naked. "But the others?" She licks her lips. "I've always imagined gods taste like Cherry Pop Rocks."

Parker's voice gets sharper. "Let Ms. Lindsay and I handle Moira and her friends without interfering, unless we explicitly tell you otherwise. Once Project Maelstrom is fully in motion, it won't matter what Moira comes up with."

"Still don't work for you," Agent One says in a sing-song voice. "But I promised Darren that I'll give your little lamb chop all the chances in the world, so I'll promise you that, too."

"Splendid." Parker grunts, shaking her head. "As much trouble as these new goddesses have already caused, you're more an embodiment of everything we stand against than any of them."

Agent One's smirk drops. She stops walking, making Parker stop, too. "You know how you make a light look as bright as it can be, Lily?" She leans forward. "You set it against the darkest dark you can find."

Parker purses her lips, remaining silent.

The ratel straightens up, her unsettlingly cheerful grin returning. "Now. It's past lunchtime, and I'm starving. I think I'm in the mood for some tacos." Her grin widens to fully expose her massive fangs. "Or a whole taquería." Cackling, she snaps her fingers and disappears in a puff of luridly multicolor smoke.

Muttering a curse under her breath, Parker strides back toward the local office.

~

Ironheart looks irritated. "At risk of repeating myself, the full details are on a need-to-know basis, Ms. Lindsay." She brings the golf cart to an abrupt stop in front of what Nunwick calls the "on-estate office," a three-story building a mile from the country club with a sweeping view of a valley below. There's construction happening on the valley's floor. Whatever they're building, it's big. When she asks what it is, no one gives her a straight answer, and it frustrates her that she's starting to get used to that.

"Something in that town was so incriminating that you altered the world's collective memory to keep people from finding it. When Moira and her new gods found it anyway, you had all physical evidence of it literally cratered, even though you'd obviously considered it valuable enough to preserve beforehand." Diana meets the lioness's eyes defiantly, no small trick given that they're walking side by side. "So at risk of repeating *myself*, I have no chance at persuading them to give you even a sliver of trust if you won't give *me* one."

"I'm sure you appreciate that we've given you far more than a mere sliver of trust already." They walk inside, heading toward Diana's office. Temporary office, she reminds herself. Even though they assigned her a personal secretary, a petite white-furred wolf girl who nods to both of them as they walk past. Even with her name engraved onto a small, tasteful sign on the door, bestowing her with the zero-meaning title "Advisory Consultant."

It's been three weeks since they gave her this office and a suite at the estate's private on-grounds resort, and she's still repeatedly struck by how *posh* it all is: the club, the hotel, even the office. She can't say it isn't nice, but she's more sure than ever it's not *her* kind of nice. While the modern, austere style of Parker's home office at Celestial Private Equity isn't hers, either, she'd have preferred it, and she's noticed that Parker doesn't spend much time here at the estate. Ironic that a former pirate captain's aesthetic is so restrained compared to her boss's.

"I do." Diana holds the office door open for Ironheart, and

closes it behind her as she heads to the huge mahogany desk and sits behind it. Ironheart takes a facing chair.

"So." She rests her hands on the desk and laces her fingers together, hoof nails clacking softly. "Moira was betrayed by the old gods, exiled by them, and abandoned by them. You left her in the dark about your existence until she started using her powers again and revealed herself as a potential threat. And now, you expect me to go to her and say, 'These new gods who've come together to keep mortals from overthrowing the natural order, to make sure your old dream of rebellion stays extinguished, need you to trust them.'"

"You're surely the best positioned among us to assuage Lady Moira's trust issues."

"Right here, right now, you're the best positioned to assuage *mine.*"

Ironheart's tail lashes. At length, she sighs. "Very well, Ms. Lindsay. We intend to break the mythological cycle. The machine we're building in the valley below is part of that project, and the Black Oak site was a test for that machine. We believe this project will enable Mr. Nunwick to end the threat of the Turning once and for all, and it's within close reach now. We keep details secret from mortals—even those who work with us—because they might cause a level of panic that, in the absolute worst case, would become difficult for us to control."

"What happened to the people who lived in Black Oak?"

Ironheart doesn't answer until the sheep fixes her gaze on the lioness, and the staring contest goes on for an uncomfortable length of time. "Sometimes sacrifices are necessary for the greater good, Ms. Lindsay. What we've learned from Black Oak should allow us to have far fewer negative externalities in production. The next, largest test is imminent, and we believe we have all issues solved."

Diana's the one who finally looks away. "And what do you expect me to say if—when—Moira asks what I know?"

The lioness stands, smoothing down her skirt. "I expect you to use your judgment. If telling the truth serves your purpose, tell the truth. Your lack of full trust in our methods and motives makes your case for us that much stronger."

"It doesn't help my case that you and Mr. Nunwick so clearly see me as a means to an end, Ms. Ironheart."

She walks to the office door, and looks back at the sheep with a raised brow. "You see us the same way, Ms. Lindsay. After all, you came to us." She closes the door behind her.

Diana stares straight ahead for a few seconds, then drops her head to the desk.

Sometimes sacrifices are necessary.

Rhiannon had been dismayed, on that first trip to Briley's farm, at realizing she *wasn't* bothered by the thought there might have been someone in her old office building when she brought it down. But Diana had been through that in her first few minutes of divinity, when she'd point-blank flattened someone under a hoof—and she'd barely had time to process what she'd done before people dropped to their knees around her.

Are you horrified because you're not horrified?

She'd told herself that moment had shaped her into being more benevolent, more mindful, later. They'd all had their moments, and they'd all learned.

But it hadn't helped any of her worshippers. It hadn't helped William.

Taking a deep breath, she straightens up. All right, she *doesn't* fully trust anyone at Celestial. Certainly not Ironheart or Nunwick. Not even Parker, even if she's somehow come to distrust the vixen the least. She has to assume she's lost the full trust of Moira, Rhiannon, and Hazel now, too; she can hardly ring them up and ask how much they know about Black Oak.

So the first step is getting the information she needs, even if that means going around Celestial's executives.

She starts to pick up her phone, then sets it down and walks out of her office to her secretary's desk. "Daisy, I need your help with a tiny project. Just between us."

The wolf looks up, wagging her tail once. "What's that, Ms. Lindsay?"

"Remember when I asked you last week about the project Ms. Ironheart and Mr. Nunwick were working on in a town called Black Oak?" She sees the wolf's ears dip, but keeps speaking, holding up a hand. "I understand that they're keeping details of that rather close and that you're not privy to everything they have, but..." She lowers her voice, as if she were bringing the wolf in on a secret. "I can't do what they've brought me on board to do without a little more information."

Daisy swallows nervously. "Like what?"

"A list of test sites related to that project. I need to know how many tests there were before, how many are left, and where the next one takes place."

"I don't think I can do that, ma'am." Daisy shakes her head firmly, causing some of her hair to dislodge and flop in front of one eye. "That's...very high level, like executive-only level."

The sheep touches a hand to her chest. "You know I'm supposed to have the highest level access. As a consultant, nothing should be off limits." Nothing in her contract says that, but as far as she knows, Daisy hasn't read that contract.

The wolf brushes back her hair, biting her lip. "I'm sure that's true, Ms. Lindsay, but..." She looks around as if someone might be watching, and lowers her voice to a strained whisper. "When I say that's top level, I mean it. Top. Level. You understand?"

Diana had quickly learned a pillar of Celestial corporate culture involved tacitly denying that the people running the show are literal gods. The majority of workers, even here on Nunwick's estate, don't know, and keep any suspicions to themselves. Those that do know quickly learn to never talk about it. She's never heard anyone but other gods use the term. Daisy, though, has worked directly with Ironheart and Nunwick before, even though she seems to still be fully mortal. She has to know, even if she doesn't want to say it.

Diana, though, has no such compunction. "You mean only for gods."

Daisy's eyes widen. She nods, barely imperceptibly.

For Daisy, the world disappears, leaving nothing but her and the goddess. The black sheep, divinely beautiful, divinely terrible, stares impassively down at her from a great height, the tiny wolf gaping at hooves taller than she is.

Crouching, Diana plucks the wolf up between two fingers, holding her in front of her muzzle. Daisy's eyes are as wide as saucers now, tail tucked meekly between her legs.

Diana smiles, showing the tips of teeth that could crush tanks like tinfoil. "Gods like me, little one." She blows Daisy a kiss—

—and abruptly the world's back to normal, Diana standing demurely in front of her secretary's desk, hands folded. Daisy slips out of her office chair to her knees, staring shell-shocked up at the sheep.

"That list, please, Daisy?"

Taking a shuddering breath, the wolf climbs back into her seat and starts rapidly typing.

By the time Diana sits down at her desk again, there's an email waiting for her, with a short, cryptic spreadsheet attached to it— columns of dates, times, location codes, and site numbers. Only six rows.

She's seen the location codes before on internal Celestial documents. Isn't there a lookup tool on the company intranet? She clicks around until she finds it, then enters the first location code, Test Site Zero, dated well over two thousand years ago. That predates the Order of Caeles by...a lot, doesn't it? Hmm. The lookup tool shows her ocean, the north side of a relatively narrow intercontinental channel. What?

The next two locations, the first from four centuries ago and the second from merely eighty years ago, are equally puzzling, but at least they're on land. She frowns. Are these towns that no longer exist? Did she have her memory of them wiped along with the rest of the world?

The *fourth* row, though, Site Three: that's dated about three months ago. And the location code is where Black Oak had been.

The next date, on the next-to-last row, is in the future, barely a week away. Fresno, a city of about a hundred thousand, in California's Central Valley. Hasn't it been in the news recently? Yes, she remembers reading an article in the actual, printed newspaper she had delivered for a while at her mountain home. All about how it had become an orderly, crime-free paradise thanks to turning virtually all government functions over to private corporations. It had sounded suspiciously like Celestial's work then; she can't imagine more definitive confirmation than this. Surely, they don't expect *that* test to do...whatever the test in Black Oak did, though? Magically making the world forget about a tiny town in the middle of nowhere is one thing, but making it forget about a city that tens of millions of people have heard of seems like much more of a challenge.

The last row has a blank site number column and a date about three months from now—and its location is Nunwick's estate.

Diana sighs, turning off the computer. She has no reason to think Moira and company have this information, but she thinks she'd better assume that they do. Which means they're going to be at that next test, probably trying to stop it.

Which means *she* needs to be there. And she has one week to figure out whose side she'll be on.

twenty-six
an orderly, crime-free paradise

As Moira drives up, what Stetson mistook for a multi-lane toll entrance turns out not to be a toll entrance at all. The lanes aren't divided between FastPass tags and cash; they're divided between residents and visitors. Fresno has erected a city gate. The WELCOME TO FRESNO sign spanning all the entrance lanes features NorthStar and Third Eye logos along with the city seal.

"Well, *this* isn't ominous." Hazel looks out from the back seat. Moira grunts, scowling, and pulls into the visitor lane.

The bored-looking tiger guard barely glances at them. "Welcome to Fresno. IDs, please."

Moira changes her scowl to an artfully confused smile. "Now, what's all this, sir?"

"You give me your IDs, I run them and give them back with passes for use within city limits. Faster and easier, gets you everywhere you're supposed to be."

"Supposed to be," Moira echoes. "I see."

He gives her an expectant look. She glances at the others, and holds out her hands for their licenses. When she passes them to the guard, he turns to the other side of the gate house, feeding them into a scanning machine.

"Third Eye has got to have a dozen bulletins out on us by now," Rhiannon murmurs.

The guard turns back to Moira. "How long will you be in town for?"

Moira flashes an unsettlingly manic grin at the tiger. "Depends on how much fun we're having."

He gives her a skeptical look, but seems to get lost in her eyes, freezing with a blush creeping over his ears. He clears his throat, nodding, and hands the licenses back to her, along with four new cards. "I've, uh, put a seven-day expiration on these, so if you're in town longer than a week you'll have to come back to a clearance office. Thank you, ma'am."

"Oh, thank *you*." She hands the cards back to the others and drives on. "There. No alarms."

"Is that because you charmed him?" Rhiannon pats the hare's shoulder. "I'm so proud of you for not eating him."

"I *can* deal with problems diplomatically." She checks out the new card. The label identifies it as a "BlueGuard® QuickPass™," with her photo, name, species, and gender printed on a light blue background, issuance and expiration dates, and a QR code.

"I've never been to Fresno before." Hazel looks out the window. If "nothing in particular" had a platonic archetype, this view would be it: a parallel frontage road, yellowing grass, what might be an almond orchard. "It looks dry, brown, and flat."

"It's also hot," Stetson notes.

"Awesome." She turns to Rhiannon. "You're *sure* the event tonight is in Fresno."

"As sure as I can be. I just hate that it took me that long to figure out the first event was Môrdinas."

Moira shakes her head. "We both know you'd have been faster at finding it if I hadn't kept arguing with you. It's not your fault I'm stubborn. It just seemed so…long ago, compared to all the others."

Rhiannon nods. "It was."

After about thirty seconds, they cross an overpass, and the edge of the city appears on the horizon. "That's bigger than I expected it to be, considering Black Oak."

"Over a hundred thousand people. They can't just wipe Fresno off the map and make the world forget about it." Stetson's ear flags, and he looks at Moira. "Can they?"

"Never say never with divinity, but the more memory of a place the world has, the more monumental a feat erasing it becomes." Moira turns off onto a long exit ramp and turns left onto Peach Avenue, following signs for the Fresno-Yosemite International Airport, a name that sounds decidedly aspirational.

It's another couple of minutes before she pulls into the Hampton Inn parking lot. At check-in, the vixen desk clerk asks for their QuickPass cards, not IDs. When she scans Stetson's, she looks up sharply, then down at her screen again. "So…you three are staying in one room, Ms. Leannán, and Mr. Halbach is in the other?"

"No, Mr. Halbach and I are staying in one room."

The vixen hesitates before nodding. "I've checked you two, Ms. Leannán and Mr. Halbach, into room 139, and you two, Ms. Harcourt and Ms. Doran, into room 237."

Hazel lifts a brow. "We can't get adjacent rooms?"

"No," she says apologetically, gesturing at the QuickPass cards. "Blue and orange."

Moira squints. Rhiannon and Hazel's cards have the pale blue background hers does, but Stetson's is orange.

"Carnivore and herbivore." Hazel narrows her eyes. "What, is housekeeping going to check?"

"Herbivore guests aren't permitted on carnivore guest floors without being accompanied by at least one carnivore guest."

Moira clenches her fist by her side. "So I can't leave my room without Mr. Halbach acting as a chaperone."

"Those are the regulations we're required to follow now." The vixen hands them their keycards. "The elevators are past the breakfast nook and down the hallway. Enjoy your stay."

Moira grabs her pair of cards, glowering. Rhiannon takes the other two.

After they check the cards work on the appropriate doors, they meet in Hazel and Rhiannon's room. The elevator won't let them choose Moira and Stetson's floor until Stetson taps his QuickPass against the control panel; there's no such protection for herbivore floors, apparently. Hazel's fuming as much as Moira is. "I'd read Fresno had been piloting some new 'anti-crime technology' bullshit, but this is a whole new level."

"Celestial's piloting it, you mean." Rhiannon crosses her arms. "A high-tech way to enforce that natural order. It's incredible how much oppression people will submit to if you convince them it's for their own good."

"It can't be a coincidence that this is their next test site." Moira shakes her head. "But what's the connection?"

"Suppose what happened to Black Oak isn't what's *supposed* to happen."

"And what happened to Môrdinas." Hazel scoffs. "And what probably happened to the test sites in between."

"But that's what I'm getting at. Suppose..." Rhiannon sighs. "Suppose Parker was right and we created a chaos nexus. What if they're trying to create an *order* nexus?"

Moira frowns. "If things are ordered enough, the test might be a success."

"Right."

"That's disturbing, but it's logical." She chews on her lip, then stands up. "Let's go for a walk."

Rhiannon's decoding of the location code gives them far more precision than they had in Black Oak. What they find, about fifteen minutes' walk from the hotel down a well-worn road lined with nondescript warehouses, is: a nondescript warehouse. There's no signage on it apart from a building number. The parking lot stands empty.

Moira puts her hands on her hips for a few seconds, studying it critically. "It looks abandoned."

Rhiannon walks along the property's edge, closing her eyes. Then she opens them again and shakes her head. "I can't sense any power lines, any data lines, any...anything."

"So this *isn't* the right location?"

"The geocodes on their list are precise down to, like, quarter-acres or so. If it isn't this warehouse, it's a neighboring one."

"But they know you're—uh, we're—on to them, thanks to Black Oak," Stetson says. "They might have scuttled this location."

"That sounds very spy movie of you. If the location is like Black Oak's, they couldn't move somewhere on short notice, though."

Hazel lifts her brows. "If the location is like Black Oak's, it's not *in* that warehouse, it's *under* that warehouse."

"Oh." Rhiannon lifts her brows. "Yeah. We still can't explain the lack of power or signal here."

"Hmm. Maybe." She looks around. "Or it could be a different building." She sighs. "And I don't know how close it needs to be to this exact spot for whatever it is they're doing to work. It could be a radius of miles."

Moira looks at Stetson. "So if we think like spy movies..."

Should we think like spy movies? "Well. Um. So." He rubs his chin. "Assume they think you have a copy of their list, but it's too late to relocate the whole operation. What they're going to want to do is find out if you'd cracked the code and gotten us here, to know if they *do* have to expect divine resistance."

She frowns. "That makes sense. Even if it's not a trap, it's going to be alarmed."

"With no power?" Rhiannon says.

"There are magical alarms, just like magical traps. If we haven't set one off yet, we will if we keep poking around."

"So what do we do? Getting giant and looking around like you did in Black Oak isn't the right answer if we're trying to be stealthy."

Hazel snorts. "I hate stealthy."

Moira shakes her head. "Honestly, I don't know. We may well have to wait until they start firing up their machinery, and locate the source then."

"That's cutting it real close."

"I know."

Stetson's tail curls. "Won't that be extremely dangerous? Maybe not to you three, but..."

"We'll keep you safe," Hazel says, looking uncharacteristically earnest.

The coyote nods hesitantly. "But there's also...well, everyone else."

Moira's tone is matter-of-fact. "They're why we're here."

Rhiannon folds her arms. "What do we do for the rest of the day?"

Stetson ventures a small grin. "I guess we enjoy beautiful Fresno."

Fresno *is* beautiful, but in a creepy way that gets creepier the more they drive around. There's no litter anywhere, not even cigarette butts; it's as clean as a theme park. No sign of any homelessness— no tents, no panhandlers. Every corner sports plainly visible security cameras, with small but stern signs promising fines and potential jail time for even the slightest offense. Checkpoints pop up for both drivers and pedestrians seemingly at random.

Bogglingly, it takes more than one try to find a restaurant that will seat them all together, even over Stetson's increasingly self-conscious protests and Moira's increasing temptation to do something Rhiannon would rightfully yell at her over. They end up grabbing fast food at the edge of a herbivore district; people who wouldn't have blinked twice at a "mixed-species" group a couple of years ago give them suspicious side-eyes.

Finding a bar that lets them in together takes two tries, too. After the hoity-toity one turns them away with a transparent excuse about "being too crowded," Moira shakes her head. "Let's look for a dive bar."

"Seriously?" Rhiannon eyes her. "You think the rowdy guys will be nicer?"

"I think they're less likely to give a damn." Moira shrugs. "Or more likely to start a fight."

"So either way, we win!" Hazel bounces. Rhiannon covers her face a moment, and goes along with a resigned expression.

As it turns out, though, Moira's right. The Bosun's Brig isn't checking QuickPasses any more than they're checking IDs. The crowd inside is thoroughly mixed and, yes, nobody seems to give a damn. Unfortunately, it's karaoke night. She sees the stage, groans, and starts to turn around.

"Oh, come on," Hazel says. "They're fun. Are you going to tell me you don't like singing?"

"I don't like *bad* singing." But Hazel's already wheeled to the bar, Rhiannon and Stetson behind her. Sighing, Moira follows.

It takes standing at the bar for nearly ten minutes before the bartender acknowledges them. Sort of. The bear looks right past both Rhiannon and Hazel, but his eyes linger on Moira. He nods, but goes to check on two wolves on their third or fourth beers.

Rhiannon glances at Moira. "Why aren't we letting a little divine aspect show again?"

"To get a beer?"

"You've been doing that for the last how many thousand years?"

"I thought you wanted me to stop setting bad examples."

"Next up is...Donna!" a voice crackles over the PA. A middle-aged cat woman steps onto the stage and starts up the lowest energy take on "Born This Way" imaginable, remaining stock still but for her tail, staring fixedly at the lyrics screen.

Moira rubs her face.

The bear ambles over, but speaks to Stetson instead of Moira. "What'll you have?"

"I'll have a Tullamore Dew, neat, and..." He motions to the others. The bear finally looks at them.

Moira gives him a death glare. "Double rye on the rocks."

"A daiquiri," Rhiannon says.

"Can't do frozen drinks."

"Straight up's fine."

He looks confused.

"Order a drink whose name is the recipe," Stetson whispers.

The squirrel cautiously says, "Rum and Coke?"

He gives her a thumbs-up and heads off to make drinks.

Donna finishes anesthetizing Gaga, and an androgynous, tipsy-giggly rat introduced as Bobby takes her place. He squeaks through the first few lines of "Perfect," but gains enough confidence to start belting them out, mostly on key, even daring to look at the audience for long seconds at a stretch before glancing back at the lyrics.

When the bartender returns with their drinks, Rhiannon leads them toward an empty table, against a wall near the stage. Its accessibility is likely more accident than intentional design, but it works. Speaking of that: "Where did Hazel go?"

Stetson blinks, looks around, then points. "Still at the bar." As he says that, the bartender hands her a pale pink drink, and she wheels their way.

"So." The coyote waits for everyone else to get settled, sips his beer, and gives Hazel an amused look. "I confess I didn't peg you for liking karaoke. Are you going to sing for us, Lady Hazel?"

"Me? Hell, no. What I like to do is get someone else in the group up singing. Preferably the one who seems the most angry about being there."

Moira eyes Hazel. "I am *not* going up on stage."

"Aw, come on. The goddess of love and war, singing in a shitty dive bar? That's the stuff legends are made of."

"Love, not music. For all you know I sing like a frog."

"I bet you don't. Love and music go together like peanut butter and banana. I'm just trying to decide if you'd choose hard rock, angry punk, or take a left turn into hip hop."

Stetson rubs his ear. "Wouldn't Moira singing anything emotional risk turning the bar into an orgy? Possibly a violent one?"

Hazel's eyes widen. "Yes!" She sounds positively thrilled

"I can control that," Moira snaps, "but there would still be... effects. Trust me, it's a bad idea."

"Totally." The pika nods. "I've already put your name in."

Rhiannon chokes back a giggle.

Moira straightens up. "Go take it out!"

"Oh come on. If you do it, I'll do it," the squirrel says. "We can figure out our songs now."

She shakes her head. "I'll sing a love song, because I literally can't help it, and it won't be—it's not the song that's important as much as—" She takes a deep breath, putting her hands flat on the table. Is she looking at Hazel and Rhiannon in particular? "What's the expression, opening cans of worms?"

Hazel tilts her head, clearly confused.

"And our next performer is…Moira!" the PA crackles.

Moira glares at Hazel. The pika shrugs, grinning.

The karaoke DJ, a middle-aged lynx dressed like he's ready for a night at the disco, glances around the room. "Don't be shy!" The rest of the audience looks around, too, a few starting to chant her name.

"Go on," Rhiannon urges.

A series of quick expressions Stetson isn't sure how to interpret flashes across Moira's face. He expects her to just stay put, force the DJ to go on to the next victim, but she doesn't. She knocks back the rest of her double old fashioned in one gulp and stands up, walking toward the stage.

"Come on up. Wow, you're tall."

"I am." She crosses her arms.

"So, Moira. You didn't write down what you were going to sing."

"No, that I didn't." She shakes her head. "Cue up 'To Make You Feel My Love.'"

The lynx motions for the audience to clap. Some do. Some hoot instead. He heads back to the DJ console. "Which version?"

"This one." She snaps her fingers. The stage lights dim except for a spotlight on her, and a spare arrangement of the song, just a piano and guitar, begins. He jumps back from his DJ console, eyes wide.

"I did not have 'folk' on my bingo card," Hazel murmurs.

Moira takes the microphone off the stand, walking a few steps away as the intro bars play, facing the audience.

She starts to sing. *"When the rain is blowing in your face…"*

Her voice is a pure mezzo-soprano, achingly beautiful, wrenchingly sincere. She doesn't look at the lyrics screen at all. She looks at the audience directly, imploring, unguarded, raw.

Most of the bar-goers except for ones close to the stage have been ignoring the karaoke, the usual parade of timid lyric reciters and drunken belters and amateur impressionists. This is something else entirely. By the time she's through the second stanza, everyone in the place, including the bartender, has come to a stop, watching, feeling her eyes locked on them as if she's singing to them and them alone.

Moira's voice rises powerfully on the bridge. As she sings, Rhiannon's smile fades. She blinks a few times, gripping the table and going pale under her fur.

Stetson tilts his head, looking at her, then around the bar as Moira continues to sing. As good as the performance is, Rhiannon isn't the only one who looks unaccountably poleaxed. The coyote rubs the back of his ear. Is the air sparkling? He's watching literal magic happen, isn't he? Again.

Moira finishes the song with a repeat of the first stanza, almost whispering the last two lines, eyes closed, bittersweet smile brighter than the spotlight.

As the notes fade, there's scattered clapping rising into more thunderous applause—mixed with the thumps of dozens of people dropping to their knees. Just as many embrace one another in kisses.

Moira walks back to the microphone stand, but pauses, fishing her QuickPass card out of her pocket and holding it up. "Don't let anyone tell you what you have to be, where you're allowed to go, just because of what you are. Don't let them reduce you to a code on a card. All the city belongs to all of you. I love you all. Love one another." She throws her card up in the air and it bursts into flame, quickly burning to ash.

A nervous, then raucous, cheer goes up from the crowd. She drops the microphone and hops down.

"I think we'll take a break," the lynx mutters hoarsely. "I need to make a long overdue call." He hurries off behind the stage, pulling out his phone.

As Moira threads her way around new worshippers—this time with a smile, not a frown, letting her fingers brush the hands held out to her—Hazel bounces in her seat, clapping. "Damn, if you ever get tired of the goddess thing, I think you have a second career ahead of you."

Rhiannon takes a deep, shuddering breath. "I don't even like that song," the squirrel gets out, and then bursts into tears. She dashes toward the restroom just as Moira reaches the table. The hare watches her with an empathetic, sadder smile.

Hazel's smile evaporates. "What the hell?"

"I did warn you. I don't know whether to be angry with you or thank you for tricking me into lighting a spark, but for now, I'll go with the thanks." She raps the table. "Back in a minute."

Stetson turns, watching Moira catch up with Rhiannon outside the restroom. He can't hear the conversation, but Moira's expression is...sweet. Sympathetic. She draws the squirrel into a gentle hug after about ten seconds.

"Hazel," someone calls from the entrance. Stetson turns just as Moira starts leading Rhiannon back to the table, hand-in-hand, and just as Hazel curses, rolling her chair toward the door.

Stetson gets up, along with most of the rest of the bar's patrons. The floor's littered with abandoned QuickPass cards. It sounds like a party's breaking out on the street.

He cants an ear toward a snippet of conversation from Moira as the hare and squirrel approach. "—going to tell her?"

"I don't—" Rhiannon mutters, and stops. "Whoa. Okay, I guess we've given up on the stealth part of the mission."

"Apparently."

Stetson points at the door. Hazel's already there, talking to a tall black sheep woman in a smart business suit. Even though she's about six feet tall now, rather than the five and a half she'd been, she's unmistakable.

Moira stares, walking out slowly.

Mexican hip-hop music's playing somewhere nearby, and, well, maybe there *is* a touch of orgy here and there. The subtle sparkling in the air expands in a slow-motion wave down the streets. Sirens sound in the distance, but it doesn't feel like a riot.

"Did you just start a rebellion by singing a love song?" Rhiannon murmurs.

"Well. I wouldn't go that far, but it's a good start." She's speaking to the squirrel, but she locks eyes with the sheep.

"Moira," Diana says, raising her voice over the music. "Let's go somewhere quieter and talk. There's not much time."

twenty-seven
starfish

As they walk away from the karaoke bar, Moira realizes the magic she's unleashed is centered on her, not the bar. The crowd doesn't follow the group of goddesses as much as loosely encircle them, growing as they move. Dancing, embracing, kissing. And, yes, there's violence, but it's pointedly directed: checkpoints demolished, guards chased away, cop cars smashed.

Hazel gives Diana a sidelong glance, voicing the obvious question. "How did you find us?"

"I expected you to be here tonight, if not earlier in the week. As for finding you right here, right now?" The sheep spreads her arms, looking exaggeratedly from side to side at the increasingly bacchanalian street party. "I picked up on subtle clues you all might be in the area."

"You *expected* us to be in Fresno?" Rhiannon looks incredulous. "How did you...figure out..." Her eyes widen in shock as she puts it together.

Moira does at the same time. She keeps her voice flat to keep herself from snapping. "She's working with Celestial."

"What?" Hazel's ears lower, and she looks between Moira and Diana. "You—you're on their side? After everything—"

"I'm on the side of not having a war between gods. You understand that's where we're heading, don't you?"

"Do *you* understand Celestial's beta-testing a full corporate dystopia here, and they're hours away from running a crazy mad science project that might wipe this city off the map?"

"Yes, Hazel, actually I do, and I don't want that to happen, either." Diana's voice rises angrily. "I also don't want the literal end of the world to happen."

Moira sighs. "There's a diner close to the hotel that should still be open. If they let us all sit together."

"They will," Diana says curtly.

They walk on without speaking, surrounded by the increasing jubilation of the divine party, and get into Moira's car, driving in uncomfortable silence to the diner.

The joint hasn't been remodeled in going on forty years: peeling tan linen wallpaper, Formica counters, a dark green patterned carpet that tries and fails to hide years of spills. The air smells of grease and burned coffee. There aren't any other customers right now. The sole waitress, a cat woman with short coiffed hair and bags under her eyes, walks over to them, looking between Stetson and the rest. "I'm sorry, we can't..." She stops when Diana flashes her QuickPass card. "Ah, sit anywhere, ma'am. I'll get some menus."

Moira eyes Diana's card. Instead of the blue herbivore or orange carnivore background, hers is steel gray. The sheep puts it away without comment, and strides toward a larger, round booth big enough for all five.

The others sit down with her, leaving her on one end, Stetson closest to her. She looks down and finally addresses him. "So, who are you?"

The coyote smiles up nervously. "I'm Stetson. Nice to meet you."

Diana keeps looking down at him, as if expecting more explanation, until Rhiannon starts speaking. "So the last goddess from Celestial we met lectured us about how we were the real villains, then either turned your high priest into a monster or let him turn into one. She watched him rampage across your neighborhood, killing your worshippers and coming alarmingly close to killing *us* before she ran him through with a sword, letting him literally die in your arms. Then she went back to Celestial and, I presume, helped coordinate the PR campaign vilifying all of us but especially *you* as terrifying cult leaders." The squirrel crosses her arms. "Got any of that wrong so far?"

Diana looks down. "Going to them wasn't easy for me."

"You're half a foot taller and dressing like a corporate VP."

The waitress comes by and pours them all cups of coffee, but some sense of the divine trips when she meets Moira's eyes. She looks around at the other women and starts shaking. "I didn't— what—"

Diana puts her hand gently on the cat's. "Coffee is fine for now, please. Don't be afraid of us."

She nods hurriedly, leaving a tray of sugar packets and artificial creamers.

"I needed to try to understand what they wanted. Why they do what they do, why they believe what they believe." Diana looks around at them. "And I couldn't get that by going back to you."

Hazel starts to snap back, but Moira holds up a hand. "So what do they believe?"

"Do you remember when we went to Hazel and Rhiannon's, the first time I met both of them? When you deified Rhiannon?" Diana tilts her head. "I told you that you were right. The natural order needed to end. You lamented that you'd believed even if you'd lost the battle, you might win the war. That mortals losing their faith in gods might lead to them upending the natural order on their own. But they never did."

Moira nods slowly. "I remember."

"Maybe they would have, if it weren't for the Order of Caeles. And now, Celestial."

Moira's eyes stay locked onto the sheep.

"They believe that mortals *would* upend the natural order on their own, if they were allowed to—but they also believe that would mean the end of this cycle. They think your war, if you'd succeeded, would have ended it, too. And the end of the cycle is the end of the world as we know it."

"So, what, then?" Hazel arches a brow. "Nunwick thinks the way to stop the world from ending is to stop progress?"

"That's not—"

"Yes, it *is.*" Hazel's tone gets uncharacteristically fierce. "I understand wanting to hold on to what you have, even if you're a god. Especially if you're a god. But what kind of world do we have if Nunwick wins?" She slides her QuickPass card across the table. "Walk around Fresno with one of *these* cards. Not yours. See where Stetson can go that we can't. Think about everything that affects. Policing. Businesses. Where you're allowed to live. Where you can bank. What kind of medical services you can get."

Rhiannon cuts in. "What else can these cards tell someone who scans them about us, or will they in the future? Species and gender might only be the start. Who knows what they're already encoding."

"I want to use my power to make the world better, too, but I can't do it if there's no world left to change!" Diana snaps, then shakes her head, taking a sip of the diner's dreadful coffee. "Celestial doesn't know I'm here. As far as I know, they don't know I found out about this test site, or about the previous one."

"Black Oak."

Diana nods to the squirrel. "Yes."

"That wasn't the first time they've done this."

"I know."

"Or the second. Are you seriously here to tell us not to interfere, given what keeps happening?"

"You've already interfered, haven't you? By setting all this chaos in motion, because none of you can help yourselves, the chances of the project going wrong have probably shot up about a hundredfold."

"Well, then," Moira says. "We'd better interfere to stop it completely."

Diana groans.

"Look." Rhiannon spreads her hands. "It doesn't sound like you *know* one way or another. And suppose what they're about to do kills just half the people in Fresno instead of all of them. Would they chalk it up as another failure, or say, 'Wow, fifty percent improvement!' and put a big fat 'X' in the success column? What gives Nunwick—or you, or me—that right?"

Diana slams her hands down on the table, rattling the coffee mugs. *"Being gods!"*

Everyone stares at her now, except Moira, who looks away. She'd love it if people would stop vocalizing fears she's trying to keep to herself.

"We affect mortals on small and large scales everywhere we go, in everything we do." She waves toward an outside window. "No one out there woke up this morning planning to stage a revolution tonight in the form of a street party. We've all treated mortals like they barely matter, and we've *also* all treated them like they're the reason we exist. Both of those attitudes are in our nature now. As many horrific things as Celestial may have done, isn't stopping the end of the world a responsibility worthy of divinity?"

Moira picks up her coffee, sips, grimaces, and dumps in sugar and creamer. "The world's *supposed* to be on a cycle, Diana. Even Daranu never said we should be trying to stop the cycle from turning. That sounds…well, very mortal." She takes another sip. Still crap.

"Prophecy is not destiny."

Rhiannon looks at Diana. "Yet your buddy Nunwick's tripling down on Daranu's whole idea of species being destiny, isn't he? I want to save the world, too, Diana." She waves a hand around expansively. "I want to save it from *this.*"

"I don't want an authoritarian dystopia any more than you do. But if it's a choice between a world that gets worse before it gets better and a world that suffers an apocalypse, let's choose the first." She sighs. "As brutal as it may be, I'd sacrifice a dozen Fresnos to save the rest of creation. Wouldn't you?"

Rhiannon twists a hand in her hair, falling silent.

"Starfish," Stetson mumbles under his breath.

Diana looks down at him.

The coyote sinks into the booth cushions, stammering. "J-just remembering an old parable, the kind of silly trite thing you learn in Sunday school or put on motivational posters. It's about a child walking along a beach after a storm, throwing starfish one by one back into the sea. An adult stops her and says, 'There are so many of them, child. Saving a few of them hardly matters.' So she thinks about that." He looks up at Diana. "Then she picks up another starfish and throws it in the ocean, and says, 'It matters to that one.'"

The sheep frowns, leaning back.

Moira sips more shitty coffee, and looks into the mug, speaking quietly. "Does Celestial know about Briley?"

Diana shakes her head. "They haven't mentioned her, and I haven't told them."

She wants to believe the sheep, but she isn't sure whether she can. Yes, maybe she would sacrifice a dozen Fresnos if she was sure of the outcome. But she isn't. "But you have talked to Nunwick."

"Yes."

"Why, in all this time, hasn't he talked to me?"

Diana shakes her head. "I don't think he trusts you, based on your history. He said I should remember that you chose war over love."

"I chose war *because* of love." Moira closes her eyes. "What do you want, Diana?"

"I've told you, I want—"

She opens her eyes and fixes her gaze on the sheep. "Not what you want in the grand scheme of the universe. What you want from *us,* here and now."

Diana looks nervous for a moment, then steels her gaze. "To let Celestial try. To watch how this test goes."

She drums her fingers on the table. "The location on the list Rhiannon decoded is just an empty warehouse. Do you have the true street address for Celestial's equipment here?"

Diana meets Moira's eyes, remaining silent.

"Do you think we could all take her?" Hazel mutters.

Moira crosses her arms. "You're going to have to meet us half-way," she says to Diana. "You give us the correct address now, and we do what we were going to do all along: wait. If we don't see a little apocalypse starting, we keep waiting. If we do, we stop it."

"Before you do anything—"

"Or," Moira continues in a flat, don't-even-try-to-argue tone, "you fuck off right now, and know that if you stand in my way, I'll end you."

Diana swallows. She looks between Rhiannon and Hazel, who might as well both have steam rising visibly from their ears, then back to Moira. "It's off Olive and Fowler, near the golf course."

Hazel rolls her chair back a fraction, looking at Moira. "So do we...?"

"We keep our word." Moira waves the waitress over. "And get mozzarella sticks."

They've put in a second appetizer order when the sun comes up again.

They all stare out the diner's windows. No, it's still night. But the buildings a block away glow so brightly they're difficult to look directly at, their edges outlined with lightning. As the goddesses watch, the light hops from building to building, bending and flickering.

Moira rises to her paws.

The waitress stops what she's doing, walking toward the window. "What is that?"

The light reaches the buildings across the street. The paint's visibly cracking and peeling, wood weathering, metal rusting. "A very bad sign," Hazel answers, and gives Diana a knife-throwing glare. "Doesn't look like they've changed so much, huh?"

"They—" Diana rises to her hooves, too, horrified. "This is exactly what I was afraid of, that what you'd done tonight would—"

"Fucking don't," the pika snarls. "They know what we did tonight, they have all the same information you have, and they're doing this anyway. *They don't care.*"

Moira glances at Rhiannon. "Where's Olive and—"

"A few blocks southeast. Look for the golf course."

The light arcs across the street, hitting the diner. Abruptly the windows become too bright to look at, and the cat jumps back with a shriek. Moira hurries to her, and the light leaps around the front half of the diner—over both the cat and the hare.

Moira winces. The waitress, though, stumbles, falling against the taller woman. As Moira catches her, she's looking into the face of a much older, frailer, terrified cat. Then she's looking at a cloud of dissolving dust.

Moira's eyes widen, and she looks over at the table—at Stetson —just as the light reaches it. Horrified realization flashes across everyone's face. Stetson scrambles back against the wall.

"No!" The hare leaps for him, even though she has no idea what to do, even though she suspects it's already too late.

Diana, though, moves faster, whirling to tackle the coyote. The light bathes both of them, and they vanish together.

Rhiannon gasps. "Are they…?"

"I don't know," Moira says hoarsely. "We have to go." She takes a deep breath and runs for the door, growing with each step, smashing out of the rapidly-decaying building.

As her vantage point rises, she sees the light flowing into a vortex, spiraling back toward a center point a couple of miles away. It's brighter at the expanding circumference, where it consumes buildings and cars and, at the brightest sparks, people. It hasn't reached downtown yet, but it's taken the freeway they'd come into town on, residential areas, part of the airport, the Hampton Inn they're staying at.

She looks toward the equally giant Hazel and Rhiannon. "Save the rest of the town before it's too late."

Rhiannon gapes. "How?"

"Improvise."

Hazel looks dismayed, but nods. They turn. Moira doesn't wait.

A hundred-foot-high hare in a full run causes earthquakes, buildings ripped up with each step, cars flying, a cloud of destruction behind her. It doesn't matter. The area she's carving a path through has already had its life pulled into the vortex. It's already gone.

As she gets closer to what had been Hank's Swank Par Three Golf Course, the force of the energy around her gets stronger. She's fighting through a hip-high hurricane. The vortex's center forms a flickering sphere of energy, multicolored lightning dancing within;

the sphere encases an intact, unaged, and incongruously normal-looking single-story brick office building. Even though the night's still hot, the ozone-scented wind cuts through her like blades of ice, and the crackling electricity bristles her fur.

She's tempted to stomp on it, to try and end it all quickly. But as little as there may be in creation that can kill a god, she knows better than anyone that other gods can. And she has to know what's in there.

Moira returns to a smaller size—still half again as high as her normal height—and staggers in the gale as it howls around her. From down here, the lightning might as well be the heart of a supernova.

She breaks into a run again, arms braced in front of her. Jeans and T-shirt transform to leather leggings and armor, short sword strapped to her back. Earlier tonight she was, for the first time in far too long, fully the goddess of love. Now, for the first time in even longer, she is fully the goddess of war.

Hitting the sphere feels like hitting electrified barbed wire. Her armor and exposed fur smoke as she barrels toward the building's front door, smashing it with a battering ram kick. She ducks through.

The three NorthStar officers, all wolves, standing closest to it aren't paying enough attention to their post. They're watching something inside. When they hear her crashing entrance, they turn. The one who moves to grab her gets demolished by another kick. One's fast enough to grab his weapon before her huge hand wraps around his face. She catches the other one the same way and slams their skulls together without breaking stride.

They'd been staring at a duplicate of the crazy underground room from Black Oak: the same massive machinery, the same long control console. Now a half-dozen men in lab coats scurry between them all. The machines roar, visibly vibrating, lightning crackling along their housings. Whatever they're doing, they sound ready to explode.

The ominous ray gun is here, too, pointed at the chair in the center of the ritual circle. It's turned on, lightning crackling around it, firing a thick, fuzzy multicolored beam at a scrawny lion in a prison jumpsuit chained to the chair. From his tortured-sounding screams, he's not enjoying the process. Surely that's not Nunwick? His aura is fatally mortal. But someone here—

"I'm telling you, if we don't shut it down, it'll take the whole city," a scientist shouts over the din. He's a lanky fox facing a tall lioness in an immaculate business suit, and he looks terrified. No wonder: the lioness isn't merely angry. She's an angry god.

"The data are more important than the city," the lioness growls back. Then her eyes widen and she looks straight at Moira. The scientists look over at the hare, too. She claps her hands once and gestures. Soldiers pour into the room from both sides, seemingly from nowhere. "Keep her occupied until we finish!"

Moira's a big target, but she's a big target in motion before they open fire. She leaps up at a high angle, vaulting off the nearest, highest machine sideways, spinning midair as she draws her sword. She plummets into the middle of one line of soldiers, sword swinging, and grabs one hapless wolf to use as a shield as his companions fall like wheat under a scythe.

The soldiers aren't quite mortal, but they're not gods, not even demigods. Her sword—and the wolf's corpse—deflect enough bullets to keep her almost unscathed as she mows through the squadron, heading directly for the lioness.

The lightning coursing around the room flickers, and the gun's beam narrows. The lion in the chair goes limp.

The lioness whirls on the hapless fox. "What's happening?"

"We're not drawing anymore!" He punches at a console frantically.

The lioness starts to respond, but Moira lunges, and her sword tip stops a hair's width in front of the other goddess's throat. "What's happening is we've saved you from turning Fresno into another Black Oak," she growls. "You're welcome."

She looks at Moira with undisguised loathing. "You understand nothing," she hisses. She clenches her fists, and abruptly Moira finds herself rocketing backward, crashing into a pump housing with enough force to shatter every bone in a mortal body. As she tumbles down to the floor, stars swim around her vision.

"We've got enough data, Lady Ironheart," she hears the fox say. "Let's go. Please."

Moira gets back to her feet in time to watch all the scientists scurrying madly, two picking up the dead lion from the chair, others hastily turning machines off. She stalks forward. "You're not going anywhere until I get answers."

Another lion walks in front of her: a broad, handsome man in a perfectly tailored business suit. His eyes meet Moira's for a moment, cool, appraising.

"To this day, I don't know what my father saw in you." He claps his hands once. The scientists and the lions all disappear, leaving Moira alone with the corpses scattered around the control room.

Moira furrows her brow, lowering her sword. Not drawing what anymore? What data do they have enough of?

His *father?*

But the noise from the machines isn't fading. It's increasing in volume, in pitch, in vibration. They haven't turned them off. They've set them to self-destruct.

In a flash, Moira's outside the building. The vortex is gone, but the lightning sphere around the building has grown bigger, more violent, sizzling. The ground itself burns, and the flames spread rapidly. The newly aged buildings in all directions are dry tinder.

Shit. She's not a god of fire suppression. A storm, maybe, wind and rain. No, a fire break—

A giantess steps out of thin air, a huge, soot-covered hoof landing in front of the hare. Her hand reflexively goes to her sword hilt as the black sheep crouches, lowering a cupped hand.

Diana's fingers uncurl to reveal Stetson, barely conscious, with new streaks of grey fur. But alive.

Moira pulls the limp coyote into her arms, breathing a relieved sigh, giving him a kiss. He returns it weakly.

"I'm sending you home," she murmurs in his ear. He smiles. She kisses him again, then teleports him away.

Moira steels herself, shifting to Diana's size. "They're gone," the sheep says. "How do we stop it?"

"I don't know. Brute force. You stop the fire." She gets larger. And larger.

Moira steps back, bringing her arms out in front of her. A mile away, a geyser erupts with the force of a newly born river. She moves her hands apart, and the water follows where her hands point, rapids rushing into a curve.

Diana, now dwarfing the hare, brings her hoof down on the building. The lightning warps around her planted foot, racing up her leg, up her whole body. She chokes back a scream, but keeps grinding.

Moira's geyser-river-lake cuts through the land until it meets itself, the two ends crashing together in a wave. As fast as the fire moves, it hasn't reached the water yet, and the moat is too wide to cross.

The lightning is gone, too. Diana collapses. Moira kneels, growing until she's big enough to gather the sheep in her arms, and turns to face downtown.

Rhiannon and Hazel tower over the buildings like mountains. Or they would, except the buildings are at Rhiannon's waist level. *Fresno is levitating.* All of downtown, most of the adjoining neighborhoods. The goddesses saved the city from Celestial's infernal machines by lifting it out of the way.

Well, most of the city. Moira walks toward them, over the ashes of the neighborhood around the golf course, stepping over the moat she created.

Rhiannon and Hazel have spotted her. The buildings and cars and pedestrians slowly lower back down, skyscrapers fusing back to foundations, infrastructure flickering back to life as power and water lines reconnect. There's a lot, a *lot* of screaming and panic, but there's just as much celebration. It's hard to tell how much the mortals understand about what's happened—hell, *she* doesn't understand it all—but it's clear many have figured out that as frightening as the experience was, it saved them from a fate far more horrifying they could literally see coming for them. And they've figured out that the beautiful, impossibly enormous women they're at the paws of did it.

She walks more carefully, joining the other goddesses at downtown's edge, in as clear a space as she can find. Diana's stirring in her arms; she sets her down and helps her stand.

"The levitating was Hazel's idea," Rhiannon says.

"It was a good one."

"I'm almost afraid to breathe at this size," the squirrel murmurs, looking down at the gathering crowds, at news helicopters, at people cheering from rooftops, at tens of thousands on their knees.

Hazel looks down, too, wide-eyed. "We're fully out of stealth mode, huh?"

Moira smiles faintly and nods.

twenty-eight
opinions on plausibility

"Well, the graphic's kind of cool," Hazel says.

Rhiannon crosses her arms, glowering at the cable news broadcast. "'Gods or demons' is lazy. The background is basically all fire and brimstone, so you know what answer they're biased toward even if you don't listen to the talking heads. And they used a halo and a pitchfork, which aren't even the right religion."

"They could be," Hazel points out. "I mean, they're not from *Moira's* religion, but our religions are whatever we say they are."

Diana looks over from the kitchen. They're all in her A-frame mountain cabin, except for Stetson, who's recovering at his own home. And Moira, who's gone out for a walk. Again. She's not sure how Moira's avoiding the spotlight, but as the hare often points out, she's been practicing it for millennia.

As for the rest of them, avoiding the spotlight fell off the table three days ago. None of them had taken care to hide their recent mortal pasts, and reporters had figured out their names within twenty-four hours. It'd taken maybe another day for hot takes to fully infest newsrooms and social media. Gods? Please! Look at where all these young herbivore women were merely two years ago! Whether *young* or *herbivore* or *women* was the key to dismissal depended on who did the dismissing.

And yet, there's the inconvenient truth of watching most of Fresno floating around Rhiannon and Hazel while Moira created a brand-new river to stop a raging wildfire sparked by a soul-eating machine. (Hazel's phrase.) They violated half the laws of physics in front of tens of thousands of witnesses, on dozens of live video streams, both amateur and professional. The people of the world— the churches, the governments, the companies—now *know* beings with divine powers don't just live among them, they're ready and able to perform miracles. Not "an anonymous benefactor saved the orphanage from foreclosure" miracles, or "the face of a saint appeared on this potato" miracles, but full-bore "those earth-shattering stories in ancient religious texts weren't just metaphors" miracles.

And the people of the world, by and large, are not happy about it.

Leaders from a half-dozen modern religions and countless denominations have appeared on news shows to condemn them as demons and false gods, or if they're religious progressives, as a supernatural distraction. A few allow the possibility that the new goddesses are avatars of *their* chosen true god or universal force. One of the biggest churches in modern life has a long tradition of claiming old gods as their saints and angels, and indeed, they've had Saint "Mira," patron of lovers and warriors, for centuries. From what Diana's gathered, there's a debate at the highest levels of that church over whether the immense, stunningly beautiful hare is an apparition of Saint Mira or of the devil.

Parker kept saying that Celestial worked in the shadows, as mortal businessmen rather than divine rulers, because the world no longer wanted true gods. As much as Diana values Moira's counsel, part of her desperately wants Parker's view on, well, everything right now. But she's pretty sure that the events in Fresno—culminating with her standing side-by-side with Moira, Hazel, and Rhiannon—qualify as what a former manager of hers dubbed a "CLM," a career-limiting move.

The front door of the cabin opens. Moira steps in, carrying a box of donuts and a quart "to go" container of coffee.

Hazel looks over. "You went to a Dunkin' Donuts?"

She sets the boxes down on the kitchen table. "I want sugar," she says. "I brought enough to share."

"It's the 'going out in public without causing a national news story' part I want to ask about."

Moira shrugs, going to the kitchen and getting a mug. "If I don't do anything divine, I'm just another tall red-haired bunny woman."

Rhiannon snorts.

The hare sits down with her coffee and munches on the donut, then licks a spot of cream off her nose and frowns. "So, I've been trying to disprove your theory about Daranu being Nunwick's father," she says to Hazel.

"You know it fits," Hazel retorts. "How could a mortal have raised himself up to be a god? He didn't. He's a demigod. Why didn't he get in touch with you when he started Celestial? Because he knows you from back in the old days and doesn't like you. What's the connection to Môrdinas? It was his temple Briley saw that first astronomical clock thing at."

"I think Hazel's right." Diana worries she's about to share secrets she shouldn't, violating some cosmic NDA, but this is mostly conjecture. Albeit conjecture she's damn sure of. "I think Nunwick —whatever his original name was—found a way to create an ascension machine, to turn mortal life into divine power. He turned himself from a demigod into a god. From what he said, the new versions of the machine are about collecting even more power, but without killing all the mortals around it."

Hazel grunts. "Not so good with that part, still."

"The end game is what?" Moira paces, waving a jelly donut. "Trying to stop the cycle from turning. How?"

"Making himself even stronger," Rhiannon suggests. "Sometimes the simple answers are the right ones."

"Maybe it's a weapon." Diana gestures at Moira. "She said they had someone else strapped to the chair and were shooting energy at him, and it killed him."

"That doesn't make it a weapon, it makes him a sacrifice to mad science. They have to make sure that when Nunwick's sitting in that chair, it does what it's supposed to. How? They run tests."

Diana winces.

Hazel rubs her ear. "How does Nunwick making himself more powerful help break the mythological cycle? Or is it just all about him?"

Shit. Is that it? Surely, it can't be it. "It might if he can make himself into the *new* Daranu," Diana says slowly. "If he becomes a creator god—*the* creator god—he might have the power to set new rules. To literally weave them into creation."

Hazel frowns. "If Daranu could do that, why didn't he?"

"Because he didn't believe it was his choice to make. He was all about the natural order, for both good and bad—and maybe the cycle turning is part of that."

"But his son thinks it *is* his choice, so he's going to just fuck it all up? Great."

"Assuming we're reading it right. I just don't..." Moira looks down at her coffee cup. "He said he didn't know what his father saw in me, but what Daranu saw in me was a betrayal. I'm still here because he never forgave me."

"Maybe he meant what his father saw in you before," Rhiannon says softly, reaching for a donut.

"Or we've got part of this all wrong." Hazel reaches for a donut, too, and she and Rhiannon grab the same chocolate frosted at the same time. The pika grins and takes one next to it. Diana catches the squirrel's faint blush, but she doesn't think Hazel does.

"I don't think you can wait for those answers." Diana pours herself some coffee. "Earlier on, Celestial was trying to manage Moira's re-emergence as a minor PR crisis. Keep pictures to the tabloids, tamp down enthusiasm for her message, reinforce theirs. But you all..." She clears her throat. "*We* have the world's attention right now in a way that hasn't happened in, well, possibly ever."

Hazel finishes her donut, licking off her fingers, and glances sidelong at Diana. "So now you think we should go on the offensive against Celestial? I thought your whole point in returning to us was talking us out of that."

"My point was trying to stop a war between gods. It still is." She shakes her head, gets up, and adds a splash of Irish cream to her coffee as she keeps speaking. "So no, that's not what I said. I don't see how going on the offensive brings them to the table."

"You saw what they did in Fresno," Rhiannon protests.

"What happened there wasn't what they intended." She holds up a hand. "And, yes, I know that they could have stopped it and didn't, and…" She shakes her head. Ironheart wouldn't have stopped, she doesn't think. But Parker? Even Nunwick?

"Yeah, and." The squirrel shakes her head. "They could have and didn't. That tells me all I need to know." She heads to the kitchen, too, and just pours a glass of the Irish cream.

Diana sits down again and slumps in her seat. She doesn't want Rhiannon to be right. Dammit, Lily.

"You still don't know which side to be on?" Hazel walks into the kitchen as Rhiannon leaves, leans on the counter, pours about half a glass of the Irish cream, then fills it up the rest of the way with Irish whiskey before heading back to her seat.

"I still don't want there to be sides."

Moira looks between her coffee and the others' drinks, shrugs, and gets up to pour herself a glass of the whiskey. "Does Celestial? They never told you Nunwick started as an old demigod. If they haven't technically lied, they've been damn selective with the truth."

"They don't have any more reason to trust me than I do them. And as much as I disliked Ms. Parker when we met, she's been a good mentor."

"I don't doubt a better one than I've been."

"That's not what I—"

"You laid into me for that the second time we met, and you were right. I'm still not that good at it." She knocks back a generous swig of whiskey.

"No," Diana admits with a soft laugh. "You're not. But for all your mortally dangerous bad temper, you have a good heart. And the goal you've always wanted is equity. A fair and just world."

"Ah, so I'm also incredibly naïve for a god."

"Maybe. But maybe that's what gods need to be."

"What if the prophecies are all way more metaphorical than Nunwick—and us—have been reading them?" Rhiannon looks to Hazel. "I mean, what you read to me a while ago was all monsters and fire and world-upending battles between gods. The death of the old gods, the rise of new ones, literally everything being reset."

Hazel nods. "Yeah."

Diana can't keep herself from sounding exasperated. "Which is why I keep beating the drum for stopping the apocalypse first, even if that means helping Celestial. *Then* we can worry about fixing their dystopia."

"No, that's the thing." Rhiannon spreads her hands. "Except for our 'chaos node' thing, there haven't been literal monsters over the centuries, and despite Parker's warnings, we haven't seen another one since. We've seen mortals screwing up the world without any magical or divine assistance. Hell, that's what we're seeing now, even *with* Celestial. So maybe we can't rely on these prophecies as some kind of ultimate guidepost. They were all written by mortals, not gods, right?"

Moira nods. "Of course."

"So what if we're *past* all those myths and prophecies and folk tales, and in uncharted territory? Those stories end with Moira's exile, hand-wave about the gods fading away, and then 'something something the cycle turns.' Nothing about Briley being here. Nothing that *remotely* suggests Celestial being here. Nothing that suggests *us* being here."

Diana shakes her head. "The 'something something' is the monsters and the fire and world-ending battles between gods. Okay, we've only seen one monster so far, but in Black Oak and Fresno, we've seen magical, all-consuming fire. And in Fresno, we literally had a battle between gods."

"So we might be playing out the prophecies whether we mean to or not." Moira rubs her face.

"We might be. And worse, we don't really know what part any of us are playing, or what part Celestial is."

Hazel throws her hands in the air. "So what the hell do we do? If we sit on our asses, Celestial's going to make damn sure the world sees *us* as the monsters, and ones only companies they secretly control can deal with."

Moira knocks back the rest of her whiskey. "We can't go back into the shadows, but maybe we can drag them out into the sunlight with us." She stands up.

"What's that mean?" Hazel turns to watch Moira as the hare walks toward the television. The cable channel's moved on to a news talk show. The host, a slim cheetah woman, faces an in-studio guest—a bespectacled, professorial mouse—across a table. He's pontificating at her about the implausibility of gods existing at all, much less appearing as giants, in *Fresno* of all places. And, why, one of them had a wheelchair!

Moira crouches by the TV and walks toward it, still hunched over, disappearing in a burst of static. Then she walks onto the show's set from stage left, now in the diaphanous silver dress she'd worn on their visit to Black Oak.

The host stands quickly, eyes wide; the guest pushes his chair back, cowering. Exclamations and gasps from the crew come over the live feed; someone audibly says, "Holy shit."

"A woman has just—just appeared, teleported, into the studio," the host says, a slight tremor in her voice. "As incredible as that is to say."

Moira walks behind the professor, who tries to shrink away from her in the non-magical sense. She puts a hand on his shoulder. "I don't mean to steal your show," she says. "But I have opinions on how plausible I am."

He opens his mouth, but barely manages a hoarse squeak.

"Steve, could we roll the Fresno tape for a few seconds, on..." The cheetah points at Moira.

The wall monitor behind them flicks on, showing a helicopter shot from that evening in Fresno, one centered on Moira, the sprawling landscape behind her. Part of Diana and Rhiannon are in the frame, but even as far back as the camera is, it's not far enough to capture all four immense women without panning.

Moira looks at the screen, too. "That's not a flattering shot, is it? In my defense, that was one of the more stressful evenings I've had in a couple of thousand years."

The cheetah woman looks between the hare in-studio and the monitor, tail starting to twitch. "You're really her. Really *here*."

"I am." She turns back and flashes a million-watt smile at the cheetah woman. "My name is Moira."

Professor Mouse manages a weak splutter, staring up. "Are...are you seriously claiming to be Moira, the ancient goddess of love and war?"

Moira looks down. "Are you seriously claiming I'm not?" She stretches out an arm. There's a sparkling blur, and the now two-inch-tall professor appears on her palm. He looks around wildly, squealing. The camera operator has the presence of mind to zoom in on him, then back out far enough to capture Moira's upper half.

Rhiannon murmurs, "Oh, don't eat him," at the same time Hazel murmurs, "Eat him eat him eat him." Rhiannon gives Hazel a look. Hazel returns a sorry-not-sorry grin.

"Please—oh, god. Uh. Goddess. I don't know—" The host runs a hand through her hair.

"Relax." Moira smiles again. "I don't think it's possible to *prove* I am who I say I am. Your viewers can't be sure this isn't all a special effect, either. So I'll have to do something harder to explain." She brings the little mouse to her lips and kisses him—

Predictably, he squeaks and shivers. But the host gasps, steadying herself with a hand on the table. The studio fills with off-camera gasps and squeaks. So does Diana's cottage. They all—and, Diana presumes, the other million and a half viewers—feel the kiss just as if they'd been two inches high and in the goddess of love's hand.

Moira sits in the chair the professor had been in, crossing her legs, then sets the now-panting mouse down by one of her paws. She taps a toe to him, and he returns to his normal size, sprawled on his back. Moira rests her paws to either side of his stomach. "That's the best I can do."

"That was pretty fucking good," Hazel mutters, sitting up

straight again on the sofa after sliding down. "Am I the only one alarmingly turned on?"

"No," Diana and Rhiannon say simultaneously.

"I'm... I'm told viewer calls are flooding the switchboard," the cheetah says hoarsely. She's breathing hard and looks flushed. "So I think it was convincing, your highness."

The professor scoots back, sitting up, then scrambles to his feet and bolts offstage.

Moira watches him, amused. "Lady Moira, if you wish, but no royal titles, please."

"All right." The cheetah warily takes her seat, glancing off-camera at a director, then looks back to the hare. "So...what... where have you been for two thousand years? Why are you back now?"

"Let's go in reverse order. I never left, but I withdrew. I rarely showed myself, and when I did, it was in small, honestly rather petty ways." She shakes her head. "But I began to feel a pull, heard a call I'd all but forgotten how to hear. A cause much like the one I took up against other gods." She half-smiles. "I don't know how much mythology you know."

"Not much at all," the host confesses.

"I fought against most of the other gods to try to overturn the idea of species as destiny, that your birth determined what you could be. I lost."

The cheetah tilts her head. "But that's not a common viewpoint now."

"Isn't it? Isn't it rapidly becoming *more* common, with more and more restrictions based on whether you're evolutionarily predator or prey? The ID cards being piloted in Fresno are the logical extreme of trends I've been seeing for decades, if not centuries."

"That's not..." The cheetah trails off, clearly working through that, and her ears lower. "And that's why you were in Fresno?"

"Yes and no. This may sound like a non sequitur, but I promise it isn't." Moira rests her hands on the table. "Let's talk about a company called Celestial Capital."

Moira's barely ninety seconds into her explanation when

Arilin Thorferra

Diana's phone pings with a curt text message from Parker. *Meet ASAP.*

The sheep slumps down in her chair.

twenty-nine
you might be surprised

If she'd had any choice in the matter other than *meet* or *don't meet*, she wouldn't have met here. She'd have picked somewhere neutral and in public. A coffee shop in another city. A diner like the one that had dissolved in Fresno, maybe with one or two of the other goddesses watching discreetly from the shadows.

If they'd have agreed to do it, at least. Diana isn't sure any would.

At least they're not meeting back on Nunwick's estate, back where Diana's ostensible office is. Parker's texts had been terse, ending with *My office is safest.* She hadn't been able to tell whether that meant safer for her, safer for Parker, or both. None of the interpretations offered much comfort.

She's only been here once before, but the path's easy enough: walk down the hallway to Parker's private reception area. Her personal secretary, the blonde rat, sits behind her desk, as before. Ms. Storm gives Diana a slight nod, identical to the one she graced the sheep with on their first meeting, then tilts her head. "You're taller."

"I'd say I'm the right height."

Storm gives her an approving nod. "It looks excellent on you. Ms. Parker's waiting, ma'am." She motions to the office, and turns back to her computer.

Smoothing down her dress, she opens the door and walks inside.

Today the window wall doesn't overlook the ocean, but it doesn't overlook what's outside, either. It's looking out over another city at nighttime, where the skyscrapers glitter, rising in tall, curved neon-outlined spires. Somewhere in Asia, more than likely. Hong Kong? Singapore?

Parker sits behind the huge executive desk, looking at her laptop. She doesn't react to the sheep's entrance. Diana clears her throat softly, closing the door and crossing over to stand in front of the desk, trying not to fidget.

After another several seconds, Parker speaks, still without looking up. "I'm catching up on the news." She rotates the laptop to face Diana, showing an article on *Vox* headlined "Celestial Capital, Explained."

Diana swallows, taking a seat silently.

"It's not a bad article, as far as the reporting I've seen goes." Parker closes the laptop, meeting the sheep's eyes with an even more steely gaze than usual for her. "I find it rather charming that it ends with a bulleted list entitled 'What we don't know' that includes 'Whether any Celestial executives are supernatural.'"

"You know I didn't leak Celestial's involvement."

"I'm frankly not sure what I know at this moment. Apart from knowing you stood by Moira's side at two kilometers high, with downtown Fresno in *fucking orbit* around all of you."

"It was stationary, not orbiting," Diana mutters.

The vixen bares her teeth slightly. "I put my personal credibility on the line to bring you into our circle, Ms. Lindsay, with the expectation that you were serious about keeping Moira from interfering with us."

"I'd successfully gotten her to agree not to interfere with whatever you were doing in Fresno, even though I couldn't explain what that was, and even though she'd been in Black Oak and saw what you'd done there—a detail Celestial hadn't seen fit to share with me." Diana can't stop her voice from rising. "Just like you hadn't seen fit to share with me that it was part of a series of tests, and that the next one would be in Fresno."

"All things considered, you have a peculiar definition of success. How did she know where the test was, if not from you?"

Diana pointed at the computer on Parker's desk. "From *that*, I imagine. When I say Rhiannon—Ms. Doran—is a hacker goddess, it's not a metaphor."

Parker frowns at the laptop.

"Beyond that, Moira only 'interfered' when our test literally began destroying the city. How many are officially missing? Over twenty thousand? If the other goddesses hadn't done what they'd done, would it have taken the whole city like it did Black Oak? Like it did Môrdinas?"

"If she hadn't disrupted the order we'd spent a year setting up, it might have taken zero."

"Maybe. But Ms. Ironheart was there. Mr. Nunwick was there, too. I know how closely you can monitor chaos, your 'weather reports,' and that means they knew whether Moira had disrupted the conditions for the experiment." She shakes her head. "They could have stopped it, Ms. Parker. I've tried to understand that, to rationalize it. I understand that sacrificing some mortals to save the rest is the lesser of two evils. But a lesser evil is still an evil, and even as gods —especially as gods—don't we need to minimize the harm we do?"

"Of course." Parker sounds affronted. "I believed that even as a pirate. You were *there*, seeing me win without firing a shot."

"But Nunwick and Ironheart *don't* believe that, do they?" Diana leans forward, meeting Parker's eyes, speaking softly, punctuating each word. "If they did, they would have stopped."

Parker keeps meeting Diana's gaze for a second, then turns away with a heavy sigh. "Even though the test hardly went as planned, there was still valuable information to gather. As I suspect you've learned on your own initiative, this was the final test scheduled, and there are no windows of opportunity for any more. A planetary alignment coincides with the Autumn Equinox barely three months from now, and that combination is incredibly powerful. If we miss it, we'll have to wait decades—and we simply do not have that time to spare."

"You're saying we have *three months* to make sure when the final machine gets turned on, it doesn't do what all the previous ones did? How many mortals will be at risk?"

"Ms. Lindsay, I didn't bring you here for *you* to grill *me*. I still believe, perhaps against the evidence, that you've been honest with me about your intentions. I need to know if you're able and willing to fix the situation you've put us in."

Diana rubs her face. This is becoming the flip side of the arguments she had with Moira, Rhiannon, and Hazel. She's not sure what else she expected. "I'm so tired of having versions of this conversation," she mutters.

"Then maybe you should—"

Diana leaps to her hooves, leaning over the desk. "Shut up and *listen* to me!"

Parker stops mid-sentence, blinking up.

"You've put your 'credibility' on the line?" Diana points out the window. "I have risked relationships with other literal gods to be here. To talk to the enemy. To *work* with the enemy." She fixes her gaze on Parker. "To work with you.

"And every step of the way, I've been told as little as possible, told my questions didn't matter, told to sweep any misgivings away. I didn't need to know the plan, I just needed to know it would save the world. And I've tried to believe that, but the more I learn about what you aren't telling me, the harder it gets. I don't even know how much of what you've told me is true. You steeled me to expect more chaos nodes, more monsters, but there haven't been any."

Parker meets Diana's eyes steadily. "There have been no more monsters, Ms. Lindsay, because you defused the situation. You began working with us."

"If that's true, then return the favor. Defuse the situation with me. Work with me. Tell me if Celestial's plan to end the mythological cycle is a plan to turn Nunwick into the new Daranu. A new creator god."

Parker's expression grows unreadable. Long seconds pass, and it takes all Diana's force of will not to look away.

The vixen finally nods. "Yes."

"How many mortals will it draw from?"

Parker shifts in her seat, now looking uncomfortable. "All of them."

The sheep's eyes widen.

"But almost none of them should die. Less than a percent. If the changes work as predicted, most will only lose a few years of life."

"If. Should." Diana fixes her gaze on Parker again. "The difference between the tests isn't in the machinery. You're trying to change the world to lessen the side effects the ascension machine has on it."

"Yes."

"But you don't know whether turning Fresno into an autocratic dystopia would have 'fixed' the machine if Moira hadn't undone it. What you *do* know is that she accidentally undid it in a single night. How do you expect to replicate what you did in Fresno across the entire world in a matter of months?"

"By starting decades ago." Parker drums her fingers on the desk. "Countries around the world have been imposing more restrictions, defining classes and castes, shaping strict hierarchies. Those aren't enough in and of themselves. But when the time for Mr. Nunwick's final ascendance draws near, there will be an event, or events, beforehand to cause as much of the world as possible to impose temporary states of emergency. Martial law. Lockdowns. They'll only last weeks, but that will be enough."

"Events," Diana echoes. "Such as?"

"I don't know the precise details. Ironic, given that I suggested the operation's name." Parker looks distant for a moment before shaking her head. "They'll be cataclysmic, but they'll be brought under control."

"You're making your own chaos nodes."

Parker frowns, focusing her gaze back on Diana. "It would behoove you not to be with Moira's group when it's underway."

"That sounds like a threat."

"Take it as you wish." The vixen gets up, walking slowly to the glass wall, and looks out into the distance. Storm clouds have rolled into the futuristic cityscape, casting it in darker shadow, making the bright lights that much brighter. "I've been working on this project for centuries, to save the world from a long foretold end. It's required me to set aside many, many misgivings over the years. To do things I still question, at least to myself. To work with beings I'm not always sure are working toward the same end I am. And the more control we gained, the more we were able to steer the course of the world, the more it seemed the world was determined to sail right into the maelstrom. But recently, finally, we had the upper hand. We had everything in place.

"And then came you. Ms. Harcourt. Ms. Doran. Moira." She bares her teeth, growling the hare's name. "And your so-called goddess of love and war so resents the idea of carnivores naturally being above herbivores that she'll fight it with all her being, even at the cost of saving the world."

Diana stands, too. "And what if Mr. Nunwick so hates the idea of herbivores being on equal footing, of breaking his father's natural order, that he'll turn the world into one that isn't *worth* saving?"

"What do you mean, his father?"

Diana looks incredulous, then tilts her head, speaking more softly. "You don't know, do you?"

Parker narrows her eyes.

Diana walks slowly toward the vixen. "Moira saw Nunwick for the first time, there in Fresno, and he told her he didn't know what his father saw in her. Maybe there's another way to read that none of us see, but I don't think so. He's—"

"He was mortal, like us!" Parker snarls. Just outside the window, a lightning bolt arcs between a cloud and a nearby skyscraper, and the crack of thunder rattles the glass. A torrential rain abruptly starts.

"Is that what he told you?" Diana shakes her head. "No. He's Daranu's son. I know you have faith in him—"

"I have faith in his mission!" There's another lightning strike in the city, another window rattle. "And who he might have been doesn't matter."

"I believe he wants to stop the cycle, to stop the apocalypse. But..." She remembers Moira's admonition, near verbatim. "A god shouldn't *rule* mortals. We're shapers, benefactors, punishers, good examples, bad examples. Not kings and queens. If he merely wanted to save the world, I wouldn't be so uneasy."

Parker turns away, lip curling. "Advice from Moira, no doubt." Thunder rumbles ominously outside as the rain intensifies.

"Yes. It's not wrong."

Parker stares out the window silently for long seconds, watching the rain. At length, she speaks more quietly. "A bit of trivia few people know about pirate ships, Ms. Lindsay: they ran as democracies. They called me the queen, but I was elected first among equals by my crew. I stayed the captain by earning and keeping their support." She glances sidelong at Diana. "For the last year I sailed, my quartermaster was a ewe. You remind me of her."

"Would you have sailed under her?"

"You might be surprised what I did under her."

Diana's eyes widen slightly, and she feels her ears grow warm.

Parker looks away again. "You understand I called you here to give you an ultimatum."

The sheep clears her throat. "I know. The question is only whether you demand I choose a side once and for all, or order me to leave because you think I already have."

"I'd hoped for the former." Parker turns and walks toward the sheep, standing less than an arm's length away. "But I do think you've made your choice, Ms. Lindsay."

Diana swallows. This is less terrifying than the fight against what William became, but somehow more nerve-wracking. "If we can avert a coming apocalypse, I'll do everything possible to help. But I'll also do everything possible to make sure the world that survives is a world that I'd want to live in."

Parker clenches her fists. There's another crack of thunder outside. "Moira is far too willing to risk chaos. She underestimates it."

"And Nunwick is so focused on avoiding chaos, he won't see that order is its own danger." She shakes her head. "The difference is that for all her faults, Moira *listens*. Can you make Mr. Nunwick listen?"

As ever, trying to read Parker's expression is maddeningly hard. But there's a shadow in her eyes, a crack in the armor. Doubt? Regret? There's another soft rumble of thunder outside. When the vixen speaks, it's soft, barely above a whisper. "He is...very committed to his course."

The sheep reaches up to put her hands on Parker's shoulders, looking at her imploringly. "We have to save the world from ending in fire *and* ending in chains."

Parker stiffens, then moves closer still. "'We.' As admirable as I find your steadfastness, I strongly doubt the happy ending you want is possible."

"But I have to try. *We* have to try."

"A word I could use instead of 'admirable' is 'infuriating.'" She lifts her hands, nearly places them on the sheep's hips, hesitates. "I wanted to work with you close by my side, Diana."

Diana's heart skips a beat, just like it had the first time she saw Parker smile. "We still can." She swallows. "Lily."

Parker's fingertips brush along Diana's sides; she can feel the heat from the vixen's body. Their noses get closer, closer, until they nearly touch. Until their lips nearly touch. The sheep catches her breath.

Then Parker draws back, expression now shockingly readable: aching sadness. "I'm genuinely sorry I have to do this," she whispers.

Diana has just enough time to blink in confusion before the vixen shoves her with both hands. "Shove" doesn't do it justice. It's as if she's been hit by a wrecking ball, driving her back through the glass out into the torrential rain, fifty stories over the city street. She can't get enough breath to bleat before she starts to fall.

She's able to right herself before she hits the ground, controlling the tumble, turning it into a hard but graceful landing at the far edge of the street. Her impact cracks the pavement and sidewalk, sets off car alarms, sets dozens of pedestrians running in panic, but she doesn't care. She could just fly back up—

But the building she's turned to face isn't the Celestial Ventures office building, of course. That's in a different city, probably on the other side of the world.

She wipes rain from her eyes, conjuring an umbrella. She still has no idea where the hell she is. Teleporting home will be easy enough, but she's not ready. Dammit, Lily was the only one at Celestial she could reach. She thought she *had* reached her. She thought...

She wipes her eyes again, sniffling.

As she reaches the next corner, the rain begins to peter out. Tilting the umbrella back, she looks toward the sky. A rainbow shimmers between the two tallest buildings.

Diana folds up the umbrella, frowning, watching the sun come out.

thirty
faithful companion

"I 'm sorry," Moira says.

They're all sitting together in Diana's living room—the big, isolated A-frame vacation cabin she lives in now, on a lake somewhere in the Rockies. Moira's talking to the sheep, who looks positively disconsolate. All the goddesses have been trying to keep Stetson from panicking about having jumped from being in his late twenties to his mid-forties a week ago in Fresno. Not even Moira can reverse the effect, for reasons she can only guess at. Now the conversation's shifted to trying to comfort Diana over a combination firing, breakup, and possibly attempted assassination a few days ago. He's listening, although he's also scrolling through his phone idly, looking at social media and news feeds. Somebody in the group has to pay attention to the news.

"It's a lot to digest." Hazel rubs the back of her head. "I'd picked up that you liked her in spite of everything, but I thought you just liked her, not *liked* her liked her."

"I didn't..." Diana trails off, and glances toward Moira. "What was it you said? Love at first sight is a seed? I felt that, but I didn't recognize it. I hadn't sensed it with another woman since college, and..." She shrugs. "It hardly matters now, though."

Moira puts her hand on the sheep's shoulder. "It does matter. She made you face a difficult choice." The hare hesitates, and smiles wanly. "And I made you face a difficult choice. I'm sorry for that. I'm sorry that I'll very likely do it again."

Diana gives her the barest of nods and lapses into silence for a few seconds. Then she pats Moira's hand. "I love you, but you give the worst pep talks."

"So she didn't give any hint as to what Celestial's response plan will be?" Rhiannon says.

"Not to us, specifically, no. But I know more about their whole plan now. The final version of the machine draws from *all* the mortals, pulling a little from each one. But only if they can successfully do what they didn't make work in Fresno."

"And if it isn't successful, then what, it kills everyone?"

Diana shakes her head. "I don't know." She sighs. "The best I can hope for is that I've planted doubt."

Rhiannon's huge tail twitches. "Would she ever go against Nunwick?"

Stetson stops at one of the articles on the feed and scans it. Is this for real? "We might not have an idea what Celestial's response to you will be, but, ah, we might have an idea *when* it's going to be."

"What?" Rhiannon's the one who speaks, but they all look at the coyote.

"Nunwick is being interviewed on *60 Minutes* this Sunday, to talk about, quote, 'the extraordinary and tragic events in Fresno,' that he wants to 'set the record straight about Celestial Capital,' and that he has a warning."

Moira drums her fingers on the sofa's armrest. "He might be going on television to deny everything I said about him. He's definitely going to spin a very different story about us."

"Maybe." Diana frowns. "But Ms. Parker said the next-to-last step of their plan, the thing that's supposed to keep the world fully ordered to protect it when they fire off their machine the last time, is an event that tips the world into temporary martial law. Something that amplifies the effects of the smaller restrictions they've been getting governments to legislate over decades, that could temporarily achieve what they were trying to do in Fresno on a global scale."

"Seriously? Given how badly everything there went?" Rhiannon looks incredulous. "They can't be ready for the final production run."

"They don't believe they have a choice. There are only certain times they can fire off that machine, and the last one for decades is just three months from now."

"So what we need to do is keep everything a *little* chaotic until then." Hazel perks up. "And derail whatever this event is. Which is…?"

"Ms. Parker said she didn't know."

Rhiannon twists a hand in her hair. "A virulent plague could cause borders to get locked down, movements to be restricted. And we'd be expected to fix it, wouldn't we? Now that we're revealed as gods."

"Do mortals expect anything of us yet? It's not like we're getting temples."

Stetson clears his throat, scrolling back to another link he'd found earlier this morning over coffee. "The Unitarian Universalist Church in Fresno is setting up a shrine to all of you, if that counts."

Rhiannon covers her face. "I don't want to be worshipped."

Hazel laughs. "I'm a UU, or at least was. Trust me, the closest they'll come to worshipping us is having earnest discussions over bad coffee about what we 'mean.'"

"*You* were a churchgoer?" Rhiannon stares at the pika. "*When?*"

"In college, a bit afterward. I stopped attending, but they're the least churchy church I ever came across. Accepting of just about anyone, dogma-free, pretty philosophical. I'm tempted to visit to see just what they're thinking about us."

"I don't know how much we should do before Celestial's grand coming-out interview." Moira shakes her head. "But the more mortal followers we have, especially if they're ones who are already predisposed to dislike the idea of natural orders and dogma, the harder we make it for Celestial to make everything nice and ordered."

"So we're going back to Fresno?" Diana says. She doesn't sound enthusiastic.

"Can we at least teleport this time?" Rhiannon grimaces. "I don't think Moira's replaced her car after it got disintegrated."

The hare scowls. "I'm still arguing with the insurance company. Anyway, yes, we can teleport." She pulls out her phone, searching the maps, bringing up a street view of the area. After putting the phone back in her pocket, she stands up, motioning for the rest of them to do so, too.

Stetson starts to, then hesitates. Is he up for this? *Should* he be up for this? He's pretty sure he knows both answers. "I think this is for the actually divine, not their faithful companion."

Moira looks at him searchingly, then nods. "All right," she says softly.

Hazel moves off the couch into her chair and rolls to the rest of the group. "I'd think you'd get an exemption from the 'no acts of god' clause."

"If they're still arguing with me in a week, you can eat the claims adjuster."

"Deal."

Rhiannon looks between both of them. "I swear, you two—"

Moira snaps her fingers, and they all disappear.

Stetson runs his fingers through his hair, then gets up and pads into the kitchen to kick off a new half-pot of coffee. Once the brew's finished, he pours a mug and starts watching an episode of "Leverage."

Why, exactly, is he still here?

"Mind-blowing sex with the literal goddess of love," he murmurs aloud. Okay, let's be real, one could come up with far worse reasons to keep hanging around.

Yet it isn't as if he *does* anything. He's tried telling himself that as the sole mortal, he helps ground them, but Rhiannon, Hazel, and Diana are mere months removed from mortality. No, the truth is, he'd stayed here because of Moira. He was the token mortal. Maybe the pet mortal, to give it a cuter spin. He wasn't sure whether he was in love with her, but she was in love with Briley, and a polycule wasn't in the cards. Why would it be? Again: mortal.

Why hadn't she deified *him*?

Does he *want* to be deified?

He leans forward, holding his face in his hands. Yes. No. Maybe? He'd never thought about it before now, and the only reasons he can come up with are selfish, venial. And if anyone could pick up on that somehow, it's Moira. Divinity isn't in the cards for him, and he thinks he's fine with that.

A sharp rapping sounds on the glass doors leading to the deck. The coyote looks up, startled, to see a short, attractive woman standing there. She waves cheerfully at him, expression hopeful.

He stifles a groan. It's a miracle no reporters had tracked them here yet, and it looks like that luck has just run out. She's seen him; he can't pretend he hasn't seen her. At least she's not leading a crowd. What even *is* she? He can't place the species.

Stetson gets up and heads to the door, unlocking it and cracking it open. "Ma'am, you're trespassing. I don't know who you're looking for, but—"

"Why, I'm looking for *you,* Mr. Halbach!" She beams, fierce teeth gleaming white against her black fur. "I wanted to avoid just inviting myself in, but I hoped we could talk for a bit out on this lovely balcony." She meets his eyes with hers, and holds his gaze with the force of a steel trap.

"I'm...not..." He tries to shake his head, to look away, but he can't. His ears lower as he realizes that's literal. He's not falling into her gaze as much as being swallowed alive by it. *Shut the door. Just close your eyes. Just...*

A victorious smile slowly creeps across her lips. "You can't really say no," she whispers.

His mouth has gone dry. He doesn't truly *want* to say no, does he? "Just...a few minutes."

"Good boy." Agent One grins wickedly, and leads him out onto the deck.

The Universalist church isn't as much on the outskirts of Fresno as in a neighboring town, at the edge of a park and community garden. "This looks more like a museum of modern art than a church," Rhiannon observes, looking at it skeptically.

"Yeah, they do that. I mean, not always. I've seen ones that looked super churchy. But the one I attended in college was a geodesic dome." Hazel rolls ahead. "Let's look around."

The church itself looks closed. But a small crowd mills around in front of it. A few glance over at the goddesses as they approach. None of them are "on," projecting any divine aspect, but four women together of their species and appearance doesn't go unnoticed.

"Hi." Hazel waves cheerfully. "Anyone know where the shrine to the new goddesses is?"

A middle-aged, paunchy rabbit's the closest to her, and the one she's looking at when she asks. "The, uh, the Thankfulness Garden?" he replies hesitantly, pointing down the sidewalk.

"Thankfulness Garden! I love it." She starts rolling in the indicated direction, and the others follow.

An older, greying vixen bites her lip. "You're not—forgive me, but you four—ah…?"

Rhiannon grins over her shoulder, motioning broadly with an arm. "Come with us."

There's distinct murmuring in the crowd now. The vixen follows, looking bemused. Others follow, too. Not all of them, but at least a dozen, including the rabbit.

It doesn't take long to find the understated shrine. Compared to what Moira knew in her heyday, "understated" is an understatement. A brick circle set back from the winding sidewalk surrounds a small native flower garden, and the garden surrounds a statue, a set of four figures standing together. Moira's statue is the closest to finished; the others are rough but recognizable. Offerings surround the statue's base: cut flowers, beads, coins, the occasional oddity like a toy or a poetry book or an old computer part. A half-dozen other people sit on one of two benches or on the brick. A burly bear kneels, back to them, chiseling away at the block that's becoming Diana.

Hazel rolls onto the grass. "I guess it's too late to ask for me to have my chair in the statue."

The sculptor looks up at them, irritated, then—as they let a glimmer of divine aspect shine—double-takes.

"Oh, my god," the rabbit whispers.

"Goddess." The vixen falls to her knees.

The crowd explodes in conversation, even screaming. Some join those kneeling, others remain standing, backing up, more than a few expressing skepticism, demanding proof.

A glasses-wearing mouse, younger than most of the crowd, strides down the path from the church, hands raised over his head. He sports a short hipster beard, casual windbreaker over jeans and T-shirt. "Please! Please!" he beseeches the crowd. They don't fall silent, but they fall back to a murmur. Then he pushes his way to the four goddesses. His expression is that of someone who's just been told they won the lottery, and can't help suspect they're being pranked. "Are you four really claiming to be…" He nods toward the statue, and looks back at them.

"I was there, at the Brig, when she sang. When—when it all started," a wide-eyed young wolf says, staring directly at Moira.

She smiles at him, and holds out her hand to the mouse. "I'm Moira."

He takes her hand, eyes widening as he looks up at her. "I'm—uh —" It takes a second or two for him to remember his name. "Reverend Miller. Mike."

She clasps his hand with both of hers for a moment, then indicates the others. "This is Hazel, Rhiannon, and Diana."

Hazel addresses the mouse. "So was the Thankfulness Garden here your idea?"

"I confess it wasn't." He smiles nervously. "Parishioners had the idea. Your appearance has been… I don't think 'inspirational' begins to cover it." As he speaks, more crowd members take to their knees, although others just sit. More than a few are on their phones, taking pictures and messaging. "You're more than a bit of a philosophical and religious conundrum."

"I've been told that more than once," Moira says dryly. She sits down on the grass cross-legged, and motions for the others—mortals and goddesses alike—to follow her lead. "Let's talk."

When they teleport back into Diana's foyer, the sheep takes a deep breath, shaking her head. "Did we just start a new religion?"

Hazel laughs. "I don't think so. But with any luck, we're helping give…whatever we'd already accidentally created an actual shape."

"I don't think I'd have placed any bets on Fresno becoming a new holy site."

Rhiannon shrugs. "Is it weirder than any other holy site?" She sees the sliding glass door to the deck's open, and Stetson's sitting outside, looking even more pensive than usual. He hasn't acknowledged any of them. She furrows her brow, walking outside. "Stetson?"

Moira narrows her eyes, looking toward Rhiannon and Stetson, and hurries in their direction. She crouches in front of the unresponsive coyote, looking into his eyes and frowning.

"What's happening?" Diana hurries over, too, Hazel trailing behind. "Is he breathing? Should I call an ambulance?"

"I don't know, yes, and I don't know." The hare snaps her fingers in front of his nose, then takes both of the coyote's limp hands. "Stetson, look at me."

He rocks, blinking once, but still doesn't respond.

Moira moves her hands to his shoulders, pulls him close, and kisses him—

The birdcage is exquisite, wrought silver and brass, classic dome-shaped top, gold chain suspending the cage leading somewhere out of sight overhead. Unlike the coyote outside, the one inside is alert, wary, curled up in the cage with knees drawn to his chest.

She kneels in front of the cage, and Stetson looks up. He can't help it; the goddess of love and war literally glows, all at once the brightest object in the universe. When she speaks, her voice is thunder. "Who put you here?"

"It was—" He stumbles as he starts to answer, putting a hand to his throat, starting to choke. Laughter peals out from far overhead.

Moira whips her gaze up sharply. She can't see who's laughing. But the birdcage is a pendant. The blackness surrounding everything is fur.

Growling, she grabs the cage, summoning her strength, and pulls—

When everyone's vision clears, their ears still ringing, Moira and Stetson sit in a sprawl on the deck, a cloud of smoke slowly dissipating around them.

Hazel's the first to voice what they're all thinking. "What the fuck?"

"You heard laughter, right?" Rhiannon glances around at the rest of them. "You *did* hear a woman's laughter."

"Someone found us here, despite the wards," Moira says. "Someone powerful." The coyote looks terrified and bewildered, but alert. Moira stands, taking Stetson's hand.

"Who?" Diana stares at the hare, then the coyote.

"I don't think I can tell you," Stetson says hoarsely.

Moira shakes her head. "He's under a geas. I don't know what the obligation is, but it includes hiding information about what happened." She leads them back in, and guides Stetson to sit down on a sofa by her.

Rhiannon's ears skew. "Can't you break the geas? You're the most powerful being on the planet."

"Maybe, maybe not. Even if I am, that doesn't mean I can snap my fingers and break a geas set on a mortal by another god." She sighs, rubbing Stetson's shoulder. "I'm a pretty shit guardian."

He straightens up and shakes his head. "She was waiting for you to leave. For you all to leave. She wanted to…" He twitches and winces, as if he'd just received an electric shock. "To, uh, talk to me. I don't…think she even came in. We just…talked…on the deck."

"Can you tell us anything about her? About what she talked about?"

The coyote's ears fold down. "She was pretty. Friendly. Intimidating teeth, though. She just…asked questions." He gets a haunted look, ears lowering. "I'm not sure what she asked. I'm not sure what I told her."

"Our biggest secret has been where we've been living, and since she found you here, obviously you didn't give that away." Diana frowns. "There aren't any other goddesses I know about at Celestial. A few elevated mortals as executives and executive assistants…"

Moira shakes her head. "She was definitely divine. Or infernal, depending on how you want to slice it."

When Stetson speaks, his voice is despondent, bordering on broken. "If I said anything, I'm so sorry."

"You didn't do anything wrong." Moira pulls him into a gentle hug. "I'm sorry I wasn't here, didn't…"

"Didn't what?" He squirms away, literally pushing her back at arms' length. "Didn't force me to go with you to keep me safe?"

"Of course not! Stetson—"

"No." He takes her hands. "I know, Lady Moira. But…why am I *here?* You pulled me along, and I never said 'no,' because it sounded like the adventure of a thousand lifetimes. It *has* been the adventure of a thousand lifetimes. I'd accepted the risk. But me staying here isn't just a risk to me, it's a risk to all of *you.* I'm the weak link here."

The goddesses look at one another, Hazel and Rhiannon both fidgeting much the way Stetson does.

"We can handle it." Moira smiles, but it's small, sad. She won't tell him he isn't right. She won't lie.

"I don't doubt it. But I don't think I can."

Diana clears her throat, and gestures at herself and the others. "If Stetson was immortal, he *wouldn't* be at risk."

Stetson rubs the back of his ear. "I'd rather she didn't."

Rhiannon tilts her head. "I know none of us handled our power very well at first, but we've been growing into it, and we'd all be here to help you."

"I handled my power fine," Hazel protests.

The squirrel looks at her. "You became giant in the middle of an intersection, caused a half-dozen car wrecks, and swallowed a loudmouth BMW driver whole."

"Like I said."

"That's not what I want." Stetson sounds tired. "I know it's ultimately Lady Moira's choice, not mine, but I don't want to be given divine power purely to keep me safe."

"No." Moira shakes her head. "For all I keep calling it 'divine whim,' choosing these three new goddesses came with a compulsion, a—a knowing. And that's not there for you, Stetson. Not yet." She sighs, and lifts a hand to each of them in turn. To Diana, "I need you as you," to Hazel, "you as you," to Rhiannon, "and you as you. No, I didn't know exactly why then, and no, I didn't prepare you well. I was still… I don't know. I was still fighting the idea there was anything left for me to do in mortal realms beyond drinking, fucking, and occasionally smiting mortals who pissed me off. But I know now, and *you* know now, too, I think."

The goddesses shift in their seats, looking uncomfortable, but no one contradicts her.

She turns to Stetson. "And I need you as *you.*"

"Even if you don't know exactly why," he says softly.

"Even if."

"And if that feeling was there? If it shifted from 'not yet' to 'now?'"

"I'll let you know."

Stetson looks down, silent for several seconds, then gives Moira a warm, lingering kiss. "If it does, I have no doubt you'll know where to find me."

She looks into his eyes and returns his kiss deeply, drawing him into a tight hug. When she lets go, he wobbles, catching his breath, then flashes a bashful, slightly goofy grin before heading out of the living room.

The three younger goddesses look at one another. Moira's not looking at any of them.

"Should we…uh…" Rhiannon mumbles, barely over a whisper, but she doesn't finish the sentence. No one else says anything.

Stetson returns with his backpack slung over his shoulder. "It's been…extraordinary doesn't begin to cover it. I'm sure I'll see you all again in person, my ladies, not just on the news."

They each give him slightly more awkward hugs. "Do you want, uh, a teleport back?" Hazel says.

The coyote tilts his head, tail swishing once. "No, thank you, Lady Hazel," he says at length. "I've always wanted to take the train, and I think it'll be lovely this time of year."

She stifles a sigh. "If you need anything, if you're in any trouble, you know any of us will be there in an instant."

He turns at the door and grins. "If at least one of you isn't there before I even know I'm in trouble, I'll be vaguely disappointed."

Once he leaves, Diana sits down by Moira. The hare's remained motionless after her last kiss with Stetson. "Are *you* all right?"

Moira opens her mouth, closes it, furrows her brow, folds her hands in her lap. "I've had so many mortal lovers over the centuries," she finally murmurs. "Yet I can't remember any of them being the one who broke up with me." She lapses back into silence.

"I'm not comfortable giving advice about this to the goddess of love." Diana smiles self-consciously.

"Have lots of dark chocolate," Hazel says. "And ice cream."

"And cheap merlot," Rhiannon adds.

The hare allows herself a small smile. "Do we even have any of those?"

Diana gets up and heads to the kitchen. "We damn well do now."

"You know you don't have to go to this much trouble, ma'am." Rhiannon watches Diana's mother set out two frittatas from the breakfast diner in town.

"It's the last chance I'm going to have, isn't it?"

Diana smiles reassuringly. "Just for a while. We have to be somewhere else for a few weeks, to regain control of our narrative."

"You've been hanging around PR flacks yourself, sounds like." She plates the breakfast while Moira pours coffee. "Maybe I should go into hiding, too. There were at least a dozen people I didn't recognize in the café this morning, and I passed at least two news vans on the road here."

Moira glances toward the door. "But none of them have made it through the wards."

The older sheep shakes her head. "One clearly did."

"You're not mentioned in the article," Hazel says. "And so far, it hasn't gone anywhere but gossip sites. You're probably safe."

"There wasn't much to that 'article' besides photos of you out on the deck with your coyote friend, and him with his honey badger friend. Even so, given how much worldwide interest there is in you, I wouldn't expect it to stay quiet."

"No." Moira grunts. "And whoever that honey badger is, she's definitely no friend."

Hazel digs into her frittata. "Could it have just been dumb luck? The wards don't keep people from seeing the house, they keep them from paying much attention to it, right? Make it hard for them to stay focused."

"No. The photos are too…" Moira shakes her head. "I was going to say they're too specific, but it's more the reverse of that. The published ones all look casual, friendly. Not like us helping Stetson to recover from a magical entrapment, or like her trapping him."

"You think they were deliberately chosen." Diana tilts her head. "Why?"

"I do think that, and I don't know."

Diana's mother shrugs. "No one but you knows that backstory, not even the photographer. The pictures make you look relatable, like you're out here on a vacation rental the same way any of us would be. It's kind of charming. You're not remote and aloof, you're goddesses of the people."

"I think we already look relatable, because we actually *do* go out among the people." Hazel spreads her hands. "We shop and cook and…well, we *used* to go out to eat, but when we're all together in public we sometimes attract attention even when we're toning down the divine aspect thing. But the point still stands."

"Although being here makes us look like goddesses of the upper middle class," Diana says dryly. "I know how expensive this house would have been if it hadn't been literally falling down when I bought it."

"That's part of the story, then," her mother retorts. "You're not demanding mortals build you a temple, you're buying a fixer-upper in the middle of nowhere."

"That's the story you would tell." Moira shakes her head. "But we don't know what story will be told with these photos. We just know we're not going to like it."

When they finish breakfast, everyone hugs Diana's mother in turn, Moira last. The older sheep looks up at the hare as they hug, expression serious. "Take care of her," she murmurs. "At risk of speaking heresy to an all-powerful goddess, you haven't been the best at it."

"I know." Moira smiles softly. "I'm trying."

"The offer for you to stay here's still open, Mom," Diana says. "If reporters get too nosy, this place might be harder to find."

She shrugs as she heads to the door. "If you all thought your 'wards' were going to hold, you'd be staying here. If I run into trouble, I'll give you a call and Miss Hazel can pop over and eat a news van."

Hazel looks at Diana accusingly. "What have you been telling your mother about me?"

Rhiannon smirks. "Clearly the truth."

After she leaves, Moira stands. "Ready to retreat to the country?"

"Just teleporting rather than driving this time?"

The hare shrugs at Diana. "Easy to hop between places we can see clearly, and we won't run into any news vans for Hazel to eat."

The pika sticks out her tongue. Moira grins, raises her hands, and snaps her fingers.

thirty-one
the real audience

The *60 Minutes* correspondent handling the Darren Nunwick interview is a gorgeous middle-aged otter woman. When Diana describes her as one of the big guns in television news, all the other goddesses except Briley look puzzled. "Seriously, none of you have even *heard* of Leslie Hansen?"

Rhiannon shrugs. "Broadcast news is kind of from another era." Hazel nods.

"It's an era I'm barely used to." Briley shakes her head as she sets down a tray of snacks. "By the time I figured out how to set the clock on my videotape gadget, it was obsolete. Y'all have been in such a rush since you electrified everything."

"Haven't they? I still haven't gotten into television," Moira says. "It's so new."

Hazel squints. "I can't tell if you mean that, or if you're just fucking with us."

Moira grins. "I know."

The segment begins with Hansen behind her studio desk. "Last week, the world saw the most extraordinary events of the new century, possibly *any* century. Giants stood astride a city in California's Central Valley, levitating buildings and citizens aloft to rescue them from a lethal magical force sweeping over the land. They claimed to be the goddess of love and war from classic mythology, and three newly uplifted gods given divinity through her." The video fades into a famous statue of Moira on display at the British Museum, enrobed in a flowing off-the-shoulder dress and holding a sword over her head. If you squint enough, it looks like the real Moira. "And they accuse one company of being the source of the strange and terrible energy that left well over twenty thousand missing and presumed dead." Now her voice plays over shots of Celestial's main office building in New York.

"While that might have been the first time many had even heard of Celestial Capital, the company's been a Wall Street power player for decades. Celestial and its subsidiaries own or have controlling stakes in dozens of companies, from global security firms to fast food chains."

"And by 'dozens,' you mean 'thousands,'" Rhiannon mutters.

The video changes to tracking shots following the otter as she walks through Celestial's cavernous, marble-floored lobby toward the elevators, meeting unsmiling business-suited security guards and lower-level executives, walking down hallways. "What Celestial *hasn't* been is visible. They don't run ads. They don't speak at conferences. They don't make public shareholder reports. They don't have a marketing or public relations department. It's challenging to even find photographs of their top executives. They've long been the subject of fringe conspiracy theories. After the Fresno Event, those theories became mainstream."

The video dissolve-cuts to a room similar to the library at the private club Diana remembers: all hardwood and red leather, sumptuous yet cozy, inviting you to sit down with an old book and a glass of whiskey. "So while it wasn't a surprise that Celestial Capital found it necessary to break their silence, it *was* a surprise that they reached out to us. Not to deliver a press release, but to set up an interview with their CEO, Darren Nunwick."

Hansen's sitting in one of those old chairs, placed near the center of the room. The camera pivots as the voiceover ends, revealing Nunwick sitting in a larger chair facing her. The three-piece suit he's decked out in might well be the same one he met Diana in that first night.

"Before we begin," Hansen says, "let's be clear with the audience that we made no agreement beforehand as to the topics we'd cover."

"That's right," he rumbles.

Moira leans forward in her seat, frowning.

"Look familiar?" Hazel says.

She shakes her head slightly. "I don't know."

"So." Hansen folds her hands in her lap. "Are you a god, Mr. Nunwick?"

He laughs. "That's a more complicated question than it might seem, Leslie. Let me tell you of Celestial's history as a secret order that I founded almost five hundred years ago."

She lifts her brows. "You're saying you're at least five centuries old."

He nods. "May I continue?" It doesn't sound like a question.

"Go on."

Briley narrows her eyes. "He damn well looks familiar to me." She gestures at the screen. "Picture him as a teenager knee-high to you, trying to look up your dress."

Moira starts to laugh, then stares. "You think he's Sotala? Seriously?"

"I can't swear to it, but it sure fits, doesn't it? Got the look, definitely got the pretension."

Nunwick's explaining the Order of Caeles in a brusque, cheat-sheet fashion similar to Parker's original explanation, about how the disappearance of the old gods left an opening for mounting chaos that would inevitably lead to the apocalypse. He doesn't use the language of the old myths as much as he uses that of the dominant religion, with a hat tip toward how many religions have a notion of the end times.

"Chaos like what happened in Fresno?" Hansen says.

He steeples his hands. "Imagine that on a worldwide scale."

"That's what your organization—the part that's still this Order of Caeles—is dedicated to stopping."

"Yes."

The otter lets that hang in the air for a moment before tilting her head. "Is the woman calling herself Moira a god?"

"You'll have to ask her."

"You must have your own informed opinion, Mr. Nunwick."

He shifts in his chair. While he keeps a pleasantly neutral expression, it's clear he's not used to being challenged by mortals. "She's another being like I am, whatever words you may choose to use for us."

"She's claimed much more than you have."

"Let's take her at her word. Where does that leave us, Leslie?" He spreads his hands. "Are the old gods worshipped now? If you went into any church in America and asked whether we should follow a being claiming to be one of those gods, what would the minister say?"

Hazel snorts. "Way to throw the mythology you're literally part of under the bus."

"They'd say she was a demon." Hansen gestures to the lion. "But they would say the same of you, wouldn't they?"

"Perhaps. But I think we can both be judged on our actions."

"According to Moira, they saved Fresno from *your* actions."

Nunwick looks patronizingly incredulous. "How much credit should a firefighter receive for saving people from a burning building when they set the fire themselves?"

Rhiannon bares her teeth, which looks more cute than threatening. "Fuck you with barbed wire."

Hansen gives him a searching look. "You're accusing her of lying. Of being the one who actually caused the devastation."

"I wouldn't use the word 'lying.' I don't doubt her good intentions. But her actions led to what happened in Fresno."

"How?"

"As I explained, Caeles wishes to stop the end of the world, to combine science and magic together to achieve this end."

She nods uncertainly.

"We are on the verge of doing so." He grows more animated, waving his hands in front of him. "So close. Fresno was a final test, *the* final test, and in certain ways it was a success—but Moira's magic, the interference she produced based on her misunderstanding of our motives, created unimaginably tragic side effects. I'm glad she and her compatriots were able to counter those effects once they saw and understood them, but if they hadn't been there, the night would have passed with no incident. No damage. No loss of life."

"The footage we have from the event, and all the first-person reports, match her telling," the otter points out. "The force sweeping over Fresno, destroying buildings and people, originated from a point she identified as your test site."

"It did."

"So how did Moira's presence affect that?"

"She's an immensely powerful magical being, sharing her power with others she brought with her, devoted to the service of chaos."

"I'm what now?" Moira narrows her eyes.

Briley pats her shoulder with a wry grin. "He's not entirely wrong, love."

The hare gives her a sour glare.

"The service of chaos," Hansen repeats. "Explain why you say that."

He spreads his hands again. "Look at the mythology she identifies with, the role that she's claimed—a lesser god who decided to overthrow the world's creator because she believed the ordained order needed to be upended. Because she believed *she* could do better. There are echoes of this in countless other myths and in religions, stories told from pulpits even today: the tragic figure whose pride leads them to rebellion and, ultimately, to their downfall."

Hansen, in the way of blunt reporters, makes the subtext into text. "You're comparing her to the Devil."

Nunwick raises his hands as if to deflect her obvious reading. "I'm simply saying the story of Moira's revolt against Daranu has echoes in other stories."

Moira sighs. "Well, it's not as if he's the first one who's made the accusation since we were revealed."

"You're not even from that mythology," Hazel spits. "And you're not a 'lesser' god, either."

"Newer mythologies always have an explanation for why the older ones were bad."

Hansen shifts in her seat as she faces Nunwick. "Let's focus on the transformation of your mystical order to a global holding corporation." She spreads her webbed hands. "Not a church, not a service organization, but a for-profit corporation that's made a concerted effort to stay in the background until now."

He nods. "Yes."

"Why?"

"States stop at arbitrary, often ephemeral borders. Markets, though? Markets are everywhere. Capital is everywhere. Business is by far the best way—the most efficient way—in modern times to bring the greatest good to the greatest number of people."

"As markets have become globalized, haven't they disproportionately favored wealthy countries over poor ones?" she counters. "Economic inequality has been growing within countries as well. Isn't the good that corporations bring largely limited to the upper economic classes?"

"I understand the criticism, but I find it...lazy. It deliberately conflates luxury goods with necessities."

Hansen lifts her brows fractionally. "Let's talk about what kinds of companies Celestial Capital invests in, then. Your primary investments are security companies, defense contractors, surveillance technologies, private military forces."

"They are."

"So it's fair to say Celestial's mission is not lifting the poorest people in the world out of poverty through the power of markets."

"Our mission is averting the end of the world, Leslie. If we're not successful, poverty levels become rather academic, wouldn't you agree?"

"Explain what you mean by 'end of the world.' There are many ways the world's threatened by the modern age. Nuclear war. Climate change. Catastrophes caused by scientific accidents." She gestures with both hands, webbed fingers spreading again. "But you mean something mystical."

"I mean *all* of those possibilities. Unchecked chaos increases the chance of the perils of war, of engineered catastrophe, whether accidental or intentional. And now, as we've seen in Fresno, and as we saw with other recent smaller events focused on the new risen goddesses—events your own network has done investigative reporting on, as I understand it—we face a mounting chance of magic catastrophe, yes."

"You're referring to reports about people turning into giants and monsters over the last year, ones dismissed by mainstream news outlets at the time but which we've tentatively validated on re-investigation."

"Yes." Nunwick raises a finger. "And those reports may still seem fanciful, may seem to pale in comparison to Fresno, but each has been worse than the last. A few mortals Moira has interfered with now claim divine power, but at least one other became a literal monster. Mix the two?" He spreads his hands again. "The next one who goes awry could become far worse than anything we've seen before. We—not just Celestial, but the world as a whole—had been making such progress toward order. Now I fear we'll all reap the chaos she's been sowing."

Hansen shifts in her seat. "Here's what I don't understand, Mr. Nunwick. If everything you've said is true, you're an immortal being who's personally been working on this project for centuries. The apocalypse you're fighting to avert is the one predicted in the mythology Moira is from, a mythology which talks about her being exiled to mortal lands. To here. And you must have known that."

"You want to know why I didn't attempt to recruit her to my cause."

The otter nods.

Nunwick looks away, silent for several long seconds, then turns back with a more stone-faced expression. "She and I have spoken, long ago."

Moira sits up straight.

"I asked her," the lion continues, "about her failed rebellion. If she had regrets. If she understood the value of order now." He shakes his head slowly. "She said she regretted nothing. She spurned me."

"That clinches him as Sotala." Briley waves a hand angrily. "Two thousand years and the kid's still got a prickly pear up his ass over you cockblocking him."

Diana makes a choking noise.

Hansen doesn't miss the choice of words, either. "That sounds personal."

"In a sense." Nunwick's tone grows frostier. "Perhaps she and I both feel things strongly."

"If she were here, what would you say to her now?"

He frowns, and looks directly at the camera. "I would say that I know, Moira, that you still believe you're acting nobly. But you not only won't win this fight, you'll take the world down with you when you lose."

Briley flats her ears. "That—that sonuva—" She growls, clenching a fist as if crushing something in her hand. The TV crumples in on itself in a shower of sparks, making all the other goddesses in the room except Moira jump.

The harvest mouse stalks off into the kitchen.

Rhiannon rubs her ear. "I didn't think of Lady Briley as having much of a temper."

"She's protective." Moira sighs affectionately. Then her smile fades into a worried expression. "She's also probably right. Nunwick made it sound not just like I could be the liar, but like I might be a villain without even knowing it." She shakes her head. "Making things worse in the name of doing good."

Briley stomps back in, slamming down several mugs and pouring hot apple cider into each one. "You're not a villain, darling."

"I don't know—"

"Yes, you damn well do." Briley stabs her finger in the air for emphasis. "What happened in Black Oak has got to be what wiped Môrdinas off the map in the process of making little Sotala into a god, because staying a demigod wasn't enough. He didn't tell the otter lady that part, did he? Or how his plan to save the world *now* is to make himself a creator god." She drops back into her seat, still visibly stewing as she picks up one of the mugs. "And besides that, he's just cruel. What is it you said he said to you?"

"That he didn't know what his father saw in me."

"Exactly. Like Daranu was your secret admirer." The mouse snorts. "It's mind games. He's aiming to make you doubt yourself. Don't fall for it."

Diana picks up a mug, but pauses as she takes a sip. What Briley's saying *mostly* makes sense, but something niggles at her. "He wouldn't go on national television just to get in our heads."

Briley looks over at her. "You felt it when he was looking right at Moira, didn't you? He wanted her attention, specifically."

"I did. It's just... I don't think we're the real audience." The sheep looks into her mug, then back at the others. "I think we're being set up."

thirty-two
there is no pattern

Parker sets down her drink and brushes back stray strands of hair the wind's blown out of place. Nunwick and Ironheart insisted on having this "casual lunch" outside at the estate's club; it's a beautiful view, but too windy. Given that they've cleared the entire patio for privacy, the level of casualness is debatable. "So this PR offensive worked, then."

Ironheart comes as close as Parker's ever seen the lioness get to a smile. "Early polling suggests it's a win. Sentiment about Celestial has moved higher, and sentiment about Moira and her band of chaos-makers has dropped considerably."

"And the opinion and influencer articles we've scanned have moved away from the 'could this be a revived old religion' tone they'd had toward a 'could this be a dangerous new radicalism' tone." Nunwick nods approvingly, waving his fork at the vixen. "The status quo always reasserts itself, Parker, and the status quo bends toward us."

"I admit it was an interesting interview. Even I learned a few things."

Nunwick cuts off another section of his steak. "Oh?"

"For instance, that you'd met Moira." She keeps her voice light. "When was that?"

"Before I deified you," he says after a moment, then shoves the bite into his mouth.

"That must be an interesting story."

He barely chews before swallowing. "It was long ago, and irrelevant to our work."

"She remains the biggest challenge to Project Maelstrom, so the more I know about her, the better."

"Of course."

"What is it that Daranu saw in her?"

He pauses with the fork halfway to his mouth.

She folds her hands on the table, her smile the epitome of professional detachment. "It's my understanding that it's something you said to her in Fresno. I can't help but be curious, given that she's become the biggest impediment to our plans."

He gives her a long, measured look. "And is your understanding of that from your failed protégée?"

"It is."

"We're sorry that didn't work out," Ironheart says. "I know you had high hopes for her."

"I'm sorry as well. Ms. Lindsay is a very perceptive woman."

"That was quite a dramatic way to terminate your relationship." Nunwick goes back to attacking his steak, a slight frown on his muzzle.

"I had to send a message."

"I agree. Just so." He shakes his head, still paying more attention to his food. "Even after Moira's rebellion, Daranu thought...better of her than he should. So I am given to understand. But I have little hint as to what positives he still saw."

"So it was a taunt to unnerve her."

"It was an expression of disappointment. But let's talk of the future, not the past. How far along is your team in the final preparation work for Maelstrom?"

"The private intelligence world is on as high alert as it can be without identifiable threats. No one knows how to respond to theoretical magical dangers, which makes it easy for us to guide plans toward rigid order. We're getting some pushback from politicians who say their citizens won't tolerate that level of restriction for very long, though."

Ironheart sneers. "Very little breaks mortal resistance faster than fear."

"And very little strengthens it faster than having literal gods on their side."

Nunwick spreads his hands expansively. "Hence the interview. You heard Ironheart. The public confidence in Moira and her girls will only keep dropping. When they can't address the crisis and we can, the world will follow our lead. They don't need to impose restrictions for very long. Simply long enough."

Parker swirls her glass of rosé. "And you're sure they can't address it?"

Ironheart gives her a pained look. "The last time they created a chaos monster, they were nearly killed."

"Perhaps so, but they've clearly learned since then. More importantly, Moira wasn't with them."

Nunwick flashes a wry grin. "You're not wrong, Parker, but that monster was the product of their incompetence. This time, our worst case is that we ride in to save the day and humiliate them. Our best case"—his eyes sparkle with anticipation—"is that we eliminate them."

Parker's brows lift. "You think you can *kill* Moira?"

Ironheart chimes in. "I told you we were investigating contingency options after Moira's re-engagement with the world. We've tested different configurations of the ascendence technology, using it to suppress divine power rather than enhance it. It can't do it completely, or for very long. But Agent One doesn't need very long to do what she does, will she?"

Parker purses her lips. "Even with technological assistance, that's a large ask."

"Moira killed the war god Segomo." Nunwick shrugs. "And just as then, a dead god would simply return to their mortal life, with memories of godhood fading to strange, uneven dreams. For her girls, it'd barely matter."

Arilin Thorferra

"Consider my worries assuaged, then." The vixen finishes another bite of her chicken salad and pushes the plate to the side.

~

Parker's suite at Celestial's on-estate office is simultaneously more modest than her real office at the VC firm and more ostentatious, outfitted in the Georgian style Mr. Nunwick adores. Abstractly, she appreciates it despite how performatively upper class it is. But it's the upper class she took to the sea centuries ago to escape. His memories of it might be fond, but hers are not.

She drums her fingers on the ornate mahogany desk, then gets up, looking out the office window. It, at least, follows the modern architectural style of high, tall panes of glass, affording an excellent view of the closest valley and its vast construction project. It has to be near the end state now. The astrarium is complete; the ornate astronomical clock, its outer wheel close to two hundred meters across, would be a modern wonder of the world if mortals knew about it. Frankly, she isn't sure what tricks Nunwick has been employing to ensure they don't. If they did, though, they'd surely have questions about the four huge energy cannons arranged in front of it at the corners of a perfect square.

A scant two months from now, Nunwick will stand between them to be shot with energy, to ascend to an even higher state. Hacking that technology to counter Moira and company's divine powers, though? No one had so much as suggested the possibility until now.

For her girls, it'd barely matter. Perhaps. You didn't start feeling being immortal for several decades, and didn't start appreciating it for many more. For gods who'd been deified less than a year ago, losing their divinity would be mere unfulfilled potential. For herself or Agent One, let alone Mr. Nunwick or Ms. Ironheart, it would be unspeakable.

She wants to talk to—someone. To ask questions she shouldn't ask. She knows who she wants to talk to, but that ship has sailed.

294

Ms. Storm would be a sympathetic, trustworthy ear, but she could neither put Parker's doubts to rest nor confirm them.

She knows who that leaves, and she hates it.

With a snap of her fingers, Parker abruptly appears by a bus stop sign, a tall pole with the number "20" in a red circle. Right in front of her is an archetypal British pub—one that advertises itself as "the most famous pub in London." While a dozen others likely claim the same, it's possible that this one truly is, even though it's barely older than a century. It's not the building, it's the location.

An elderly civet woman waiting for the bus startles and stares. "Where in bloody hell did you—"

Parker touches her shoulder. "Nowhere."

The woman's stare goes blank.

The vixen steps forward, looking through the pub's glass doors and wrinkling her nose. It's crowded, busy. So not likely she'll find who she's looking for inside; she's not much for crowds, unless they're running away in panic.

Parker sighs. This is a foolish endeavor. She's not much for crowds, either, but she could do with a walk to clear her head. And maybe a drink. She heads a couple of blocks west to the Whitechapel station, just in time to catch the southbound Overground train.

She'd hoped to reassure herself at lunch with that bit of faux-innocent subterfuge, asking Nunwick about what Daranu saw in Moira. Those hadn't been Diana's words, though: she'd said the lion said *his father*, without giving a name.

Yet he hadn't caught that and corrected it, which he surely would have if his father had *not* been Daranu.

Nunwick's always been an elusive, private man. His plans, though—they've so far always succeeded. His assurances have been gold. And his confidence in her has been sustaining. She has spent centuries at his left hand.

And yet—

Parker gets off the train at Wapping. She can smell the Thames, glimpse it through alleys as she walks east.

And yet, he *lied* to her.

That lie, inevitably, leads her to face other lies. He lied about his origin. His age. His relationship to the mythology behind the cycle they're trying to upend. And his connection to Moira. Can she trust there are no ulterior motives behind his decisions? Behind the project itself?

Does it matter?

The name of the pub she's heading toward has changed more than once since she visited it as a mortal, but she'll always think of it as The Pelican. It was already old when she was a young, fearless pirate. Despite its arguably bigger claim to historical significance than The Blind Beggar, it's fairly empty.

Parker's rarely here more than a few times a decade, but often enough to watch the changes. Lately—well, this century—they've played up the maritime connection with the inside decor. She sits at the bar, ordering a St. Andrews from a taciturn bear. She's pretty sure he's been here the last two or three visits she's made, but if he somehow recognizes her, he gives no sign.

When he sets down her pint, he says, "Friend o' yours?"

She lifts her brows. "What?"

He nods toward a table in the back corner.

Parker turns to see Agent One sitting there, looking directly at her and grinning. The ratel finger-waves, popping an olive into her mouth. Well.

"An associate. I wouldn't say 'friend.'" She picks up the pint glass, giving the bear a curt nod and receiving a matching one in return, then heads toward Agent One's table.

"Why, it's the Captain! I'd welcome you to my old stomping ground, but this pub's more yours, isn't it?"

"It was."

"So is this just a pleasant coincidence, or did I miss another appointment with you?"

"Neither. I..." She flicks her ears, hearing faint screams. Her gaze settles on the bowl of olives, and her brows shoot up. The olives have been stuffed with little people, just their heads poking out, all crying and whimpering, some struggling futilely.

Agent One sips her beer. "Pimientos are so run-of-the-mill, don't you think?"

Parker purses her lips. "So you're eating random innocent bystanders."

Agent One looks sternly into the bowl. "Oh, they *know* what they did." She lifts an olive up; the mouse inside it shrieks. "Don't you?"

Parker can barely make out his tiny voice pleading. "I swear I'll never do anything like it again, please—"

She makes a cooing face at him. "Of course you won't, dear." She pops the fruit into her mouth, chewing noisily. The tiny wails from the bowl grow in frenzy.

The vixen glances around quickly. None of the few other patrons are looking over.

"Oh, give me credit. No mortal sees—or hears—anything besides olives with bits of blue cheese and almonds."

"And what did he do?"

"How should I know?" Agent One flashes an impish grin. "Everyone's guilty of something." She picks up the bowl and holds it out to Parker.

The vixen pushes it away with a sigh. "I need—I want to talk to you about Operation Maelstrom."

Agent One laughs. "So that's what this is about. Sent to check up on me?"

"I'm leading the operation—"

"At least in name."

Parker pauses, then looks to the side and bares her teeth. "Yes, precisely. I barely know what your part in all this is."

"And I barely know yours. I'm fine with that."

She looks back to the ratel. "I'm not."

Agent One's expression brightens to glee. "Oh, you're fishing!" She leans forward and steeples her fingers, lowering her voice to a melodramatic stage whisper. "Are we about to conspire together?"

"We absolutely are not." Parker's ears lower. "I'm as loyal to Mr. Nunwick and the project as you are."

The honey badger smirks. "Oh, but aren't I an embodiment of everything you stand against?" She folds her arms.

Parker glances pointedly at the olive bowl.

Agent One rolls her eyes. "You had a few decades of both goddess *and* pirate. I bet you were more fun then." Then she tilts her head at the vixen. "That was a curious jump right toward asserting your unwavering loyalty, though, Captain. So what's this really about? Questioning mine?"

"You just all but confirmed I should be."

"Did I? All right, let's spell it out." She picks up another olive, this one holding a frantically squirming vixen, and holds it to her lips. The ratel sucks the woman out, then nibbles the empty olive as she speaks. "Ironheart's loyal to Nunwick. Whatever he says, she'll do without question. Her trust is in him." She points a finger at Parker. "You are loyal to the project. Your trust is in the mission." She cups her chin in her hand. "That leaves me, and Glorious Leader's. Are you here, refusing to partake in my olive tray, because you're concerned with where *my* loyalties lie, or where his do?"

Parker sighs heavily, looking away. "You know you're the last person I'd choose to confide any doubts in."

"Of course. While I know you can trust me, I know you can't trust I'm telling the truth about that." She winks. "So you share something you shouldn't with me, and I'll share the same with you."

"Mr. Nunwick has...lied. About things that I'd like to believe are small, inconsequential, but I don't know."

"Oh, my dear." Agent One sighs, looking disturbingly sympathetic. "You don't see it, do you? If you're right about me—and make no mistake, you are—he's been lying to all of us from the start."

She tilts her head warily.

"He chose us to be his divine instruments." The honey badger starts rolling one of the olives around with a claw, the rabbit trapped inside it wailing. "To help fulfill his grand vision of a perfect little world, everything snug in its perfect little place, us as its perfect little new gods. He fits in that shiny, happy, stifling future. Ironheart fits. You *think* you fit. But me?" She abruptly spears the olive with her claw. The rabbit's eyes go wide with fatal shock. "No place there for someone like me," she finishes, sing-song. "Never was. Never will be."

"He wouldn't..." Parker trails off.

"Don't lie, now. Especially to yourself." She pops the olive into her mouth.

Parker falls silent for several long seconds. "What will you do?"

"Ah." Agent One looks away with a small, curiously wistful smile. "I've been on borrowed time for over a century, Captain. I owe him. We both do, don't we. This is the part I've been destined for all this time." She looks back, grin getting sharper. "So I'm going to play it fucking gloriously, that's what I'm going to do. But what about *you*, pray tell?"

"I still believe in the project, and I don't see any other path forward. But I'll have my eyes open." She takes a long drink of her ale and regards the ratel. "You haven't told me just what that part is."

"Be the maelstrom, of course."

She grunts. "They still haven't told me where or when."

Agent One grins. "They couldn't even if they wanted to. They don't know."

What? Parker can't help but look incredulous. "So you're keeping it secret from everyone? They're letting you?"

"You misunderstand me, Captain." Agent One shakes her head, finishing her beer. "I don't know, either."

Parker furrows her brow.

"You're making the mistake of thinking I plan." She laughs. "I *never* plan."

The vixen's expression grows more confused.

"That's why all the amateur sleuths looking for me to this day never get closer than the police did." She leans forward, a hint of a long-suppressed Cockney accent slipping in. "See, they all pull out a kill here. A kill there. Say, why look, there's a pattern! These five are so surgical, so precise. They must be connected. Maybe those, too, but *definitely* these. Just find the pattern! There's always a pattern!" Her eyes lock onto Parker's. "So they don't see all the other kills. So very many other kills. They never find me because *there is no pattern.*"

Parker's faced down warships and hanging judges, been the scourge of both seas and boardrooms, and been a terrifying supernatural force on multiple occasions herself. Her ears still go flat against her head.

Then the ratel sits up straight, the spell broken, and her voice returns to its typical ironic pleasantness. "Anything else on your mind, Captain, or shall we go back to staying out of one another's way?"

"That sounds excellent."

"It does." Agent One beams. "Now, I suspect you'd prefer a more boring plate of olives, so..." She holds out one hand and snaps the fingers of the other, and the remaining dozen little tourists appear on her open palm. Then she tilts her head back and shoves all of them into her mouth at once. "Mmm. Mmm." It takes her several chews and swallows to get them all down.

"Thank you," Parker mutters, eyeing the honey badger's briefly bulging throat.

Agent One licks her lips and stands up, then puts her hand on the vixen's shoulder, looking dismayingly sincere for a moment. "Goodbye, Lily." She walks out of the pub.

thirty-three
the best shot of
your life

"We're building the generators into this warehouse. It's close enough to blanket most of the downtown area with the effect field." Ironheart circles the warehouse on the projected map with her laser pointer, then circles the wider area around downtown Los Angeles. "We *may* be able to direct it more precisely, but the results have been inconsistent at best, so you're going to have to assume…are you paying attention?"

The mortals in the room—high-level executives and security officers, all with a touch of magic power themselves—all nod quickly, nervously. The immortal she's talking to doesn't nod, though. The honey badger looks completely disinterested in the lioness's speech, instead playing with a Rubik's Cube.

Ironheart's eyes narrow. "Agent One."

"I'm going to have to assume that the field affects me, too," she says, without looking up. "Does that mean I won't be able to do any *new* magic once I'm in the field, or that it'll just be difficult? And how will magic I've already used be affected?"

A wolf to the ratel's left snorts. He's been giving her an irritated side-eye the entire time. "If you've already *used* the magic, what does that matter?"

She keeps fiddling with the cube rather than looking at him.

"Pretend I'd made you the size of a tiny, helpless doll. Would you remain that way if I brought you into the field, or would you return to your normal size? I need to know if I can crush your insignificant little body under my heel, or if I have to disembowel you." She holds up a hand, fingers splayed, claws gleaming.

He clears his throat.

"From our tests, whatever previous changes you go into the field with, you keep. New feats will be difficult to impossible within the field. I couldn't do much more than parlor tricks, and I'm the strongest among us apart from Mr. Nunwick himself."

"And Mr. Nunwick?"

"We can hardly ask the CEO to participate in tests."

"I'm trying to take down the one being left in creation older and possibly more powerful than he is, whose unexpected re-emergence threatens the plan you've been working on for centuries." She smiles blandly. "So shouldn't he dance Mambo Fucking Number Five on my command if it gives me a higher chance of succeeding?"

Everyone mortal in the room flinches visibly.

The lioness's tail lashes. "I'll ask him," she says after a moment.

"Wonderful. You start promoting your 'only order will save us' spiel after the second hit, and I'll make sure I don't show up anywhere that's already stiflingly authoritarian. Then you set up your magic trap after I've hit, hmm, the third city, and it'll be ready when they think they have a chance of stopping me in the fourth."

Ironheart nods again, and looks at the rest of the room. "I think we've covered all we can. You all know what to do and what to be on guard for. In the event of," she waves at Agent One, "unusual activity, evacuate field offices by teleporting directly to the estate here. Don't wait for confirmation."

Everyone nods and stands up. The wolf glances at Agent One nervously and bolts out of the room.

As Agent One heads out, Ironheart gives her a piercing look. "You understand how much Mr. Nunwick is counting on you."

"I'll do my part. You do yours."

～

The honey badger sips her latte, looking out the coffee shop's window toward Wacker Street. She should have a newspaper in front of her. Back in the old days, she'd always have a newspaper to pretend to be looking at when she staked out an area. She tries not to be a stick-in-the-mud complaining about modern technology, but countless tiny things have fallen by the wayside in the last few decades. No matter how much their replacements objectively improve on them, they simply aren't as *satisfying*.

But, why quibble? She's about to do what she's been dreaming of for much longer. Since she'd been given the ability to. Since she'd been chosen. Divine Lord Darren might profess to hate chaos, but he *needs* it once in a while. Now, his entire plan depends on it.

She grins, finishing the latte and licking her lips. Lily, Tierney, they don't see what she does when she looks at the lion. They don't have the eye for it. They're both admirably ruthless and brutal in their own ways. Lily was a pirate captain, for God's sake! If she'd stuffed the olives with Royal Navy captains, she might have tempted her into eating a few. And Tierney's almost as powerful as Darren and twice the fanatic. But the lioness is a natural-born follower; she'd unhesitatingly rip her own liver out on Darren's command.

Darren, though? He's the one who's most like her. He's just better at hiding it from everyone. He's so good at it, he's hiding it from himself. But she sees him.

She stands up and stretches. "I think," she says out loud, "it's time to be a monster." Smiling, she walks over to the nearest customer, a middle-aged rat nursing a tall coffee, grabs his head, and smashes it into a table. There's a wet crunch, and he falls, leaving a red smear behind.

By the third head-bash, the Starbucks is in full pandemonium, some customers bolting for the door, others pulling out their phones to call 911 or get her crime on video. Two burly tigers make the mistake of trying to tackle her. She stretches out her arms and whirls, gutting each one as they come close. Oh, this is fun!

She strides back to the center of the store, leaning toward a rabbit who's dared to keep his phone camera held up this whole time. "Are you getting my best side?" She holds up her bloody claws and grins manically.

"I-I'm uploading this all!" he squeaks, backing up. "Right now! Live!"

"Fabulous! You're about to get the best shot of your life, I guarantee it." She raises her arms, curls her hands into fists, and grows rapidly. Ten feet. Twelve. Clothes shred and fall away. She punches through the ceiling. Fifteen. Twenty. Thirty. Fifty. The rabbit's last shot becomes her paws, then the underside of one paw, then blackness, frantic screams cut off with crunches and cracks.

She backs into the street, close to a hundred feet tall now, pausing and looking up at Willis Tower. From what she's heard about the thing Moira's "chaos nexus" had inadvertently created, it didn't look much like a mouse when it got its murder on. To be authentic, she should turn herself into an ugly tentacle monster—but to set the trap, she needs to stay recognizable, identifiable. She prefers that. It's delightful to see *how could someone so pretty do this to me!* in people's eyes as they die.

But, she may have to look possessed. Less...smart. All right. Hmm. She crouches, facing down the street, curling her fingers in to accent those claws, and does her best feral roar. When she stamps a paw, she makes sure it comes down squarely on cars in the traffic jam she's caused.

She stomps around the building to the south, continuing to grow as she follows the street, taking care to step on the fanciest cars and tightest knots of pedestrians. When she reaches the Shake Shack, she rips off its roof, scooping up a fistful of shrieking patrons to crudely shove in her mouth and bite down on. Some of them—or pieces of them—fall back to the ground. *Now* she's getting a solid panic going on. She can hear helicopters and sirens approaching.

She looks up at Willis Tower again and grins.

∽

Rhiannon races into the living room and turns on the television.

Moira looks up from where she's sitting by Briley; the hare's reading an old mythology book, as if to refresh herself on her own history. The mouse hasn't even looked up yet, concentrating on her needlepoint. "What's up?"

The squirrel fiddles with the remote, grumbling, until she hits a news channel. "This." On the screen there's an aerial view of a massive, 1970s-modern glass skyscraper, one built with multiple square towers clustered together, so tall that it all can't fit in the camera's view at once. But what the live shot's tracking is the giant climbing its side.

She's nude, her back down to her tail a salt-and-pepper mix of white and black, becoming pure black on her arms and legs, with pure white head-fur. Pretty, although when the camera zooms in enough, the blood on her teeth and claws is visible. She's scaling the building by digging those massive claws, on both hands and paws, into its side, leaving a trail of gaping holes punched behind her.

Briley stares, setting the needlepoint aside. "Well, didn't have that on the bingo card for today."

The network anchor's trying to narrate what's going on, but stammers, repeating the obvious ("a giant honey badger, estimated to be close to two hundred feet tall"), the uncertain ("reports of casualties all around the base of Willis Tower, no estimates of how many people may be inside"), and the ominous ("rescuers are reporting trouble accessing the building due to debris and blocked entrances"). Meanwhile, the ratel pulls herself up onto one of the shorter towers, and punches all the way into one of the floors she's now at eye level with. Pulling out a handful of people, she tilts her head back, dropping them carelessly into her mouth. At least a third miss and keep falling.

Rhiannon looks stricken. "She can't be a monster from—from—"

"From us, like William?" Moira shakes her head. "No."

Hazel's rolled into the room, too, with Diana close behind. "Holy shit. Is that the honey badger who was in the photos with Stetson?"

Moira stares.

"So are we going to watch," Hazel continues, "or are we going to stop her?" She doesn't wait for an answer, disappearing in a flash. Diana blinks twice, then disappears, too.

"I was going to ask if we could do anything from here." Rhiannon runs a hand through her hair. "Just…visualize her not on the building."

"That's not working for me, so it's not going to work for you." Moira stands up.

"That's bad, isn't it?"

"Yes."

Briley makes a *hurry-shoo* motion at both of them. "Go. Go."

They appear on the street at the base of Willis Tower, in front of the remains of the Starbucks. It looks like the images of a bomb blast you might see on television, but the gore is fresh, visceral. Rhiannon puts a hand to her mouth, gagging.

Moira stares up. The woman's climbing again, even though the higher parts of the building don't look strong enough to support her. She still can't just will her down to the ground, down to normal size, but now she knows why. The ratel is another god.

Where are Hazel and Diana?

Before she can turn to Rhiannon, a blast of ground-level thunder provides an answer: all at once, Hazel's standing right to the south of the tallest building in the city, at its same height. She's as impossible to take in all at once as the building itself. Fortunately, it *looks* like she's got her paws planted in areas that were already green space—or already flattened by the honey badger.

"Oh, fucking hell. Rhiannon, figure out what's blocking the entrances and try and let people out." Moira crouches, then kicks off, leaping into the air—and not dropping. She rockets toward the pika.

Rhiannon stares open-mouthed, then crouches and hops in place. She does it again, and a third time, looking angrier each time she fails to take flight. Groaning, she stops and starts racing around the building on foot.

The pika's reaching toward the tower, and the honey badger has —inevitably—shifted her climb to the north face. Hazel reaches, pauses, reaches another way, curses, realizing her dilemma: if she keeps her paws where they are, she can't reach all the way around Willis Tower without having to brace against it, which will bring it down. If she *doesn't* keep her paws where they are, she'll have to find somewhere else to set them.

When Moira reaches Hazel's head height, she's made herself closer to the ratel's size. She stops in front of Hazel's face. "What the divine fuck are you doing?" she yells.

"If I can't magic her off the building, I can use brute force." The pika slides a paw forward with comical care.

"If you lose your balance, Chicago loses three blocks!"

She glares. "I can stand just fine."

"You can also *fly* just fine. At a safer size."

The pika looks simultaneously annoyed and chagrined.

On the ground, Rhiannon's come to the tower's main entrance on its east side, and come to a dead stop, staring. The entrance isn't blocked by debris, it's—it's—she doesn't know *what* it is. It's twisted into a shape that looks non-Euclidean, less Escher than Giger, weird organic curves spiraling up at least two stories before merging seamlessly and disquietingly into the normal facing. She can see people inside and out trying to climb it and failing, sliding right off.

"What does a building normally look like?" the squirrel mutters aloud, glancing around at other skyscrapers, then back at this one. She takes a deep breath, spreading her hands, and *pushes*, molds, re-imagines. It feels like the building's fighting back in a way she's never experienced, like it *wants* to stay in its new shape. But it's bending back. She thinks. Hopes.

At the tower's top, Moira circles around to face the ratel, who's almost reached the roof, unbothered by the central tower visibly swaying under her stress.

The woman turns and speaks before Moira can. "Hello again, Moira!" she shouts.

"Who the hell are you?" She clenches her fists.

"You don't know? Aren't we both on the same side? Or am I one of your chaos monsters?"

"No, and no!"

"You say that *now*, dear, but perception is reality." The ratel grins widely, showing off a dazzling array of teeth. "Let me show you a neat trick."

She kicks off the building with her legs, but keeps her hands dug in—and starts sliding down. Fast. This doesn't merely punch holes in the side of the tower, it rips giant gashes, glass and debris spraying up like a boat wake. As she builds up speed from gravity, the damage gets worse; within seconds, she's peeling off half the outer wall with her hands.

Moira swears. She sees Hazel—now smaller, although still massive, and thankfully flying—diving after her, and Diana giant-sized on the ground. What's she planning to do, *catch* the woman?

She focuses on the building. Is the top starting to tilt? Stop falling. Hold that. Seal that. Mend the damage. Dammit, there's too much, she can't picture it all, she needs to focus on—

The ratel disappears a split-second before she hits the pavement. The pressure wave building from a two-hundred-foot giant plummeting at terminal velocity, though, hits with the force of a bomb. Cars, people, existing debris blows back.

Willis Tower's bundled-tube construction relies on its outer frame for support, and the tallest support section has been mortally wounded. The entire structure bends impossibly for a moment as the shockwave hits it, and starts to crumble, falling in on itself, starting to cascade down in a rising cloud of dust and debris.

Moira doesn't think she can put it back together, but she can damn well hold it in place. The tower's collapse slows and then stops, everything hanging in midair. The hare dives into the suspended cloud of debris, shielding herself, levitating objects out of the way.

Objects. Not just concrete and glass and steel, but furniture, paper, computers, office equipment. And people. Hundreds of people. Maybe thousands. She can't tell how many are still alive.

Diana's alive, but she barely looks it, covered in concrete dust and her own blood. Moira helps the giant sheep stumble out into a clearer area. Rhiannon and Hazel are in better shape. The mysterious ratel—naturally—is nowhere to be seen. By all rights, she should be more fucked up than Diana is, but if she's recovering from her fall, she's doing it somewhere else.

"Holy shit!" The squirrel helps steady her.

"Get the people out of the blast radius." Moira motions at Hazel and Rhiannon.

"We should be able to...snap our fingers and put the building back!" Hazel says, voice trembling. "We're fucking goddesses!"

"We can't—it's not—" She doesn't know how to put it in a sentence. Maybe (maybe) if it was a simple earthquake, a mortal bomb, but it wasn't. It was an act of another god. She can't undo it with magic. And if she can't, Hazel certainly can't. "Get them out. Please," she says, hoarsely.

Hazel swallows, and focuses on the cloud. Rhiannon joins her, hand on Diana's shoulder. People separate from the debris. Moira lets the rest of the building come down as gracefully as possible.

When the four goddesses are together again, they return to their normal sizes, Hazel slumping in her chair. Diana still looks like she's stepped out of a war zone. Bystanders and survivors watch the goddesses now, from a distance, looking more fearful than worshipful.

The police have been joined by fire trucks and ambulances. As responders flood into the area, cops surround the goddesses in a wide circle with guns drawn. They all advance slowly; the four women draw closer together.

"Do they think we did this?" Rhiannon says in a low voice. "Weren't they watching?"

Diana coughs and winces. "The published photographs. Of us with Stetson...and Stetson with a honey badger. *That* honey badger. Both out on my deck."

Moira runs a hand through her dusty hair. "And Nunwick used his interview to warn everyone that our 'interfering' with mortals would turn more of them into monsters."

They're all silent as the cops advance, one with a megaphone warning them to stay still.

"I suppose it'd look even worse if we didn't cooperate," Hazel says tiredly. Rhiannon puts her hand on the pika's shoulder; Hazel reaches up and laces her fingers with the squirrel's.

Moira lets out a slow sigh.

thirty-four
never much of a god

M oira reads it in Rhiannon's eyes before the squirrel speaks. "Another one."

She nods.

"Where is she? Can we get there in time?"

"This is Grand Cayman Island. Was." She shows the video on her computer, a satellite view. The honey badger takes up most of the island, sprawled on her side, at least twenty miles long toes to head. She casually wipes buildings away with a single finger.

Moira stares, muzzle open.

As if she can hear them, Agent One rolls onto her back and blows a kiss at the sky, then vanishes. The air rushing in to fill the sudden vacuum where the mega-ratel had been pulls ocean with it, tidal waves crashing over the island, filling in the depressions across the landscape caused by her weight and movement. Rhiannon's use of the past tense proves terrifyingly accurate: little land remains above sea level now.

"That's a tiny city compared to Chicago and Paris, but given that it's likely 100% casualties, an order of magnitude more deaths." Rhiannon sets down her laptop and face-plants into Briley's sofa, although she keeps speaking. "And it's an international tax haven. There are—were—literally more companies incorporated there than people living there. So she's ramped up the atrocity level *and* punched the entire global financial system in the solar plexus."

"I'd call that a silver lining if it wasn't for the blowback coming our way." Hazel sighs. "Third in two weeks, and this one so fast it was over before we could do anything."

Moira rubs her forehead. The police back in Chicago—and officers from more state and federal law agencies than she knew existed—weren't mollified by the truth as the goddesses told it, but they had no reason to hold them. (Nor, it was left tactfully unsaid, the ability. Hazel's honesty in responding to "will you come quietly if we need you to" with "fuck no" hadn't helped matters, though.)

"Given the press we're getting, trying to help might only make things worse." Diana folds her arms, brooding. "No one understands why we can't snap our fingers and undo it. Hell, I barely understand."

"We can't reverse acts of another god. And we apparently can't make mortals understand she's working for Celestial. The story's out there, but 'the gods that failed' got even more traction after Paris. After this…"

"What she did to the Eiffel Tower's hardly your fault." Briley waves at Diana. "I might not be creative enough, but I'm not seeing how Celestial imposes a grand new world order by having a crazy-ass giant honey badger squash cities."

"I don't know what the plan had been before us. Maybe they always intended to come out of the shadows right before they engineered monster attacks, then argue everyone needed to be off the street and locked down under martial law to protect them. Now, though, they're tying it to our magic."

Hazel drums her fingers. "So they'll show up at the last minute and pretend to take the honey badger out, doing what we never could do."

Rhiannon nods. "That makes it look like they were right about us all along, and they'll say, 'to keep this from happening again, follow our lead.'"

"So how do y'all find a way to stop her?"

Moira points at Rhiannon's laptop. "We can't do a damn thing when she does something like that. Our best chance was the first time in Chicago, and we—I—failed. The last two attacks were so fast we couldn't even try to respond. Unfortunately, we're stuck on their schedule. We need to get her in a position that lets us fight her on our terms, not hers." She runs a hand through her hair. "I need a trap."

Hazel's brows shoot up. "You want to set a trap for a god."

"It's what I did with Segomo. But I knew him, though. We don't know anything about Rampaging Ratel Girl." She looks to Diana. "Do we?"

"No more than the last time you asked." The sheep shakes her head. "They were all 'need-to-know' when it came to talking about future plans. I was lucky to get what I did out of Ms. Parker before…" She trails off for a moment. "And she mostly just confirmed what I'd already guessed."

"Right." The hare starts pacing. "Okay. So you bait a trap with what the target wants. What does she want?"

"We know what Celestial wants," Hazel says. "They want to take us down, one way or another."

"So we bait the trap with us?" Rhiannon looks skeptical.

"I didn't say that."

Moira stops her pacing and furrows her brow, folding her arms. "But what if."

"What if you come up with a plan that doesn't make me worry y'all got zucchini between your ears?" Briley snaps, putting her hands on her hips. "You just watched Miss Psychoclaws literally wipe an island off the map, and you want to go off and be helpless in front of her?"

Hazel sounds defensive. "If we'd been able to plan better first, we might have gotten her that first time. We *are* gods."

"So is she, and she's meaner and nastier than all of you to boot." She points a finger at Moira as the hare starts to open her mouth. "Yes, including you. Just because nobody wants to cross you when you're in war-bunny mode doesn't make you—make you *that*." The mouse's voice catches at the end.

Moira's expression softens, and she takes Briley's hand. "I know it's scary, love. But this…" She looks into Briley's eyes. "This is what I crawled out of the ale barrel I'd been in the last thousand years to do. I didn't know it at first, but I know it now. And so do you."

Briley takes a deep, slow breath, nodding a fraction.

Diana clasps her hands in front of her. "Being bait is the easy part. How do we get her to take it?"

Moira shakes her head. "Discrediting us is good, but ending us is better. She'll take the chance if she has it. We need to give her that chance, get to where she is next time *before* she leaves."

"So…we convince her she has the drop on us. Get smaller, look for her in the wrong place."

"Which leaves us smaller and unprepared." Rhiannon's tail twitches. "How do we turn the tables?"

Hazel flashes a lopsided smile. "She can't get all of us, right?"

Briley gives the pika a worried glare.

"I killed one god of war on my own. Now I have you three. We can kill another."

When Moira appears on the sidewalk in front of Los Angeles City Hall, she stares dumbly down the street at the birds.

This time, the honey badger started out walking casually down the middle of the street at a normal size, maybe five and a half feet high—shrinking cars and people alike to toy size as she approached them. The crumpled bits of metal and disquieting splotches show she stepped on anything in her direct path. The rest, though, the city's birds have discovered. The air reverberates with tiny screams as sparrows, pigeons, gulls, and crows flock to the streets.

Seething, Diana flings her hands in the air as they walk, bringing everyone who's left—who hasn't been splattered or made into bird food—back to normal size. Some scramble to their paws and run; others run at the birds. Most just lie where they are, sobbing.

"Keep your eyes open," Moira says. "We have to let her find us, then trap her." The ratel's not *right* here, but she's close by, somewhere. She feels it. The question is whether she'll take the bait.

After they've almost reached the Disney Concert Hall, Hazel frowns. "She went this way, but where—"

The hall collapses in a rising cloud of debris and dust. Agent One strolls out of it like an action movie villain, a good ten stories tall, moving straight toward them.

"So this is part of the plan, right?" the pika says, voice rising uncharacteristically.

Moira nods, setting her jaw. "Now we—"

She stops, feeling *something* change.

The honey badger grins. She's at least a hundred feet away—maybe two good strides, at her size. "Now you all get big and take out the evil monster!" She clasps her hands together. "Woe is me. Whatever shall I do?"

Hazel scowls, concentrates—then looks dismayed. "What's happening?" she hisses to the others.

"Moira…" Diana gives the hare an alarmed glare.

"I don't know." Moira scowls, too, backing up. She *should* be two hundred feet tall now, but she isn't. She isn't summoning ropes to bind the ratel, either.

"Oh, dear." Agent One looks concerned, tilting her head. "Why, it seems something's blocking our powers. But I'm already giant, and you're not." She grins, showing off all her teeth. "I'm about to have *so* much fun."

Rhiannon's backing up quickly. "What do we do?"

Moira's backing up, too, gaze fixed on the giantess. "Run like hell. Maybe we can triangulate on whatever's blocking us. If you get your power back, become big, fast."

All of them dash away in different directions.

Agent One sweeps a finger around. "Eenie, meenie, miney, moe." She strides after Hazel.

Hazel doesn't wait. Fortunately, she still has enough arm strength to build up speed. Unfortunately, this isn't a racing wheelchair, and there's only so much speed she can build up. Dammit, she can *feel* the magic; she just can't make it do what she wants. Get bigger: no. Throw shit in giant psycho bitch's way: no. So go faster.

A giant black paw smashes down a few yards behind her.

Go faster!

She manages a turn to the right that she's sure a wheelchair couldn't do without magic, zipping down a narrow one-way alley. How did she do that? If she could just—

A tremor stronger than the giant's walk shakes her wheelchair. She doesn't lose control, but she brakes hard to keep from slamming into a wall. What the hell?

Rubble cascades through the alleyway just behind her. A moment later, Hazel sees the ratel ahead of her. She's run through that building, bringing down a wall at the far end of the alley, too.

Hazel's eyes widen. Debris blocks both exits. She's trapped.

Agent One leans over and waves. "I'm going to go crush your squirrel friend and come back as fast as I can with an insensitive 'meals on wheels' joke." She pounds away before Hazel can react.

Rhiannon looks out from a hotel lobby, in the midst of a cowering crowd. Too many people have stayed on the street, too many gawking rather than fleeing. As she watches, though, the screams rise, and everyone starts running in the same direction— down sidewalks, through the streets, tying up frantically honking traffic. She puts her hand to her mouth as a Lexus, horn blaring, rams into a crowd of pedestrians and tries to keep going even with people under the wheels. She can't help herself from running out, at least a few steps, before she stares up at the source of the sudden shadow.

The ratel's paw comes down squarely on the Lexus, flattening it, its occupants, and everyone caught around it. She stops, looking around at the panic, leaning down. "Are you trying to hide in the crowd, little squirrel? Hopefully you're not...there!" She stomps her other paw on top of another knot of fleeing bystanders.

Rhiannon all but dives back into the hotel.

"Ha!" The honey badger's paw follows her, smashing into the lobby entrance over the crowd's head. Over Rhiannon's head. She tries to push through the tight crowd, but can't get far enough away before the toes curl and come down, pulling dozens of people—including the squirrel—with them, tumbling them out onto the sidewalk and street. Rhiannon lands in a sprawl on her stomach.

Then a toe bigger than her body nudges her onto her back. The paw moves far enough away that she can see all the woman's towering body; her face is difficult to make out with this angle and distance, but the sense of her smirk is overpowering. "I don't know if I'm more thrilled or disappointed that killing a god is this easy." The paw moves back over her. "But you never were much of a god, were you?"

Rhiannon tries to scramble back, then just hopes it'll be over quickly.

Unexpectedly, there's the sound of a car crash. The ratel curses, and her paw smashes down just *next* to the squirrel. "What the—" Rhiannon's view becomes the honey badger's butt and tail as the giant pivots.

Diana's just rammed an SUV into the ratel's other foot after carjacking it a half-block away. The impact's knocked the breath out of her, leaving her momentarily dazed against the airbag. She hasn't recovered before the roof rips off.

"Oh, you're Captain Lily's little lamb chop!" The honey badger crouches.

Diana scowls. She can feel *some* magic in her, but can't deliver the hoof to the face the woman desperately deserves. "You won't get away with this!"

Agent One's eyebrows lift. "You actually *said* that?" She bursts out in delighted laughter, reaching for the sheep. "Oh, I haven't heard that in so long! No wonder she liked you so much."

Moira's plan—using the word very loosely—had been to see if she could find the edge of whatever damn thing was dampening their power. That's a whole heap of assumptions, but it's the best she has to go on. Or was. Unfortunately, one of those assumptions was that the other goddesses wouldn't immediately be in danger of being killed.

New plan: run like hell *toward* Crazy Monster Lady and hope to draw enough power that she can do…something.

Whatever technomagic Nunwick's set up makes what should come as naturally to her as walking feel like wading through molasses. Every step is a fight. But every step is still a step. By the time she's near Rhiannon, she's armored, armed. She's still just six feet tall and change, though, and only as strong and fast and talented as a mortal warrior could be.

But she's as strong and fast and talented as a *fucking badass* mortal warrior.

As Agent One picks up Diana, Moira leaps onto the ratel's closest paw and slashes with her sword. The giant drops the sheep and jerks her foot off the ground with a yell, sending Moira and her sword flying. Diana lands on the SUV's hood with a pained bleat and slides off. The hare hits the sidewalk and rolls, scrambling back to her paws just as the honey badger's eyes lock onto her.

"Oh, you've found some magic, haven't you, little war-bunny." The ratel crouches, hands held defensively in front of her. "But not much, or you'd be large enough to be a challenge."

Moira runs straight at Agent One, sword raised.

The honey badger grins and reaches forward with both hands, claws forward, forcing Moira to come to a stop. She tries to grab the hare with one hand, then the other, but the sword's not just suddenly in motion, it's all but a blur. The giant's expression slips from confidence to frustration, and she starts flicking at the little warrior. It takes three tries for the side of one of her claws to knock Moira's legs out from under her.

As the hare tumbles, Agent One looks smug, rising from her crouch and smashing a paw down toward the hare—but not fast enough to keep Moira from rolling, sword held out with both hands, straight up. The ratel's eyes go wide, and she topples over with a choked-back scream, spectacularly taking out a low building as she falls.

Moira's cut a long gash in the ratel's center paw pad, ending with her sword driven in almost to the hilt—not what she intended, but the giant's own weight did most of that work. As the giant falls, Moira loses her grip, tumbling back to the ground.

Agent One pushes herself into a sitting position, breathing hard, twisting around to look at her paw. She pulls the sword out, biting back another scream, and hurls it blocks away.

As the giant tries to get back to her feet, Moira rushes to Diana and Rhiannon. "Are you all right?"

Diana nods, although the way she's holding her side and limping makes it clear she isn't. Rhiannon nods more quickly. "Are *you*? You were just stepped on!"

"She didn't get much weight down on me. Probably just a few cracked ribs."

"'Just,'" Rhiannon echoes.

Before she can say anything else, there's a growl from above as Agent One falls back to her knees. When she looks down at the little goddesses, there's no trace of cruel humor in her expression now, just pure snarling venom. "You are so *fucked*," she roars, and launches herself at them, hands out.

They run, but there's only so far they can get. Rhiannon disappears with a muffled cry under Agent One's chest as she lands. Diana makes it a few steps before the honey badger's right hand closes around her; Moira makes only a few more before she's wrapped up in the left.

"You, I'll peel," she spits to Moira. "*You*, lamb chop, I'm going to just crush." She squeezes, and Diana lets out a wheezing bleat. "And your little squirrel's under my left tit, and her struggles feel *good*." She wriggles, taking a deep breath, and there's another, higher-pitched yelp. "Yes...mmm...oh, I think she's getting weaker." She arches her back, groaning, then says in her sing-song voice, "I think she's gone."

Moira growls, pushing against Agent One's hand. She thinks she can move a finger at a time, but that's useless.

Agent One grins manically, focusing back on Diana, still speaking in a sing-song voice. "And now, pop! goes the sheep girl." She slowly begins to clench her fist. Diana's bleating becomes terrified, then frantic.

"No!" Moira pushes and twists even harder. She can feel pounding from somewhere, and can't tell if it's an earthquake or someone running or her heart.

Arilin Thorferra

"Little rabbit love god, dressed up as a warrior. You're going to be delicious—"

Abruptly Moira's world spins like a roller coaster. Agent One's on her back, staring up incredulously at another giant crouched over her. A *furious* giant, chest heaving enough to strain her country dress, one arm back behind her.

Agent One brings an arm up, but not fast enough to fully deflect the blow. Briley swings the cast iron frying pan right into the side of the honey badger's head.

thirty-five
the darkest dark

A half-dozen live news feeds fill different monitors around the makeshift control room, each showing Agent One beating the shit out of Los Angeles and, more importantly, Moira's young goddesses.

Ironheart watches, barely containing her excitement. "She might be able to kill them all at this rate."

"She hasn't killed a single one yet." Nunwick rubs his chin. "Moira won't let them go down without attempting a rescue—and that will be the most risky moment for us. Agent One has to kill or incapacitate Moira herself before we disable the field generator, or there's a good chance she'll be killed by one of them before I can."

"Moira is at a serious disadvantage. You won't be. And Agent One won't be expecting you to attack her."

Parker breaks the silence she's kept since they've arrived by making a skeptical grunt.

Ironheart gives her a baleful look. "You've been vocal enough with your displeasure over the years about her deification. Surely you're not, at the last moment, expressing displeasure over her end?"

"I'm expressing caution over assuming she's an ignorant naïf."

Nunwick frowns. "Do you have reason to think she expects us to turn on her?"

Parker's silent for a long moment before shaking her head. "No."

He frowns, turning back to the screens. "She caused a great deal of damage to our finances by destroying Grand Cayman."

Ironheart glances at Parker as she answers. "To me, that suggests she may be an ignorant naïf after all."

"Unless Parker is right, and it was a none-too-subtle message. If the last few months demonstrate anything, it's that I made far too many rosy assumptions on this journey." Abruptly, Nunwick squints at one monitor, that feed tracking Moira's entrance onto the field. "Speak of the devil."

Ironheart narrows her eyes, tail lashing. "How does she have armor and a sword?"

"She's an old god." Nunwick places a hand on her shoulder. "The field suppresses magic, but can't fully deny it to a being like her."

When Agent One stomps on Moira, Ironheart sucks in her breath, but Nunwick grits his teeth, as if he can foresee that's a bad move. The lioness roars angrily again when the honey badger stumbles and falls. "How can a tiny damned rabbit—"

"She's still the goddess of war," Parker murmurs.

As the ratel recovers, though, her expression moves from furious to crazed, letting her weight fall on the squirrel, grabbing the sheep and even Moira herself.

Ironheart fixes her gaze back on Parker. Even as Agent One starts to crush Diana in a fist, the vixen keeps her expression impassive.

Nunwick lifts his brows. "Moira may have just made a grave tactical error."

"Prey animals always do. Even divine ones. We should get ready to—"

One by one, each news feed quickly refocuses on an impossibility: a new giant. A mouse woman, well over a hundred feet tall, runs full speed toward the combatants, a plume of debris rising from her path. She looks more like a farmer's wife than a warrior, and the cast iron pan she's brandishing over her head might be comical if it wasn't twenty tons of metal.

"Who is that?" Ironheart's roar edges toward unhinged, the cool professionalism she usually projects lost in her anger. *"Who the hell is that, Darren?"*

"I don't know."

"Has she created another damn goddess? She can't have—"

"I said I don't know! She looks…" Nunwick's eyes widen. "It can't be." He clenches his fists, and a growl starts at the back of his throat, rising in force until the walls begin to rattle.

As Agent One goes limp, Diana and Moira tumble from her hands. Briley drops the frying pan. She still looks furious, but now the fright's clear in her eyes, too.

"Briley!" Moira wheezes. "You can't—it's not safe for you."

"I can damn well see that, but who else was left to save you? Are y'all okay?"

"No. But thank you." Moira smiles, trying to catch her breath. "Set me down by Rhiannon, please. Check on Diana."

Briley follows her directions, setting the hare down by the squirrel and leaning over the sheep.

"I'm okay," Diana gasps, then rolls over and moans.

"Where do you hurt?"

Diana weakly indicates a half-dozen places.

"Try not to move." Moira kneels by Rhiannon, moving gingerly, acutely feeling her own injuries. "Rhiannon's breathing." She looks up at the mouse. "Can you feel it? That we've lost magic here?"

Briley nods hurriedly. "I felt it just kinda *stop* when I ran past that building." She points at a squat office tower a couple of blocks away.

"Then I was right. It's a field effect." She shakes her head. "I don't want to ask you to help more, but I'm afraid I have to. Pick me up. We can circle around and figure out where the generator is."

Briley nods, then freezes as she sees Agent One roll onto her side. The honey badger moans, a low, guttural noise, and holds a hand to her head, struggling to sit up. She's between the mouse and Moira.

"Damn you, stay down!" Briley swings the pan again, but this time Agent One, as weak as she is, deflects it with an arm. She hisses, grabbing at the mouse's wrist with her claws. Briley jerks her hand back, dropping the pan.

The ratel breathes quickly and raggedly, looking unsteady and pained, but fixes a gaze of pure hatred on the harvest goddess. "You...big mistake...mousie." The honey badger's voice is raspy, slurred, but she speaks with absolute conviction. Briley's expression edges toward terror.

Moira stands, and winces with momentary pain. Where the hell did the ratel throw her sword? Can she summon it to her?

Briley takes another step back, gritting her teeth with determination, then dashes away in the direction of the building she'd pointed at a moment earlier. Moira swears.

Agent One looks at the mouse dumbly, eyes unfocused, then down toward the little goddesses. She raises an unsteady fist over Diana, moves it to wobble over Moira, then watches Briley as she quickly jogs in a zigzagging line, trying to avoid buildings and traffic. Her fist unclenches and her brow furrows. Then her eyes widen, realization piercing the fog of concussion. She lurches toward a nearby building, gripping it and painfully pulling herself up to her paws.

Moira runs after her, ignoring the protests from her ribs. Even when—if—she gets her powers back, she won't be able to just snap her fingers and heal herself and the others. One crisis at a time, though.

Her sword won't come back to her, but it doesn't matter. The hobbled ratel can't chase Briley at full speed, she can't do it without yowling with pain when she takes a bad step—but she still moves faster than Moira. The hare stops running, letting out another frustrated curse. "Dammit!"

Briley sees Agent One running at her. She jumps backward, causing a cloud of debris to rise around her paws, then narrows her eyes and snaps her fingers.

The ratel abruptly disappears.

"Yes!" Diana manages a weak cheer.

Briley looks down at the building she'd accidentally leapt onto. "Sorry," she mumbles apologetically. She resumes zig-zagging, looking toward the center of the rough circle she's making. "I think I'm getting it!" she calls.

Moira searches the street futilely. "She's still there. I just don't know where." She raises her voice. "Briley! Get the honey badger!" But the mouse can't hear her.

Wincing at the pain from her own cheer, Diana counters, "She's small. Not dangerous now."

"She gets her powers back when she's on the other side of the field, too, and she knows exactly where the boundary is. If we can't get to her first, and it's just her and Briley facing off…"

Diana lets out a weak, worried bleat.

Nunwick quickly paces, hands to his head. He talks quickly, just to himself. "Has she been here all this time? She must have been. But did they know? No, they couldn't have. Every old god had to leave for the cycle to turn. They all knew it. Moira was supposed to be the last. How could *Briley*, out of all of them, stay hidden from us?"

Parker furrows her brow.

Ironheart hurries behind. "Could—could Moira have hidden her?"

"I don't know—no. No. We'd have known. No, somehow they found each other because of Moira's damned new crusade. It somehow brought them together." He stops pacing, glancing at the screens, frowning as Briley jogs away from the battle. "What's she doing?"

"I don't know." She watches, looking dismayed.

Parker watches, too. What *is* the mouse doing? Back and forth—Oh.

"She's not trying to get out of the suppression field, she's trying to find its circumference. And therefore, its center."

Ironheart's eyes widen. The center, with the suppression machinery itself. The center where they are.

"Mr. Nunwick." The vixen's voice remains soft, but the gaze she fixes on Nunwick is blade sharp. "They knew?"

He turns from the screens, giving her a blank look.

"You said the gods knew they all had to leave for the cycle to turn."

The irritation becomes—something else. Anger, but more than that, an emotion she isn't sure she can read. "This is not an appropriate time for a mythology lesson, Parker."

"She's up!" Ironheart points wildly at the screen.

Agent One wobbles, but stands, starting to run in an obviously pained fashion toward Briley.

Then the honey badger disappears. Ironheart yowls.

"Our margin of safety is closing." Parker puts her hands on her hips. "Do we have an evacuation plan better than waiting for Briley or Moira to destroy the generator and hoping we can teleport out before we're drawn into open battle?"

"Maybe we *should* be in open battle," Ironheart spits. "The world's already against Moira, already believes Agent One is her creation, not ours. If we kill them—"

"No. Ms. Parker is right." Nunwick clenches his fists, looking pained. "We've portrayed Moira and her compatriots as misguided but still well-intentioned, suggested Agent One is her *accidental* creation, one she and her goddesses have been futilely fighting against. We can't go to war with Moira without a better story than we have."

"Then—"

Nunwick cuts Parker off with an acid glare. "Let's not count Agent One out yet."

Parker purses her lips, and silently gestures back at the array of screens. Briley has stopped circling and dashed back into the generator field. Toward the other stranded gods. Toward the field's center.

Ironheart's ears lower.

～

Briley double-takes as she looks to the side of the path, seeing Hazel trapped in an alley between two piles of debris. The pika's trying to get the chair over one rubble stack, using sheer force of will.

Hurrying over, the mouse crouches, offering Hazel a hand. The pika stares open-mouthed for just a moment, then rolls on.

"How are you even here? Where's Miss Psychoclaws?"

The mouse straightens up, hand cupped around Hazel and her chair. "I whopped her with a frying pan. She got back up—the damn woman's like Rasputin with nice tits—but I shrank her, too, so she's out of commission."

"Only if you stomped her into two dimensions. How're the others?"

"All kindsa messed up, and since it's mostly due to another god, nobody's gonna snap their fingers and recover quick. You and I are the ones in the best shape." She makes her back to Moira and the others, setting Hazel down near them.

Hazel squeaks when she sees Rhiannon, still lying motionless. She rolls over and drops out of the chair, feeling around for the squirrel's pulse. "Oh, no. Stay with us." She looks at Moira desperately, then back at the squirrel. "Stay with me."

The hare puts her hand on the pika's shoulder, trying to look reassuring, and looks up at the mouse. "I'm sorry. I don't—you shouldn't have to—"

"What I have to do is get you back to godhood. You're the fighter, not me." Briley leans over and blows Moira a kiss. "And I gotta find this thing fast. Somewhere where they can bring in a lot of power…"

"If you see her, Briley, you have to kill her. Don't wait for me."

She bites her lip, nodding, then stands and scrambles off down the street. Moira swallows hard.

A few blocks away, the mouse stops, running a hand through her hair. The fashion district stretches in front of her, low warehouses full of importers and florists and fabric wholesalers. She can't see the honey badger, but this is just about the center of the circle she was making. Whatever's blocking them has to be right here. Somewhere. Do any of these have "a lot of power"? Nothing has high-tension lines coming in to make it obvious.

But one of those adjacent blocks is one big building, a combination of parking garage and multi-tenant flower market. Huge solar panels cover the roof.

Quickly circling the structure, she sees most of it looks industrial and commercial, a thin strip of retail along one side. She takes a deep breath, and calls down to anyone below. "Sorry I gotta do this!"

She smashes her paw down on the building, knocking a massive hole in it, and begins kicking, stomping, sweeping both paws back and forth.

Blocks away, Moira clenches her fists again, running—limping —toward the boundary. "Come on," she murmurs. "Come on—"

A rumbling starts near the concert hall's ruins. Agent One, battered and raging, reaches the edge of the field—and grows. And grows. And grows.

Moira changes course and runs toward Briley, as fast as she's able, yelling. It puts her in the path of destruction. It makes it all too likely she'll end her immortal existence ignominiously crushed under a paw. But she has to get there. She *has* to.

Briley's focused enough on her work—the debris cloud so thick, the noise so loud—that she doesn't see Agent One until the honey badger, now twice her size, starts stomping toward her. Each furious step is a small earthquake.

Eyes widening, the mouse smashes down the building frantically. "Dammit to hell, shut off. Shut off!" She circles, trying to keep space between herself and Agent One.

"I'm not going to use magic on *you*, little god-mouse. I'm going to gut you. I'm going to watch the light in your eyes fade."

The ratel turns, flattening a fire station on the outskirts of the warehouse Briley's been demolishing. Huh. If she'd walked straight through the retail section across the street, directly at the mouse, it'd already be over. That means—

Briley dives for the storefronts just as Agent One grabs for her. She's not sure if a belly-flop onto a concrete building would have hurt less if she'd had her full powers, but it sure hurts without them.

As she obliterates the roof, she gets in a couple of good pounds with her fists before the bigger giantess grabs her leg. Briley digs in with her fingers and claws, raking them through what's left of the building as she's dragged backward. She can't make out what's inside the storefront she's wrecking, but the tanks and wires look a lot more mad science than any flower shop she's ever seen. When the power cuts out, she *feels* it.

And some of those people running away from the building—

"Sotala!" she gasps, just as Agent One lifts her fully off the ground.

The running people all disappear in abrupt, decidedly magical flashes.

Moira and the other goddesses feel it, too. Abruptly, the hare's giant once more, sword in hand, armor repaired. She still feels every wound the ratel's given her, though. She forces herself not to stagger.

Hazel and Diana grow, too, and the pika teleports Rhiannon into her carefully cupped hands. "I'm the only one of us who isn't injured," Hazel whispers. "But I can't—I can't leave…"

"I know." Diana squeezes her shoulder.

Agent One howls, body-slamming Briley back down into the rubble. "This was my time! *My* time!"

Briley grabs one of her arms. "Don't fuck with old gods, girl." She's wincing with pain, blood trickling from her mouth, but still smiles defiantly. "Even harvest gods."

The ratel's eyes widen incredulously, then narrow. She raises a fist—

Vines and tendrils and stems burst out of the ground all around the gigantic ratel, rapidly tangling her up, binding her, encircling her torso and limbs. Then piercing. She screams, huge body bucking and thrashing.

Yes. They've got her. Moira runs. She doesn't create *much* more rubble than was already there, but caution isn't first on her mind. Almost there.

Agent One makes a final lunge, immense claws straight out, digging deep into the small-to-her mouse. Into her sides, her chest, her stomach. Ripping. Tearing.

"No!" Moira yells, raising her sword. Too late. Too late.

Agent One's face blooms into a fevered smile as she lifts her claws, blood and gore streaming off them. She laughs, raggedly, wildly. "I *got* you!"

The mouse sets her jaw stiffly, meeting the ratel's gaze. Just as Moira reaches them, Agent One's eyes go wide as branches and flowers burst out of her mouth, sprout along her body, tear through her fur.

As the light in her eyes fades, she never stops smiling.

The honey badger's form shimmers, fur shifting from black to iridescent, the light growing blinding, as bright as the sun. Sparkles drift away like embers, leaving nothing behind but the wild garden that's all but replaced the ruined flower market building.

Diana stares. "Is that what happens when gods die?" she whispers. Hazel shrugs helplessly.

Moira falls to her knees by Briley, dropping her sword. "You did it. You..." She tries to smile reassuringly, but she can't keep the horror off her face, can't tell her that everything will be fine. They both know it would be a lie.

Despite the tears of pain streaming down her cheeks, Briley manages a smile. "I know," she gets out, fumbling for Moira's hand.

"You're supposed to be the one who stays behind." Moira's voice breaks, and she clasps Briley's hand tightly. "I'm supposed to be the one who fights."

"I couldn't..." Briley coughs, the sound of wet, ugly ripping. "... choose my fruit over you again."

Moira smiles, sadly. "Oh, Briley. You should have—I should—"

"Moira." The mouse squeezes her hand back hard, and her gaze sharpens. "Listen. Your real power ain't war. Anybody can kill. Even me." She smiles wryly, then winces. She finishes in a whisper, breathing shallowly. "Be love. You understand? Be love."

She nods shakily. She doesn't think she does understand, but she nods.

Briley blows her a weak kiss.

Moira leans over and touches her lips to the mouse's, as Briley's fur starts to shimmer and shine, overtaken by brilliant iridescence.

Hazel gasps. Diana lets out a small, disbelieving sob.

When the hare straightens up, she's alone, grasping a handful of flowers. She stares blankly into the distance, slowly letting her fingers uncurl.

thirty-six
a thousand years too late

I t takes a good five seconds of Diana holding out the coffee mug before Moira looks up and takes it. "Thank you." She gives the sheep a wan smile, takes a perfunctory sip, and returns to looking distant.

The sheep sits down next to her and sighs, looking around Briley's farmhouse. It remains as it was the last time the mouse had been here. Well, almost: boxes and old ledger books cover the kitchen table, where Rhiannon, Jerry, and Jerry's boyfriend Trevor sit going over Harvest Dance's finances. At least, they're supposed to be. Jerry's a sniffly mess, with frequent dips into blubbering wreck. Trevor, she's told, has accounting experience, but between trying to comfort Jerry and trying to handle being one of two mortals in a room full of damaged goddesses, the black-footed ferret is kind of checked out.

Diana can't blame him. Part of her selfishly wishes she could check out, too. It's been two weeks since Briley's death, and she's still got weeks left to heal, as does Rhiannon. Hell, as does Moira. Hazel's the least injured of the group, but she's clung solicitously to Rhiannon as she heals. The squirrel looks gratified by that, maybe a touch embarrassed. Does she have a crush on Hazel? Was Diana being thick in not picking that up before now? Has Hazel figured it out yet? They're all messes.

All except Moira, and that makes Diana nervous. She's been quiet, melancholy, but not visibly angry, or sad, or emotional, period. From all appearances, she's as stoic as she was when they'd first met, tempered by the love goddess tenderness she's been showing more of lately.

Diana sets her mug down. "I know what you've said about this," she says softly. "But I still think—"

"I know." Moira pats Diana's knee. "And you're wrong." She says it without rancor.

"Even if it's difficult, isn't it worth it?"

Moira falls silent so long Diana doesn't think she's going to answer. When she speaks, it's curt. "As I've said several times now, I don't truly know how a god's death works. Even if there's a mortal version of Briley—"

"But that's *not* what you said. You said you'd asked the god of death about it when you killed Segomo. He didn't say 'if,' did he?"

"It won't be her!" Moira snaps, then rubs her face, speaking more quietly again. "Yes. There's a middle-aged mouse woman out there, right now, a 'what if' version of Briley. What if she'd been born as a mortal? If I found her, I'd have that answer. It's the one way history can be rewritten, for gods to change the past. Change *their* past. By dying.

"But she *was* my flower, Diana. Was. Past tense. A mortal Briley, whether she exists now or is yet to be, won't be the goddess of the harvest. Maybe she'll be good with plants. Maybe her mortal parents will have named her Briley. But she won't have a history with me. She won't even *know* me, except through legends and folk tales. I'll be a god, and she'll be a mortal. We could have a brief dalliance, but...only that."

Diana looks down.

Moira pats the sheep's knee again. "I'll be all right. I *am* all right. I'm fine. We're going to have to prepare for whatever Celestial does next, so we can't take too much of a break." She stands up, picking up her coffee. "I'm going for a walk."

She leaves the farmhouse, Hazel, Rhiannon, Diana, Jerry, and

Trevor all turning to watch her. Hazel looks at Diana, brow raised. "Have you seen her cry yet?"

"No. I haven't."

"Just stoic and serene like that?"

"Stoic and serene."

"And do you think she's really all right?"

"I absolutely do not, and I don't know how to help other than just...not pushing." Diana shakes her head. "But she's right about preparing. Celestial might be stopped for the moment, but they're going to regroup."

"You're as close as we've got to an enemy gods expert," Rhiannon points out. "What will they do next?"

She shrugs helplessly, spreading her hands. "We can only guess as to what the plan was in the first place—that they'd hoped the honey badger would take us all out, and then they'd be able to stop her."

"That sure as hell didn't go well for them. They're still avoiding the media."

Hazel chimes in, "Why are *we* still avoiding the media?"

"Lady Moira talked to reporters briefly back in L.A."

"Really briefly." The pika shifts in her seat. "I ended up being the one explaining god business to the mortals. That was, uh, awkward."

"You're good at it." Diana smiles slightly. "You explained who Briley was beautifully. And you did a better job than we had before of getting people to consider the possibility the honey badger *wasn't* a chaos monster, and that maybe Celestial *isn't* as benevolent as Nunwick made them out to be."

"And you did it without smiting anyone for asking stupid questions," Rhiannon adds.

Hazel nods, looking distant a moment. "That was a challenge."

Diana clears her throat. "Anyway, even if the world doesn't understand most of the details of what happened, the trust level in Celestial has dropped through the floor."

Jerry closes the book he and Rhiannon have been looking at.

"I'm going to heat up a pie, ma'am. Is there a kind y'all want?" He looks around at the others, too.

"Peach," Rhiannon and Hazel both say, then grin at one another. Rhiannon adds, "Please," with Hazel echoing it a moment later.

"Peach would be lovely," Trevor confirms.

"Coming right up." The fox bakes when he's stressed; the last few days, they've all had *way* more pie than probably wise.

"So..." Hazel nods after Jerry, and looks back to Trevor inquisitively. "Are you two going to be able to take over Briley's farm business?"

The ferret lets out a puff of breath, looking poleaxed by the question for a moment. "I think so, Lady Hazel. If I can convince him that it's not going to all fall apart without Briley's magic touch."

"He has a magic touch, too." Rhiannon stretches, then winces. "Ow. You'd think being immortal would prevent back pain."

"You got crushed under a giant god's boob." Hazel crosses her arms. "You were like one sharp inhalation away from the most ludicrous epitaph in history."

The squirrel snorts. "Anyway, I don't think all this relies on Briley. I mean...it's all still from stock she grew, and he worked with her for over twenty years. And it's not as if the concept of harvests depends on Briley being..." She trails off.

Hazel forces a smile. "Maybe one of us can be the god of harvests once this is all over. You're like the god of technology or something, but Diana and I are still uncommitted."

"I'm not sure any of us have aspects the way the gods of Moira's pantheon do."

"Celestial's gods don't seem to, either. I can't imagine what the aspect of Miss Psychoclaws would have been."

"Chaos." Diana looks away. "As much as we say that we're the chaos in opposition to Celestial's order, she was the kind of chaos that I think—that I *thought*—they were truly, sincerely trying to prevent. And yet they deified her."

"And they never even hinted anything about her to you." Hazel grunts. "You think they have any others they didn't bother to tell you about?"

She shakes her head. "By definition I can't say for sure, I know. But it doesn't seem like creating gods happens that often. Moira may make it look easy, but she's said she hadn't deified anyone before me since the mythological days."

"We don't know if Celestial's playing by those rules." Rhiannon spreads her hands. "What about whatshisname, Max, the one who introduced Moira to Celestial?"

"True." Diana rubs her chin. "I think Celestial's created a fair number of people at least on the power scale William was, and a few closer to Max's. Ms. Parker's administrative assistant, Ms. Storm, for instance."

Hazel blinks. "Her assistant? So she's a secretary who might magically stomp mortals who get pushy with her?"

"No 'might' about it. I saw a salesman try to barge past her once. She turned him into a coffee cup."

"Okay, I gotta admit, that's cool."

Rhiannon leans forward in her seat, furrowing her brow. "So what can we do for Moira?"

"I don't think there's anything we can do for her that we couldn't do for mortals," Hazel says.

Rhiannon nods slowly, frowning. "I guess loss is how all *mortal* love stories are destined to end, one way or another. But not divine love stories. Gods might break up, but they don't...outlive one another."

"You can never know, even if you're a god." Hazel rubs the back of one of her ears.

"No. I guess you can't." Rhiannon hesitates, biting her lip, then abruptly stands up. "Going to get some coffee, too." She heads into the kitchen.

Hazel watches the squirrel leave, looking faintly puzzled.

Diana looks between the two, then feels her phone ping. She pulls it out and gapes. It's a brief message from Parker. *Diana, you were right. I have to meet with Moira ASAP.*

"Hmm?" The pika looks over inquisitively.

Could this be a trap? Yes. Should she ask? Maybe, but she knows what answer she'll get. After another moment's hesitation, she sends Parker the farm's address and closes her eyes. "I hope this isn't a terrible mistake," she mutters.

Hazel arches one brow high. "Diana?"

"I'll be back shortly, unless Moira kills me." The sheep gets up and hurries toward the front door.

Moira walks from the farmhouse into the closest orchard. Apples, right? She should know how to tell one tree from another without looking for fruit. But yes, apples. They're still on the trees, reddish-orange streaked with yellow and green. These must be Briley's beloved pippins.

A few weeks ago, a stroll here would have calmed her, but now it makes her feel hollow. She closes her eyes, takes a deep breath, and strides out toward the road. Maybe she needs to be somewhere else. Anywhere else.

Visit Stetson? No. She all but promised to leave him alone, and doesn't want to break her word. Besides, what would she say? What would she do?

Oh, she knows what she would do. A fling, like so many over the centuries. Briley had hers, too. Nothing wrong with that. And how is she out here whimpering silently to herself that a mortal somehow deserves better than an intimate night with her? She's the fucking *goddess of love.*

Could Diana be right? She literally watched Briley die. And yet the truth is, Moira could find a now-mortal Briley and—

And hate herself for what amounts to using divine power to stalk her.

She slows down, and comes to a stop at the road's edge, in front of the HARVEST DANCE ORCHARD & FARMS sign. She drops to sit cross-legged at the sign's base, finishes the dregs of her coffee, and leans against a thick square post to stare up at the sky.

What *does* come next? What *is* her plan? For all her bravado, she's a horrible tactician. She tried to set a trap for the honey badger goddess and got trapped herself. She hasn't been outwitting Celestial, she's been getting lucky.

Except when she hasn't.

Well, come on. She'd spent the last millennium assuming she'd lost Briley, along with all the other gods when they up and vanished. This is just—just the status quo. Back to her on her own again.

She's fine.

Moira closes her eyes, rubbing them, and looks straight ahead to find a crow across the driveway peering at her. When she peers back, it tilts its head one way, then the other, hopping sideways a few times.

No, not a crow. It's a raven, like the ones gods used to send messages with. Like the ones she sent Daranu. Like the ones Daranu never sent back.

"If you're here with a note, you're a thousand years too late," she mutters.

The raven eyes her and squawks.

"Screw you, too." She tosses a pebble at it, lightly. It flaps away a few feet, lands, and gives her a distinctly annoyed look. After another few seconds, it takes off.

Sighing, she leans back again, then realizes the raven flew off because someone else is walking down the driveway. Diana.

"I wasn't gone that long, was I?" She tries to sound light, but suspects she sounds bitter.

"No. I did want to find you, though." Diana stops a few feet away. "Were you talking to that bird?"

"Yes, but I wasn't expecting much of a response. Good thing, too." She waves after the bird. "What god's left to send messages that way now? Even Briley would have just given me a phone call. And we know it wasn't from her, was it?"

Diana crouches by the hare. "Moira, it's all right to mourn her."

"Stop worrying at me, Diana." Moira tosses another pebble into the grass. "I thought Briley was gone for good long ago. But we got to reconcile. We had another few months together that I'd never expected. And we got to say goodbye." She smiles brightly for a second or two, then falters. "I just—I just..."

Diana puts a hand on her shoulder.

Moira speaks more softly. "We—all of us, mortals and gods—justify war by saying it's about *protecting* us, protecting *things*. Our family, our friends, our freedom. That's usually a lie. It's a desire for power. For resources. For revolution. For revenge.

"But once—once in a while, it truly *is* about protection. It lives up to those stories and those songs. And when I had..." Her voice breaks. "Had to protect her..." Her face crumples, and her breath starts coming out in abrupt, choking gasps.

Diana pulls her into a hug, and Moira finally can't stop the tears, loud, wracking sobs flooding out of her. "I'm sorry." She buries her face against the sheep's woolly shoulder. "I'm so sorry."

Diana holds her more tightly, and stays silent.

A full minute passes before Moira pulls away, looking up at the sky again. "You know, I think of you as the den mother of this little group." She sniffles and wipes her eyes. "Gods know I'm not qualified."

Diana rubs the hare's back. "Like I am? Being the goddess of love makes you more qualified than...goddess of whatever I am. Assuming us new gods even work that way."

"I don't know." Moira shakes her head. "I don't remember a time when I didn't have my aspect. My first aspect, at least."

Cars don't travel down the country road the farm stand's on too often, but a handful have passed since she's been sitting here. The one approaching now catches her attention for two reasons: it's an electric blue sports car, and it's slowing down.

Moira sniffles and wipes her nose again. "Briley did have an interesting mix of customers," she mutters, rising to her paws.

Diana stands up with her. "I...think that's someone who messaged me a few minutes ago and asked to meet."

Moira looks at her, confused. Then her eyes widen and narrow in quick succession.

The car turns at the sign, and comes to a stop in front of them. It's not merely a sports car, it's a supercar, a two-door Ferrari convertible. The driver's door opens, and the silver vixen inside steps out.

Diana nods fractionally, taking a deep breath. "Ms. Parker."

"Ms. Lindsay." Her words and demeanor are as professional as ever; with her designer sunglasses still on, standing in front of a half-million dollar car, she looks ready for a glamour photoshoot.

Moira locks her eyes onto the vixen, but hisses at Diana. "She asked to meet you after *pushing you out a window,* and you said yes?"

Diana glances up at the hare, but before she responds, Parker cuts in. "I had to send a message."

Moira wipes her eyes again, and growls under her breath. She does *not* want to look like she's been crying now, of all times. "And you don't think she got it the first time?"

The vixen takes off her sunglasses, putting them in her jacket pocket, and looks directly at the hare. It breaks the spell of her appearance: she looks weary, uncharacteristically haggard. "The message wasn't for her, Lady Moira."

Diana blinks, looking back up, and fidgets.

"I *am* glad to see Diana. But the truth of the matter is, if you'll allow me, I'm here to speak with you."

Moira gives Diana a sidelong glance, and the sheep nods to her.

Turning back to the vixen, she grits her teeth. "Convince me not to smash you and your overpriced gas guzzler into two dimensions, and I'll allow you."

"The SF90 is a plug-in hybrid. I want to talk about why the old gods, your pantheon, left."

"I don't know!" Moira snaps, voice rising with an edge of thunder. "I haven't known for a thousand damned—"

"I might."

Moira freezes.

"What I don't know," Parker continues, "is why they left you behind. But I'm sure it's not what we've both believed."

thirty-seven
the whole raven thing

Based on the irritated expressions of both lions, the stoat knows his presentation hadn't been welcome, but he puts on his bravest face. "I know it's not the public relations campaign we'd prefer to pivot to, but—"

Nunwick cuts him off with a hand-wave. "We can't paint ourselves as victims."

"But w-we *were* damaged by Agent One," the stoat stammers. "Placing that front and center builds sympathy and casts doubt on the accusation that we're responsible for her creation."

"It's an admission of weakness." Ironheart glares. "Cast doubt another way."

"How, ma'am?" He can't keep the frustration out of his voice. "A blanket denial followed by silence won't work this time. The world *saw this live on television.* There are cities wrecked, hundreds of thousands of people dead…"

She bares her teeth. "Hundreds of thousands and one."

"Ma'am?"

With a clap of her hands, he's inside her mouth, looking at the back of those bared teeth. She snaps her jaws shut, muffling the scream, and chews twice perfunctorily before swallowing.

Nunwick sighs, leaning back and crossing his arms.

"I trust you don't think he had a point." She licks her lips.

"I don't know." He grunts. "It *is* an admission of weakness, but we need to wrest control of the narrative back from Moira and company. We have a short time before my ascendance, and the majority of governments in the world need to fall in line beforehand. If they don't..." He spreads his hands.

"We risk bringing about the end of the world, just in a different fashion than the one we've been fighting to prevent." She scowls. "If only that damned honey badger had done her job."

Nunwick shakes his head. "She did magnificently. If Briley hadn't shown up, Agent One might well have killed all four of them."

"She *could* have killed them, if she hadn't insisted on being showy about it."

"A criticism Ms. Parker might well have made. She never liked that I deified that ratel."

"She never saw the value in using chaos against itself."

"No. And I sense she has increasing doubts." He drums his claws on the conference room table, brooding. "But there's no value in re-litigating this now. We need options, and pointing out our losses is a viable strategy."

"We need to convey a reassuring sense of strength. I don't see how we can project that with 'we share your pain' as a message."

"We could play off the idea of 'stronger together.'" He makes air quotes with his fingers. "The core message that we need strict order to prevent another monster from erupting remains the same, but we tug at a sense of community."

Ironheart looks skeptical. "When has community ever unified mortals? They respond to authority, rally around great men they expect to save them. Even self-proclaimed communists slap figureheads on their flags and create authoritarian states."

He grunts. "Rallying them around me was the plan, but the plan clearly has to change."

"Does it?" She stabs a finger at him. "We can tug at community all we want, but if leaders follow us, follow *you*, their followers will follow them."

"Based on what? The Fresno experiment should have created a

model of order, and it ended in disaster that cast us as the villains. We *almost* rewrote the story successfully, got them to argue for us that Moira's meddling accidentally created Agent One. But now? They treat her counterarguments as credible. We're back to demons rather than gods."

"Perhaps we can use that confusion to our benefit."

"How?" he roars. "Confusion is chaos, and chaos is that fucking rabbit!" He slams his hands on the table hard enough to crack it, and begins pacing around the room furiously.

Ironheart swallows, ears back for a moment, but waits patiently. He'll come up with a plan when he calms down. He always does.

Hazel raises one brow when Moira slams the front door open, scowling hard enough to set tinder aflame. When Diana follows, looking nervous, her other brow goes up. "What's going—"

Parker steps in a moment later. Diana closes the door behind the vixen.

"—on."

"Hello, Ms. Harcourt." The vixen nods to the pika, then the squirrel. "Ms. Doran."

"Hi." Hazel works on keeping her voice perfectly conversational. "Long time no see." In the same tone, she says to Moira, "Is there a reason we're not killing her?"

"Reply hazy, ask again later," the hare mutters, dropping into a seat and watching Parker. Diana sits with the vixen on the sofa, but keeps a distance.

Jerry enters the room, carrying a pie on a platter along with several dishes. "Fresh out of the oven…oh. I didn't know we were having guests."

"I didn't, either."

Jerry glances between Moira and Parker. Hazel's glaring as much at Parker as Moira is; Rhiannon looks conflicted. Diana looks uncomfortable. Finally, Jerry clears his throat and addresses the vixen. "Would…would you like some pie, too, ma'am?"

She smiles disarmingly. "That would be lovely."

"I'll get you a plate, too. And start a pot of coffee." He hurries back to the kitchen.

"All right." Moira faces Parker. "Talk."

"According to Ms. Lindsay, you met Mr. Nunwick in Fresno, and he said one thing to you in passing: that he didn't know what his father saw in you. Is that correct?"

Moira gives Diana a sour look, then nods to Parker.

"And you assumed that meant Daranu."

"Are you going to tell me that's wrong? Briley and I are—were—both damn sure who your Mr. Nunwick really is."

"No, I'm not. I didn't believe Ms. Lindsay then." She looks away. "I didn't want to. It would have meant he'd lied to us, very early on. But I confirmed to my satisfaction that it was indeed a lie. A small lie, yet one at the very heart of the enterprise."

Rhiannon crosses her arms. "Our hearts bleed for you."

Parker looks at her. "That lie *also* means that Mr. Nunwick knows far more about the old gods than he'd told us for centuries."

Jerry comes in with another plate, then starts carving pie slices.

"And, since the time you pushed Diana out a fifty-story high window, he just happened to tell you why they left?" Moira takes a plate, eyes locked on the vixen.

"He was so discombobulated by the appearance of another old god that he let something slip." She takes the offered plate from Jerry. "Thank you."

"You're welcome, ma'am." He hands out other plates, ears back, then disappears into the kitchen again.

Parker purses her lips. "Ms. Harcourt, I'm given to understand you're the expert on the old mythology, barring Lady Moira herself. Is it the gods leaving the mortal realm that causes the cycle to turn?"

Hazel snaps out of entertaining images of nibbling the vixen's limbs off and clears her throat. "All the myths say is that they *do* all leave before it turns."

"Do the stories record the old gods *desiring* the cycle to turn?"

"No. Why would they want that?"

"Why indeed. You'd think they would have fought to stop it, the way we—Celestial—are. And yet. Mr. Nunwick was surprised by Lady Briley's appearance in part because, he said, the gods knew they all had to leave for the cycle to turn."

Rhiannon furrows her brow. "Briley never said that, and neither did Moira." She looks to the hare, who shakes her head, too. "Either he was lying or you misunderstood him."

"I don't think either of those are the case, Ms. Doran."

"No matter what, they knew they'd left *me* behind." Moira glares, setting her plate down. "They knew I was still here."

"Yes." Parker nods slowly, looking at the hare.

"But the gods didn't *want* the cycle to turn!" Hazel can't believe this is even up for discussion.

"The cycle has turned before," Parker counters. "The old gods left, and new gods arose. Is it a question of *want,* or a question of *should?*"

"I would have known!" Moira clenches her fists, her voice growing raw, caught between anger, denial, and a welling despair. "You think that after centuries of spurning me, keeping me in exile, they realized that the cycle *did* have to turn? That the only thing keeping it from turning was me being here? Briley being here? If they wanted it to turn, they would have made her come with them! They would have—" Her words catch, and she looks away.

"Forgiven you," Parker finishes softly.

Jerry returns, wide-eyed, with a tray of coffee mugs. He sets them down and scurries away to the kitchen table.

"This is an uncharacteristic amount of conjecture for you, Ms. Parker," Diana says, not quite meeting the vixen's eyes.

"Perhaps, Ms. Lindsay. But whatever Mr. Nunwick heard his father—Daranu—say that he saw in Moira, he heard it *after* her banishment. If Daranu had come to a new understanding, Nunwick is the only being left in creation who would know."

"Briley," Hazel sputters. "Lady Briley knew more than Moira did, and she'd surely have—"

"She didn't. Not really." Moira runs a hand through her hair.

"But she's also a tremendous hole in whatever theory you're grasping at. And so am I."

"She may well be. But I don't believe you are. Both Daranu and his son knew you were here."

Moira frowns. "Meaning...?"

Hazel can't hold back now. "No. Look." She makes a time-out gesture. "When we first met, you monologued a batshit theory to us, one I'm still not sure wasn't all gaslighting. It's not lost on any of us that for all your warnings about 'chaos nodes,' the closest thing to a monster we've seen since William was the honey badger your team fucking created. Now you're back with another one. You think Daranu *did* forgive Moira, and that he, what, just forgot to tell her? Oopsie doopsie?"

She meets the pika's eyes. "I told you the truth then, Ms. Harcourt, and I'm telling you the truth again now. I am guilty of taking advantage of your creation of that chaos nexus, but not of creating it myself. If anything, it seemed to be incontrovertible proof of Celestial's premise."

Hazel looks at Moira. "What about the whole raven thing? You sending ravens up to Daranu with notes asking if he'd forgive you and them always coming back with 'no, fuck you' notes?"

"In so many words, yes."

"So I'm going with gaslighting." She gestures at Parker. "Can I step on her? I know I usually run people over, but I'll make an exception, since she stepped on me."

"I brought my shoe down precisely *around* you without harm. If I'd wanted to kill any of you that night, you know full well I could have."

Hazel narrows her eyes. Before she can speak, Moira holds up a hand. "If anyone kills her, it's me." She focuses on the vixen. "Tell me why. Why you've come here and told us all this. Why we should believe you."

"Because I need to know what else I've been lied to about." Parker doesn't raise her voice, but it takes on a sharp edge for a moment. "I gave up the life of an outlaw to take up one devoted to order, to guiding mortals away from chaos toward a—a perfect future that seemed clear to me a mere half-year ago. A future you threatened. And a future I've started to question, thanks to you and Ms. Lindsay."

"But you were all right with Nunwick's glorious ordered future even when you knew step one was 'let a psychopathic honey badger god destroy major cities?'" Hazel snaps. "Because I want to get a reading here on when you finally thought, 'Oh, maybe this guy preaching ultimate order while releasing a literal monster on the world might be a touch hypocritical.' Was it when she did *things* with the Eiffel Tower? Wiped out the Caymans? Killed Lady Briley? Nearly killed—"

"Yes!" Parker snarls, clenching her fists. "I didn't question the plan to create *some* catastrophe as the final pretext, and yes, I knew the plan involved Agent One. But I didn't—" She stops herself, closing her eyes. "I suppose I didn't know it all because I didn't want to."

"'Agent One?'" Moira murmurs.

"In all that time, I never learned her real name. I don't even know if Mr. Nunwick chose that name for her or if she bestowed it upon herself."

"Who was she as a mortal?"

"An infamous serial killer."

Everyone in the room stares at Parker. Diana's the first one to speak, voice shaking. "All your talk of order, the danger of chaos. The way you made me feel about creating a 'chaos nexus.' And your great plan for saving the world involves someone like *that*, doing things like *that*."

"I had to believe our project justified deifying a psychopath."

"And did it?"

Parker stares down into her coffee. "The last conversation I had with Agent One was, in one small way, like the last conversation I had with you. You showed me a lie of Mr. Nunwick's I preferred not to see, and she showed me another, one that I should have seen from the very start. Although truthfully, I don't know what I would have done if I had."

"You were very committed to your course."

She flinches.

Hazel shakes her head. "You come here out of the blue when we're all grieving over the death and destruction your friend Agent One caused, telling us surprise, you've realized we're actually right and you're on our side, so—"

"Agent One was never my friend, I have not once suggested I am 'on your side,' nor have I suggested you are, in some grand cosmic sense, 'right,'" Parker snaps. "I still believe in order over chaos. But I also still believe, have *always* believed, that intentions matter as much as actions.

"And so do you." She looks around. "So do *all* of you. Because, like me, you are gods, with all the power and all the hubris divinity entails. The outcomes of our actions literally shape the world."

Moira responds in a softer tone. "Which makes our intent that much more important. And you no longer trust Sotala's."

Parker looks up at her, then nods.

Hazel looks between the two, and stares at Moira. "Wait. Do *you* trust her? Are we all supposed to be friends now?"

"Friends? She just told you she's not on our side." Moira shrugs. "But I know how Diana's spoken of her in the past, and she has good judgment. Probably better than I do."

Parker looks to the sheep, ears coming forward, and offers a slight, near-bashful smile. Diana sinks in her seat slightly, looking embarrassed.

"But I don't have any answers for you," Moira continues, looking back at the vixen now. "As far as I know, what Daranu saw in me was a misguided fool brought down by her refusal to accept the truth of the natural order. Sotala may have reinvented himself as Darren Nunwick, but even that name's clearly a nod to replacing his father. He wants the same order, the same power. He's just carrying on the tradition."

Parker rubs her muzzle. "And yet the few times Mr. Nunwick spoke of his family, of his father, it sounded as if no love was lost between them."

"So he's not as much carrying on the tradition as trying to prove he's better than Daddy." Rhiannon looks at Moira. "Does that sound right? How did Daranu and Sotala get along?"

"It was fraught. Maybe more so than most parent-child relationships. There were signs even then that Sotala thought he could do a better job than his father, but he played along well enough, most of the time." She drops into a seat again, at least picking up her slice of pie. "In the end, though, Daranu trusted him. Possibly more than he should have."

Then she pauses with a bite of pie halfway to her mouth. "Possibly more than ravens."

Hazel's eyes widen. "You think *he* had the message for you?"

"If there even was a message. He might. I don't know." Moira purses her lips. "But if there was, if he'd given it to his son before the gods moved out of contact with the mortal realm…"

"Then Sotala just had to wait until Dad bounced off to the Great Beyond." Rhiannon narrows her eyes, tail twitching. "And as long as you were here—and Briley, even if he didn't know that—he had as much time as he wanted to make himself a new creator god."

"I think you all have an educated guess after all. An unfortunately plausible one." Parker sighs, picking up her plate and looking at her pie glumly.

"We still don't know what the message was," Diana says. "But, if we're right, Mr. Nunwick does."

"Yes." Parker looks at Diana. "But I doubt I'm in a position to make inquiries without arousing suspicion."

"You *are* in Mr. Nunwick's inner circle."

"My recent questions, my signs of doubt, haven't gone unnoticed. If I ask about this…" She shakes her head. "I can't make any promises."

Diana slides closer to her on the sofa. "But you can follow your heart."

"It's rather atrophied from disuse, Ms. Lindsay. I can only implore you to believe that if I wasn't trying to do so, I wouldn't be here."

The sheep nods. "I do."

The vixen takes a bite of pie. Her brows lift, and she takes another bite. "This is the best pie I think I've ever had."

Moira smiles, more sadly. "Peaches were Briley's favorite fruit."

Parker looks down. "Ah." She's silent for a few seconds, and takes another bite before setting the plate down, looking self-conscious as she stands up. "I suspect I've taken up more than enough of your time. Thank you for entertaining my questions."

"I wouldn't have really stepped on you," Hazel mutters.

"Then I wouldn't really have trapped you in the brig of a ship in a bottle until you learned to behave."

Hazel blinks a couple of times. Diana covers a grin.

As the vixen walks to the front door, Moira looks up at her. "Are you going to be safe?"

Parker lifts her brows at that, considering the question. "We'll see." She half-smiles. "You're not what I was led to believe, Lady Moira, which only raises more questions. Do take care."

As she opens the door, Diana leaps to her hooves and hurries to intercept her. Parker pauses.

"It's…" The sheep swallows. "I was going to say 'good' to see you again, but I think the right word is 'complicated.'"

"I understand." She shifts on her paws a moment, hesitating, and looks into the sheep's eyes. "Diana, I'm sorry. I wish many things had gone differently. I wish we'd had more time to get to know one another."

"Maybe in the future, when things…aren't what they are now."

"The future seems less certain now than it ever has." She squeezes Diana's hand, and starts to let go.

"Lily."

Parker stops, looking into Diana's eyes.

The sheep gives her a soft kiss. After a moment, the vixen wraps her arms around the shorter woman, the kiss's temperature rising rapidly.

"Whoa," Hazel murmurs under her breath.

The kiss holds for long seconds before Parker pulls back, stroking the sheep's cheek lightly, then quickly walks out.

thirty-eight
an appropriately
modern mythology

"You keep saying I need to have a better argument for not trusting Parker than her having led the enemy forces for centuries, and I keep circling back to: do I? Really?"

"I know. It's been over a day, and I'd like to stop circling." Diana sighs, rubbing her face. "People change, Hazel. *We've* all changed in just a half a year."

"A half year ago, we were mortals. That seems like an extenuating circumstance."

"You don't know her the way I do."

"Yeah, we picked up on that."

Diana narrows her eyes.

Before she says anything, Moira raises her hands. "Both of you, relax." She tilts her head at the pika. "I take your point, and I'm wary, too. But everything she said tracks with what we know, and what I feel. And I trust Diana."

"How do you know she's not blinded by love?"

Moira crosses her arms. "It's not as if I know much about love, of course, but…"

"Come on, you know what I mean."

"I don't know if love really blinds you," Rhiannon says. "Paralyzes you, maybe." She twists a long lock of hair in a hand.

Hazel gives her an odd look. "What?"

Moira looks back and forth between them. "You two have *got* to talk. At any rate, what Parker came to us with was a good theory, but only that. Perhaps Daranu truly did forgive me. Perhaps he sent a message to me I never received. Perhaps I was left behind for a final task. We can guess about that all, but the only being left in creation who can confirm it is Sotala."

"So we're relying on Parker to get answers. Wonderful." Hazel sighs.

"And I don't know if she can." Diana grimaces. "As someone who's been with them since they were the Order of Caeles, she gets a lot of leeway. But if it becomes clear she's doubting Nunwick's leadership, she'll be in serious trouble."

Jerry takes the pot of coffee and stands up, refilling everyone's mugs without prompting. "You're almost disquietingly solicitous," Moira tells him.

"Sorry, ma'am. Keeps my mind occupied while Trevor and I work out a plan for re-opening Harvest Dance. Now that news stations have put together that this farm stand used to be owned by a goddess…" He shakes his head.

"Yeah, I know." Hazel glances out the front window along the farm's long driveway. They're tough to see from this distance, but a few dozen people stand outside a newly planted fence surrounding the property and blocking off the driveway. "I swear you should have let me electrify the fence, or plant carnivorous flowers there or something."

"Carnivorous flowers don't eat people, you know," Rhiannon says.

Hazel grins. "Mine would."

Rhiannon rolls her eyes. "So, what *are* our guesses about the message?"

"I don't have a clue." Moira sighs, sipping her coffee. "The only thing that makes me special is that I'm the one who rebelled, and who says, 'You know who I need for a special, all-important last task? The one being in all creation who went to war with me.'"

"Unless it's a task that he could *only* trust you with." Diana drums her hoof nails on the table. "What can you do that Sotala can't?"

"Create new gods," Moira says after a moment's thought. "Sotala can do that too, now, but he couldn't have back then. But Daranu could have done it himself and picked exactly the mortals he wanted."

"Which wouldn't have been anyone like us."

Moira shakes her head. "No."

Rhiannon tries to think through this more. So if Moira had to create the new gods, why tell Sotala instead of sending a raven-gram? "Maybe Sotala was supposed to tell you whom to deify, but he decided the right way to do this was to make himself a god and do it himself."

"Yeah, I'm sure 'pirate captain' and 'serial killer' were just what Daranu had in mind," Hazel says dryly.

Diana says, "If Moira's whims mean something, maybe so do his." She looks to the hare. "But if your whims *do* mean something, maybe you didn't even need to get the message."

"That feels like a comforting stretch."

Hazel shrugs. "It's not the strangest thing I've heard in the short time I've been a goddess, so surely it's not the strangest thing *you've* heard."

"Mmm." Moira sits up, looking less defeated, but still skeptical. "This theory is too much like what I'd want to hear, isn't it? Daranu had the power to uplift Sotala himself if he'd wanted to, to bring him from demigod to full god. Then he'd have someone to make new gods he'd know to trust. Not me."

"He could have trusted Sotala to pick other gods, but not to be one himself. Which his kid might have taken as a real slap in the face."

"Maybe, uh." Jerry runs a hand through his short hair. "Maybe he just knew you'd do a better job of it, Miss Moira. You lifted up these three wonderful women."

"We're wonderful!" Hazel looks at Moira beseechingly. "He's cute. Can we keep him?"

"I have first dibs!" Trevor calls from the kitchen.

Jerry's ears color.

Rhiannon looks to Diana. "Nunwick's mad science machines depend on being able to maintain a certain level of rigid order across all the mortals they draw from, and his whole ascend-to-supergodhood plan requires drawing from literally all the mortals. And they can only pull off whatever juju they do-do on certain days. The fiasco with Agent One means they're going to miss the one next month, because nobody's super interested in taking orders from them right now. And didn't Parker tell you it'd be decades until the next window?"

"She did."

"That's more than enough time for them to regroup," Hazel says. "Mortal memory is pretty short."

"It's also more than enough time for us to find answers to this, and figure out how to keep public opinion turned against them."

"It's not much time at all," Moira mutters.

The other goddesses all look at her. So does Jerry.

"Assuming you all keep your immortality through this, you'll feel the same in a century or two." She glances to Rhiannon with an amused look. "'Whatever juju they do-do'?"

The squirrel shrugs, returning a lopsided grin.

"So I suppose we just have to keep major world governments from imposing martial law." Diana furrows her brow. "I know it's come up in some countries, including this one, and I don't know if it's off the table yet."

Rhiannon snorts. "With some legislators, it's never off the table. Since we made ourselves known to the world, I've inspired a dozen new trans panic bills around the country, and when it came out that the goddess of love was, gasp, not straight, a whole new round of anti-LGBT shit got prepped."

Hazel looks at her. "There's also been countless people inspired by you and Moira. Don't underestimate how validating it is to see yourself in literal fucking *gods.*"

"Yeah." Rhiannon glances toward Hazel's wheelchair and back with a smile.

"None of that's martial law, at least," Diana says.

"No, but enforcing conformity is imposing a kind of order." Moira sighs. "It's not going to be enough for them to safely suck mortal energy into Sotala in a few weeks, but if things keep trending that way over a couple of decades…" She shakes her head. "Well, at least that's a *little* time to try to turn the tide."

"Okay!" Hazel slaps her thighs. "Let's drop by Fresno."

"What?"

"We've been hiding from our worshippers since Stetson left and the paparazzi started staking out Diana's lake house. Now they're staking out *this* place. We should probably go talk to those reporters soon—"

Rhiannon smirks. "I thought you wanted to feed them to flowers."

"Only the ones from ATN. My point is, we should get back into the world, but face a friendly crowd first. Kind of a sanity check."

Moira nods, looking reluctant. "And you have a friendly crowd in mind?"

"You know I do."

∾

On their first visit, there'd been a small group outside the church, even though it wasn't a Sunday. Today isn't a Sunday, either, and there's still a group, and at around two dozen, not all that small.

"Okay, not what I was expecting on several levels," Diana murmurs. She leads them along the sidewalk toward the Thankfulness Garden. Nobody's noticed them yet; they're too focused on the statues of the goddesses to notice the casually dressed genuine articles approaching.

The tiny garden encircling the statues has a different mix of offerings than it did on their first visit, more eclectic and personal. More scraps of paper with requests for blessings. More photos. The statues of Moira and Diana are finished now, with Hazel and Rhiannon close to completion. Hazel's still standing, but there's a new addition: a form behind her starting to take the shape of a wheelchair.

No, there are *two* new additions. A fifth, rough statue's joined them, close to Moira. Shorter, plumper, unfinished, yet—to them—completely identifiable. The bear who's been sculpting them is working on that one.

Moira stares, walking forward slowly. As she pushes through the crowd, there's more focus on her, more murmuring.

The sculptor looks up, and his eyes go wide. He stands, then awkwardly drops to his knees. "L-Lady Moira!"

The crowd explodes in conversation, all turning toward the hare and the other three. Diana shifts on her hooves uncomfortably. Moira, though, barely notices, eyes fixed on the statue as she addresses the sculptor. "You're...you're adding Briley."

He swallows. "I thought—if you don't think I should, my lady, I'll stop, I swear I didn't mean any disrespect, it's just—"

She kneels beside him and pulls him into a tight hug. His eyes widen so much they look like they're going to pop out of his head, but he manages to hug back awkwardly.

The crowd applauds, many dropping to their knees, too.

The bear pulls back enough to look into Moira's eyes, then drop his gaze bashfully. "I d-didn't know you were coming. Nobody said—"

"Nobody knew," Diana says. "Including us until a couple of days ago."

Rhiannon wiggles her fingers. "We work in mysterious ways."

"Are there any other old gods?" a vixen asks.

"Or new gods?" a nervous-looking young wolf adds.

Suddenly everyone's speaking over one another.

"Or ones that Celestial company's made?"

"Can you offer blessings?"

"Are they devils?"

"My son's husband is sick, and..."

"No such thing as the devil."

"What about that honey badger?"

"Don't be speciesist, Bob."

Hazel raises her hands over her head and claps once. It sounds less like a hand clap and more like a thunderclap. Everyone jumps, including Rhiannon and Diana. "Hello!" she says loudly, breaking the abrupt silence she'd created. "It's good to see you all again, too, and we're less interested in giving you divine pronouncements than in hearing what you think about...well, everything of late. But we might have to be more organized than just answering shouts."

Reverend Mike, the mouse they'd met before, hurries toward the crowd from the church.

Moira waves casually to him and addresses the crowd. "There aren't any other old gods we know about, I haven't made any new ones, I can't speak for Celestial, and blessings and devils are both complicated. Although—" She nearly says *Agent One,* but that's a name they could only have learned from someone with inside knowledge, and she sees there are already phones out, undoubtedly livestreaming her. "—that honey badger qualifies as much as a devil as anything I've met."

"And she wasn't created by a 'chaos nexus' like Celestial's CEO was talking about?" Mike asks.

Moira lifts a brow fractionally, but from his expression, she guesses he knows the answer and is deliberately steering the conversation. Okay, she'll follow. "No." She gestures to Hazel. "As Hazel's told reporters, we're sure she was created by Celestial."

Some people in the crowd gasp, but most nod grimly. "Maybe that kinda makes that Nunwick the devil," Bob—a portly retiree-aged grey squirrel—offers.

"Do we really believe in devils?" an androgynous punkish possum asks, spreading their hands.

Reverend Mike smiles lopsidedly. "Do we really believe in gods? I think many of us might have had a different answer a few months ago."

"I think Mr. Nunwick sincerely believes what he's doing is right," Moira says. "But what he did was create a literal monster with the intent of unleashing it on the world, all so he could be the hero who saved you all from it."

"He wanted to create a chosen one narrative," the possum says. "With him as the chosen one."

Rhiannon nods. "Good way of putting it."

The possum points at her. "But aren't you a chosen one that Moira created? And you? And you?" They point at Diana and Hazel.

"I..." Rhiannon furrows her brow and tilts her head. "Okay, that's a discombobulating question."

Hazel bounces in her chair. "I love UUs." She looks at the possum. "I've thought about that question, too. A lot. It wasn't like Moira came to me and said there was a great quest only I could embark on, if I was willing to accept immense power and promise to use it responsibly. Honestly, I thought she selected us pretty much at random, couldn't give us a good reason *why* she chose us, and we hardly started out as paragons of responsibility. None of us, including Moira, saw what was coming, either."

Moira clears her throat. "Not entirely random," she mutters.

"Yeah," Rhiannon says, "but you couldn't explain it then. I mean, I was an atheist before..." She raises her arms over her head and momentarily glows, with the sound of an angelic choir echoing from the air around her for a second.

A few people look confused or wary; the possum blinks rapidly, then grins, folding their arms. "So you were fallible mortals who became fallible gods, had no idea why, got drunk with power, but found yourself facing world-ending threats only gods can deal with and rose to the occasion."

"I don't know—" Diana begins.

"I'm not sure I'd say—" Rhiannon starts.

"You got it," Hazel says, shooting the possum dual finger-guns.

"That's an...appropriately modern mythology. I seem to be leading your first church, and even I still can't say I'm sure quite what to make of you." The reverend gives them a thoughtful half-smile, then sweeps his arms around to take in the whole surrounding area. "But I *am* sure that you saved us. It's quite possible none of us would be here if not for you. If we were, we'd be living under an apartheid system Celestial wanted to sell the rest of the country, even the world, on. When you take how well that system did for those at its top and combine it with the threat of literal monsters, they might well have pulled it off."

Rhiannon looks toward the church. "Can we go inside and turn this into a coffee klatsch?"

"Absolutely," Mike says, motioning them along. "It's as close to a holy sacrament as we have."

It takes nearly a day for the "coffee klatsch" to make national news, for reporters to besiege the UU church. The goddesses stay at Briley's farmhouse for the next few days, occasionally inviting in reporters at random for quick conversations. It's not until next Friday that something unexpected happens. Not another new dangerous god, or bulletins from Celestial (they're keeping an even lower profile now), or even just a bad—or good—news story. It's a knock on the door.

Jerry starts to head for it, but Diana stops him. "No reporter should be able to get through the wards."

"Oh." His ears fold back as he contemplates that.

Moira frowns, and heads to the door, opening it.

The rat woman standing on the porch wears a long red trench coat, gloves, and a matching wide-brimmed hat, giving her the air of an international woman of mystery. "Lady Moira?" She speaks timidly. She's clearly scared.

The hare narrows her eyes. Whoever the rat is, she's not a reporter. She's a god. A lesser god, but a god nonetheless. All the goddesses have turned to stare at her, too.

Diana makes a soft, surprised bleat. "Ms. Storm?"

"Ms. Lindsay." She looks relieved to see the sheep, but still frightened. "I need your help."

thirty-nine
the final phase

Sunlight bounces off the gargantuan astrarium in precisely the right way to hit Parker's glasses. She shades her eyes with a hand. Much of the surrounding machinery has the retrograde mission control look she's seen before. The skyscraper-high technomagical clock itself, though, is a fervid steampunk fantasy, and the four monstrous energy beam guns at the corners of the wide square plaza in front of it look straight out of vintage sci-fi.

The calamity in Los Angeles had brought the work to a hard stop. When it resumed, though, it resumed with a frenzy. In the past two weeks, the plaza has transformed, the vast concrete square now polished to a high sheen, a raised terrazzo platform supporting a chair at its center. No, not a chair. A throne. A Victorian-era throne scaled to monument size, to the astrarium's scale.

Construction workers swarm over the plaza, paying her no mind. Scientists around the control apparatus who recognize her, though, flash wary glances when they think she's not looking. She approaches a wolf in a lab coat, barely managing to hide his nervous grimace. "Everything's on schedule, ma'am." He holds up a finger. "Or ahead of schedule."

"I'll trust your assessment on that, Mister…?"

He smiles nervously. "Meridrew, ma'am."

She nods, and gestures toward the throne. "Yes, you've been working with a great urgency lately."

He swallows, nodding. "The construction managers had put the last phase on hold, so we've had to scramble." He sweeps his hand to indicate the mission control consoles. "But on a technical level, we've been ready for months."

"Of course. We used your work here in the field in Los Angeles, correct? Just a matter of reversing the...flow."

He waggles a hand. "After a fashion, ma'am. We took the idea of the power flow and applied it in a novel way to create a field effect."

"To suppress power rather than concentrate it." She nods thoughtfully. "Was the technology designed to be reversible?"

"I wouldn't say 'designed.' It's intrinsic to the nature." He points at the retro-futuristic ray guns, the size of modern battleship cannons. "Think of it like sending light through a series of lenses. It's meant to focus everything there, on the target." He sweeps his hand toward the chair. "But going the *other* way..." He waves his hand back. "In theory, it'd disperse energy *from* the target over the whole area it would normally draw from. In practice, it'd probably just explode."

She purses her lips and looks back at the throne. "So the orders to finish building came recently, then. After Los Angeles."

"That's my understanding." His ears lower. "I don't, ah, have anything to do with that side of the project." He waves his tablet at the control consoles. "I just check the schedules and make sure we're ready for the firing window when we get the final word. Ah, if it's a go, of course."

"Of course." She hears Agent One's gleeful *oh, you're fishing!* in her head. "There's still uncertainty on that point?"

He gives a twitchy shrug. "Given how long things were set in stone, I was surprised when they were called off, but not completely surprised. I know there's been all that, ah, all that trouble with the rabbit goddess and her friends. But I gather it's been worked out. Ah, hasn't it?"

"She's a hare," Parker says absently. "Apparently it has. So we're expecting a go, not a no-go."

The wolf nods, left ear flagging in confusion. "I imagine you'd know that better than I would."

You'd think. "Have a pleasant day, Mr. Meridrew."

Parker keeps herself from visibly fuming until she's back in her car, door shut, and glowering at the throne through the windshield. She grips the steering wheel without starting the car yet.

So: two possibilities.

One, Meridrew's read is simply wrong. The site construction resumed not on the hopes the world could be sufficiently re-ordered in time for Nunwick's original ascension plan, but for a future astronomical alignment in a few decades.

Two, Nunwick and Ironheart have a salvage plan they haven't informed her of.

She punches the car's start button and roars back onto the roadway. Even at her speed, it takes ten more minutes for the winding road to climb from the valley floor to her office building. She parks, starts to head up to her suite here, but pauses. With a finger-snap, she's back at Celestial Private Equity's New York headquarters, walking down the interior hallway toward her private suite.

"Ms. Parker." Her secretary looks up from her desk. "I didn't expect you in the office today." She doesn't look surprised, of course. Ms. Storm rarely does. It's one of the things Parker treasures about her.

"I hadn't, either. But this office and its predecessors have always been more conducive to deep work for me, and that's feeling more true than usual today."

"I understand," the rat says, with the assurance of someone who's worked for the same employer long enough to read all the subtext. "I'll see that you're not disturbed."

"Thank you." She tilts her head. "There hasn't been any substantial world news I've missed in the last day or two, has there?"

"Such as?"

"Martial law declared somewhere. Anywhere. Governments rolling out control plans similar to the one we'd piloted in Fresno."

Ms. Storm shakes her head. "No. Is there any...corporate news I should be aware of? Watching out for? All that's on your calendar is the weekly executive lunch meeting tomorrow."

"I think there may be, but I haven't been informed of it yet." Parker smiles wryly. "I trust there's nothing *you've* heard that you think I should know about."

"If I had, you'd have heard it, too, ma'am."

Parker heads into her office, shutting the door behind her, and pours herself a drink. She changes the panoramic window view to the same as her office on Nunwick's estate: overlooking the astrarium and throne construction site.

Did they somehow solve the problem with the ascension machine killing mortals it draws from when the area isn't sufficiently ordered? The chatty Meridrew would likely have volunteered that information, brought up how exciting or stressful this last-minute change to "his side of the project" was. So tentatively rule that out.

The astrarium? The astronomical clock is a focus mechanism, if also more of an ornate affectation than Nunwick would ever let on. Perhaps they found a way to make the process less dependent on precise time alignment with the heavens, so they could proceed whenever mortals became sufficiently subdued.

But, again, no—that contradicts what Meridrew told her about being ready for the "firing window."

She sits on the sofa, brooding. The technomagery to fulfill Nunwick's ascension had been *theoretically* possible for centuries. Practically, though, it had required not merely the industrial revolution, but the recent micro-electronics revolution. The alignment less than three weeks from now is the first one since the tests had worked —mostly worked—suitable for the end goal, the goal they'd been working toward for centuries. Waiting another two or three decades for the next one should be nothing to a god, but Nunwick and Ironheart would treat it as snatching defeat from the jaws of victory.

Dammit, Lily, even if Nunwick's motivations *aren't* entirely pure, whose are? The plan is still picking up where the old gods had left off, preventing the chaos and the resulting turn of the cycle, preserving and strengthening the world. Doing what the old gods couldn't.

Or doing what the old gods decided, at the end, they shouldn't. A decision Nunwick knew about. Lied about.

Are you here because you're concerned with where my loyalties lie, or where his do?

Parker takes off her glasses and rubs her forehead. Had Agent One truly seen things more clearly than she has? She doesn't know what that says about her, but she's damn sure it's not good.

The next morning, Parker's in the office early, reviewing the most recent weather report. The turbulence isn't as high as it was during Operation Maelstrom, but if she eliminates those data points as outliers, it's higher than it's been in months. Even before Moira's meddling, Fresno's regional reports had barely hit what they'd forecast as the required minimum for the ascension machine to work without...side effects. The median across the world now approaches twice that, with hot spots blossoming in dozens of cities.

She taps a pen on the desk. Hot spots. Chaos nodes? No, but the potential grows. As far as she knows, the one that destroyed Diana's house, nearly destroyed the three young goddesses, was genuine, an artifact Moira and company inadvertently created. It was the perfect encapsulation of what the Order of Caeles was fighting against, what the world would become if the cycle turned. Why would the old gods possibly want that?

Moira thought the most serious flaw in that theory had to do with Daranu forgiving her, but it isn't. That question is. No one—not Moira, not her new goddesses, not even Agent One—would seek that kind of madness. Either Parker has wasted Moira's time and put herself needlessly at risk, or the old gods understood something she doesn't.

And yet again, the answers continue to circle around getting the truth out of Mr. Nunwick. Sotala. Does she want to risk that kind of confrontation?

No. But maybe she has to.

She finishes the report she's working on, and gets up, heading out of her office. As she passes by her secretary's desk, she stops, deliberating. "Ms. Storm, how long have we been working together?"

The rat looks up curiously. "Two months shy of one hundred and fifteen years."

"There's something I want to ask of you, but it may risk putting you at odds with other executives at this company. With all the danger that entails."

Storm remains silent for a moment. "Ms. Parker, I'm here because of you, and *for* you. Not for anyone else, no matter their title. And you know I'm not here merely for a paycheck."

She does know that, although that paycheck is as high as any partner in any of the firms Parker's run—a secret only one partner ever discovered, back in the 1950s. (He made the mistake of threatening the rat and found himself transformed to a tube of lipstick, a fate Parker found admirably unsettling.) "I do." She takes a deep breath. "I *should* return to the office later this afternoon, but that depends on…many variables. If you haven't seen me back in the office by Friday, I need you to get in touch with our former associate. Ms. Lindsay. Ideally in person."

The rat blinks slowly. "I see." She nods. "If I need to, I'll find a way."

Parker smiles, unusually warmly. "Thank you, Amelia."

She blinks again at the use of her first name, and watches Parker closely as the vixen leaves.

Taking the elevator to parking, Parker shifts locations as she steps out, walking not into her office's garage but the one a continent away on Celestial's estate. Teleporting there would be just as easy, but she finds the time alone driving—and riding or walking—a small, relaxing solace.

Every so often, they hold their weekly lunches outside on the patio, a change that has less to do with the weather than with Mr.

Nunwick's mood. Lunch today, though, is in the private area of the bar she'd taken Diana to for her initial meeting with Nunwick and Ironheart. This is where he'd first discussed the schedule for the final tests and ascension, the schedule Moira unknowingly unraveled. The last time they met here, it was to listen to him talk elliptically about how they needed to use The Event both for its original purpose and as a weapon against the "former love goddess."

She makes her way past the security guards into the empty bar, past another set of guards to the back. Even though she's ten minutes early, Nunwick and Ironheart are there in quiet conversation.

He looks up as she approaches. "Parker." Ironheart looks up, too, but doesn't greet her.

"Good morning, Mr. Nunwick. Ms. Ironheart." She sits down in the booth, opposite the lions.

"You were touring the astrarium site yesterday," Ironheart says. "Did something catch your attention?"

Is Ironheart—or Nunwick—surveilling her? She can't rule it out, but Meridrew's chattiness could also be to blame. Both of the other gods have a keen interest in the site and visit regularly. "I haven't seen it from ground level for at least a year. But yes, what caught my attention over the last few weeks is the renewed construction."

He nods. "The pause after Los Angeles put us behind schedule, but we've caught up again."

"The project's no longer on the schedule it had been, is it?"

"That's the primary discussion topic for today."

A squirrel waitress comes over with their customary drinks and a plate of appetizers. Nunwick doesn't thank her, but says, "Have the room cleared." She nods.

Once the guards have retreated and closed the door, Nunwick leans forward, resting his hands on the table and fixing his gaze on Parker. "I've thought for weeks on how to move forward, since Moira made it impossible to follow through on our original plans. And I've come to the sobering conclusion that my grand plans for order, martial law, the desired hierarchy on a worldwide scale... they were foolish of me."

Ironheart shakes her head. "They were idealistic."

He grunts. "The effect is the same."

"So the project is..." Parker stops herself from saying *over.* If it were over, there wouldn't be construction going on. "...changing?"

"We've dropped all operations involved in influencing world politics, in controlling mortals, and are proceeding directly to the final phase."

"You've found a way to prevent what happened in Fresno?"

"In most respects, the operation in Fresno was a success," Ironheart says. "You saw that data, and know it proved that—"

"It proved that mortals in the field of influence would still be killed, and the field of influence for the final phase is the entire planet." Parker fails to keep the sharpness out of her voice.

"You're missing the larger picture. As was I." Nunwick spreads his hands, sounding more animated. "At the end of that final phase, I will be a creator god, at least the equal of Daranu." He raises his arms over his head, and his voice edges toward soft thunder. "The world as it is now doesn't matter—let it be swept away! I'll have the power to create a *new* world, permanently ordered the way it should be!"

Parker stares at both of them. Ironheart looks infuriatingly adoring. Nunwick looks—like a god. Projecting the same awe that he did the first time she saw him, chained in her prison cell. She almost wants to fall to her knees again.

But only almost.

She clenches her fists, digging her claws into her palm pads. "So the 'larger picture' is that the best way to save the world is to destroy it."

Ironheart's smile slips. "It's a larger picture only gods can see."

"I *am* a god, Ms. Ironheart."

"Then stop thinking like a mortal!" Nunwick snaps. "We create on a scale unimaginable to them and rule over that creation!"

"For all the time we've been working together, all the time since you deified me, you've said we've not just been following the tradition of the old gods—the ones Moira rebelled against—but doing what they wanted to do but couldn't. Not just preventing the cycle from turning once, but for the eternal future."

"Yes."

"But that's *not* what the old gods wanted, is it? They wanted the cycle to turn."

"That's a *lie.* Who told you that? Ms. Lindsay?" He leans forward, teeth slightly bared. "Moira?"

She locks her eyes onto his. "You did."

His angry look grows uncertain.

"Right after Briley appeared. When you said the gods knew they all had to leave for the cycle to turn."

The anger floods back, and he stands, voice rising. "The old gods were fools, all of them!"

"Even your father?"

"*Especially my father!*" he roars, then grits his teeth.

"Father?" Ironheart glances between the two with a confused expression.

"We both understood that Daranu was Mr. Nunwick's chosen namesake." Parker glances at the lioness. "But there's more to it than that." She looks back at Nunwick. "Why did the old gods change their minds?"

He glares without answering.

Parker rises to her feet, too, voice becoming imploring, unusually passionate. "Maybe the old gods *were* fools, Mr. Nunwick. Maybe you were right to violate their trust by not bringing the message you were given for Moira."

Ironheart rises to her paws, looking dismayed less at the mention of the message but at Nunwick's silence, lack of denial.

"So please." Parker lifts her hands. "Tell us the *whole* truth. Tell us the message. Show us you haven't violated *our* trust."

"Don't say 'us' and 'our.'" Ironheart leaps to her paws, growling. "I trust in *him*, Parker, and that's all both of us should need!"

Nunwick smashes the table between them out of the way, wood splintering, glassware shattering.

Parker takes a reflexive step backward. "This new plan isn't what we've been working toward this entire time. It's a monstrosity." She looks into Nunwick's eyes. "There's not just one hole in this plan. There are over seven billion holes."

He clenches his fists, breathing hard, but speaks softly, tone less angry than resigned. "I'm disappointed you, of all beings, can't see the value in simply starting over. But I'm not surprised, given that you've already been working against us."

"That's—"

Both lions raise their hands, and everything around her changes, colors flowing together, paint spilling onto a canvas. Parker's world becomes an artist's abstraction.

Her eyes widen, and she tries to stop it, to keep her reality stable. But she can't. It's two against one. The colors become oppressive, closing in on her, darkening.

"As someone who's so clearly studied the old mythology," Nunwick's voice comes, "I'm sure you're familiar with stories of lesser gods being imprisoned. Perhaps you'll come around with time to think. If not, the machine can draw your power into me as easily as it can that of mortals."

The painting around her comes into focus, greys and blacks, musty and cold. She's lying on a floor, but not the floor of the bar. This is cold, rough-hewn stone. The light remains so dim it's barely above darkness. She shakily tries to stand, but can't get any farther than sitting. She's chained to a stone wall, iron manacles on her wrists. And it's all too real.

Cursing, she pulls with what should be superhuman strength, wills the manacles to shatter, the light to brighten, anything, any change. She can *feel* her power, the magic, but it's not…it's not…

Her ears lower. She knows this prison. The light through the bars. The texture of the stone. The scent of the air. The weight of the chains. She's still in her modern clothes, still her, the executive, the goddess. But this is the prison Nunwick found her in, centuries ago, awaiting her execution.

Parker presses back against the wall, the chill seeping through her fur, and shivers.

forty
just skip to
that part

Hazel speaks to Diana, but keeps her eyes on the tall rat woman. "Friend of yours?"

"Ms. Storm is Ms. Parker's personal secretary, if I've gotten the title right. Did something happen to Lily? Ms. Parker?"

"Executive assistant, these days. And, I don't know, but I fear it has. May I come in?"

Moira steps aside.

Storm walks inside, sitting down beside Diana on the sofa. "On Wednesday, Ms. Parker had a lunch meeting with Mr. Nunwick and Ms. Ironheart. This is a weekly event. Nothing I would normally be concerned about."

"But you are now." Moira takes a seat on a nearby chair.

"She hasn't been back in the office since. That wouldn't concern me normally, but she gave me explicit instructions Wednesday morning to contact you, Ms. Lindsay, if I hadn't seen her by now." The rat bites her lip. "Ms. Parker hasn't…hasn't been a double agent working for you, has she?" She glances around the room.

All the goddesses shake their heads. "No." "Not at all." "Like we'd trust her."

Diana glances at Hazel for that last one. The pika shrugs. "How do we know this isn't a trap? Something to get us to go on a rescue mission that'll give them another opportunity to take a shot at us."

"It's not as if I can force you to do anything," Storm says, sounding slightly wounded.

Diana says, "No, Ms. Parker isn't a double agent. But she's recently come to believe that Nunwick has been lying to her, and others, for a long time, and that casts a lot of doubt on his motivations."

Rhiannon nods. "Like, for instance, he's actually the son of the original creator god, and might have screwed over Moira a thousand years ago because he wants to prove he's a big boy or some other divine daddy issue shit."

Storm's ears skew.

"There's also the whole turning a psychopathic murderer into a goddess," Hazel adds. "Although apparently Parker didn't have a problem with that at first."

"She was never comfortable with it. In today's corporate parlance, she's good at being a team player. But that doesn't mean she agreed with them all the time." She bites her lip. "I'd like to think they wouldn't out-and-out kill her just because they had suspicions. Nonetheless, I'm sure something has happened. She's not answering her phone, so either it's not with her, or the signal is blocked. They always hold the lunch meeting at the estate clubhouse, but it could be in one of several places, and if she's being held somewhere, it could be anywhere."

"No." Moira shifts position, crossing her arms. "She's the third or fourth most powerful being in creation right now, behind myself, Nunwick, and maybe Ironheart. You can't just lock her in a storage room while you figure out what to do with her. You need to find a place that can hold her."

"So we're supposed to break her out of a prison built to hold a god?" Hazel glances at Rhiannon. "Rescue mission, see?"

Storm lifts her head. "Ms. Harcourt, isn't it? Ms. Parker talked about you on occasion."

"Yeah, she and I don't exactly get along."

"I'm aware. She admires you more than you might think, though."

"Great. But look, all you have is the claim that Parker didn't show up for work two mornings in a row, a claim we can't even verify. And the only place we can look for clues to her possible disappearance is the stronghold of super-powerful gods who tried to murder us with a honey badger."

Storm nods after a moment, looking away. "I understand your skepticism. I doubt I would believe me if the situation were reversed, and…" She trails off, swallowing. "I honestly don't know what I imagined you could do. I was just following her last instructions without fully considering…not *last* last, I hope, but…" She clears her throat and stands up. "I think I've rather made a fool of myself. Ms. Lindsay, if I hear anything from her, I'll let you know. I think she'd want that either way."

As the rat starts to walk toward the door, Diana stands, too. Hazel holds up a hand and sighs. "Wait."

Everyone, including Ms. Storm, looks at her.

"Diana's about to blurt out that she'll help, I'll half-heartedly object because we still don't know this isn't a trap, Rhiannon will glare at me but not exactly contradict me, then Moira will commit us all in some definitively laconic fashion. Let's save time and just skip to that part."

Diana beams at the pika. Rhiannon frowns at her, and Hazel gives her a *see, like that* smirk.

"We'll get to work, then," Moira says.

"Well, there aren't any alarms going off or private security forces immediately converging on us, so that's something." Rhiannon glances around Parker's office on the Celestial estate, where Storm teleported them all directly from Briley's porch.

"The alarms could be silent." Hazel rolls toward the window overlooking the valley. "This is pretty swanky. I've never been in a CEO's office before. Also, is that a giant god-making machine?"

"This isn't as nice as her main office. It's still nice, though." Diana looks out the window, too, and her eyes widen. "That's what they were building out there? It's massive!"

Storm looks perplexed. "What do you mean by 'god-making machine?'"

"What did they tell you it was?" Moira asks. She's walking around the office more slowly, looking at everything. It *is* nice, in an austere way. Nothing about it screams divinity. Certainly not the way a giant damn throne does. She's not sure how Sotala planned to square that in the public eye with his benevolent billionaire persona. Maybe he figured he wouldn't have to. He likely thought Agent One would kill Moira, he'd flip off the magic suppression gizmo and kill the honey badger, and the world would joyfully submit to his command. If that was the plan, it severely misunderstood the modern world.

"They didn't, to be truthful." The rat looks annoyed. "I knew it was the culmination of the project they'd been working on since before I was deified. Ms. Parker is circumspect about it in the way she is when talking about anything classified, though, and I seldom dealt with Mr. Nunwick and Ms. Ironheart beyond managing Ms. Parker's calendar. But I thought all of their work had been directed toward saving the world from a descent into chaos."

"Yeah, well, you also thought we were the bad guys." Hazel looks over at Rhiannon. "Can you find out what she was looking at on her computer the last time she was in this office?"

The squirrel heads over to Parker's desk and sits down, pulling the keyboard toward her.

"I don't have her passwords," Storm says. "She's very conscious about security."

Rhiannon's already touched one hand to the keyboard and the other to the docked laptop. Windows start opening and closing on their own on the display. "Yeah, I see. This is good security, but not *magical* security." She hmms. "Unfortunately, nothing looks real interesting here. A lot of actual executive-level work crap, disappointingly few secret plans to take over the world." She squints at windows, pausing one as it flies past. "Her regular meeting yesterday got moved to, quote, 'the back of the library bar.' Mean anything?"

"It's where I first met Mr. Nunwick," Diana says.

"Ms. Parker said whenever they held the lunch meeting there, it usually meant something big, and I had the distinct impression she didn't mean that in a complimentary manner."

Rhiannon concentrates, and new windows open. "There *is* a private prison on site, but nothing in the records from yesterday or today looks suspicious at first glance. Other than having their own private prison on site in the first place."

"Celestial is in a 'special jurisdiction,' as if it were an independent city-state," Storm says, frowning. "Police, emergency services, telecommunications, even taxation—companies they own run everything."

"So you've got your own cyberpunk dystopia, but with the fashion sense of Wall Street finance bros?"

"I'd call it more Edwardian."

"Shame. You'd look good in mirror shades. Anyway, in detective shows, they'd retrace her steps at this point, but the more we snoop around openly, the sooner we're going to be discovered." Rhiannon drums her fingers on the desk for a couple of seconds, then stops, a twitch running down her tail. She looks at Moira. "That viewing-only time travel trick you did at the Black Oak site, using my memories to go back there and then move forward in time. Could you do that with Diana's and this meeting room?"

"Maybe. But if I could, any of you could."

"Nice you're getting your sense of humor back, but is this really the time?"

"I'm serious. All of you have been growing in power and confidence. You can't do everything I can yet, but you can do more than you think."

"Rhiannon, you have a photographic memory," Diana points out. "I don't."

Ms. Storm lifts her hand slightly. "What about my memories and Ms. Lindsay's together? I've been to that room on more than one occasion."

"I don't know." Diana furrows her brow, then slowly walks toward the tall windows looking out over the valley. "Ms. Parker liked to change the view of her *other* office to look out over other places she's been and liked. She was doing this, wasn't she? Projecting memories. Maybe..." She touches the glass and closes her eyes, concentrating.

What was it she'd thought when she'd first walked into that bar? Mobster movie. The deep mahogany wood of the furnishings, the rich leather cushions, the polished brass fixtures. The long mirror behind the ornate bar. Parker hadn't called it the "library bar," but there *were* bookshelves along one wall, weren't there? Old cloth-bound books, that fine musty paper smell mingled with the aromatics of expensive whiskeys. Every table was far enough from its neighbors to be private, but Nunwick's favored meeting booth was close to the back, even more secluded—and, of course, he ordered the whole bar clear when he held executive-level meetings there.

"That corner there is the rare whiskey cabinet," Ms. Storm says, close to her right. Diana startles, eyes opening. The window-wall's view has changed to the bar, Nunwick's favorite booth centered. As she watches, shadows—places she hadn't seen, or perhaps hadn't noticed—fill in as the rat looks from side to side. "And the cigar case."

The other three move closer. Rhiannon looks a little awed. "Back when I was in my college goth phase, I'd have loved a room like this. Also hated it because of the over-the-top capitalist club vibe, but it's such an aesthetic."

"You're still in your goth phase," Hazel says.

"We've been over this." Rhiannon plucks at her multilayered colored skirt (today's theme color is lavender), waves her hands at the silver bangles and jewelry she habitually wears. "Not goth."

"Pastel goth?"

"I am not a—"

"Children." Moira claps her hands. "Focus. You need to bring the view forward in time now, like we did in Black Oak."

"Like *you* did," Diana says, turning back toward the hare. "I have no idea how you did that. And how do I bring it back to two days ago? I can't visualize what I wasn't there for."

"Not exactly, no, but these are very recent events. The room still remembers them."

Diana stifles a frustrated bleat. "What the hell does *that* mean?"

Hazel tilts her head. "What is it Parker said to you on the night when we first met about visualizing stuff you can't visualize?"

"To not be concrete and to focus on the end state." She lets the bleat out. "I didn't know what that meant then, either."

"We know they'd be sitting in that booth," Ms. Storm says. "Ms. Ironheart and Mr. Nunwick sit...if we fear this was a confrontation, they'd sit together on the same side facing Ms. Parker, and it would be that side," she points, "because Mr. Nunwick *always* sits on that side, so he can watch the entrance."

Diana groans silently and pictures the two lions sitting in the booth, zooming in on Mr. Nunwick's Patek Philippe watch to show the meeting time and date.

"Parker would have arrived early," Storm notes.

She pulls back, and Parker's sitting opposite them, drinks and a plate of appetizers on the table. She jumps, blinking, and the scene grows shadowy, indistinct. Cursing, she focuses again. The meeting would be like this, yes. Empty room, quiet conversation. It seems real, but she can't tell if she's making it up. Everything around the three she's locked onto flickers and blurs like ruined watercolor.

Silent conversation, technically. "Is...there any way I can make this vision be auditory? So we can hear what they're saying?"

"It's possible, but challenging." Moira steps forward, watching. "The more details you want, and the farther it is in the past, the harder it is to call. This is recent enough that it's mostly the room rather than you."

"But if it was a year ago, it'd be mostly me?"

"Since you hadn't seen it a year ago, it'd be *all* you."

Rhiannon looks over at the hare. "For divine magic, the rules are a lot more complicated than I'd have imagined."

Moira shrugs. "They're rules the way physics are rules."

"We're routinely defying gravity and the square-cube law."

"That's visualization."

The silent conversation they're watching grows more animated,

Nunwick raising his arms over his head like a revival preacher, Parker's dismay clearly rising.

"Maybe we don't need the soundtrack," Hazel murmurs.

It's clearly become an argument, the lion rising to his feet, the vixen to hers. Then Nunwick smashes the table.

Storm's eyes widen. "Oh, my."

Both lions stand now, raising their hands, and Parker disappears in a blur of rapidly shrinking, darkening color, lines ripping around her like a three-dimensional frame.

As the vixen vanishes completely into the whirlwind of magic, Diana puts a hand to her muzzle.

"What the hell?" Hazel's the one to put it into words, naturally, pointing.

Ironheart leans over and lifts up—

—a painting?

"I don't...understand..." Diana's voice barely breaks a whisper.

Nunwick and Ironheart both walk away, but Ironheart pauses, smirk returning, and strides behind the bar, hanging the small framed piece of artwork just to one side of the mirror. Then she and Nunwick leave the bar arm-in-arm.

"Did she—turn Parker into a picture? Is that even possible?" Hazel squints.

"I've turned people into objects for years." Ms. Storm frowns. "But I'd think it would be difficult for even those two to do that to someone with Ms. Parker's power." She looks at Moira questioningly.

The hare waggles a hand. "Maybe. But like I said, holding a god is the hard part."

Diana looks at the painting, walking closer to the image, bringing it closer to her. "That's so...familiar."

"It looks like an old fort," Rhiannon says.

Diana nods slowly. Then her eyes widen. "I know it. She showed me this place. After the Royal Navy captured Captain Lily, they held her here. Awaiting execution." She looks to Moira. "I don't think they turned Parker into this painting. I think they captured her in it."

Moira's gaze hardens. "Playing off her memories could be a way to hold her, too."

"A cruel one." The sheep clenches her fists. "I'm going after her."

Hazel lifts her brows. "By doing what, walking into the painting?"

"I—I guess so, yes."

"We're still looking at the recent past," Moira says. "Let's see the bar as it is now."

Diana brings her hands forward, and the bar's image blurs like high-speed film for a moment. Now Nunwick's booth is empty, but the room has people in it: the bartender, Celestial executives, wait staff, unsmiling guards in black suits. The painting's still there.

"All right." Moira rubs her chin. "We can wait until evening—"

Diana sets her shoulders. "I'm not waiting."

"Diana, I understand, but—"

"Come with me or not." Diana marches forward, walking through the glass—and right into the bar. They can't hear the exclamations of surprise, but they can see them. Diana looks just as surprised, as if she'd expected to be able to bypass the bar and walk right into the painting. Then the guards start to react, reaching for their radios—and guns. The room erupts in panic.

"Daranu's nutsack," Moira swears, stalking after her.

Rhiannon and Hazel look at one another, then at Ms. Storm. "This isn't a trap, right?" Hazel says.

"Frankly, I have no idea, Ms. Harcourt." The rat hurries forward.

forty-one
what gods
should do

When she appears in the dead center of the library bar, Diana's as surprised as anyone. Why couldn't she walk right into the painting *here* from the office *there* without inconveniently going through physical space?

Well, nothing to do for it now. She hurries toward the painting.

The black suit security guys watch her, two wolves moving to intercept. It's the ones reaching for their radios she's worried about. She waves a hand and their radios turn into hissing snakes.

"Shit!" The snakes get hurled away in a panic. Pandemonium breaks out as the other goddesses appear—Moira first, then Ms. Storm, Hazel, and Rhiannon right behind.

One of the two wolves who'd been going for Diana reaches out to grab her. "All right, that's enough of—"

She thrusts her arm out toward him, palm out. He rockets backward, smacking hard into a booth. The other wolf follows a moment later.

Phones are out now, people calling for backup as they scramble for the exit. Ms. Storm snaps her fingers, and everyone freezes.

No, *almost* everyone. At least a dozen, including two of the remaining security guys, look startled but still move. "We're not all that easy to take down," one growls. He snaps his fingers. Time starts moving again. He grabs Storm's arm. "You're Parker's secretary, aren't you?" He rips her hat off; the rat's ears fold back. "All of you, stay put."

"We're not that easy to grab, either." Moira claps her hands over her head. Everyone besides the goddesses—and Storm—drops to three inches high.

Storm grins near demonically. She turns around, waving a hand, and the doors slam shut. Several tiny people who'd almost made it out get caught in the slam.

Wincing, Rhiannon glares at her. "Was that necessary?"

"Everyone here who isn't security is a high-placed executive with Celestial, Ms. Doran." Storm reaches for the wolf who'd harassed her, now busy trying to stay away from her high heels. When she lifts him up, she shakes her hand like a magician with a handkerchief, and now she's holding a replacement hat.

"Wow!" Hazel looks delighted. "I should do that with people I don't like."

Storm grins obliquely as she puts the hat on. "Or with a more intimate garment, people you do like."

Hazel blinks, then blushes deeply.

Diana strides toward the back of the room, shrunken patrons scrambling to stay away from her hooves. As she walks around the bar, she studies the painting. She should be able to simply keep walking, shouldn't she? Right into the image. The energy doesn't feel right, though. It could merely be her imagination, her nerves. She walks forward, hand held out in front of her—

Her hand smacks into the wall.

She backs up, and focuses, trying once more. Same result.

"Dammit." What's she doing wrong? Is there an enchantment, a ward? Maybe. But this isn't a door or a window. Focus on the end state. She doesn't want to walk to the fort, she wants to be *at* that fort. "But we can't go back in time," she murmurs aloud, looking at Moira as the hare walks up, Storm close behind. "She can't *really* be at that fort. She can't be trapped in the past."

"No." Moira shakes her head. "She's trapped in memories."

Two of the tiny guards open fire on Rhiannon, a strange, high-pitched firecracker sound. She glances down at them. "Seriously?"

"Eat them," Hazel says.

"Squirrels don't eat wolves!" one of them yells. "A wolf is a fucking *predator*, and I don't care how big you are, you are *not* stepping out of the natural order. There's a *hrrk*—"

Rhiannon's grabbed him in a fist. "Prey on this, asshole." She shoves him in her mouth and tilts her head back. His legs kick frantically to either side of her square front teeth. Then she squeezes her eyes shut and swallows hard, twice, white throat ruff rippling.

Hazel stares, then covers her muzzle with both hands, looking like a teen girl who's won front-row tickets to a concert by her favorite band.

Ms. Storm looks mildly confused at Moira's words. "I can't tell if you're being literal or figurative, Ms., uh, Ms. Moira. Memories can't literally hold Ms. Parker, can they? She has to be somewhere physical."

"Physicality gets complicated around divinity, as I'm sure your hat could attest."

"But how do I *get* there?" Diana stomps a hoof.

"You said you've seen this place before, that Parker showed it to you. But she didn't take you there physically. Do what she did."

Diana stares at the painting. What *did* Lily do?

When they moved from the *Silver Rose* to the fort, it was foggy. She closes her eyes, remembering. Cold—no, *warm* air, humid, heavy. A cobblestone road, uneven, soft scraping against her hooves as she walked. Streetlamps flickering. The faint scents of the lantern gas, of hay and grass, of salty ocean air. And a high, black iron fence surrounding the fort, separating it from that road.

She reaches out, and her hand touches one of the fence bars.

Diana opens her eyes. She's there.

It's not past dark this time, though. It's daylight, just as in the painting, and the port town—the memory of it?—is busy. Carts move down the street, shoppers walk in and out of the storefronts behind her, and guards stand by the nearby gates.

And unlike her last "visit" here, she's disquietingly visible. Horses pulling a nearby wagon rear up as she appears, whinnying, and passersby cry out. One woman screams. The guards have turned to see what's going on, shouting to soldiers back inside the fort. Rhiannon and Hazel appear behind her, adding to the panic.

Okay. Deep breath. She doesn't understand the rules—where and when she truly is, if anything around her is real in any objective sense. What she does know, though, is that she's a goddess, and she makes her own damn rules.

With a wave of her hands, the fence rips apart. The black sheep strides forward, the other goddesses following. Some soldiers facing her scatter, but others regroup, aiming their rifles and opening fire.

At least, they try to open fire. Sprays of rose petals come out of their rifles, and they stop, looking confused. Rhiannon smirks. When some of the enraged soldiers charge the group, Hazel speeds up, meeting them with chair flying and arms spread wide open. Diana isn't entirely sure what the pika's doing, but they're all left motionless in the dirt, as if they'd been run over by a heavy truck rather than a wheelchair.

Hmm. The soldiers can't truly be *real*, can they? They're pulled from memories and stories, not only Parker's but Nunwick's and Ironheart's.

Even so, if they're part of what's trapping Parker here, she can't take for granted they can't hurt her. She's not just in a hostile god's territory, she's in a hostile god's *creation*. This calls for getting in and getting out fast. Where was the part of the prison the vixen had burst out of? That corner, maybe. Well, near that corner. Her memory is clear but not precise.

"Where is she?" Rhiannon asks.

"I don't know. Somewhere in that corner." She points, walking in the same direction. "But I don't—"

A cannon cracks off a booming shot. A moment later, dirt explodes in a spray, barely two yards from Hazel's chair. The pika yelps as she disappears in the blast.

"Hazel!"

Both Rhiannon and Diana race to her. The chair's knocked over, but the pika's already climbed to her paws, wincing. She gestures grandly in the direction of the ramparts the cannon shot came from, and a hailstorm of cannonballs drop out of thin air. The walls don't collapse as much as disintegrate.

"Fuckers," she mutters, wincing again.

"You okay?" Rhiannon worriedly puts a hand on Hazel's shoulder.

She looks at her leg. It's bleeding, but more of a big scrape than anything else. "I'll be fine. But this wound isn't letting me magically heal it."

"So everything in here hurts us like damage from a god. Terrific."

Diana looks back worriedly, but strides ahead into the building, waving walls out of the way. She reveals a group of cowering soldiers in the first room, their weapons shakily pointed at her. "Where's the silver vixen prisoner?"

A tiger glares defiantly at her. "I won't talk, devil woman! Do your worst! You can't—"

She snaps her fingers and he bursts into flame, immediately collapsing into ash. "Where's the silver vixen prisoner?" she repeats.

All the soldiers point down and to the left. "Prison's below street level," one wolf gets out. "I th-think her cell should be about twenty feet to the right of where I'm standing."

She points.

"Yes. Yes."

"Thanks. Get out."

They make a mad dash for the exit, barely a second before the walls and floor start flying apart, Diana magically flinging stone and brick to the sides as she "digs" to reveal the prison. As sunlight pours into the suddenly ceiling-less cells, emaciated prisoners stare up at her, terrified, wondering. Most cower; others dare to scramble away, looking for freedom. The sheep glances their way a moment, but mostly ignores them. She sees she'll have to be even more careful, though, to make sure she doesn't knock down any walls—there might be prisoners chained to them. She can't let any stones fall from the ceiling, either—

"Diana," Rhiannon says sharply.

She jerks her head to look where Rhiannon's pointing, down at a newly revealed cell. A silver vixen in an incongruously modern business suit huddles against a wall, ankles and wrists chained to it. She stares up, seemingly more confused by what's going on than frightened or thrilled. It's hard to tell if she even understands what she's looking at, let alone recognizes the goddesses staring in.

"Lily!" Diana leaps down to the floor beside her. The vixen flinches, trying to draw away. "It's all right." She lays her hands on the heavy iron manacles, dissolving them, and takes one of Parker's hands in both of hers. "It's all right," she repeats.

The vixen, still in a half-crouch, stares up at the sheep woman, as if she can't bring herself to believe what's happening.

"We're here to get you out, Lily." Diana smiles as reassuringly as she can.

"Hey," Hazel calls from above, looking off into the distance. "I'm no naval history expert, but I'm pretty sure that's a fleet of warships sailing into the harbor there, so we might want to hurry with the 'getting out' part."

"Right." She puts her arms around Parker, and levitates up to stand by Rhiannon and Hazel.

"How...how are you here?" The vixen isn't crying, but her eyes brim.

"Ms. Storm came to get us, and..." She looks toward the harbor, with soldiers starting to stream off the boats, cannons starting to fire. "Long story we don't have time for yet. Let's go."

"Okay." Rhiannon pauses, tail flicking. "How?"

"Visualize the library bar and move into it."

"That's what I'm trying to do, but it's the visualizing getting from *here* to *there* that's difficult." She flinches as one of the still-intact buildings nearby collapses under cannon fire.

"Go forward," Parker calls, voice hoarse. "Go forward and change the world to fit."

"Uh—" Hazel points at the approaching army. It's growing larger. Not in number, but in size: the soldiers are literally growing.

"This is no longer historically accurate," Rhiannon hisses.

"Nunwick and Ironheart know we're here." Diana takes a deep breath. "Do what Ms. Parker says." Without waiting for acknowledgement, she marches ahead. Rhiannon and Hazel pivot to follow close behind.

That building, there, should be a table. And that one. That one, too. The rubble crunching under her hooves should be carpet. The light should be dim, the sky should be the old-fashioned hammered tin roof. Fences should be bookshelves. The air shouldn't smell of ocean and gunpowder, it should smell of leather and whisky—

The world flickers between the library and the approaching giant army, wolves and tigers and lions towering over the town, marching over it, brandishing their bayonets. The more Diana pays attention to them—the more any of the goddesses pay attention to them—the more solid they remain, the more they merge with the bar.

"Picture the bar! Only the bar!" Diana yells. Another step, another, another—

—her hooves hit carpet.

All at once, the goddesses are back in the bar. Several soldiers come through with them, back at normal size, drawing short and looking around in confusion before they flicker out and vanish.

The vixen takes a deep breath and groans, wincing; the sheep puts an arm around her to steady her. Parker buries her face against Diana's shoulder.

The bar itself has emptied, half the furniture overturned. Moira and Storm are in the midst of a fight with new security forces, and even though they're outnumbered, it's not a fair fight. Storm looks tense, but the much larger tiger she's in hand-to-hand with looks increasingly terrified as she lands three or four blows for each swing he takes and misses.

Moira doesn't even look tense. As she grabs one of the wolves and catapults him hard enough at the wolf next to him that both canines smash into the nearest wall hard enough to leave cracks, she looks disturbingly serene. "You got her."

"We got her." Diana has enough time to smile before more guards rush in from the main café toward the bar. And she can sense something—someone—behind them.

Storm manages to push the tiger off his feet, breaking his

concentration enough to allow a final magic shot rather than a physical one. A small stuffed tiger toy wearing a business suit and a shocked expression falls to the floor in front of her. She stomps, spiked heel sending up a spray of stuffing.

"We should get going," Rhiannon says nervously. "Like, right—"

A tall lioness stalks into the bar behind the guards, expression pure ice, a genuine chill in the air blowing in front of her. Blue light crackles across the room.

Diana swallows and starts shifting the room back to Briley's farmhouse. Or tries to. The surroundings shimmer, blur, but they stay put.

"Ironheart, right?" Moira's voice is conversational. "We met in passing once back in Fresno."

"Where I beat you in a fight."

Moira starts walking casually toward her. "You got in a good hit, I'll admit. You're powerful." Without changing her walking pace, the hare backhands each of the three guards converging on her, sending them flying, and punches one of the wolves threatening Storm into the other one. She smiles and cracks her knuckles, eyes on the lioness. "But believe me when I tell you we haven't fought yet."

The lioness's ears lower.

"And you're facing all four of us now," Diana says.

Storm clears her throat. "Five."

Parker silently holds up five fingers on one hand and the middle finger of her other. If the lioness's expression remains a glacier, the vixen's is the fire of a thousand suns.

Ironheart curls her lip. "Your love goddess has done a poor job explaining how divine power scales. Parker has been a god for centuries, and I trapped her as easily as a cub. You all have been gods for less than a year. You're mere insects."

"I'm about to be a fucking murder hornet," Hazel murmurs under her breath.

Moira shoots the pika an amused glance, then looks back at Ironheart. "I haven't been the mentor I should have, no. But I don't think Sotala's done a good job of explaining what divine power is for. You may understand what gods can do, but you don't under-stand we *should* do."

The lioness's voice rises, her cool composure slipping. "You have no idea what Mr. Nunwick is capable of. You have no idea what *I'm* capable of."

Moira looks steadily into Ironheart's eyes, and raises her hands slowly, palms up. The room starts to vibrate. Subtly, at first. As the hare's hands rise, it feels like a train rumbling by outside, faster and faster, even though the only sounds are the rattling of glasses and bottles and chairs.

Ironheart sets her jaw and stalks toward Moira.

Moira's hands reach her shoulder level, and she bursts into light, starting to rise off the floor. The light doesn't come from her as much as all from around her, as if she's always between it and whoever's looking at it. One by one, the lesser gods in the room—all the security guards, even Ms. Storm—find themselves falling to their knees, staring at her. Diana, Rhiannon, and Hazel all feel it, too. From the lioness's expression, just as open-mouthed as Storm's, she isn't immune.

"I know you, Tierney Ironheart."

A commanding voice with an edge of a roar to it comes from the doorway. "Then you know she is devoted to me." Nunwick stands there, immaculately dressed as ever, scowling as he points accusingly at her. "You have no right to be here, Lady Moira. Not in my temple."

"She is." Moira's response is soft, edged with regret. "You were so full of arrogance and bluster when you were a cub, little Sotala. In all this time, have you not grown?"

"Rich from the woman who tried to overthrow the order of creation to accuse anyone else of arrogance. And I was no 'cub' when you rejected me, the son of the creator god, to stay with Briley, the harvest goddess." He spits out the mouse's name. "I am certainly not one now."

"And yet you still, after all this time, don't understand why I did. You still can't see anything but yourself."

Nunwick clenches his fists, but keeps his voice level. "You're not worth a fight. You never were." He turns away with a contemptuous snarl. "Take the vixen. In a few weeks it won't matter." He walks out without looking back, Ironheart close behind.

The light around Moira and her compatriots intensifies, and she teleports them to the field outside Briley's farmhouse. Storm looks startled, trying to catch her breath.

Moira walks to Parker. The hare's back to merely a tall, extremely attractive bunny woman. "I'm sorry."

"For what?"

"Blowing up your life."

"Better my life than the world, Lady Moira. The 'few weeks' Mr. Nunwick referred to are the days until his ascension."

"Wait." Rhiannon raises a hand. "The whole other half of your crazy project besides Operation Divine Daddy Issue was forcing enough order on the world to keep all mortal life from basically disintegrating. Are you saying they solved that?"

"No, Ms. Doran." Parker slowly shakes her head. "I'm saying they no longer care."

forty-two
in the moment

"All right, here's the chicken pot pie." Jerry sets down a rectangular baking pan on a trivet on the dining room table in Briley's farmhouse.

Trevor follows behind. "And here's the vegetable pot pie." He sets the pan down by the chicken pie, pulling out a seat for Jerry before sitting down himself.

Hazel, Rhiannon, Diana, Parker, and Storm already sit around the table. Moira heads to the table from the living room, moving gingerly.

"Are you all right, Lady Moira?" Trevor says, looking worried.

"I'm feeling queasy. Either I need to eat or not eat. I'm not sure which."

After everyone's served themselves and dug in, Hazel says, "Okay, so why can't a couple of us just go back to Nunwick's estate and destroy the god-making machine?"

"They're absolutely going to be watching for you—and me— after today's events," Parker says.

"They can watch all they want." Hazel waves a hand. "But what do they do if Diana grows to a mile or two high and grinds a hoof down on everything?"

"Mr. Nunwick and Ms. Ironheart have power that, with all respect, I doubt any of you except Lady Moira can match."

Diana nods. "Also, I stomped on the test site in Fresno, and it *hurt*. It spat out magical fire and lightning. This final incarnation of it might literally be a million times stronger, so taking it out with that kind of brute force might not only kill me—or whoever else stomped on it—but everyone and everything for a thousand miles."

Rhiannon gestures at Parker. "From what she says, *not* taking it out kills everyone and everything, period."

"Yes, but if we win, we have to work with the world in whatever state it's left in. They don't have that constraint." Diana glances at Parker. "What else could we do to stop them?"

The vixen spreads her hands. "Destroying or disabling the machine is necessary, but not sufficient. You'll eventually have to either persuade Mr. Nunwick to abandon his plan, or kill him."

Diana's eyes widen.

"She's right." Moira sighs. "And he's had a long time indeed to convince himself of his own unassailable righteousness, so convincing him that he's in the wrong about anything's going to be a hell of a battle."

"But stopping the machine at least buys us time." Hazel looks between Parker and Storm. "You know more about the thing than we do. If we can't curb-stomp it, how do we pull its plug?"

Parker looks dour. "There's no one plug to pull. As I understand it, it draws on not only its own generators but multiple national power grids. And the security is surely designed with the idea of foiling literal divine intervention."

"Yeah, but with you and Storm helping us, it's six gods against two. They don't have Agent One anymore."

"I still can't believe she did that to the Eiffel Tower," Jerry mumbles under his breath.

Ms. Storm shakes her head. "There are three C-suite level gods, and Ms. Parker's defected, true. But that leaves dozens closer to my level scattered around various Celestial offices and campuses. They'll converge on the estate in a heartbeat to defend it."

"Oh." Hazel frowns. "No offense, but aren't we so far above you that—" The pika cuts herself off with an alarmed squeak as she appears at figurine size by the edge of Ms. Storm's plate.

"That doesn't mean you can't be taken by surprise," the rat says.

Hazel snaps her fingers, returning to her original place and size, and clears her throat. "Good point."

Parker leans back, folding her arms and brooding. "I don't know if we can *disconnect* it, but if we can *reverse* it, that would either diminish Nunwick's power or destroy the machine. Or both."

Moira tilts her head. "We can do that?"

"So I'm told. A lead scientist on the project got rather chatty, and compared it to reversing light through a telescope. Instead of focusing power on the target, it pulls *from* the target, dispersing the power everywhere. Or explodes."

"How do you do it?"

"I don't know. Mr. Meridrew described it as a side effect rather than intentional design, so it may not be simple. I didn't press for explicit details on how to subvert the project, as I suspect that would have drawn suspicion even from him."

"So we'd have to learn how it works and modify it." Rhiannon rubs her face.

"Maybe we can brute force that," Hazel says. "Grab the ray gun and just turn it around."

"There are four guns."

"So each of us grabs a ray gun and turns it around."

Rhiannon half-grins. "With the remaining two literally holding off the army of the gods."

"Sure."

"I admire your bravado."

Hazel snorts at Parker. "Why do I hear 'foolhardy' when you say that?"

"They're often close cousins, Ms. Harcourt." The vixen looks distant, and gives a slight shrug. "I've been thinking of my old mortal life more than usual recently, of the blurry line between bravery and foolishness, pride and self-importance."

Moira's ears lift, and she looks at Parker intently. "Why that last one?"

"Because of you, Lady Moira." Parker pushes her glasses back up her muzzle, then waves around. "You and your... I don't know if 'team' is the right word. Companions. You've chosen them well."

"I think I have. Even though I just acted in the moment."

"Something led you to those moments, though."

"A sense that the world was in serious need of chaos, and we were the right ones to add it," Hazel suggests.

Parker nods. "Ms. Harcourt is correct."

"I am?" Hazel beams.

"Not chaos, precisely. But a new direction. Or an old one, the one Lady Moira tried to take the world in long ago. You all, I suspect, felt the injustices of this world as keenly as she did.

"But us?" She smiles wanly. "Ms. Ironheart, Agent One, and I were all in positions where Mr. Nunwick not only gave us power, he gave us reprieves. Ironheart had lost everything in a brutal revolution, and was on the cusp of a life as an indentured servant. I was a mere day from execution. Agent One…" She snorts. "A serial murderer given an opportunity to not only escape punishment for her crimes, but continue them in undreamed-of fashion."

"He didn't think his vision alone was persuasive enough?" Diana shakes her head.

"Indebting them to him added another level of security." Moira stands, helping Jerry clear plates. "Sotala wasn't always that arrogant, but he was insecure, and insecurity and arrogance often go together."

"Perhaps." Parker frowns. "But he's never been short on pride."

"I have no grounds to criticize anyone over that," Moira responds, tone dry. "Maybe he and I aren't as dissimilar as I want to think."

"But you're not—" Rhiannon runs a hand between her ears. "Moira, I'm sure you're arrogant and proud in a way only a goddess who's been around since the start of creation can be, but I can damn sure tell you what the difference between you and Sotala is."

The hare tilts her head.

"Even when I was fighting the whole bloody 'you're a goddess now, sorry about your atheism' mess as hard as I could, I was learning about you. From books. From her." She jerks a thumb at

Hazel. "And I realized you were the secret cool hero of your mythology. You were willing to put your power on the line for what you believed in. Now I've seen you do it again, more than once. I don't doubt for a moment you'd sacrifice yourself for the world. Sotala wants to take the world for himself. *That's* the difference. And it's monumental."

Moira shrugs. "Sometimes love means…" Then she tilts her head, eyes unfocusing. "That's it, isn't it?" she murmurs. "That's it."

"What's what?"

"The message." She sets the plates down, voice growing excited. "What Daranu saw in me. How to fix everything. Maybe."

Everyone's looking confused now. "What?" Hazel says.

Moira's heading to the living room and grabbing her jacket. "There's someone I need to go see."

Diana stands up. "Moira…"

The hare pulls on her jacket. "Save some peach cobbler for me." She waves and vanishes.

Everyone's silent for several seconds. Then Jerry clears his throat. "So who wants dessert? I'm sure we'll have enough left over for Lady Moira."

After Jerry brings out bowls of cobbler and homemade cinnamon ice cream, they move to the living room, Rhiannon and Hazel sitting on the sofa, Parker and Diana taking a loveseat. Jerry sits with Trevor, fidgeting.

"What is it, love?" the ferret prompts.

"Oh, all that talk about the end of the world. Gods fighting, cycles turning. Even if *everything* doesn't end in a few days, *this* will end, won't it? The farm." He looks to Diana. "Your time here. If you win, you'll all have to go do…god things, whatever that might be. And if you don't…"

Hazel looks like she's about to say something smartass for a moment before recalibrating. She frowns, taking a big spoonful of cobbler. "Well, if the world *doesn't* end in a few days, I don't see why you won't still have this farm. Assuming we all make it, I imagine we'll still be visiting. I can't swear to any of that, because it turns out even gods can't predict the future." She swallows the bite before continuing.

"But, Jerry, you worked with a literal goddess for decades. You learned how she farms. How she cooks. You got a little of her magic." She waves her spoon. "And now you're hanging around with five other goddesses. Whatever happens, you don't get to look back and say, 'if only my life had been more exotic and unusual.'"

He laughs after a moment, rubbing the back of an ear. "Definitely not, Lady Hazel."

Diana looks at Parker. "You're the only one of us who *had* an exotic and unusual life when you were still mortal."

The vixen sets down her mostly finished dessert, and lifts her brows. "This sounds like the opening of a conversation starter about whether I miss it."

"Oh, I know part of you does. I remember watching you stride across the deck, how in command and sure you were. And how you looked watching your past self. That grin." Diana shakes her head. "At that moment, with that joy on your face, you were...so much not what I'd expected."

Parker looks down. "I would say the same of you. We'd only met once before and had hardly parted on good terms, yet..." She shakes her head.

Diana smiles and takes Parker's hand. The vixen entwines her fingers with the sheep's.

"I know you've been through a lot today," Diana says after a moment. "Are you up for a walk? Not far, but there's a lovely meadow close by, right up the hill behind the farmhouse, and watching the sun set over the vineyards to the west would be very..."

"Romantic," Parker finishes with a soft smile. "I'd like that very much."

Once the two head out, Hazel leans back on the sofa with a bemused expression. "They're such a weird couple."

Trevor tilts his head. "Why do you say that, Miss Hazel?"

"Because they met when Parker accused us of turning Diana's mouse sidekick into some kind of chaos monster, then ran said monster through with a giant sword. It's not exactly your rom-com 'meet cute' moment."

"Ah. Hm. No." He blinks twice, then clears his throat and starts picking up plates. "I'll, uh, get some things cleaned up." Jerry follows.

When they're alone, Rhiannon looks thoughtful. "I don't think I've ever had a 'meet cute' moment."

The pika grins. "I'd say you eating the idiot wolf guy, except we've known each other a few years. How was he?"

"Awful." Rhiannon laughs. "And that's a very on-brand take for you."

"You know me pretty well."

The squirrel nibbles on her cobbler in silence for a minute, then chews on her lip before speaking again. "Have you been in love?"

Hazel hmms. "I've had one fling, singular, that stomped my heart flatter than a car under Diana's hoof. I've had crushes on people since, maybe more in one case, but I've kept it to myself. And since the goddess thing, I haven't exactly had much dating time."

Rhiannon nods. "No. Right. Yeah."

Hazel looks at the squirrel speculatively; Rhiannon doesn't turn to meet her eyes. "How about you?" she finally prompts.

"I went on exactly two dates pre-transition, and they weren't great experiences. Afterward, I threw myself into my work for a while, and then, like you said, the goddess thing." She takes a deep breath. "I've fallen in love once. But I haven't worked up the nerve to tell her."

"Oh." Hazel's watching her closely. "So it's someone you're in love with...now."

Rhiannon nods, pulling her tail into her lap to keep it from quivering.

Hazel looks away, clearly chewing on this, then looks back to the squirrel and slides a few inches closer. "Well, with the world maybe ending in a couple of weeks, you might want to tell her soon, huh."

"Good advice." The squirrel nods, sounding like someone desperately trying to sound casual. "But it's hard. I don't know if she'd… I mean, I wouldn't want to screw up the relationship we already have."

Hazel reaches up and gently tilts Rhiannon's head toward hers, so they're looking into one another's eyes. "You won't."

Rhiannon swallows hard, and moves closer until their noses touch, freezes, then lets her lips just brush Hazel's.

After holding that lightest of kisses for a second, Hazel wraps her arms around the larger squirrel and pulls her down on top of her. Rhiannon chitters in surprise, eyes going wide, and sucks in her breath as Hazel nuzzles at her neck. She returns the nuzzle, breathing faster, then turns it into another muzzle-to-muzzle kiss, this one deep and fierce. Hazel keeps holding the kiss, her hands running down Rhiannon's back toward the base of her tail.

Walking out of the kitchen, Jerry catches sight of them before they see him. He blinks twice, ears coloring, and backs silently out of the room with a goofy grin.

Moira isn't sure where Stetson's apartment is. She's navigating with half divine intuition and half pragmatic triangulation. He'd said he didn't have a car, and he used public transit when he could. So unless his circumstances have changed drastically since she last saw him, he's near a light rail station, and in walking distance of the brewpub they had their second meeting at. And, probably not a luxury apartment complex, unless it's "luxury" in air quotes. This one, here, feels right. Two stories, unpretentious but well-maintained, blending into the neighborhood.

She scans the sixteen doors facing this street, then heads up to the second floor, walks to the fourth door (apartment "K", apparently), and knocks on it. No response. She knocks again, harder.

After another second, she hears shuffling inside, followed by a startled bark. The door swings open wide. "Lady Moira!"

"Stetson." She spreads her arms, inviting a hug, not sure if he'll take her up on it.

He doesn't hesitate, though, hugging her back tightly. "It's good to see you. Amazing, even, all things considered."

"It's good to see you, too. It's…not been as long as it feels like."

"And you're the immortal one." He steps back and motions her inside. "Come in."

She steps in, and he closes the door behind her, leading her to the couch. The furnishings are sparse, but nice, in a "decade-old Ikea catalog with a few thrift store finds" way.

"So. Can I get you anything to drink?" He hesitates. "Am I going to want a drink, for that matter? I bet this isn't just a random social call."

Moira gives him a lopsided grin as she sits down. "Two of those barleywines might not be a bad idea."

"Ah. Unfortunately, I don't have—"

She snaps her fingers, and two full tulip glasses appear on the coffee table.

Stetson blinks, laughs, and takes a seat by her. Picking up one of the glasses, he waits for her to pick up hers, and clinks them together in a toast.

After they each take a sip, he puts a hand on her shoulder. "I'm so sorry about Lady Briley."

"Thank you." She takes a longer pull of the beer, and sets her glass down. "We've learned a lot since then. I've had my view of the world tumbled over as much as I'm afraid I tumbled yours."

He cocks his head to the side. "Dare I ask?"

She goes over what they've learned since she last spoke with him—and what's changed.

"So Nunwick—Sotala—still wants to stop the cycle from turning, but he's decided that instead of waiting to get the world so ordered he can do it without killing everyone, he'll go ahead and kill everyone anyway, because he'll have made himself so powerful he can snap his fingers and bring them all back."

"It's less about bringing them all back than about creating a new set of mortals who have his idea of the 'natural order' as part of their DNA, but otherwise, yes."

"And unless you stop it, this happens under two weeks from now."

"Right."

"Ah." He looks into his glass. "And...you somehow need my help to stop it."

"Maybe. But it's the other part I know I'll need your help with."

He lifts his brows. "Other part?"

"When we met at that brewpub, you told me that even though I didn't know why the other gods had left, I might still be here because it's where I needed to be. I think you were right. I think I'm still here to make sure the cycle *does* turn. And to plant the seeds for what comes next."

"You've picked up seed metaphors from Briley. So the goddesses you've deified are the seeds, then?"

"Yes. And I think they've been the right balance against Celestial." She tilts her head. "But—assuming we stop the world from ending, or at least get it to end *our* way—we'll need more than those three women, as wonderful as they are."

Stetson looks off into the distance, silent for long seconds, then half-smiles. "Do I have a choice?"

"If I say yes, will you say no?"

The coyote knocks back most of his glass of barleywine, and takes a deep breath, looking into her eyes. "You know I won't."

She smiles, taking his hands.

forty-three
back to life

When Moira holds the door open for Stetson, Diana's the first one to exclaim, race over, and hug him. "Stetson!"

"It's good to see you, too, Lady Diana." By the time he gets the words out, Rhiannon and Hazel have both stood from where they'd been sitting against one another on the couch.

"I didn't think...you..." She trails off, staring.

"I didn't think I would, either. Well. I'd hoped I'd see you again, but..." He waves at himself. "I assumed I'd still be boringly mortal."

Rhiannon gives Moira an accusing look. "You said you needed him 'as him,' as in not one of us."

Stetson holds up a hand. "Please don't chew on Lady Moira. When she says she needs my help, I trust her, even if I'm utterly bewildered by the idea."

"It's news to us as well," Hazel says. "Was it your choice?"

The coyote gives her a lopsided grin. "It wasn't not my choice."

Parker rises from where she's sitting, holding out a hand. "I don't believe we've met. Lily Parker."

He takes her hand. "Stetson Halbach. Uh, Ms. Parker, with..."

"I've had a recent change of employment status."

"I see." He blinks, taking a seat. Shortly everyone's sitting again, Diana by Parker, Hazel and Rhiannon so close they're almost in one another's lap.

Arilin Thorferra

"So Stetson's the one you rushed out to visit," Rhiannon says. "I admit I didn't guess that."

Hazel smirks. "And spend the night with."

The coyote clears his throat, looking away.

Parker readjusts her glasses. "One could argue we all needed a night of recovery."

Diana squeezes the vixen's hand lightly.

Hazel and Rhiannon both giggle softly, moving closer still. "Yeah, I guess so," Rhiannon says. Hazel gives her cheek a nuzzle.

Stetson looks between the vixen and sheep, then the pika and squirrel.

Moira waves a hand at Rhiannon and Hazel. "I thought I was going to have to smash their faces together and scream, 'fucking kiss already.'"

Rhiannon sinks into her seat, ears going red. Hazel crosses her arms, looking simultaneously annoyed and glowingly pleased. Stetson arches a brow at Moira, looking amused.

The hare shrugs. "Love and war make an uneasy balance."

Jerry comes in with Ms. Storm. "I have coffee brewing." The fox beams at Stetson, albeit with an edge of nervousness. "Hello. I'm Jerry, the... I'm used to saying caretaker or assistant for the farm here, but I suppose I'm the co-owner now."

The rat sets down a tray of tarts. "And I'm Amelia Storm, Ms. Parker's assistant."

Moira gestures at the plate. "Have a tart. Whatever Jerry makes is spectacular."

As Stetson picks up one of the miniature pies, Jerry says, "These are Miss Amelia's creation."

"With Jerry's kind assistance," Ms. Storm quickly adds.

Ms. Parker smiles. "Don't be too modest, Ms. Storm. I've had your tarts on a few occasions."

"I bet that's a euphemism," Hazel stage-whispers to Rhiannon.

Parker and Storm both narrow their eyes at her.

The pika shrugs, flashing a sorry-not-sorry grin, and picks up one of the tarts, too. "So if you put on your god of war hat, do you have a plan for an attack or do we just improvise and hope?"

"I know what we need to plan for. I don't know how to do it yet." She takes a big bite of one of the tarts before continuing. "These *are* good. Anyway, I've been kicking the can down the road for a thousand years. When I brought you all into this, even I didn't honestly know what I was starting. Or restarting. But we need to finish it."

"Meaning...?"

"You want to not just destroy the machine, but kill Mr. Nunwick," Parker says after a moment.

"It's not a matter of want." She finishes the tart, and folds her hands in her lap. "Sotala's spent centuries trying to keep the cycle from turning, failed, and now plans to blow up the wheel. We need to stop him, yes. But setting the world right means starting the cycle's turn."

Diana stares at her. "What?"

She nods. "I didn't know that's what my revolution would have brought about, but maybe Daranu did. And it wasn't the right time. But at some point after the gods left, it *was* the right time, and now it's long overdue."

"Th-that's the end of the world, isn't it?" Jerry stammers.

Hazel shrugs. "I mean, yes, the turning of the cycle is described as the end of the world as we know it in folk tales, but what does that actually *mean*? It probably doesn't mean wiping out all evidence of life and starting over from scratch. It's a new age with new rules, but not a new creation myth."

"New rules." Moira nods, and sweeps a hand around. "And a new pantheon."

Rhiannon sits up straight. "What now?"

"You're brand new to being gods. You're of this place and time. You've all got ideas on how you'd do things, what you'd want to be hands-on with, what you'd want to leave alone. I know you're all literally chosen ones, but I also know you're capable of rising above that. You won't be like Daranu, or Nunwick, or even me. You're perfect for the new cycle."

"Whoa." Rhiannon runs a hand through her hair, looking discomfited.

Diana takes a deep breath. "But destroying the machine and dismantling Celestial, killing Nunwick, isn't enough to make the cycle turn."

"No. We have to reverse the machine, and do it while it's focused on Nunwick," Moira says. "Well, Rhiannon has to figure out how to do that without making it blow up. We have a couple of weeks, though."

Rhiannon lifts her brows. "Even if it doesn't blow up, what does that actually do? Spit all of Nunwick's divine magic over the world? Does that make everybody gods?"

"I can't imagine it would, but it might infuse the world with magic in…surprising ways. Honestly, though, I'm not—"

"That's not what I meant!" Diana cuts her off, voice fierce and trembling. "That's not what I meant by not enough. And you know it."

Moira meets the sheep's eyes. "I know," she says softly. "Let's focus on this. Please."

Stetson's ears skew. "Uh…"

"So we need to get to the machine as close to the time of Nunwick's ascension as possible," Moira continues after a moment, ignoring Diana's continued glare.

"Not necessarily," Rhiannon says. "If we can sabotage it ahead of time without them noticing, it'll be safer for us all, won't it?"

Parker turns a searching gaze away from Moira, and shakes her head at the squirrel. "It will be just as securely guarded, and the longer the time between any successful sabotage and usage, the more likely they are to discover the problem."

Moira nods. "And we need to be there when it's used regardless. We can't rely on subterfuge."

"We can't exactly walk into Sotala's technomagical ascension ritual without being noticed." Hazel spreads her hands. "What, we disguise ourselves as lab interns? Pizza delivery drivers?"

Stetson tilts his head. "What if we're small?"

Everyone looks at him.

"I know being mega-huge is way more fashionable in this crowd, but you—uh, we—can change size the other way, too, right? Small can be hard to see, and might be able to get into machinery."

"Huh." Rhiannon rubs her chin. "I don't know if it'll make us harder to detect. I mean, we're all still gods."

"If we can do it right then, while the ritual's going on, there's gonna be a *lot* of magical energy flying around," Hazel points out. "It might end up being easier, as stupid as that sounds."

"It might." Moira starts to get up. "I'm going to start coffee and check if Jerry needs kitchen help. You all strategize."

Diana's voice rises again. "Moira, sit down!"

Everyone in the room feels it. It's not just an anguished cry, it's a divine command. And a forceful one, too. Everyone but Parker and Moira flinches.

Moira grits her teeth, but relents. She looks back at the sheep, folding her arms.

"What am I missing?" Stetson looks bewildered.

Parker pushes her glasses up her muzzle. "For the cycle to turn, Mr. Halbach, all the old gods have to leave."

He blinks twice, staring at Moira. "And go where?" he says at length.

Moira sighs. "I've said what I need to say already. The world needs a *new* pantheon. This is why I'm still here. To find all of you. To hold the door open for you. And then to clear the way."

"But…" Hazel runs a hand through her hair. "By immortal standards, you've barely had time to meet us." She gestures at Stetson. "And he's been a god for, what, like, eighteen hours?"

Moira allows herself a small smile, but turns away. "I really need that coffee now. And seriously, strategize. We're going to be trying to kill literal gods in like a week and a half, they're all but certainly expecting us to try something, and we won't have the benefit of our own weird magic-suppressing technology." She heads into the kitchen.

Stetson leans forward and lowers his voice. "So we *are* going to figure out how to keep her from flying off to the land beyond the land of the gods, right?"

Rhiannon nods. "We are. But she's right—we need to stop Sotala from destroying the world first." She looks between Parker and Ms. Storm. "And as the ones who know the most about Celestial's estate, that puts the ball in your court."

Parker frowns, crossing her arms and drumming her fingers on her side. "The idea of being too small to be easily noticed has value, but I'm not comfortable with the risk."

"They're not going to be able to suppress our magic without screwing up their whole plan, so our only disadvantage will be physical size." Hazel shrugs. "And a tiny god is still a god."

"But still tiny." Rhiannon's tail flicks. "Surely we can do the spooky action at a distance thing. Most miracles don't involve gods standing right there being miraculous, right? They're visions and things moving under their own power and all that."

"If we were talking about taking over a competitor's corporation, yes. A series of nightmares, a fortuitous accident, Ms. Storm meeting a key executive for lunch." Parker waves a hand. "But we're not."

Hazel looks at Ms. Storm. "By meeting them for lunch, she means you ate them, right?"

Storm smiles demurely.

"Well, you *are* the longest-lived god here, other than Moira," Diana says. "What other options do we have?"

Parker's silent for long seconds, then takes off her glasses and rubs her temples. "As much as I wish otherwise, I can't see any plan as effective as being there physically, and Lady Moira's insistence on doing this as the ascension starts is likely correct." She puts the glasses back on and sighs. "The advantages of being small may slightly, *slightly*, outweigh the peril. To have a chance of survival, let alone success, we'll have to be extremely disciplined, though."

Hazel grunts. "That's not exactly our thing."

"Fortunately for you, Ms. Harcourt, it is mine."

All the deities—Rhiannon, Hazel, Parker, Diana, Ms. Storm, Stetson, Moira—stand on the farmhouse porch. They're looking out, but not at the driveway. The view "outside" is that of Celestial's grand estate, specifically the valley with the giant astrarium, with Nunwick's chair-slash-throne. It looks for all the world as if they've perched the house on the side of the hill under Parker's office building, maybe a hundred feet off the valley floor.

And the site is *packed.*

A dozen scientists stand at the control consoles, twiddling dials and checking screens. Meridrew stands off to the side, speaking with Nunwick, Ironheart, and several black-suited security guards. At least two dozen more guards, again mostly wolves and tigers, roam the perimeter of the plaza, right behind high metal barricade fences they installed a week ago. Other guards stand by each console, as well as the single gate through the fence.

Beyond the fence, a crowd of spectators fills the side facing the astrarium. A *massive* crowd, at least a thousand people, waiting for their divine CEO to crown himself king of the universe.

"I'm guessing most of those aren't gods, at least," Hazel mutters.

Parker sweeps her gaze around. "I recognize multiple high-placed executives who are gods themselves, both inside and outside the fence. Assume all the guards have some power, as well." She turns to Rhiannon. "Have they made changes that you can detect?"

The squirrel twists her long hair in one hand. "I think…ugh." She squeezes her eyes shut, then opens them again in a few seconds. "No."

"And it's operating as we surmised last week."

Rhiannon nods and points. "The consoles along the rear lines are monitors, watching the input power—electricity, hydraulics, uh, souls sucked in through black magic, whatever. The front line has controls for output." She gestures with her hands, drawing a circle in the air to act as a magnifying glass. She zooms in on the center, back, forth, almost back to the center again. "The big dial, there, is output power. Now the bad news: power's running through it all now, and I can't sense any circuit that reverses polarity. Maybe when we get on the ground, I can find a way, but right now I'm doubtful."

Hazel shrugs. "The silver lining of that is that if you rewire it from inside, they might not catch it until it's too late."

"It ran for quite a long while back in Black Oak, though." Diana shakes her head. "If Mr. Nunwick's sitting on his throne and suddenly starts screaming—"

"It'll be really funny?"

Diana eyes the pika. "They'll turn it off."

"No." Parker shakes her head. "His obvious pain won't be enough for anyone else to act. No one truly has an idea of what to expect when dealing with this much raw power, and they'd be terrified to fail him. He'll have to give them an explicit command to shut it down."

"Which his ego and pride will compel him to resist doing as long as he can." Moira crosses her arms. "So we'll need to have secured the area at that point."

"Since Mr. Nunwick will obviously be, ah, occupied, does that mean that Ms. Ironheart is the one to truly worry about?" Stetson asks.

"She's the one to worry *most* about," Ms. Storm says. "But as I pointed out to Ms. Harcourt the other evening, don't underestimate 'lesser' gods."

Moira looks over the plaza again. "We'll need to find a way to secure the area around our console, and do it the moment we're discovered."

"We're nearly out of time." Parker points to Ironheart and Nunwick, but it's unnecessary. As the two lions walk toward the throne, the crowd goes wild—and gets even louder as both of them begin growing larger.

Moira looks at them. "This is less planned than Ms. Parker and I would like, but it's the play we have. Rhiannon gets physically inside the system; the rest of us act as lookouts. I have ideas on how we can secure the area when the time comes—and it *will* come—but there's no guarantee it will work. And if Rhiannon can't do it, we fall back to Hazel's plan."

"Wait, I have a plan?"

"Brute force it."

"Right!" The pika gives her a thumbs up. "I do like that plan."

"Anyway, I need you all to know…" Moira trails off. "Thank you, all of you. You've brought me back to life. Thanks to you, I found not just worshippers again, but friends. A new pantheon. I found Briley. I found…" She shakes her head. "I found myself."

Abruptly, she hugs Diana. "Den mother." Diana bites her lip, hugging back tightly.

Then she embraces Rhiannon. "Technowitch." Rhiannon laughs weakly and hugs back.

She leans over and clasps Hazel, too. "Chaos muppet." Hazel snorts, but returns the hug.

"Guiding star." The coyote blinks rapidly at that appellation as she embraces him, awkwardly hugging back.

Moira regards Parker for a moment, and the vixen smiles slightly. "I'm not part of your new pantheon, Lady Moira."

"We'll see, captain." The hare gives her a hug, too. Parker swishes her tail, returning it.

Finally, she comes to Storm. "I don't know you well. I believe you have a little welcome chaos in you, though." The rat laughs, returning the hare's snug lightly.

Moira's smiling at the end of this all, a smile like a rainbow after a storm.

"Who are you and what have you done with Lady Murderbunny?" Rhiannon murmurs. Moira only laughs, which makes the squirrel squint.

"Mr. Nunwick's taking a seat." Parker points. "We'll teleport in at the base of that console, under the center dial. Ms. Doran makes her way up through the interior and reports back whether this is even feasible. The rest of us can only keep our eyes and ears open, and stay out from underpaw. Are we ready?"

"I sure hope so," Rhiannon mutters.

Parker stares at her. "You've always been pugnaciously assertive with me before, Ms. Doran. This is no time to stop."

She clears her throat and straightens up. "Ready, bitch."

"Better." The vixen snaps her fingers.

Abruptly all of them stand on what looks, at first glance, like a city street, under an odd, brutalist skyscraper. But they're all barely an inch high, looking up at the console's underside. The shift from the house to the frantic bustle of the technomagic ritual envelops them in a cacophony: voices far above, thunderous footsteps close by, the buzz of machinery everywhere. The air smells of metal and heat and ozone, and the concrete has become a rough, hot plain. A scientist's paws loom close by, each toe dwarfing any of them.

"All right," Moira yells. "Go!"

forty-four
hares are bigger

R hiannon faces the sheer metal wall of the console, going over the plan she and Parker had worked out. With a few swipes of her claws, she cuts a mouse-sized hole into the base, runs inside, and creates a will-o-wisp to light the way ahead of her as she flies up toward the controls. Moira pointed out that they could approach the space in the fashion Parker and Diana had back in the vixen's memory of the *Silver Rose:* stay invisible and, as much as possible, intangible. It wouldn't protect against anyone who could detect the supernatural, but it would reduce both their physical and magical footprint. It won't keep them hidden for very long, but it just has to work for long enough.

So far, at least, it's still working. The group splits up, making sure at least one pair of eyes covers every possible angle on the console.

Moira's eyes, specifically, are on Nunwick—Sotala—and his giant chair. He's so enormous compared to her that he's difficult to make out, but it looks like he's staring at the huge ray guns trained on him. She can read the trepidation in his eyes.

At the other end of the console, Parker and Storm do their best to catalog the lesser gods they recognize in the crowd, both inside and outside the fence. "There's no way we can do this without a higher view," Storm mutters. Frowning, Parker nods, and motions up. They rocket into the air.

Hazel, Diana, and Stetson have stayed together. "So we just...sit here and sound an alarm if we have to?" Hazel drums her fingers on her wheelchair's arm.

"And offer assistance if we have to." Stetson steps back closer to the console as a security guard, this one a burly arctic vixen, walks close by. He stares up, muzzle slightly open.

"This is a disquieting view of the world," Diana mutters. She risks stepping out further, looking quickly around, and her eyes widen. "They're starting."

"What?" Hazel rolls forward a few feet—inches, she reminds herself—and looks, too. The scientists are taking position along the consoles. A fox walks directly toward them; fortunately, his eyes are looking up, fixed on Ironheart and Nunwick. She grimaces and moves backward against the console as the fox stands directly in front of the control panel Rhiannon's trying to subvert.

"How much serious opposition can you spot?" Parker circles in the air.

"If we count elevated mortals, well over a hundred." Ms. Storm points down at various spectators. "Only the guards are strategically positioned, but when we disrupt the festivities, they'll have a serious advantage in numbers."

"Our advantage in power may be a sufficient counterbalance." Parker waves toward Ironheart and Nunwick; the two giant lions talk softly, Ironheart leaning over the chair. "They'll be the true challenge. Lady Moira will handle Mr. Nunwick, but even she may not be able to handle both of them along with the distraction the mob will cause."

Storm glances at the vixen as they hover. "Can *we* handle Ms. Ironheart?"

"If we keep her on the defensive."

Ironheart straightens up, faces the crowd, and raises her hands over her head. "Tonight!"

The crowd bursts into cheers.

"Tonight, we fulfill the culmination of all our work." She lowers her hands to spread her arms wide. "The work Celestial has been doing for a century. The Order of Caeles, for centuries before that. You are all here," she looks around, down, "to witness the ascendance of a new Creator. The birth of a new world. A world free of chaos."

The roar of the crowd grows.

Inside the console, Rhiannon barely hears Ironheart's words, but she feels the current pulse, the pressure change, as console switches flip and dials turn. She zooms from connection to connection, wire to wire, panel to panel. Dammit. Exactly what she feared: reversing the polarity of the main circuits won't matter. Running the guns in reverse requires a mechanical change.

She flies back out as the crowd builds to a deafening frenzy, as Ironheart walks forward, as she steps over all the consoles at once to stand behind the astrarium. Meridrew, the short fox towering right in front of Rhiannon, Hazel, Diana, and Stetson, turns the power dial.

With four piercing cracks, the ray guns snap on. The whine of turbines quickly overwhelms the noise of the crowd.

Not all the gods are in a position to see it, but Moira is, and Parker and Storm certainly are. Thin white beams hit Nunwick, and he growls softly, eyes widening. His hands clench at the throne's armrests. Light pours out of the back of the guns, a liquid glittering wave moving up the walls of the valley, visibly flowing *backward* toward the devices.

"No no no," Rhiannon hisses, putting her hands to her head. She speaks to all the gods at once, willing the power into existence, trusting that she can. "It's mechanical. We can only reverse it at each gun."

Abruptly Moira's standing in front of her. "How?"

"I'm still working—"

The turbine whine mutates into an unearthly howl.

Moira claps, and all five of the ones who'd been on the floor appear on top of the console, close to Meridrew's chest level. They're out in the open, but they have a good view of the guns. The beams have become rough, multicolor torrents of lightning.

Nunwick's claws come out, digging into the throne's arms. He has the stoic expression of someone trying not to show the pain they're in.

And the light flowing into the guns boils over the valley walls, forming raging photon waterfalls, the lake of energy greedily swelling. The crowd couldn't be heard over the din even if they were still cheering, but they're not. Most watch Nunwick raptly, but some have turned to watch the light. So far, none of them have noticed the office building overlooking the valley—the one Parker and Diana both had their offices in—starting to decay.

"If you cut the power, will it buy us more time?"

"We can't. There are so many redundant systems here it makes the Pentagon look like a mall Radio Shack. We might be able to trip it off for a few seconds at most." Rhiannon runs a hand through her hair. "But something Ms. Parker said is the key. Telescopes. They're like telescopes. We can reverse the effects by physically flipping them."

Moira looks at one of the guns. "So just spin them around?"

"They're not built to spin. We have to flip them without breaking the electrical connections and, uh, magic tubes."

She nods, then looks up to see Parker and Storm flying down—and Meridrew staring at them all, open-mouthed. "Hi." She waves.

He looks back and forth between them, ears flicking. "I, uh, oh my. Uh. Uh." He backs away and starts pointing at them.

As Parker lands, the scientist vanishes and reappears in her hand. She lifts him up to her muzzle. "Mr. Meridrew," she hisses, "do you understand what that machine is about to do?"

"S-save the world!" He scrabbles around in her palm. "It's too late for you to stop it, either!"

Her ears lower. "It's going to do the entire world what it did to the parts of Fresno that Lady Moira and her friends weren't able to save."

"No. That's not—it can't—we can't stop it now. There's no way." He looks stricken, then steels himself. "You're lying, you vile—"

She tosses him at Ms. Storm. The rat catches him and shakes

him once. Now she's holding an exquisite paper doll, a perfect watercolor version of the fox. She crumples it.

"You're terrifying," Hazel says, with clear admiration.

"Company!" Stetson gestures at the guards now running toward where Meridrew had been. Ironheart's turning her vast head down to look at the commotion.

"New plan," Moira announces, thrusting her arms out to the side with her hands raised. The guards closest to them stop as if they'd smashed into an invisible wall, others comically piling up behind them. "You four," she points at Hazel, Rhiannon, Diana, and Stetson, "Get to those guns. Rhiannon, figure out how to turn them around."

"Got it." Rhiannon nods, flickers—and stays where she is, expression registering shock. "I can't just visualize myself right by one." The others murmur agreement.

Moira shakes her head. "They're ready for us magically, so we're going to have to go physical. Parker, Storm, and I will handle Sotala and Ironheart and buy you time."

Hazel raises a hand. "Just to check that I understand what I'm hearing here—"

Parker answers, "It's time for brute force, Ms. Harcourt."

The pika pumps her fist.

"Let's do it." Moira claps her hands. Abruptly all seven of them appear to one side of the massive plaza, at the same enormous size as Ironheart and Nunwick. Ms. Storm looks mildly surprised; Stetson yelps in momentary panic.

Ironheart looks shocked for a fraction of a second, then bares her teeth. She brings her hands together, and the pressure of the shock blows them all backward. Parker and Moira keep their balance; Hazel rolls several dozen yards. The others get hurled across the plaza, tumbling, crashing into the fence. "Even you can't stop this, *Lady* Moira," she growls, making *Lady* into a curse.

Nunwick groans, and gets out through gritted teeth, "The divine machinery...will draw in your power, too. Always the plan...always the inevitable end for you." He manages a triumphant smile. "Just... a matter of when you give your power to me."

Moira gestures at the others. "Go. Go."

Stetson looks down at the crowd he's fallen into and on top of. "You know Nunwick and Ironheart aren't truly on your side, don't—"

Some of them open fire on him; others shoot lightning and fire bolts.

"Right. Never mind." He hops to his paws and dashes toward one of the guns. Hazel moves toward another, Rhiannon toward a third. Diana scrambles to her hooves, looks at Parker, then hurries toward the fourth gun.

Ironheart roars, plasma crackling along her fur, and gestures grandly to the spectators beyond the fence, inviting them. Empowering them. They surge against the barrier—then start to push it down. Or take to the air and fly over it. Or grow, simply stepping over it. Mortals with magic powers, lesser gods, they all move in for a fight.

Nunwick's expression freezes in ecstatic pain as the beams continue to bathe him. Moira, all the gods, can sense his power growing.

The hare straightens as she, Storm, and Parker face the crowd, the other gods starting to fight, physically and magically, against the assault. Hazel looks grimly thrilled; Diana and Rhiannon just look grim. Stetson looks panicked.

Parker brings her hands together, her cutlass appearing between them. Her outfit changes, too, business suit changing to blue waistcoat, blouse to ruffled short and corset, sandals to boots.

Moira's armor swirls into existence around her. Drawing her sword, she strides forward. Parker follows on her right flank, Storm—outfit shifting to a more Victorian take on the red outfit she'd worn when she'd first met Moira—on her left, a sword in her hand as well.

The gods and demigods of Celestial, the guards and executives, middle managers and secretaries, meet them with fists and knives and guns, with fire and lightning. They meet them at six feet tall and fifty feet tall and three hundred feet tall.

And, as they rush forward, some of them change more than size.

Muscles. Claws. Spikes. Tentacles. The transformations become disquieting mirrors of William's turn, what seems like decades ago. The self-proclaimed gods of order use chaos, once again.

For a minute or two, Nunwick's divine/infernal army nonetheless seems dramatically outmatched. Moira and the gods fighting with her stand strong, massive, determined. Diana unerringly spots the most capable captains on Sotala's side and makes sure they end up under her hooves, sometimes directing the others or calling out advice. *Get to the guns. Focus on the end state.* Meanwhile, Rhiannon knows the opposing forces *are* executives and middle managers and secretaries, bristling with smartphones and tablets and computers—all of which fall under her spell. They distract, they spy, they simply explode on her command.

For her part, Hazel fights as chaotically as the monsters she faces, smashing creatures together, levitating smaller foes right down her throat, even leaping to her paws at unexpected times while her wheelchair rolls over enemies on its own like her mechanical sidekick. Stetson marches with purpose toward the gun he's been tasked to reach, setting the pace for the others; he hasn't had much time to learn how to be a god, but he catches on quickly, sending the enemy flying away not with physical force but divine command.

And the trio of Moira, Parker, and Storm fight like a divine army all by themselves: an onlooker who'd successfully kept out of the fray might be hard-pressed to tell which, between the vixen and the hare, was the god of war. Moira's shield becomes not only defense but as much a weapon as her sword, smashing into opposition, twice launched into crowds and returning to the hare's arm. A leopard, nearly as tall as the gargantuan Ms. Storm, makes a leap for her and finishes it transformed into a buckler for her. Parker, for her part, doesn't fight as if she needs armor, the immense sword moving so fast it seems to knock even spells out of the air when it's not slicing through enemies.

But there are so *many* enemies. And they keep coming.

As Storm fails to turn a group of knee-high lesser gods

attacking her into dolls and resorts to stabbing and kicking them, she gasps, "Am I getting tired, or are they getting tougher?"

Moira dispatches a wolf, and checks on the progress of the others, of her new pantheon, struggling to reach the guns. They hold their ground, but they've stopped advancing, and her group is too occupied to give them cover. They *are* getting tougher. But how?

She glances quickly between the two lions. Sotala still looks like he's in pain, but he's focused now. And he's grinning. So is Ironheart. "They're getting power from Ironheart. And Sotala."

"You handle him," Parker says. "We'll handle her." Storm swallows, but nods her assent.

Moira hesitates.

Parker gives her a steady look. "What you have to do is, as you said, long overdue."

Moira gives her a quick embrace. "I'm glad you're by my side, Captain Lily."

"I'm glad to be by yours, Lady Moira. Go."

Moira turns, and walks—not runs—toward Nunwick.

Parker and Storm stride toward Ironheart. The defenders get in strikes against both the vixen and the rat now. It doesn't save any of them, from wizards ending up in Parker's boot prints to the threatening security wolf who lands a single punch on Storm before she turns him to colored sand. He has enough life left to look shocked before the sand collapses.

Ironheart, though, pushes other defenders out of the way herself. "The last time you challenged me, I trapped you in a painting." She curls her lip.

Parker slows her walk. "I didn't challenge you. I appealed to you." She changes her grip on her cutlass, holding it by her side deceptively casually. "I'd hoped it might still be possible to reason with you and Mr. Nunwick."

The lioness sweeps her gaze up and down Parker's outfit. "You're lecturing me about reason, and you're dressed as a pirate queen." She sneers, then claps her hands over her head.

Parker feels the magic hit her, try to trap her again, just like she'd expected. Ironheart's shown strengths over the centuries, but creativity's never been one of them. She brings her sword up, catching the spell, twisting it. The vixen spins right at the lioness, blade coming back down.

"How—" Ironheart grabs the vixen's arm with both of hers. She stops the cutlass when it's right against the side of her neck, close enough to shave fur. Her eyes widen.

"No, Tierney." Parker looks straight into her eyes and grins wildly. "*The* pirate queen."

Ironheart snarls and pulls away, shoving Parker backward—then whirls in furious surprise as Storm swings her sword at the lioness. She ducks, vaulting backward, landing outside the plaza with an earthquake drop.

Even so, she barely has enough time to summon a shield to deflect Storm's next thrust before Parker takes another swing at her. She pulls away from that, too, but the vixen wings her leg. She yelps, then growls, all three hundred feet of her vaulting into the air, rising quickly above the battlefield. The other two giantesses give aerial chase.

As Ironheart's attention shifts to her own defense, the magic deployed against Diana and company weakens. They all make progress toward their guns—but slow progress. All have collections of wounds now; Stetson's limping, and Rhiannon's tail has been painfully singed. Even so, the squirrel reaches hers first, and frantically studies the machinery's mounting, as well as she can while still under constant attack.

Moira reaches Darren Nunwick, sword at her side.

He takes a ragged breath, and his stare manages to be imperious despite the immense force he's under. "You know it's...too late to stop. You can't beat me, Moira. If you fight me...you *will* lose."

She stops in front of him, out of his immediate reach, two beams sizzling past her arms to either side. Her armor and weaponry shimmers, melts away, replaced by the diaphanous dress she wore at Black Oak. "We're not going to fight, Sotala."

Everyone's attention is on her, for at least a moment; the mortals and demigods and tentacled horrors simply stop fighting, continuing to stare. Nunwick does, too, as his expression grows uncertain, then incredulous. "After all these centuries, you think you can...come to me now...dissuade with your mere favor? I'm no longer...the lovestruck child you spurned."

"No. I don't."

Both Parker and Storm press their attack in midair on Ironheart, the lioness hurling lightning bolts, casting magic nets, trying to catch either sword, strike either warrior. She's bleeding in a dozen places, but they're small wounds. Her fury at her inability to dispatch her inferior opponents visibly grows with each second.

She drops to the ground outside the plaza, her landing an earthquake—perilously close to the whirling streams of light being sucked into the closest ray gun, the one that Diana's just reaching. Ignoring the black sheep for the moment, she spreads her arms wide. Both Parker and Storm jerk in midair, as if physically grabbed.

"*Enough!*" she bellows, clapping her hands together. Parker and Storm smash into one another in a puff of flame and drop out of the air unceremoniously, trailing smoke and fire. The vixen smashes into the ground on her back. Storm falls into the pool of light, dissolving into iridescence.

Diana screams.

Ironheart looks down at her, narrowing her eyes. The sheep looks back up defiantly, preparing to attack—

The lioness's eyes widen as she senses danger, too late. She spins around just in time for the pirate queen to thrust her cutlass into Ironheart's chest, running her all the way through.

"Ironheart," Nunwick breathes, looking past Moira, expression stricken. As the lioness slides backward into the light, he roars as if he'd been stabbed himself. "Tierney!"

Parker staggers, falling to her knees.

Diana abandons her position, running to wrap her arms around the vixen, coating her hands and arms with blood and charred fur. "Oh, Lily."

The vixen nuzzles her. "I didn't expect to make it out of this." Her breathing is labored. "You didn't expect me to, either."

With Ironheart gone and Nunwick's attention completely diverted, the remaining opposition to Hazel and Stetson melts away, and they find positions at their ray guns.

"Did you love her?" Moira asks. Her tone isn't smug, or skeptical, or reproaching. It's sincere, guileless.

Nunwick stares at her. "I…"

"I'm sorry."

He slaps her hard enough to rock her backward. "Don't you *dare* pity me!" he thunders.

Rhiannon yells, "I have it! Break the mounting points at the bottom and lift straight up. Then turn them around *without* letting the back point at any of us."

Parker gives Diana a kiss. "You have to go."

"But…" She looks at Moira as the hare gets back to her paws.

Parker squeezes the sheep's hands. "Keep me in your heart."

Diana whines and gives the vixen a fierce kiss, then moves to the gun.

"I can remake her along with everything else!" Nunwick yells into Moira's face.

"You can't. A simulacrum won't be her. The new world you make won't be this one. And it won't be what this one's supposed to become."

"My father was a fool to trust you!"

"I was the one meant to do this." She tilts her head. "You took this on yourself, and you can't."

"He wanted us both to die!"

"He wanted the new cycle to start. But it can't, not until new gods are ready to take our place…and until we've left. They're ready." She takes one of his hands with both of hers. "It's time for us to go."

Rhiannon's already uncoupled her gun and started to turn it around. She pauses, staring at Moira.

The hare turns around. "You'll all do wonderfully. I'm so happy I got to know each of you…and so proud." She smiles, and for a moment that seems brighter than any of the magical energy flooding the valley.

Nunwick stares, then roars. "No!"

Abruptly Moira's twice his size, gathering him into her arms, holding him there, gently but firmly.

"Moira!" Rhiannon calls, voice breaking.

Diana looks back toward Parker. She can see the vixen turning iridescent, and her vision blurs. "I'm happy I got to know you, too," she gets out, not sure if she's speaking loudly enough for Moira to hear, and hefts up her gun. Hazel and Rhiannon do the same. With a whimper, so does Stetson. The energy that had been focused on Nunwick shoots up along the valley wall now, digging into the dirt, making the earth itself glow bluish-white.

Sotala stares up at her as the light swirls around both of them.

"There should have been another way." She smiles down sadly at him. "Maybe I was meant to spend a century or two making you understand it, maybe there was a path we were both supposed to find. Maybe..." Her voice falters for a moment. "Maybe Briley should have been by my side. But I've already put myself, my divinity, on the line for the world before. Daranu knew that when I had to, I'd do it again in a heartbeat."

"Why?" he whispers. "Why would you do that?"

"Because I'm the goddess of love." She strokes his side. "And sometimes love means sacrifice."

He tries to get up, but he stumbles and slides backward. They're both weakened now by the force of the light. "No. No. I—I will not be denied by a prey animal. By a damned rabbit."

"You know I'm a hare, Sotala." She pulls him gently against her as her fur starts to shimmer.

As his fur begins to sparkle, too, he trembles, closing his eyes, speaking hoarsely. "I'm scared."

"I'm with you."

He opens his eyes and looks up at her, fearfully, wonderingly. She smiles down.

This time, the iridescence glows brighter, brighter, outshining the sun itself. The ray guns vibrate with unspeakable force, the beams pouring out of them becoming sprays, ripping the machinery apart, the noise becoming all-encompassing, deafening.

Each of the gods shrieks as they're surrounded by starlight, racing out in concentric circles up the valley walls, up into the air, across the sky.

The world turns blinding white before slowly fading to black. The next moment might be a split second, or it might be a thousand years. No sound, no sight, no sensation.

Then, the moment fades.

Diana rubs her eyes as vision returns, as she feels wind against her wool, cold ground under her. She's still in the valley; the valley's still recognizable. Nunwick's throne is gone, though, along with the guns, the astrarium, the stones of the plaza. She looks around quickly. The other three gods are still there, too, although Hazel's wheelchair seems among the casualties. No one else is left on the battlefield.

She gets up and walks toward the spot the throne had been. Stetson follows; the others do, too.

Rhiannon's the first to speak, looking around. "Uh...Moira..."

Diana shakes her head mutely.

Hazel looks around, wiping away a tear. "Is that it? It's just... over?"

Stetson points up. "Look at the sky," he says hoarsely.

They look up. It's nighttime, blacker than any of them have seen it, the stars brighter than ever against it.

"Okay," Hazel says doubtfully. "What am I supposed to see?"

Rhiannon looks back and forth. "Orion and the Big Dipper, for two. They're not there. All the stars are different."

Diana furrows her brow. She traces a line with a finger. "It's... it's...the mango tree." She traces another one. "And the sea serpent."

"Those aren't real constellations."

"No. They're not. I made them up. I drew them in kindergarten."

Rhiannon stares at the sheep, then back at the sky, mouth open. She starts walking, then sprinting, up the road out of the valley. The others follow, Hazel conjuring up her wheelchair and rolling on ahead. What's left of Celestial's estate looks like Black Oak did: no life, buildings aged into ruins.

"I think maybe we need to check on the rest of, uh, everything," Stetson says. "Back to the farm?"

Hazel shakes her head. "My old place in the city." She snaps her fingers without waiting for a response.

They're standing on a sidewalk, back at their normal size. The city's not only intact, it is, as usual, full of cars and pedestrians.

Diana breathes a sigh of relief. "Maybe everything else is…" She trails off, watching a pair of winged vixens zoom by overhead, screaming in delight.

"Normal?" Stetson finishes.

A giant cervine head appears over the nearest building, the deer woman leaning down and looking at them.

"Hi," Rhiannon says cautiously.

"What…" The woman waves around, then at herself. "…the hell."

Rhiannon opens her mouth, closes it, shrugs helplessly.

Over the next minute or so, a lynx casts fireballs and shrieks in apology when he sets fire to a car. A mouse races down the street bare-pawed at impossible speed. An apartment building down the block abruptly vanishes. People start to stop and notice the gods, point at them, gasp, occasionally fall to their knees.

A roar sounds overhead. What can only be a dragon, easily the size of a jumbo jet, flies past.

They all look back at each other. Hazel starts laughing. "Holy shit."

forty-five
festival

H azel looks around as she and Rhiannon head up to the farmhouse. "The place hasn't changed much at all."

"You say that every year." Rhiannon knocks on the front door.

"That's because it's true every year. This is literally the farm of the gods!" She spreads her arms wide.

The door opens, and Trevor flashes her an amused grin. "And you know we'd rather not let it get out."

She stands up from her chair and gives the ferret a hug. "You two are such stick-in-the-muds for gods, Trevor. I bet you and Jerry haven't even eaten anyone yet."

He returns the hug. "Bring someone over who goes well with his honey apple wine, and we'll discuss it. Hello, Rhiannon."

"Hi, Trev." The squirrel gives him a hug, too.

"We will most certainly not!" Jerry calls from the kitchen as Trevor ushers them in. Hazel walks, her chair rolling of its own accord behind them. The fox comes out to meet them, inevitably carrying a tray of food—in this case, appetizers he sets down in the living room. "I swear, Hazel, are you ever going to stop trying to be a bad influence on my husband?"

"Of course not." She and Rhiannon both hug him once his arms are free.

Diana and Stetson smile from where they're sitting together, but don't stand up. "Welcome back from…" Diana waves the hand that isn't holding a wine glass. "Nepal, right?"

Hazel drops into a seat, her chair parking itself nearby. "Yep. I climbed Mount Everest."

Rhiannon sits next to her and pokes her side. "Touching your hand to the top of a mountain does not count as 'climbing.'"

Stetson lifts his brows. "I'm afraid to ask what that does to the tourist destinations around the base."

She waves a hand. "They'd been worrying that there were too many tourists. I'm helping."

Diana shakes her head and takes a sip of her wine. "We're supposed to give nudges to mortals here and there, but mostly leave them to their own devices."

"I *mostly* do that," Hazel says defensively.

Trevor crosses his legs and smiles at the sheep. "You and Stetson don't stay entirely in the background, either."

"I know I don't always practice what I preach, but last fall was a special case. It wasn't just that they were appealing directly for our help; they were facing unusually brutal wizards."

Rhiannon grunts. "It might be a new world, but it's kept too many old patterns."

"I know. Were we supposed to end up with a world filled with monsters, wild magic, and unpredictable catastrophes?" Diana makes a little half-shrug gesture. "And incredible political instability on top of it all."

Stetson gives her cheek a quick nuzzle. "It's barely been a decade, dear. Give it a couple of generations."

"And some of that political realignment could end up being a net good," Rhiannon adds. "There's a lot of mess now, but people are emboldened, experimental. For the first time in forever, we might be on track for less imperialism and capitalism, more egalitarianism and socialism."

Diana grunts, eyeing the squirrel. "It's certainly curious how many oppressive regimes over the last few years have found their firewalls and information blackouts falling apart."

Rhiannon nods solemnly. "Most curious."

Trevor says, "Any candidates for filling out the pantheon you've advanced?"

"There are a few I have my eye on, but I haven't had the sense of...rightness that I did with you and Jerry yet. I don't think we need to rush."

As Jerry serves dinner—a lemon garlic roast chicken paired with a panzanella salad, both served in simple family style but executed with Michelin-star quality—he asks, "So. Are any of us showing up to a festival tonight?"

Hazel helps herself to a generous measure of the salad and a drumstick. "The way you're asking suggests the answer is 'no' for you and Trevor, huh."

"You know we like keeping low profiles. Just simple farmers with good produce."

"Produce people can find either at high-end restaurants or food banks." Diana smiles.

Jerry shrugs self-consciously. "Briley used to give away a lot, too. And we're reaching out to other farmers around the world to help improve crops. Better yields without pesticides, better flavor, more variety."

"I keep telling him that one day someone's going to figure out those peaches are *literally* divine."

Jerry blushes at his husband.

Hazel laughs. "Well, Rhiannon and I usually put in an appearance at the temple in Fresno, and we'll probably do that again tonight after dinner."

"Is...what's the possum's name...Reverend Sidney still there?" Diana asks.

"Yeah, and they're just as challenging as ever." Hazel laughs. "What about you, Diana?"

She shakes her head. "The festivals—and the remembrances—shouldn't be about us. You know how it is. If we draw too much attention to ourselves, we get treated like ceremonial heads of state. Stetson and I were thinking of going to the festival up in San Francisco, but staying faces in the crowd."

Rhiannon smirks. "Until people notice you and drop to their

knees."

"Hopefully, we'll have an hour or two of staying incognito."

Trevor nods. "We've always liked the way you've said we're stewards, not rulers." He smiles. "Even though you four were also catalysts."

"We had to be there, as things played out, but the catalyst was Moira." She sighs, smiling. "And I'm paraphrasing what she used to say. Gods might be all sorts of things, from role models to bad examples, but they're not rulers."

He smiles and lifts his wine glass. "To Lady Moira."

Jerry adds, as he lifts his, "And Lady Briley."

Everyone else lifts their glasses, clinking them together.

After grabbing margaritas in plastic cups from a vendor outside the Ferry Building, Diana and Stetson stroll along the Embarcadero, hand in hand, as the sun sets. On purpose, they've missed the most somber parts of the ceremony, as well as the official parade. An impromptu parade continuation, though, edges toward a bacchanalia, many participants losing most of their clothes. A few are giants, usually "small" giants twice the size of normal people, although a curvaceous red panda wearing nothing but strategically placed tassels stretches out on her side across most of Rincon Park, toying suggestively with admirers who seem quite enthusiastic about being toyed with. Fireworks—small ones, but ones impossible before the Turning, little physics-defying animations of fluttering butterflies and birds—fire off regularly.

"I have to admit, the city's nicer without cars," Stetson says. Six years ago, the mayor had spells cast that disabled combustion engines within city limits.

"And with giant nude wahs?"

He laughs. "I won't pretend she isn't a lovely sight, too."

"She is." Diana sips her drink and grimaces. "Oh."

"That bad?" He takes a sip of his. "I don't know. For a margarita in a plastic cup, this is top-notch."

"I suppose we have to grade on a curve."

As they reach the Bay Bridge underpass, propeller noise comes from overhead, and he tilts his head up to watch a zeppelin sail past. "It's patently ridiculous that one side effect of this all was airships making a comeback."

Diana nods, looking up at it. "There's still a feeling as if anything is possible. New things to discover, new dangers to face." She grimaces. "A *lot* of new dangers to face. Dragons, trolls, giant carnivorous plants, who knows what else. And countless newly empowered mortals testing limits, intentionally or not. It's going to take me another few decades to fully understand the new rules."

The coyote shrugs. "True for all of us. And all of them." He waves a hand. "I don't think I've seen anyone eaten yet tonight, at least."

"I suspect that's another quirk that's our fault, given the way we —I mean me, Hazel, and Rhiannon—behaved at first."

"I don't know. I'd give Moira a healthy share of the blame there."

She chuckles. "Maybe."

"And, as I said—" He's distracted by the brief sound of a water-fall as a giant otter woman walks out of the water up onto Pier 30, bay water cascading off her. "My. Uh, as I said, give it a couple of generations." The otter catches him staring and grins, waving a huge webbed paw as she strolls onto the Bay Trail. He waves back.

"I know, I know." She sighs and shrugs. "As much as I can tell my way of looking at the world has changed, it's still challenging to think on a divine timescale."

"Give that a few generations, too."

She squeezes his hand and chuckles. "I think you've adapted to this better than any of us."

"And I think I'm just good at faking it." He returns the squeeze.

As they approach Brannan Street Wharf, Diana points at a group of a half-dozen foxes in the small park there, all dressed in red and black leotards, sparkling faintly and floating in the air. Music streams from decidedly non-magical outdoor box speakers.

He lifts his brows. "Performers?"

"I think so. At first, I thought it might have been a magic class, but…"

As she speaks, the foxes twirl in the air, an acrobatic dance in time with the music—ballet set to a rock beat, but choreographed in three dimensions, with multicolored will-o-wisps darting in and out among the dancers. They stop and join the small crowd gathering to watch.

"I hadn't imagined we'd be ushering in new art forms," Diana murmurs.

Stetson grins, tail wagging.

As the song ends and everyone bursts into applause, Stetson pauses, eyes widening. He puts a hand on Diana's shoulder and points at one of the other spectators.

She follows his gaze, confused, then sucks in her breath. That can't be who it looks like.

The woman is turning away, starting to leave. Diana hurries after her, Stetson close behind. "Diana, wait. What if—"

"Moira?" she calls sharply.

The hare stops, turning around as the two run up.

She looks the same as Diana remembers from over a decade ago. Same build, same hair, same arresting green eyes.

But she's mortal.

She tilts her head. "Yes?" Her confusion is plain on her face. She has the same lyrical voice, too.

"I thought—you…" Diana stops and swallows. "You were someone else."

"Someone else named Moira?" Skepticism starts to overtake her confusion.

"Yes. Someone I…" She trails off. "Used to know. I'm sorry."

The hare—Moira, but not her Moira—starts to turn, then double-takes, looking back at them. "You…are you…both of you…" Her eyes widen, and she starts to fall to her knees.

Stetson's ears fold back. He steps forward quickly, catching her. "Please don't. If you start, everyone will."

She swallows, nodding shakily, looking between them with a

starstruck expression. "I-I just never...never thought..." She runs a hand through her hair. "You thought I was *the* Moira?"

"You look..." Diana smiles lopsidedly. "You look a lot like her."

"I'm named after her, Lady Diana."

"You were..." She feels her voice crack, and forces it to be level. "You were named well." She smiles. "We didn't mean to keep you."

"It's all right. It's more than all right." She smiles nervously, then turns as someone else strides toward them, a plastic bottle in each hand.

"I swear, if they charged any more for pop, these'd be solid gold bottles." The mouse shakes her head, handing Moira one of the sodas, and looks at Diana and Stetson quizzically.

Diana drops what's left of her margarita.

Moira puts a hand on the mouse's shoulder. "This is my wife, Briley," she says, voice shaking.

Briley nods to the sheep and coyote with a wary expression, picking up on Moira's *this is a big deal* vibes. "Hi." She looks back to the hare, to the sheep, to the coyote. Her eyes widen, too.

Stetson puts a finger to his muzzle.

Briley swallows and nods again.

He glances at Diana, who looks frozen. He smiles curiously. "You're *both* named after goddesses we knew. That's...an extraordinary coincidence."

Briley nods. "We, uh, we get that a lot. People sometimes joke it was destiny, but when we met, it was just...uh, just..." She shrugs.

"You were the seeds for each other's flowers," Diana murmurs.

Moira tilts her head, and smiles brightly. "I like putting it that way."

"I know." Diana clears her throat. "I mean...never mind." She swallows hard.

Briley puts a hand on Moira's shoulder. "Meeting the king and queen of the gods would be a great excuse to be late with anyone else, but you know Lily. She'll cast off with or without us."

Moira snorts, and smiles apologetically. "We're going out on a friend's sailboat for a sunset cruise."

"That sounds lovely. Don't let us keep you," Stetson says. "And we're very much not royalty. No titles. It was so nice to meet both of you." He clasps Moira's hand, then Briley's.

"It was nice for *you* to meet *us?*" Moira laughs, then squeals as Diana gives her a hug. Briley makes a flustered squeak at her hug, too.

"More than you know. Take care." Diana watches them head off, surreptitiously wiping her eyes.

Stetson takes a deep breath and exhales slowly. "They're both at least in their late thirties, so they were...born a couple of decades before the Turning?" He lifts a brow.

Diana starts walking more slowly again along the trail. "Moira said the death of a god is the one thing that can rewrite history." She furrows her brow. "They don't have any memories of divinity, though. They're fully mortal. And somehow they still found each other."

"Maybe it's a sign this truly *is* the way everything was meant to work out."

"Maybe."

He puts a hand on her shoulder. "And they found their friend Lily, the boat captain."

She nods, smiling wanly.

"You know they'd have taken you to meet her if you asked."

"That's why I didn't. They're not truly our Moira, our Briley, our Lily. They have their own lives."

They walk on in silence for another minute, before Stetson tilts his head. "Do you think—"

"No."

"You're sure you know what I was going to say?"

"You were going to ask if I thought they could be deified again. Truthfully, I don't know, but...they shouldn't be." She looks up at him. "We both know that if our Moira were here, she'd tell us that."

"You're right. Although she'd find a more profane way to put it." She grins.

"Do you think this means there's a mortal version of Sotala and Ironheart out there, too?"

"There must be."

"Do you think they're going to find one another?"

"If they do, I hope they'll be happy together. And I hope they won't do anything that invites me to leave them in a hoofprint."

He laughs. "I hope not, too." The coyote tilts his head. "Should we go somewhere to watch the sunset ourselves? Somewhere secluded, before more people notice us?"

"I think we should." She gives him a kiss, and both of them vanish with a silent shimmer.

epilogue

The security guard turns sharply at a noise, but as usual, it's nothing but leaves rustling in the wind. The Flower District Park—what used to be LA's actual Flower District, before the battle between the gods that leveled several blocks and left magical foliage overrunning the original Flower Market—is a strange area, and not always safe. Especially lately.

Shaking his head at himself, the tiger heads along the empty path, his patrol taking him deeper into the park's heart, toward the pond. When he completes one more circuit, he can lock the last open gate for the night.

Someone sits on the bench by the pond, back turned to him. He grumbles and walks up toward her. "Early closing time, ma'am." No response, so he walks closer, waving his flashlight. "Come on. We've got an after-dark curfew this month."

She stands up. "I've heard about that. Some sort of magical serial killer in the area."

"Nobody said he was magical." He waves his flashlight again. "Let's get going."

"Oh, I assure you she's magical." The honey badger grins widely. "Let me show you."

acknowledgments

The Turning would never have made the transition from a series of vignettes about an irascible, unnamed bunny woman to an actual, hopefully coherent story without the help of the Novel Architects, Kij Johnson's long-running residential workshops that started at KU's Center for the Study of Science Fiction. Erin "Quake" Lee helped as a sensitivity reader (and beta reader and generally cool person). My writing group, the Unreliable Narrators—Kyell Gold, Jakebe, and Ryan Campbell—offered helpful comments and insights which I have probably failed to follow in the final draft. They were my local writing group for years, and have shown great forbearance in keeping it up after my cross-country move. And I'd like to thank my publishers, FurPlanet, for taking the chance on supporting this kind of crazy work.

Lastly, all of my Patreon patrons deserve thanks and gratitude. This may not be a career (yet?), but your support and faith have been immeasurable to me.

about the author

Arilin Thorferra has been involved with the furry and macrophile community since the 1990s, writing dozens of short stories and several novels under both this name and their real one. As Arilin, their published work from FurPlanet includes *Goddess* and *Saida & Autumn.*

Arilin's website:
https://giants-club.net/

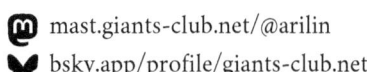 mast.giants-club.net/@arilin
bsky.app/profile/giants-club.net

about the publisher

FurPlanet productions is a small press publisher serving the niche market that is furry fiction. They sell furry-themed books and comics published by themselves and most major publishers in the community. If you can't get to a furry convention where they are selling in the dealers room, visit their online stores: FurPlanet.com for print books and BadDogBooks.com for eBooks.

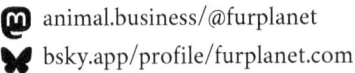 animal.business/@furplanet
bsky.app/profile/furplanet.com

www.ingramcontent.com/pod-product-compliance
Lightning Source LLC
Chambersburg PA
CBHW071343020726
47502CB00001B/223